Wandering Soldier

Angela W. Buff

Word of His Mouth Publishers
Mooresboro, NC

All Scripture quotations are taken from the **King James Version** of the Bible.

Print ISBN: 978-1-941039-48-9
Printed in the United States of America
©2024 Angela W. Buff

Word of His Mouth Publishers
Mooresboro, NC
www.wordofhismouth.com

"Be strong and of good courage; be not afraid, neither be thou dismayed: for the Lord thy God is with thee whithersoever thou goest.

Joshua 1:9 KJV

Chapter One

The sound of her laughter tickled his ears. He could not help but smile as she playfully and easily pulled from his embrace. She teased him as she turned away, glancing over her shoulder playfully, beckoning for him to follow her deeper into the alley toward her home. Her long, dark, silky braid bounced behind her as she ran. He could still smell the perfume he had given her recently as he began to chase her, quickly catching her and pulling her back into his arms.

There was the laughter again that he so loved to hear as she relinquished her body into his embrace, wrapping her arms around his neck and pulling his head toward her own so that their lips met in a tender, yet passionate kiss. Again, she pulled away, this time backing away slowly until she was just out of his reach. She rounded the corner, and before he moved to follow, she peeked back around to see if he was advancing in her direction. Her dark eyes were passionately inviting him to continue the quest and to follow her quickly. Nazim moved in the direction she had gone, tiring of the game but allowing her this moment of intrigue and seduction, nonetheless. After all, his victory would be all the sweeter for it.

As he rounded the corner, he reached out for her, expecting her to be just beyond the bend, but was surprised when he touched nothing. There was no sign of her at all. He paused a moment, staring down the dark alleyway. He was met with complete silence in the dim light. Not even the sound of her footsteps met his ears.

"Rahab?" he called in question. The alley was long and straight. There were no more corners for her to round, no doorways in which she could escape, the windows above all well out of her reach. He looked above his head and as deep into the alley as the darkness would allow, calling her name again.

"Rahab!" he called louder this time, puzzled as to where she may have gone. A moment of confusion passed before he heard tortured screams coming from just beyond his view, right past where the darkness began. Drawing his sword, he began to rapidly advance down the alleyway, moving in the direction of the cries— Rahab's the loudest among them all.

"Nazim!" he heard her scream. "Nazim, where are you?"

"Rahab!" he returned in desperation as he ran, faster now. On and on the alley continued, an endless trek that seemed to stretch into infinity. To his surprise, he suddenly reached the end. A solid wall appeared in front of him, the mass of stone and mortar stopping him abruptly in his tracks. Rahab's cries continued as Nazim searched frantically for a door, a window, whatever avenue she had found to escape the alley. To the far left of where he stood, an open door evolved in the stone. He was certain that doorway had not been there just before. He raced toward it as her cries intensified.

"Nazim! Help me!" she cried in desperation. He could hear a low rumble beginning that sounded like the earth trembling beneath him, but his steps were firm and sure on the ground underneath. Reaching the opening of the portal, he burst through it, scarcely believing the sights that surrounded him.

The darkness was obliterated as fires blazed high in every direction. Women and children screamed as they ran through the streets, attempting to escape the chaos and turmoil. The great walls of Jericho, the walls they were certain could never be breached, were fiercely crumbling all around him as he ran, leaping over the corpses of men, his friends whom he had fought beside in so many battles.

Rahab continued to cry out for him, her scream far louder in his ears than all the others, as she continued begging for his aid. Finally, in his frantic search, he caught sight of her. She was on her rooftop, the only building in all the land that was continuing to stand. Her tower stood tall, but she was surrounded by the flames blazing high in every direction.

"Nazim! Help me," she cried again and again.

"I am coming, Rahab," he yelled to her as he tried over and over to get through the door, which should allow him access to the stairs, but it held fast. In all his strength and with all his might, he tried again and again, using his entire body weight against it, but he could not budge the door. It was as if it were being held fast by some unseen force, a force with strength such as he had never encountered before. Her cries continued to ring in his ears as he searched for a way to reach her.

In desperation, he backed away and took a running leap, grabbing hold of an open window above him. He pulled himself up and, using the stones in the wall, began scaling the side of the building in an effort to gain the rooftop where Rahab stood.

Suddenly, as he climbed, the rumbling sound gave way to motion beneath him, and he could feel the earth and the tower he was gripping begin to shake violently. Nazim could feel his grip loosening on the stone that held him to the tower. Rahab's cries continued as he lost his grip and began to fall in what seemed like slow motion. The only sound in his ears as he fell toward the earth below him was Rahab screaming for him to save her. Nazim braced his body for the impact of the ground below and… woke up.

His eyes shot open wide, and he leaped to his feet so quickly that he stumbled backward. The wall of the cave where he had slept the past few nights caught his body, keeping him from crashing back to the ground. Nazim stood against the cave wall, his head enveloped in his large hands. He allowed himself to yell once, long and loud, just to drown out Rahab's screams that continued to sound over and over in his mind. He had heard stories of people being possessed by demons, and if that even resembled what he felt now, he had empathy for anyone who had ever experienced such.

As her screams slowly began to fade from his mind, silence surrounded him once again. Rahab's screams finally abated; he released his head and attempted to calm his own breathing. His heart continued to race, but slowly, he gave himself liberty to slide down the wall of the cave and collapse onto the ground below.

It was the dream. Again. Night after night after night, it was always the same, yet it was always different. Rahab was in his grasp, content and happy in his arms before fading away into danger and torment in a place he could not reach. He attempted in every way possible to get to her, to save her from her torment, but the same unseen force continually blocked his path. Tonight, it was the door that was held fast. Last night, it was the alley that would never end. The night before, an unseen barrier, she on one side, he on the other. Some nights she was within his reach before she would be the one to fall into the abyss, and other nights, as was this one, it was he who fell. Regardless, the dream always ended with him failing in his attempt to rescue her.

Nazim rose slowly and stumbled from the cave to the stream that ran alongside his campsite. The only light to aid him was from the moon, full overhead, and the stars that twinkled as they mocked him. He was fortunate to have found this place in the middle of the desert. The stream was narrow, but the water was clean and had yet to run dry. Kneeling by the stream, he reached into the cool water, splashing it onto his face and the back of his neck, then tied his hair into a small knot on the back of his head.

Settling himself by the stream, he compared the similarities in his recent dreams. On a few occasions, the Israelite, Salmon, would make his way into the nightmares. Nazim clenched his teeth at the thought of him and rubbed his forehead in frustration. How he hated that man. In his dreams, the Israelite would sometimes rescue Rahab right in front of Nazim, then mock him in his victory.

When Nazim could get beyond his pride, he would almost admit that there was a small sense of relief in that aspect of his torture. Oh, he detested the man. With every fiber of his being, he longed to run him through with his sword, but Salmon had, in truth, kept Rahab safe when Nazim could not. And apparently, from what he had witnessed not so long ago along the riverbank when he had finally found them, the Israelite continued to keep her safe, even now. He had searched for her for over a year after the walls had fallen.

The walls of Jericho. So many questions continued swirling through his mind of the things he had seen upon his return to Jericho that day. Nazim stared into the darkness as those scenes played again in his mind. He could still smell the smoke from the fires that burned, still see the faces of his brothers, whom he had won countless battles alongside, now lying dead in the streets, their final battle lost. He could still feel the dust encompassing him, burning his lungs as he fought to breathe, as the mighty walls continued to crumble and settle in heaps around him like sand on the seashore.

He remembered the short-lived feeling of relief he had experienced when he first realized that the one section of the wall that stood, seemingly unscathed, was the wall in which Rahab had her home. He had taken the steps to her dwelling by twos that day, racing to the top expecting to find her hiding, trembling in fear, but instead, he had found her rooms as empty and as cold as the alley in his dreams.

He had left her tower, still completely intact, and moved to the ruins of the palace where he himself had resided. The Israelites had taken plenty of spoils, and little was left in the king's treasury. Nazim was able to find a bag of coins that he had hidden away himself, however, and that bag of coins would be more than enough to sustain him for quite some time. He had walked away from the ruins of Jericho that day, for the first time in his life, feeling completely lost and empty.

Nazim reached deep into his vest now, pulling out the pendant he still kept tucked safely inside. It was the pendant he had given Rahab not long before that fateful day. At one time, she had cherished it and never removed it from her neck, but not that day, the day his world had literally crumbled. Upon his return to Jericho, he had found the pendant rejected and lying on a table by the window where the scarlet cord had once hung. He rubbed across the beautiful red jewel held firmly in the center. He had been burdened by so many questions. Had they taken her by force? Was she now enslaved by them? Had she gone of her own free will? Did she even live?

His heart had told him that she lived. He had no doubt, and the pendant, so perfectly laid aside, seemed to prove that to him. He was even almost certain that she had gone with them willingly. Nazim assumed that the Israelite had promised her safety and security, and she had been too interested in the beliefs of their people to have needed much convincing.

When Rahab first met the Israelites, it was only natural that she would have questions about the God they served. After all, their people had been hearing rumors in Jericho of the miracles this God had performed long before the Israelites had ever made their presence known to the city. Rahab had always been curious about other religions, never catering to the gods and idols of Jericho. Though she had been raised there, she never felt a connection to the gods of her ancestors. Nazim had dismissed her curiosity as simply that. Once she had begun to show a real interest in this

"Jehovah" God of the Israelites, he still waved her interest aside, aligning Him with all the other idols and foolish notions they had heard about from time to time. He could honestly not care any less. Nazim felt gods were only as powerful as the people who worshipped them, and he felt powerful enough to be his own god. Why did he need something to worship and to sacrifice anything to?

He thought back now to the night she had tried to talk to him of this God. "Why did I not listen to her?" he rebuked himself aloud as he stood slowly to his feet, tucking the pendant back into his vest. He should have paid attention when she tried to tell him of the "one true God" Who she now claimed to serve, not because he himself would ever have an interest in serving the so-called God of Israel, but because perhaps he could have learned something, something that would have enabled him to seek and destroy whatever this "spiritual being" was who had taken Rahab's affections and twisted them for His own.

This Jehovah God of Israel, Whom she claimed had brought her such peace and happiness, had caused him nothing but trouble. He crossed his massive arms and stared into the darkness. Aside from this God, Who could not be seen, was the Israelite man who very much could be. And this God the Israelite had taught her of used and manipulated these Israelites to do whatever He willed them to do. Nazim pondered on that thought.

He shook his head in disgust with himself. On the riverbank that day, he could have easily killed Salmon and taken back what belonged to him until he saw the baby that Rahab cradled in her arms. The child was small and obviously belonged to her and Salmon. Her smile lit up her face as she cooed to the baby she held so tenderly, and Nazim would never forget the peace that he had witnessed in her at that moment. She seemed so happy and so content in the world that she had created. A world without him. A world that involved the Israelite, her child, and the God she herself had tried to share with him.

The Israelite was keen, and Nazim's presence had not gone unnoticed. He had been warned, though no words had been spoken, to remain hidden and to remove himself from their location. Nazim had succumbed to the warning. Not because he was afraid of the man, it would have been an even fight for sure, but Nazim was certain he could have won the battle. No, he had remained hidden that day, truthfully, because he was afraid of Rahab's rejection.

She had loved him once; he knew that without question, but that was before. Before she had met the Israeli people, before she had learned of their God, and before she had surrendered her life to Him. That God, Whom she had now given her life to so freely, had taken everything from Nazim. Rahab's newly discovered God had used the Israelites to destroy his home. They had destroyed his life, and they had destroyed his relationship with the one person Nazim felt was truly worth fighting for.

Of course, he had been loyal to his king, the king who was now dead beneath the rubble of what had once been Jericho, and of course, he would fight alongside his brothers in arms, all who now also lay dead beneath the ruins of the city, but Rahab was who he saw each time he closed his eyes. Rahab is who he had thought of each time he went into battle. She is who he had thought of each time he returned home, and hers was the house he could not wait to get to at the end of each journey.

He knew that at one time, he had the chance to have her for himself, but his greed to advance among the ranks had taken precedence then. The rank he had coveted, he had quickly achieved, but now, none of that mattered. It was all gone, all but Rahab, and she was now simply out of his reach. All because of the Israelites and their God.

Nazim moved to the fire he had made hours before. He clenched his jaw once more in an effort to control his temper even now. Stoking the ash and debris, he watched the slumbering coals ignite, and a flame began to dance once again. Silently, he repeated the vow he had made to himself the day he had found Rahab on the riverbank, the vow he would keep until his quest was completed. He would search the world if he had to until he found this so-called Jehovah God of Israel if it was the last mission he completed in life.

He wanted to find out everything he could about this being. Were the stories of the miracles this God supposedly performed even true? How had the Israelites wandered the desert for so many years yet continued to reign victorious over and over again? How had the Israelites breached and destroyed the walls of Jericho? Had

11

some unknown force really been responsible for the conquest of this and such other major cities? So many questions.

It had been months since Nazim had seen Rahab, her child, and the Israelite on the banks of the river. He had not fought Salmon that day, a decision he had constantly regretted, but he reminded himself once again that it was ultimately the God of the Israelite he was after, not the man He was hiding behind.

Nazim had traveled the Jericho Road ever since, deciding on his next plan of action. He had fought beggars and thieves, killing when needed for his food and for his shelter, all in an effort to gain control of himself and his emotions. He had allowed himself to become a vagabond, convincing himself that rules did not apply to a person in his condition, and he found self-justification in every action he took. His home, Jericho, was gone, and Rahab had moved on. He may never have her in his arms again, but he would not rest until he had taken vengeance on who, or what, had taken her from him.

He tired now of wandering the Jericho Road, searching, fighting, and seeking for satisfaction that never came. He was not a patient man, and he was ready to complete this task. Once he had answers to how the Israelites had defeated his and many other cities and who exactly it was that was behind it all, he would find a new home and a new mission to fulfill whatever time he had left on earth. He was ready to form a plan and to act on it.

Before Jericho had fallen, Nazim had traveled as far as Bashan in his attempts to find out how the Israelites had won the battle against King Og. It was there, in Bashan, that he learned that the Israeli troops had ascended on Jericho in his absence, and from there, he had fled to return home. The thought had crossed his mind on more than one occasion that if he had remained in Jericho and had not been away searching for answers which he had not found, would even he have survived the battle of his homeland? By the looks of all he remembered, unless he had been in Rahab's home at the time of the attack, he too would have met the ill fate of his fellow soldiers and citizens of their city. Nazim knew himself well enough to know that he would not have been hiding in Rahab's rooms during such a battle; he would have been fighting in the streets alongside his colleagues. He shook his head to dispel the thought and continued to focus on formulating a plan.

His questions would not be answered as long as he remained in solitude. He would move into civilization once again. He would not yet return to Bashan but would instead visit Heshbon, where the Israelites had also defeated King Sihon. He had heard that the wandering Israelites would sometimes leave behind part of their citizens after the defeat of a city in an effort to rebuild and transform the area into a new nation built on their own beliefs and principles while claiming the land was their inheritance. Perhaps, if that was so, there he would find the answers he was searching for. He would learn all he could of these people, their customs, and practices, and in doing so, he would learn the secrets of their victories and of the God who they claimed brought them.

The sun was beginning to break the horizon when his stomach rumbled. He was not in the mood for more porridge, and he felt an urgency to kill. Taking his quiver and bow, he moved quietly along the rocks next to his camp. It was not long before a hare was roasting on a spit over his fire. He ate until he was content, fed and watered his horse, and broke camp. He figured he was only about a day's journey from Heshbon. This night, be they friends or foes, Nazim would dwell among people once again.

Chapter Two

Nazim unwillingly made quite the spectacle as he rode into Heshbon late that afternoon. The sun was low in the sky as he approached. It was obvious that he was not a local, and the people of Heshbon did not hide their curiosity over his arrival at this time of the day. He could have arrived from anywhere, really, as travelers and those buying and selling wares came and went through the town at will, but his stature was hard to ignore. He was unlike the others who often came into their town. Obviously, he was not seeking to trade, and he was definitely not a shepherd. Nazim was a man of great strength and possessed the look of a warrior. That he was, or at least had been, a soldier was of no doubt in anyone's mind who took notice of him. And many did.

The entrance to the town looked similar in comparison to other towns he had visited, though no fine palace stood in the background. No temple coveted the attention of those passing through; no stone idols leered over the city gates. No towers of gold flanked either side, beckoning for visitors to enter. Instead, great pools of crystal-clear water were situated on each side of the gate, honestly quite stunning, though he noticed that many paid no mind to them as they came and went eager to finish their day and return to their homes. Nazim noticed, as he entered inside the gates, several smaller roads leading in separate directions away from the city. He was curious, but tired, and decided those roads would be better explored another time.

He continued his course through the center of town where children played in the streets, women fetched water from the town well, and shepherds herded animals down back alleys, no doubt from their trading, buying, and selling during the day. Nazim continued through the center street, making his way slowly until he caught sight of an inn just on the outskirts of town. He halted his steed as he approached and began to dismount.

"May I stable your horse?" a young voice asked suddenly from behind him. Nazim turned to see a young lad, no doubt in his early teenage years, who appeared more than eager to assist him.

"Are there rooms available?" Nazim questioned, his voice steady.

"Yes, sir," the boy responded. "My sister is just inside and will have you settled in no time."

Nazim handed the reins over to the boy with a final pat on his horse's neck. He loved this creature; he was the only thing he had left in the world.

"I will take good care of him, sir," the young lad promised.

Nazim flipped a coin in the direction of the boy.

"See that you do," he instructed firmly, his face stern. He watched as his horse was led behind the establishment. From where Nazim stood, he could see that the stables looked to be well-maintained and in decent condition, with fresh hay and large troughs of water separating one from the other.

From outside the inn, though a few minor repairs needed to be made, it too looked to be a fairly reputable structure. *"This will be as good of a place to begin as any,"* Nazim thought to himself as he approached the door to the inn. It opened freely, and inside, he noticed a central meeting room. Several men, most likely travelers passing through, were seated at small tables scattered throughout, with one long table standing in the center of the room. Nazim spotted an unoccupied table in the back corner and chose his destination. Two women stood in the opposite corner of the room, and though he could not hear their words, it was evident he had been spotted as soon as he entered and that the conversation they shared was about him.

"Who... is... THAT?" Uma asked, watching the tall, dark, and extremely handsome stranger now walking slowly across the room. His massive presence filled the small area, and even the men who sat at the tables he passed cast sideways glances of caution in his direction.

"Let us pray he is not trouble," her dearest friend spoke softly from her side, watching as he selected his seat at the corner table.

"I wonder where *he* came from," Uma asked, her eyes never leaving him.

"Gather your wits," Eliana ordered with a small smile as she elbowed her co-worker.

Nazim took his place in the corner as far back as he could go. He liked this spot; everything around him was visible from this vantage point, yet he could almost go unnoticed in the shadows. He leaned forward, resting his elbows on the table to ensure he would be seen and served.

Eliana turned and began gathering food for the stranger as soon as he was seated. "I will serve him and get him out of here quickly," she informed her friend, noticing that Uma was continuing her unrelenting stare in the stranger's direction. "He does not look as if he is one to be toyed with, Uma," she spoke firmly and with surety, finally taking Uma by the elbow to get her attention. Eliana demanded to be looked at and stared straight into her friend's eyes. "Uma, I am serious," she spoke, a little louder this time.

"Alright, alright," Uma conceded. "But you get to serve all the good customers," she pouted playfully.

"No, I protect you," Eliana reasoned, "from yourself," she finished. The two friends shared a quiet laugh as Eliana balanced the entirety of a meal on a single board. "Pray he does not intend to stay for long," she instructed as she straightened her face and began to move toward the stranger. "We do not need any trouble."

Nazim's face was firm as he waited, though he did not have to wait long before a young woman approached him.

"I am Eliana," she spoke as she sat a bowl of stew and a cup before him. "If you require a room, we have several available. If you require a bath, one can be drawn at your request, and if you require only a meal, you can pay when you are finished and then continue on your way."

Nazim watched her speak, her eyes never rising to meet his face. She instead focused on her task, speaking lines she, no doubt, had repeated hundreds of times. She completed serving his meal by setting a cake of bread before him. He could not help but notice what a lovely maiden she was and how innocent she seemed, though her disposition seemed quite frigid. Something within him stirred at the sound of her voice.

"And company for the room and bath?" he questioned simply.

"As I expected," Eliana thought to herself before she continued. *"Trouble with a capital T."*

She spoke her next sentence firmly and raised her eyes to look directly into his face so she was certain she would not be misunderstood. "This is not that kind of establishment. If that is what you are seeking, you need to look elsewhere." She did not flinch and was very matter-of-fact, even after seeing the playful look in his eyes. Nazim grinned sheepishly and held up his hands in surrender.

"Fine," he answered finally. "*I*," he emphasized, "will require a room and a bath." He paused before continuing. "How about some company for the meal?" he tried more gently. "I have traveled a great distance and would appreciate some conversation," he finished, motioning for her to take the seat across from him and smiling slightly as he did so. He was ready for answers to his many questions, and he would not mind the company of this woman, even if only for conversation. Her candor with him proved that she was not a woman to be trifled with, and he liked that about her instantly.

Eliana never wavered. "Reuben," she called, "come to talk with this man," she instructed. Nazim's face fell as the young lad who had cared for his horse came bounding to his side, taking the seat across from him. This was not the company he had been referring to, nor that he had expected.

"I have work to do," she said directly. "The room to the left at the top of the second flight of stairs will be yours. I will collect the dishes and payment from the table when you have finished your meal," she called over her shoulder as she turned and began to walk away. "The morning meal is included with your night's stay. We break the fast at sunrise."

"Hi! I am Reuben!" the young lad began, now happily seated across from Nazim. Nazim took a deep breath and, in doing so, inhaled the aroma of the food that had been placed before him. This morning's hare was long gone. He had not stopped for a midday meal, and he was hungry. The food smelled wonderful. He broke off a section of the bread before him and dipped it into the stew. It tasted as delicious as it smelled.

Reuben placed both of his hands quickly on the table before him.

"Sir, you must wait," he instructed quickly. You have not yet given thanks to Jehovah God for the meal," he explained, noticing the confused expression on his guests' faces.

"*Israelites*," Nazim thought as he slowly chewed the food in his mouth while returning the bread in his hand to the table. *"I have landed directly in an inn owned by Israelites. How perfect could this be?"* He did not speak but motioned for Reuben to pray for him.

"Father, God, we come to you with thankfulness for the food our guest is about to partake of," Reuben began, "and ask that you will use this food for the nourishment of his body and that you will use his body for Your service. We pray blessings on my sister who prepared this meal, and may you bless this new friend who has come into our presence. Amen," he finished. "Now, you may eat fully," he instructed, a smile across his face.

Nazim nodded his head slightly in acknowledgement but spoke not a word. He was sure that if this lad knew who he was or from whence he came, he would have left off the ending to his prayer. Nazim had no intention of becoming a friend to anyone, especially Israelites. He picked up his bread and began eating again.

"You have a fine animal," Reuben began. "Does he have a name?" he asked. Nazim was in no mood for conversation with this child. He simply glanced at the boy as he chewed. "Well, everything should have a name," Reuben continued, "but because he is your horse, you should be the one to choose it." Again, Nazim spoke nothing but simply stared at the boy as he continued his meal.

The lad cleared his throat. "You have met my sister, Eliana," he continued as he motioned to his sister, who was busy filling the cup of another patron. "And that is her dear friend, Uma," he stated as he motioned to the woman still standing in the corner. She looked away quickly as Nazim turned to look in her direction before moving completely out of view, embarrassed at being caught gawking.

"Our grandfather, Eliana's and mine, owns this inn. His name is Eli, and Eliana and I live here with him. She was named after both our grandparents. Eli and Anna. I never knew our grandmother, she passed long ago, and our parents passed in the desert, and grandfather was too old to continue the journey to the Promised Land, so we stayed behind here, in Heshbon, after the conquest of this city. I remember little of it, but I believe Eliana remembers, though she rarely speaks of it." Nazim listened intently to the wealth of knowledge spewing from the mouth of this child. He ate slowly as the boy continued, with no need to speak a word of his own. Not that he would have been able to.

"Uma is from here, in Heshbon," the lad continued, "she and her parents were spared in Israel's conquest of the city. Her family is well-established in the town. They are potters and turn out beautiful work as well as practical pieces. Uma has befriended us, and she and Eliana are now the best of friends. She has learned much of our God and has forsaken the pagan gods the people of Heshbon served before we overtook the land. Grandfather has taught me much, and Uma has learned much from him, too. I believe he knows all there is to know of our Jehovah God."

Eliana approached the table and filled Nazim's cup.

"Uma's father made that!" he grinned, pointing to the vessel his sister filled.

"That will be enough of your chatter, Reuben," she spoke with surety. "I believe our guest has had all the company he needs this evening," she smiled at her younger brother. "Leave him in peace now," she instructed. "Grandfather will be looking for you soon," she reminded him, "for your evening devotions and prayer time."

"Very well," he obeyed kindly. "I will go check on your horse first," he promised as he moved away quickly, darting back and forth between the now-empty chairs blocking him from the door. Nazim watched him leave, then looked to the woman standing over him who was doing the same. She smiled slightly as she watched her younger brother exit through the door in the direction of the stables. Her mind seemed to have wandered to another place. Nazim now had a full stomach, and the journey of the day was catching up to him. Suddenly, he was growing very tired. He pushed back from the table, taking one more long drink from the cup in front of him. His motion broke her trance.

"Pardon me," she begged, looking away from where her brother had departed. "Where are my manners?" It was clear that she was embarrassed by her wandering mind.

"Top of the second flight of stairs to the left," Nazim clarified as he stood. He towered above her, and she realized, standing next to him now, just how massive he was. She nodded her head and cleared her throat. She had felt much more assertive when he was seated and not looming over her as he was now. She looked down and quickly busied herself by clearing his meal from the table.

"Yes, just up there," she pointed, not looking again at his face. "Reuben has already moved the belongings you had on your horse into your room."

Nazim acknowledged his understanding with a nod as he laid more than enough coins on the table than what was necessary for one night's stay.

"I had Uma draw a bath for you," Elaina continued, "before she departed for the evening," she concluded, making sure it was apparent he would bathe alone. "The wash house is just beyond the stables. It is for the private use of our guests," she clarified. "You will not be bothered while you are there. Just make sure the door is latched. Drying cloths are available on the shelf above the door for your use."

Nazim paused and looked at her. She was so direct with him earlier, but she looked almost frightened of him now as he looked down at her, and a strange feeling of empathy stirred within him. He nodded his head then moved to his room for his fresh clothes before heading outside to the wash house.

The room was simple but clean and would be more than sufficient to meet his needs. One window peered out to the street beyond, streets that were now beginning to empty as patrons began retreating to their homes for the evening. A cot stood in the middle of the room against the wall, with a small table beside it holding a single oil lamp. A wash basin and towel lay on a smaller table near the window. Though he was tired, he still preferred a soak tonight and moved now to enjoy the water that was waiting for him.

As he passed the stables, he heard the boy inside speaking to his horse. "Perhaps I can learn your name soon so that I can call you something other than Horse," Nazim heard Reuben say. Nazim could not stop the smile that lifted one corner of his lips.

Just a few moments later, he sank into the warm water, allowing it to soak into his skin and relax his tired muscles. It had been well over a year since he had sat in a bathing tub. He had to admit that the warm water was much more soothing than the harsh coldness of bathing in a river, though something about that was refreshing as well. He breathed deeply and listened to the sounds around him, allowing his mind to recount the information that had been so freely handed to him by the boy, Reuben. Nazim could not believe his fortune. He had landed directly inside an inn of Israelites, the very people he had claimed as his mission to learn all about. He must be patient and learn all he can from this family.

Nazim felt certain he could gain countless information from Reuben, such a simple child, and he must meet this grandfather he had spoken so highly of, this grandfather whom Reuben claimed seemed to know all there was to know about Jehovah God. But Nazim recognized that he must be careful with Eliana. There was something about her, something he could not quite put his finger on, yet something that intrigued him nonetheless. Reuben had said that Eliana remembered their time in the desert as their people had searched for the Promised Land but that she seldom chose to speak of it.

Nazim sat up slowly in the bath water as a thought began to form in his mind. Eliana would be a wealth of information. More so even than Grandfather on some accounts. Her mind was younger and sharper, and her observations would have been keener. He thought over their encounter inside the central room where he had dined. As assertive as she had been with him at their first encounter, she had seemed almost afraid of him as he took his leave. He would have to break down her resolve. To learn what he really wanted to know, he would have to make her want to tell him. He needed to get close to her, and one way to achieve that was to get closer to her younger brother. He could tell there was a very strong maternal instinct toward Reuben where Eliana was concerned.

His body now clean, Nazim began to wash his worn clothes as he formulated a plan. It would take some time, some work, and some patience, the latter being the hardest for him, and if he saw in the near future that he was getting nowhere, he would move on to the other side of town and go from there, but for tonight, he had a plan which satisfied him for the current time. He would get closer to Eliana and closer to this family of Israelites he had so easily happened upon. He would gain their trust, and though he was not yet sure how, maybe their dependence upon him as well. It would not be easy, especially with Eliana. He would have to pace himself and not appear too eager, but at least he had a plan, which was more than he had just a few hours before.

Chapter Three

Rahab ran ahead of him, laughing as she bid him to chase her. The field was full of flax ready to be harvested, and he watched as she hid behind a cluster of the tallest stalks. Nazim slowly moved toward the spot where he had watched her hide and began to speak gently as he approached in an effort to coax her from her hiding place. When she failed to appear, he reached behind the stalks to playfully force her from her seclusion, only to find she was not there. He called to her but heard nothing but the breeze as it began to stir through the tall reeds. He listened intently as he continued to wander through the field, calling her name, noticing the wind which was beginning to intensify as he walked. The gentle whisper swiftly turned into a howl, and suddenly, he found it difficult to stand as it began ripping the stalks from the ground, turning the beautiful field into a mass of tattered reeds.

As he watched and attempted to shelter his face from the stalks of reeds whipping through the air around him, the howl of the wind was replaced by the sound of sickening laughter. Nazim looked around him in an attempt to find who, or what, it was that mocked him but saw nothing. The wind calmed abruptly, and he expected for a brief moment that the worst was over, but then watched in confusion as a glowing ember floated past him, and then another, and another. Smoke began to fill his nostrils, and the field became a blazing inferno. In the distance, he spotted Rahab bound to something, something he could not identify but something that held her so tightly she could not free herself from it. The fires burned close to her body as the sound of the mocking laughter continued to surround Nazim, stifling Rahab's screams from reaching his ears but not clouding the vision of the torment he saw on her face.

He ran toward her, shielding his face from the blazes now beginning to swirl around him. There was a clear path to her which the fire had not yet touched, and Nazim realized that if he could reach her quickly enough by that path, he would be able to free her. He sprinted in her direction until suddenly, his feet began to feel like lead beneath him. He continued to fight, Rahab now just out of his reach, but something was binding his feet. Pausing long enough to see what it was that held him, he realized that he was sinking, the ground beneath him beginning to pull him beneath the surface. He had heard stories of sinking sands in other lands, but he had never heard of it being experienced here. Where did this "sinking sand" come from? The earth continued to pull him deeper and deeper into itself as he struggled for his freedom. The sinking sand reached his knees, then his waist, then his chest. The resounding laughter continued to deafen his ears, and Rahab's face continued to show her mounting distress as the flames moved closer and closer to her body. He watched her helplessly as he continued to sink, the sand now reaching his neck and then his chin. He took one last breath before it consumed him as he watched her continue to struggle, knowing the words that were coming from her mouth were pleas for his aid. The flames reached her body at the same time the sand completely covered his head and finally… he snapped awake, the blanket that had been covering him now wrapped in tangled knots around his neck and head.

Nazim ripped the blanket from his body, soaked with sweat, throwing it across the room, and then quickly sat upright on the edge of the bed. He rocked back and forth, enveloping his head in his hands. He remembered his location only a split second before he allowed his own angry yell to exit his throat. He could not release his own voice here, even though it was his ever-present attempt to stop the sound of Rahab's screams, which continued to ring in his head after each terrible nightmare. Without the audible release he was accustomed to, he had to work harder to calm his breathing and his heart, which was once again attempting to beat out of his chest. He kept his place at the edge of the cot until finally, after what seemed like an eternity, the sound of Rahab's screams abated in his mind. His own breathing slowed, and finally, his heart began to return to a normal rhythm.

With a final deep breath, Nazim stood slowly and moved to the window overlooking the street in an attempt to distract himself. How he tired of these endless nightmares! He was a warrior who had fought in battles he never should have survived, yet these dreams left him trembling like a mere schoolboy. Rahab had survived the fall of Jericho; he had witnessed her alive and well for himself. Why, then, did her safety and well-being continue to torment him?

He knew the answer before the question had fully formed in his mind. It was because he had failed her. He had not been with her when the world had literally crumbled around her. The final words they had shared had been unpleasant, the terrible argument coming back to him again and again. He had said things to her that he would never forgive himself for, and obviously, neither would she. If he had been in Jericho to save her, would she have stayed with him after the horrible things he had said? Or was the confession that she had come to trust in the God the Israelis worshipped her way of telling him goodbye? Would she have still chosen this God and the Israelite who rescued her if she and Nazim had not had such a terrible argument? And how did those petty Israelis destroy the indestructible walls of Jericho anyway?

Nazim rubbed his forehead. He had so many questions, yet, without question, Rahab had made her choice. She had left her former life, and she had left him. It was time for him to find the answers he sought to the questions that had plagued him for over two years and then it was time for him to move on with his own life. Who, or what, was this God that had overpowered her and so many others, and how could he be destroyed?

Remembering the wash basin in the corner, Nazim moved to splash the cool water on his face, then dressed himself for the day, pulling his hair into a familiar knot at the back of his head. The same ritual he performed every morning, but today, in someplace new, and today there would be no need for him to hunt for his first meal. This morning, he would have food to break his fast, ready and waiting for him downstairs.

Reminding himself of the plan he had formulated the night before, he took a final deep breath, now fully composed, and opened his door. Moving quietly, he descended the stairs to find he was among the first in the central meeting room. He could hear noises coming from the cooking area and decided to take the same seat he had previously occupied. As he crossed the room, it was Reuben who first noticed him and came bounding to his side.

"Good morning, kind sir!" he spoke, much more friendly and enthusiastic than Nazim felt this early in the day. More friendly and enthusiastic than Nazim felt any time of day, actually.

"I have already visited your horse this morning and made sure he has fresh water and clean straw. He has been fed and brushed and is ready for whatever plans you have today. What plans do you have today? I do hope you can stay with us for a while. You do not plan to leave quickly, do you?" Reuben continued, quickly firing one question after the other, yet failing to pause long enough for Nazim to answer even if he had chosen to. "I do hope you will remain for a few days at least. I must go for my studies this morning, but I will return this afternoon and..."

"Reuben!" Eliana called to him firmly as she approached the table where he sat with Nazim. She softened once she had the boy's attention, "You must go now and stop bothering our guest with your endless chatter. Off with you! You will be late!" Her tone was firm, but she was still kind in speaking to the young boy. Nazim admired the way he quickly obeyed.

"Yes, sister," he said obediently. "Do not forget to pray over your morning meal," he reminded Nazim quickly and quietly. He then grabbed his book and parchment and began to speak loud enough for his sister to hear. "I will go, but please plan to remain here, kind sir, so that we may talk again!" he yelled in Nazim's direction as he ran through the door.

"Please, forgive my brother," Eliana began as she sat a cake of bread, a small bowl of berries, and a large bowl of porridge in front of Nazim. "He loves meeting new people, and talking." That she herself was quite uncomfortable in his presence was obvious. Still, she continued in perfect hospitality, though she failed to raise her eyes to look at him. "I trust you slept well?" she questioned as she filled the cup she had sat before him.

"I did," he lied as he took in the fare she placed on the table. His lack of sleep had nothing to do with the accommodations, they were quite adequate. *Be cordial. You must be kind to her,*" he reminded himself. Nazim cleared his throat. He decided to attempt somewhat of an apology, which was something he was unaccustomed to doing. "I fear our initial meeting last evening was ill-regarded, and I apologize if I offended you in any way. Thank you most kindly for the perfect accommodations," he paused, "and for the delicious meal."

Eliana looked at his face for the first time this morning and stared at him in shock. Her eyes were wide, and her face did not hide the fact that she was surprised not only at his apology but also at his compliment over the food. It was clearly evident that she was taken completely off guard, and she turned to leave before she remembered herself. She paused in her departure but did not completely turn back to look at him.

"You are quite welcome," she spoke slowly and softly, glancing quickly over her shoulder. Nazim allowed a small grin to lift his lips, which Eliana acknowledged with a nod of her head. Other travelers were beginning to fill the common area now, and Nazim took note that more came from off the street than what came from the sleeping quarters above them. The food was good and plentiful, and Nazim noticed that Eliana was much more comfortable with the other guests as she served them, mostly locals, he imagined, than she was with him. Her demeanor was more relaxed, he noticed a smile continually light her face, and everyone could hear the soft laughter she shared with guests on more than one occasion.

Nazim ate heartily, quite heavily for a morning meal, and was more than satisfied with the food before him. He took his time to finish and used the time to ponder his next move. What to do in his waiting had not really occurred to him until this moment. Eliana had made her way back around to his table. She moved to fill the cup before him but stopped when he held out his hand to halt her.

"I am quite full, thank you," he said politely. Nazim could not remember the last time his voice had sounded so kind, and he almost did not recognize it himself.

"I would like to secure my room and board for the remainder of the week," he began. "I will be…" he suddenly realized he had no idea what he would be doing. "I will be working in the surrounding area and will need a place to stay," he finished.

"Very well," Eliana agreed, though he almost thought he saw a hint of disappointment cross her face. "Your room last night was suitable?" she asked, glancing at him for confirmation.

"Very," he agreed.

"Ellie!" a portly, older gentleman yelled, waving his cup in the air.

"I am coming, Abner," she acknowledged before directing her attention back to the man in front of her. "Then it will remain yours for the week. Let me know when you need a bath drawn or if our normal mealtimes do not suit you. I will be happy to accommodate your stay as best as possible. You may leave your payment on the table." Her speech was, again, well-rehearsed and had been spoken similarly many times in the past, he was certain. She moved away quickly to fill the old man's cup who had called to her, obviously finished with their conversation.

Tables were filling up rather quickly now, and Nazim noticed that most of Eliana's customers seemed familiar to her. She moved quickly and efficiently from table to table, never halting in her duties and remaining ever kind and friendly to each person who entered.

Nazim stood and again left more than enough on the table to cover the remainder of his week's food and lodging. He decided he would explore his surroundings today and familiarize himself with the rest of the town. He felt he would attract less attention on foot than if he mounted his horse, and since he did not plan to travel an abundant distance today, he opted to stretch his own legs and allow his animal a day of deserved rest. His speculations regarding being able to stay low-key, though, were very wrong.

Those he passed did not hide their curiosity or their concern over his presence. On more than one occasion, citizens stopped in their path and watched him as he passed by. Merchants paused in their sales, and women ducked behind their men. Children scampered as he approached, and on one occasion, a young child tripped and fell in her hurry to flee his presence. Nazim could not figure out how such weak and timid people could overcome even a small city, overthrow its king, and claim it as their own, much less the great city of Jericho.

He did not return to the inn for second meal but decided to purchase figs, a piece of bread, and a small flask of water from a street vendor in the marketplace. The woman served him quickly, thanked him profusely, and then ducked inside her tent after his purchase as if she were frightened of his presence.

"What is wrong with these people?" Nazim thought to himself as he walked through the streets to the edge of town. He was attracting far more attention than he was comfortable with. Though he had been in solitude for months, he now found himself needing to think, needing to complete his plan of action. He took his meager meal and decided to get out of the middle of everything. He decided to explore one of the roads he had noticed at the entrance of the city. Moving toward the outer gate quickly, he could almost feel the townsfolk's relief with each step he took away from their presence. He was used to people being intimidated by him, a characteristic that had served him well as he patrolled the streets keeping peace in Jericho, but this was something more. He could not describe it, nor if he was honest, did he particularly enjoy it.

In Jericho, women had flocked for his attentions – here, they seemed to abhor him. Men had watched him in envy –here they eyed him warily, almost angrily, as he passed. Children had not been overly obsessed with him, though he was more than one young boy's hero. Here the only boy who had even spoken to him was Reuben. He was a man among men in Jericho, and he missed the respect he had earned there. He realized now that he missed his situation in Jericho, almost as much as he missed her.

He stopped and pinched the corners of his eyes as Rahab's face swam into his memory, then shook his head to dispel the image. Would there ever be a time that he did not think of her? Finally, he reached the city gate and took the first of the roads that he had passed. It did not take long for him to realize that this road was a short one, though one would think the distance to the end would have been much farther away. What he was met with quickly, however, at the end of the short road, took his breath away.

Nazim did not consider himself a sentimental person by any means, but even he marveled at the scene before him. The trees opened up revealing a beautiful pool of crystal-clear water settled in the middle of a deep green meadow brimming with wildflowers. The few trees that had voluntarily popped up here and there were giants with branches that bowed low, almost touching the earth beneath them. The branches were so mighty, in fact, that Nazim selected one at just the right height and easily sat upon it, stretching

31

his long legs out before him comfortably. The trunk behind him cradled him as he leaned back, where he ate his meal, reveled in the solitude, and then allowed himself time to take in the beauty before him. He could not believe a location such as this remained unoccupied. He had found the right place to explore for certain.

He could honestly say that even in Jericho, he had never seen such a landscape. Beyond the meadow lay a wooded area, almost begging him to approach and explore, but he refrained today. For now, he remained on his comfortable perch and allowed his mind to wander and contemplate his next plan of action.

He had always worked to keep himself at a distance from those around him. That had always come naturally to him, and he had easily succeeded in his efforts, except for Rahab. She was the only person he had ever allowed to get close to him, to know him for more than just the soldier he was, and his allowance of that had proven many disadvantages. However, if he were to learn of this "God" and the secrets of the Israelis, Nazim realized he would have to appear to be genuinely interested in these people. He would have to appear as if he desired to be close to them, and that would indeed be a difficult challenge.

He scoffed at himself. He had always used his stature and his position to get what he wanted from anyone. Information, affection, whatever the situation called for. But here, in Heshbon, he would have to gain his information differently. Being a blood-thirsty soldier would gain him nothing in this battle. Before he could learn anything about this God and the secrets of these people who both fought for and worshipped Him, he knew he would have to get close to the people who served Him. Going against his own natural instincts could prove to be a much harder challenge than any he had ever faced.

He remained in his state of solitude for longer than he intended before finally deciding he would head back to his quarters. He had been gone long enough to appear to anyone interested that he had attended to some sort of business for the majority of the day. The sun was not yet beginning to set, and Nazim expected the central meeting room would not yet be occupied by those looking to end their day with a hot meal. He was correct.

Nazim entered the inn alone, no one in sight save for one old man sitting alone at a table in the corner closest to the stairs. As Nazim entered, the man paused his carving and watched him as if he had been anticipating his return. The elder stared at him intently, never wavering, never blinking as Nazim moved past. The old man's knife held still in midair, as Nazim continued with his plan to ascend the stairs and retreat to his room until the third meal of the day was ready to be served.

The old man's gaze was pointed, however, and Nazim returned the glare, his pride refusing to allow him to look away. Finally, the ancient man lifted a crooked finger around the piece of wood in his hand and beckoned for Nazim to approach. Nazim was not accustomed to taking orders from civilians, or from anyone other than his former King, as far as that went. He scoffed at the old man and moved to take the stairs to his room, finally breaking his focus from the withered face.

"Nazim," he heard in a broken voice that was weak yet strong enough to be heard. Nazim paused, his foot in midair at the sound of his name coming from the stranger's lips. He turned slowly to lock eyes with the old man, now once again motioning for him to approach.

Nazim turned slowly, redirecting his steps and moving slowly to the old man's table. The man seated before him did not stand but instead beckoned for Nazim to take the seat across from him.

"What brings you to my inn?" the old man asked as Nazim sat down slowly.

"'His' inn...ahh...this must be the grandfather, Eli," Nazim thought to himself.

"How do you know my name," he retaliated bluntly, refusing to be the one to break the stare.

Satisfied that he had won and gained an audience with Nazim, Eli went back to his carving before he began to speak. "Word of a mighty soldier such as yourself does not remain hidden in a town no larger than ours," the old man answered, plainly blowing carving dust from the wood in his hand. "We have heard of the very few who did not perish when our people overtook the city of Jericho. You are either of the house of Rahab, which I do not expect, or you are the soldier she has told our people of. The one soldier, who was not present in Jericho when the walls fell. That makes you the only remaining citizen of what was formerly Jericho…"

Fear coursed through his body, and Nazim stood so quickly that his chair nearly toppled behind him, "Rahab…" he began.

The old man looked slowly in Nazim's direction as he spoke, "…aside from Rahab and her family," he finished slowly. Nazim regained his seat, his breathing labored, but remained quiet as he motioned for the man to continue his conversation.

"You have been rather unsettled, from what I have been told," the old man spoke slowly. "Keeping yourself 'occupied' along the Jericho Road for quite some time if the stories are true. The 'wandering soldier' they call you. I am curious as to what has brought you out of hiding and into my inn," he finished plainly, laying aside his wood and knife, then intertwining his fingers and finally looking up at Nazim. His weary eyes did not appear unkind, but neither were they welcoming. Nazim suspected that in his youth, the man before him now would have been a force to be reckoned with.

"How do you know of the house of Rahab?" Nazim questioned, attempting to control the curiosity in his voice.

The old man looked straight into Nazim's eyes as he spoke, completely confident in whatever it was he intended to say. "I have not had the privilege to meet the wife of Salmon," the old man continued, "but one of Salmon's dearest friends, Garrick, who fought alongside him in the battle of Jericho, as well as many other battles, is my nephew, and he visited to inform us of the victory of our people finally overtaking the city of Jericho in their quest of The Promised Land. He also told us of the few survivors who remained, those being the family of Rahab and the one soldier who was not present when the walls fell. So, I ask you again," he continued slowly, "what brings you to my inn?"

Nazim sat back in his chair, his gaze never leaving the old man's face. Salmon. Nazim rolled the name over and over in his mind. He detested that name and swallowed hard in an attempt to control the anger coursing through him at the sound of it from the man's lips who sat before him now. Salmon.

Nazim cleared his throat. He had to weigh his next words and his next actions carefully. He reminded himself of the challenge before him, the challenge he had made to himself just a few hours ago. He would learn nothing of these people and their God were the old man to send him out of the inn and into the street. He took a deep breath before he began to speak, confident he could do so without conveying the animosity he felt at that mention of the name he had just heard repeated.

"Very well," he admitted. His voice was smoother than even he expected. "I *am* the soldier from Jericho, as you anticipated. As you have heard correctly, I was not present when your people breached our city walls and destroyed my home, and I have, as you claimed, wandered the Jericho Road ever since. Everyone I knew and everything I had, save my horse, who was with me outside the city walls, was destroyed. I have no home, no family, nothing other than the horse in your barn, the clothes on my back, and the few things in that room upstairs to call my own."

"What brings you to my inn?" Eli repeated more pointedly this time, interrupting him.

Nazim leaned forward, his elbows resting on the table. His temper almost got the best of him as he envisioned grabbing the old man's own carving knife lying right in front of him and running it through his aged chest as he spat his intentions to find out exactly how these puny Israelites continued to take city after city, claiming it was through miracles from an unseen God. Suddenly, he remembered once more the vow he had made to himself as well as the old proverb he had been taught as a boy about catching flies with honey.

He smirked as he continued. "I had nowhere to go," he spoke honestly, shrugging his shoulders and leaning back casually in his chair. "I was tired of wandering the same road, being forced to kill for food and shelter. I was passing through, and this inn looked comfortable enough."

The old man continued to stare at Nazim, their gazes locked. Nazim felt as if the old man was searching the depths of his soul and finally broke the gaze himself before the man could discover more than he wished to reveal. Eli had seen something in his eyes, but unknown to Nazim, the prayer in his weary heart had been heard and answered by Jehovah.

"Show me your way, Jehovah. Give me Your direction," Eli had prayed silently. As he waited and prayed, he saw question

and curiosity in Nazim's eyes; then suddenly, it was Nazim who had broken the trance. Though Eli was hesitant, Jehovah's direction to him had become clear. For what purpose, he did not know, but for the time being anyway, he was to allow this wandering soldier to remain in his inn without interference.

"Very well," the old man spoke finally, picking up his carving and beginning to once again shave thin strips of wood from the block. "I am Eli; you have met my grandchildren, Eliana and Reuben. Do not cause any trouble, and you are welcome to remain our guest for as long as you can pay for your room and board. Eliana sees to our guests, and she will make sure your accommodations are adequate and that you have nourishment for as long as you remain in our company."

Nazim was shocked. He was not sure what he had been expecting from the old man, but as intent as he had been upon gaining an audience with him, Nazim certainly did not expect to get off so easily. He sat for a moment in anticipation, waiting to see what would be said next. Eli continued his carving and began to sing quietly to himself as he worked.

"For all our days are passed away in thy wrath: we spend our years as a tale that is told," he sang. *"Who knoweth the power of thine anger? Even according to thy fear, so is thy wrath. So teach us to number our days, that we may apply our hearts unto wisdom. O satisfy us early with thy mercy; that we may rejoice and be glad all our days. Make us glad according to the days wherein thou hast afflicted us, and the years wherein we have seen evil."*

Clearly, Nazim was dismissed. He listened to the old man's words as he sang softly, curious as to the story he seemed to be telling, before slowly pushing back his chair and rising to stand. Was it a story? Or was it a prayer? Nazim was confused yet intrigued by the old man's words set to a sweet and reverent tune. Eli never looked up at him but continued with his carving and quiet melody.

Nazim slowly approached the stairs to his room, his mind still contemplating whatever had just transpired and still able to hear the old man as he quietly continued his song. He paused on the lower step as something caught his attention at the back of the room. It was Eliana, readying herself for the coming guests of the evening. She did not see him as he watched her weave her long dark hair into a thick braid at the back of her neck before replacing a veil overtop her head. He closed his eyes as he remembered watching Rahab as she made the same motion on so many occasions. Biting his lip as he so often did when she came to his mind, he moved to his room trying to think of something, of anything, else. He could not get this inward battle behind him fast enough.

Grandfather laid down his carving, watching, unknown to Nazim, as Nazim watched his granddaughter. As the soldier slipped up the stairs, another silent prayer now echoed in the aged man's heart. *"Help me to trust Your will in this, Jehovah. And Dear God, please. Please protect my family through this as I seek to do Your will, and Yours alone."*

He would go so far as to tell Eliana from where this man came, but for now, Eli decided, that was all he would tell her of this wandering soldier who had currently found his way into their home.

Chapter Four

For the first time since the walls of Jericho had fallen, Nazim slept soundly that night. Perhaps it was formulating his plan that had occupied his thoughts enough to keep the nightmares at bay, for one night at least. Perhaps it was the short, odd conversation with Eli that plagued his thoughts more so than the memories that usually lured him to sleep each night. Regardless, he slept peacefully until morning.

He rose when the first rays of sun crept into his room, washed his face in the basin by the window, and descended the stairs to partake in the morning meal. He took his normal corner seat, closest to the cooking area, almost in the shadows, but was quickly spotted by Reuben, nevertheless. The lad wasted no time bounding to his table and taking a seat.

"Good morning, sir!" he spoke excitedly. "I attended to your horse again this morning. He is such a fine animal. I talked with him as I brushed him. I said to him, Horse…"

"Ares," Nazim spoke, interrupting him.

"Pardon me?" Reuben questioned.

"My horse. His name is Ares," Nazim clarified, folding his elbows on the table in front of him and leaning in so that the boy could hear him clearly.

"The Greek god of war!" Reuben answered, excitement filling his voice, his own elbows on the table now. "The Greek culture is so very new: do you worship the gods of the Greeks?" he asked.

"I do not," Nazim clarified. "I just like the name. Does the name surprise you?" Nazim scoffed. "You, yourself, have commented on what a magnificent animal he is. Is there any other name that would be better suited for him?"

Reuben appeared to think on this statement. "His name suits him well," he finally agreed, a grin splitting his face.

"Reuben," Eliana called as she came from the cooking area. "Your studies are waiting," she reminded him as she approached with bread, figs, and porridge, tossing her head in the direction of the door. "Off with you now," she instructed, her face firm but her eyes kind.

"Goodbye, sir," he called to Nazim as he ran quickly toward the door. Then, stopping abruptly, he turned and ran quickly back to the table. Laying his hand alongside his mouth, he moved to whisper something into Nazim's ear.

"Do not forget to pray blessings over your meal before you partake," he instructed softly. Nazim allowed a small smile to lift one corner of his mouth as Reuben quickly bounded out the door. He watched the boy go and then decided to use the opportunity that had been presented to him.

"What is that all about anyway?" he questioned his hostess as she placed his meal on the table.

"What is what all about?" Eliana returned, clearly uncomfortable speaking with him but minding her polite manners at any rate.

"The lad, your brother. He is very adamant about blessing the food when I am about to eat. I am aware that you people pray. And often," he scoffed. "Yet, I am not familiar with the purpose of the custom."

"We thank our Father, Jehovah, for the food He provides," she stated simply as she sat the last of the food in front of him.

"But *your* hands have prepared this meal for me; why would I thank something else for it?" he asked sincerely.

"Not some*thing*, but Some*one*," she explained. Nazim caught the urgency in her voice as she answered him. "Jehovah has allowed you the finances to purchase the meal, and He has allowed me the ability to prepare it for you. He encouraged the wheat to grow, and He allowed the animals to provide the meat. Without Him, none of this would be possible. We thank Him for His provisions and ask for His blessings over it."

"I work to earn the money I need to pay for the food," Nazim retaliated.

"Yes, but He allows you the health and strength you need to work and earn those coins," she spoke with surety.

Nazim realized he had provoked a passion in Eliana. She was very devoted to this Jehovah. She was talking to him openly, almost forgetting how shy she was in his presence. She may be a timid female on some accounts, but her faith was definitely not something she was timid over. This he would remember in the future for further conversations he planned to have.

"Grow up eating nothing but manna for years, and you too would be thankful for figs and porridge," she grinned with a small laugh. Nazim noticed her face soften when she smiled, and the sound of her laughter brought a small smile to his own. Clearly uncomfortable and surprised with herself at how honest she had become, she quickly schooled her features, swallowed deeply, and filled the cup she had placed in front of him. She abruptly turned then to see to her other guests.

The seats were filling quickly now as people hurried in, eager to break their fast and begin their day.

"Eliana," an old man called to her. He sounded gruff, but Nazim watched as she approached him, laid her hand on his shoulder, and then leaned low to kiss his withered cheek.

"Good morning, Abner," she spoke kindly to the elder patron, and Nazim noticed again how easily she conversed with the others. She wasn't particularly shy in nature he observed, only in the presence of himself.

"You have hungry customers, and you have nothing more to do than stand around jabbering in the corner?" he scoffed.

"I will be right back with your porridge, Abner," she promised with a smile.

"And maybe one of those fig cakes like yesterday," he yelled over his shoulder.

"Yes, Abner," she smiled, moving quickly to the cooking area. Eliana was very efficient in her task. Her customers seemed to be content, and her service to them was impeccable. She obviously enjoyed her work and she seemed to honestly enjoy the people who appeared to be regular guests in the establishment. Eliana stayed busy, and Nazim watched as she laughed easily, paying special attention to each and every person. She even returned to his table, filling his cup when it had gotten low. She did not converse with him but simply nodded as he thanked her.

Nazim took his time eating, continuing to observe the people around him. He had just finished the last bite of his bread, laid his napkin on the table beside his plate, and pushed back his chair when a thunderous racket sounded from outside in the street. Out of habit, he was quick to his feet, his hand going to the dagger at his side as he moved quickly toward the door. Eliana quickly set down everything that occupied her hands on the table nearest her and reached the door of the inn before he did, pulling it open and exposing a tremendous cloud of dust. Quickly, she covered her mouth and nose with her veil and ran straight into the cloud toward the street beyond.

"Well, she is not nearly as timid as I originally believed," Nazim thought as he continued quickly toward the door, fascinated at her bravery. Other patrons simply kept their seats and craned their necks to see what was going on. They were curious but clearly not anxious to become a part of whatever was happening in the street.

Nazim exited the door shortly behind Eliana, and through the haze, he spotted her standing in the middle of the street facing the inn. A large beam on the far corner of the building, which had held the roof over the entrance to the structure, had collapsed, taking the corner of the roof with it. Fortunately, it appeared to have only affected the stoop over the doorway and had not removed the roof over the inn itself. Still, it had caused quite a mess and had left the integrity of the entire roof now in question.

"Well," Eliana spoke first as the dust continued to settle, "this presents a problem," she spoke calmly, one hand on her hip and the other continuing to cover her mouth and nose with her veil. Nazim was amazed at her composure. He would have expected tears and flailing at the discovery. Instead, Eliana calmly took in the scene before her. The majority of the dust had fallen as she now approached the mass of broken wood and crumbled stone carefully as she attempted to survey the damage up close. Nazim noticed that many others in the street continued about their day, only pausing to gauge how to move around the mess the collapse had created and being careful not to trip over the rubble.

"I knew that beam was going to give way sooner or later," someone yelled angrily to her, approaching the doorway from inside the inn. "We have been warning you to fix it!" he yelled from the open portal.

"Yes, Abner, it appears you were correct," Eliana returned simply, and Nazim recognized him as the older man from inside the inn.

"Is everyone well, Eliana? Did anyone suffer?" another woman called to her who was passing by on the street.

"No, Sarah. Everyone is fine. Thank you for your concern," Eliana called back to her. The woman continued then, moving on her way, but Abner approached where they stood, carefully stepping over stones and broken beams until he reached Eliana's side.

"Better get this mess out of the road before Kylus comes through town," he spoke again, though softer now. Nazim realized that although he appeared to be a bitter man, this man she had called Abner now seemed to be issuing a gentle warning.

"Kylus is returning soon?" she questioned, looking at Abner. From his vantage point, Nazim could not see her face clearly, but he could hear the anguish in her voice at the mention of this "Kylus."

"You know it will not be long," Abner assured her. "He has not been through here in weeks. He is expected any day. Especially if he hears of this."

Eliana took a deep breath and sighed. Nazim did not know why, but for some reason, her obvious concern of this man, Kylus, stirred anger within him.

"Who is this Kylus?" Nazim asked, now from his place behind her.

Eliana turned to look at him, her discomfort at speaking to him obviously being temporarily replaced with the unfortunate situation before her. She paused only a moment before answering.

"A self-appointed leader of our city," she answered honestly, looking up at him over her shoulder. Nazim moved to stand beside her as she spoke. "He lives on the outskirts of town between Heshbon and Bashan. He goes between the two of our cities to ensure we are following the commands of Jehovah and not 'falling prey to the gods of the lands our people have conquered,'" she explained with emphasis on the latter statement.

"He will consider this mess an 'unholy sight,'" Abner explained. "And he will expect a penalty to be paid for anything he feels is not enabling the rebuilding of the cities in a manner that is befitting Jehovah God."

"He calls them 'righteous tributes,'" Eliana continued.

"Yet, there is nothing righteous about them," Abner snapped, spitting in disrespect on the ground.

"Another perfect opportunity presents itself." Nazim thought again.

"Then I should get busy," he spoke aloud as he moved toward the rubble.

"And you are?" Abner asked, bitterness consuming his tone once again.

"Just passing through," Nazim spoke as he lifted a large boulder with ease. Abner's mouth dropped in astonishment as he watched Nazim easily carry the boulder to the side of the inn and drop it with little effort to the ground.

"Seems like you can handle it well enough," the old man huffed as he turned to leave, mumbling under his breath about the mess as he once again moved along his way.

"Sir, please," Eliana began, directing her attention back to Nazim. "I cannot allow…" she began.

Nazim looked at her as he lifted a broken beam with barely any effort.

"It does not appear to me as if you have much of a choice," he spoke with a sideways grin as he balanced the broken beam easily on his shoulder.

"But I cannot pay you for your work," she clarified.

Nazim carried the beam to the side of the inn and placed it beside the boulder. He returned to Eliana and looked down at her, a plan once again formulating in his mind. He could sense her uneasiness return at his near proximity to her, yet she did not look away from his face as he spoke.

He began to speak, crossing his arms in a disarming manner. "I am here," he began with certainty, "and I have nothing pressing that requires my immediate attention. You, on the other hand, have a rather large task, which does seem to be rather pressing at the moment. Perhaps we can work out an exchange," he offered.

"I am listening," she countered hesitantly, now crossing her arms as well as she stood looking up at him. He almost smiled at the curiosity that marked her features but did not want her to feel he was belittling her.

Nazim took in the task before him. The debris would have to be cleared, even if they chose not to rebuild the stoop. He was sure with careful planning, he could make the project take as long or go as quickly as he needed, giving him as much time as he desired to acquire the answers to the questions that plagued him. And, he would never have to leave the proximity of the inn. He had wandered for over a year. Having a soft bed and provided meals, even if it was temporary, somewhat appealed to him.

"I will do what it takes to complete clearing the debris," he offered, "for a room and food for myself and my horse until the task is completed."

Eliana looked again at the huge mess before her. There was no way she could complete the job herself, and Grandfather would kill himself if he even attempted to do it. Reuben could prove helpful, but the task before them was far too big for him to attempt alone. She also knew she could never afford to pay anyone the sum that would be asked to have the debris cleared and to complete the necessary repairs. And then there was Kylus. Eliana sighed in defeat.

By the looks of the giant before her, he could make easy work of the task which, not only seemed but was, in all actuality, impossible for her. She could not see that she had any other choice.

"It appears Jehovah has sent someone to aid me in my time of trouble," Eliana spoke in agreement with his offer.

"Something like that," Nazim answered, once again a sideways grin playing at his lips.

"I shall need to know your name if you are to be with us for a while," she stated.

"Eliana!" a scream echoed through the streets. Uma ran as fast as she could to her friend grabbing her in a fierce hug at her approach. "Are you well? Whatever happened?" she asked, breaking the embrace and looking up and down at her friend to make sure she was not harmed.

"All is well, Uma. Breathe," Eliana instructed, calming her friend. "The beam finally gave way, but…" she stumbled, realizing she still did not have his name, "our guest is going to help me with the repairs," she finished, motioning to Nazim.

Nazim stood before them, his hands planted on his hips. Uma stared at him, her mouth gaping. Until now, she had been so overcome with the scene she had come upon that she had paid no heed to his presence. Uma, noticing him now, was overtaken with the man before her. Without a word, Eliana used one finger to lift Uma's chin, closing her friend's gaping mouth firmly.

"I should really get to work," Nazim stated motioning to the debris at his back. "Ladies," he nodded as he moved to continue his task.

Uma took Eliana's arm and ushered her quickly around the inn to the back entrance.

"Tell me EVERYthing!" Uma demanded as soon as they were out of earshot.

"Uma, there is nothing to tell!" Eliana spoke sternly, shaking her head at her childish friend. "The beam collapsed; Abner mentioned that Kylus would be coming through soon; our guest overheard it and offered to stay on to make the repairs for room and meals. That is EVERYthing," she mocked her friend.

"But who IS he?" Uma asked, sneaking a peak around the corner of the inn, hoping to catch another glimpse of the handsome stranger.

"I have no idea," Eliana answered sincerely. "He could be a thief or a vagabond, for all I know. But what I do know is that he is here and that I could really use his help just now. So, please, leave him be, and let him complete the task at hand quickly. I cannot afford a "righteous tribute" at the hand of Kylus right now. We are doing well just to keep food on our tables to serve our paying guests without having to gouge them for what little change remains in their pockets," she answered honestly.

"I will leave him be," Uma promised, "but if you were honest with yourself, you would admit that he is very handsome. Look at how easily he handles those boulders!" she whispered excitedly.

Eliana stole a look and shook her head, a puzzled expression on her face. "Handsome he may be, but there is something unnerving about him," Eliana admitted quietly to her friend. "Like he is hiding something…" Eliana paused, not able to give words to the thoughts in her mind as she continued to watch him navigate through the rubble.

"I know," Uma laughed quietly. "Is he not mysterious?" she giggled.

Eliana threw back her head in defeat and sighed. "Uma, please," she begged. "We have guests inside who are waiting for their morning meal. Please help me serve them so they will continue to be *paying* guests."

"Alright, alright. But you have to promise to tell me everything that happens while he is here," Uma giggled.

Eliana rolled her eyes and shook her head as she escorted her friend through the back door of the inn.

Chapter Five

Nazim worked throughout the morning, clearing the largest pieces of debris from the path. When he had first begun, the villagers had paused, watching in awe as he lifted the massive boulders and beams, but as the morning wore on and people became consumed with their day, he became less of a novelty among the people of the city. Nazim allowed his thoughts to wander as he worked, ignoring the spectators, allowing his mind to go back to the day he had frantically arrived in Jericho to find the massive walls collapsed and the city in ruins. Anger still burned through his veins as he remembered the destruction clearly, and he used that anger to fuel his strength for the task at hand.

By mid-afternoon, the majority of the largest beams and boulders had been cleared. The path into the inn was now free of rubble and debris, allowing guests to access the main entrance with no problem and no danger to themselves. He had also removed the remnants of the stoop directly over the entrance, assuring there was nothing that could potentially cause harm to anyone as they entered the establishment. There was still much work to be done. The rather large stoop had wrapped around the building, and none of it was safe now that one of the main beams supporting it had broken. The entirety of the stoop would have to be completely removed, and the roof that covered it, but not just now.

His task this day had been great and had worn on him physically, his anger being exactly the fuel he needed. His stomach reminded him suddenly that he had not even thought to stop for the midday meal. Now, he was near exhaustion, yet his pride refused him the luxury of a lingered rest.

Leaning on a large broken beam, he stood and observed the damage. There was simply no way he could make the repairs necessary without giving some attention to the earth which had supported the entire structure. It appeared that not only was a broken beam the issue but also the sagging ground below which

49

had begun to recede and give way. He would have to find a way to stabilize the earth before he could begin to efficiently repair the stoop.

From her place in the cooking area, Eliana could see Nazim from the back entrance as he studied the situation. She had been scorning Uma all morning for continually sneaking peeks at him from the same doorway. Currently, her friend had busied herself with the tent maker's son. He was a lively boy who was enjoying the innocent attention Uma was giving him. Eliana rolled her eyes to herself. *"Well, he does not have the best reputation, but Ezra is a much safer target than some others,"* Eliana reasoned, turning her own gaze out the door to the soldier beyond it once more. *"This one is very handsome,"* she admitted to herself, *"but he also seems very dangerous,"* she honestly admitted. *"Any attention you show him could be easily misconstrued by men such as himself. But still, he is doing you a great favor, and you must be hospitable to him. And he is a guest."*

She continued her silent argument with herself as she began to gather bread, meat, and cheese, as well as a flask. She put the provisions into a leather satchel and filled the flask with water, grabbing an apple to add to the fare, before exiting the back entrance. Nazim watched her as she approached.

"You have made great progress, and quickly," she observed in amazement, offering him the satchel and water. "You missed the noon meal, and you have expended a lot of energy. You must be hungry."

Nazim accepted the satchel and peeked inside. Seeing the food, his stomach rumbled once again. He moved to a large boulder and sat, using a small amount of the water from the flask to clean his hands before taking a long draw from it. It was the first water he had drank all morning, and Eliana felt ashamed that she had not thought to bring him water earlier as he continued to drink. In only a moment, the flask was empty. As he finished, he realized she continued to stand across from him.

"Thank you," he remembered to say, wiping his mouth with the back of his hand.

Eliana held out her hand for the flask. "Let me refill that for you," she offered. Nazim nodded as she took the flask from him, then smiled as he pulled the apple from the sack.

"My favorite," he commented with a grin before taking a large bite. "How did you know?" he chided her.

"You need nourishment," she said matter-of-factly. "I thought you could use something sweet as well." She almost returned the smile but caught herself and quickly schooled her features. She must not give him any false pretense for her kindness. "I will be right back with more water," she stated plainly as she turned away.

Nazim continued to eat from the sack, enjoying every bite of the food she had provided. He could not remember when meat and cheese had tasted so good. Eliana returned with the flask, once again filled to the brim, offered it to him, and then turned to leave as soon as he had accepted it.

"Your brother would rebuke me," he stated as she walked away. Eliana stopped and turned back to him.

"For?" she asked, though she expected she knew the answer to her own question.

"I failed to pray before my meal," he stated just as she had anticipated, a small smile lifting one corner of his mouth.

"That would be an issue for you to take up with Jehovah, not Reuben," she answered, her face solemn as she turned to leave once again.

"Your Jehovah has no desire to hear from me," Nazim spoke with certainty around a bite of bread. Just as he expected, he struck a nerve, and Eliana stopped immediately, turning her body to face him once again.

"What do you know of our God?" she asked simply, watching him from where she stood. Nazim pulled his knee up on the boulder and took a long draw from the flask she had refilled. He must be careful with his response, and he took another long drink to prolong his answer. He finally decided to be honest, which would ensure a continued conversation with Eliana.

"Not as much as I would like to," he stated, speaking honestly while again wiping the water from his mouth. Eliana watched him, and although her desire was to turn and walk away, she could not leave him wondering about the God she so loved and respected. Everyone deserved to know of Jehovah. Slowly she began to approach as he spoke.

"I know that He is apparently very powerful and that He's capable of using common men to do great things," Nazim spoke with surety. "I also know that He expects much prayer, and I am assuming worship, from things I have heard, from those who have chosen to serve Him," he continued.

"Israel did not choose Him," she spoke softly, "He chose Israel." Surprisingly, Eliana took a seat on a boulder across from him, and Nazim accepted the silent invitation to continue the conversation.

"Whichever the case," he retaliated, "I have known nothing but destruction from the hands of your God. He obviously defeated the gods of my people and took everything I had as well in His conquest. I have nothing to offer Him, and obviously, He cares little for those who are not willing to sacrifice much for His purpose, whatever that purpose is," he finished. Nazim leaned forward now, his feet planted firmly on the ground beneath him, his elbows propped on his knees. He felt his back protest as he assumed this position and realized he may have pushed himself to the limit by lifting so many large beams and boulders in such a short span of time.

"You still have your life," Eliana answered sincerely, "which is all Jehovah requires. And it is far more than the other citizens of Jericho can say. Apparently, Jehovah has plans for you outside the walls of the city of Jericho, much as He did Rahab. She chose to serve Him, and now, she is the wife of Salmon, who is a prince among our people. She and her family are quite happy and very well cared for. Far more than they ever were inside the walls of Jericho. Jehovah must have a plan for you as well, else you, too, would have perished in the destruction of the city."

Nazim breathed deeply as he turned his head slowly in her direction. His eyes were like pure steel as he glared at her, cold and menacing. He had not expected the name of Rahab to come from her lips, and it took everything he could muster to control his temper at the mention of not only her name but of her newfound happiness. Eliana was stunned at the rigid look she witnessed coming from him and jumped so quickly to her feet that she almost stumbled.

"I should let you get back to your work," she spoke softly as she gathered her skirts and almost ran to the back entrance of the inn. Once inside, she slammed the door closed, leaning against it in an effort to control her features and catch her breath. She was not sure what she had just said that had provoked such anger in him, but she was sure that she would do everything in her power to avoid any further conversation with him. How could she have dropped her guard and been so outspoken? Why had she even cared what he knew of Jehovah? The quicker he finished the task he had promised to complete, the quicker she would be rid of him. He was a grown man; he could find his own water. And God forgive her, but someone else could tell him of Jehovah. She would not put herself in that situation again.

Nazim kept his place, not even turning to watch her flee. He realized instantly that he had frightened her; he had caused grown men to retreat from his presence with that look. He had not meant to cast it in her direction. Still, the name of Rahab and her happiness coming from the lips of Eliana had caused his blood to boil. And how could she even fathom the care Rahab had inside the city? He had always protected her!

Nazim remained seated in the position he was in, forcing his blood pressure to calm. At this moment, he felt he could have ripped the boulder beneath him into two equal parts.

Grandfather had been cautiously watching the entire exchange from the window above. He expected Eliana to be hospitable to any of their guests, but he also expected her to use extreme caution in the presence of men such as Nazim. He must speak to her and find out what exactly had caused her to retreat so quickly from Nazim's presence. Perhaps simply telling her who this soldier was and that he hailed from Jericho had not been enough to rouse the caution in her that he intended. Perhaps he should have told her more.

He had tried to be as discreet as possible and not divulge all of Nazim's sins to his granddaughter. After all, everything he had been told of the man was hearsay; the battles he had fought, the men he had killed, the reputation that he had earned, and Eli expected much of it was embellished as those stories often were. Still, Nazim had, in fact, been a mighty warrior in control of many men, and he was a man who was used to getting his way in any situation presented to him. The fall of the city he protected, at a time when he was not present, was not something he would easily accept. This likely provoked an anger in him unlike any other, much of it toward the Israeli people, and Grandfather must make sure that Eliana understood the danger in that.

Slowly, he took his walking cane and descended the small flight of stairs that led to the main room. Uma continued to sit with the tentmaker's son talking and laughing. A few others were scattered around, prolonging their midday break before moving to complete their tasks and end their day. Eli moved to the cooking area where he expected Eliana to be. He entered the room silently, and once there, he watched as she continued leaning against the door, her eyes closed, working to calm her breathing.

"Eliana," he spoke softly.

"Grandfather!" she exclaimed in surprise, working effortlessly to control her features. "What do you need? What can I get for you?" she asked, jumping into action and pulling a stool over to him.

"Nothing, nothing, my dear," he assured her calmly as he took the seat she offered and motioned for her to take one across from him. Eliana did as he asked and sat.

"I was watching from my window as you and the soldier were conversing," he began. "I must say, you left him rather quickly. May I ask what provoked such a hasty retreat? Did he say something inappropriate?"

"No, Grandfather," Eliana began to explain, "but I fear that perhaps I did," she blushed.

"Eliana?" he questioned in surprise. "Please continue."

"I took him some nourishment, for he has done much work in a short amount of time and had failed even to break for the noon meal. He is doing us a great favor, Grandfather, and though you warned me of him, I still assumed you expect me to be hospitable to all of our guests."

"I do," he confirmed. "Continue," he instructed.

"Reuben has already spoken to him about praying over his meals, and he almost mocked that he had failed to do so. But as we talked, I realized that he knows nothing of our God. He sees Jehovah as harsh and unyielding, out for nothing other than the destruction and demise of great cities, great cities such as his Jericho. He went on to say that our Jehovah would not care to hear from him and that he had nothing to offer Him." Eliana stood and began pacing in front of her grandfather, wringing her hands in front of her. "All I said, Grandfather, was that Jehovah must have plans for him outside the walls of Jericho to have spared his life in the way He did. And I told Him that He obviously had great plans for Rahab and her family as well, seeing as how since she had come to serve Him, she had married Salmon and was happier and more cared for than she had ever been while inside the gates of the city of Jericho."

"Ah," Grandfather said, holding his hand in mid-air, signaling for Eliana to stop.

Eliana rushed back to her stool and sat, taking her grandfather's hands in her own.

"What was it, Grandfather? What did I say to provoke such anger in him? He looked at me as if he could have taken my life on the spot! I have never seen so much hate in a person's eyes before." She shook her head to dispel the image that still caused chills to race up her arm. "He frightened me, and I ran."

Grandfather hesitated before he spoke. Eliana was always very passionate about Jehovah. He did not want to quench her spirit when speaking of their God to others, so he must be careful with his instruction to her.

"Ellie," he spoke calmly, using the name only he had ever been allowed to when referring to her. "Men like Nazim are very prideful in their abilities to protect and to rule over other men. I told you that he has been a great man of war, but I fear you do not understand the complexities that come with that stature. Reminding him of the destruction of his city is like rubbing salt in an open wound. And revealing how much happier citizens of his former city are, now that they are free from it, is like piercing a dagger through his heart."

"So, I offended him," she realized. "But he still had no right to look at me in that way," she reasoned.

"I fear you did, and you are correct. However," he continued, "when I told you who he was, I had hoped you would pick up on the subtle warning I was offering you. Because you did not, it is I who should apologize to you for my not being more clear in my warning," he finished opening his arms for a hug.

Eliana leaned into his embrace. "I love you, Grandfather, and it is I who should apologize. I should not have been so naïve when dealing with a man such as him."

"You have little experience with men of war, Ellie. And your passion to share the love of our God is to be commended. Oh, that others would share the love of our Jehovah as you and Reuben do!"

Eliana pulled from his embrace but did not let go. "We were taught by the best," she smiled to him. "I do not know how to apologize to him," she stated honestly.

"It will work itself out," he assured her. "Perhaps you are meant to tell him of Jehovah, Ellie, but be most careful and use much precaution when dealing with his past. It is best to leave it where it is, in his past."

"I will, Grandfather," she promised with another hug. As if by design Uma chose that moment to bound into the room.

"Eliana, you will not believe it," she began as she came through the door not even looking up as she moved to place cups and plates on the table for washing. "I just had the most wonderful conversation with Ezra, the tentmaker's son! He is such a delight...Oh! Grandfather Eli," she started as she finally took in the additional company in the room. "I did not see you there," she paused and stared at the scene in front of her. "Wait, what did I miss?" she asked innocently.

Grandfather chuckled and stood to excuse himself.

"Just an old man who needed a moment with his lovely granddaughter," he grinned as he walked past them. "It is time for me to go back to my room," he stated, patting Uma's arm as he moved about his way.

Eliana watched him go and wondered to herself what she would ever do without his guidance. She decided quickly that she would not tell Uma just now of the exchange with Nazim. She wanted the interaction to remain between herself and her grandfather.

"We must get ready for the evening meal," she said to Uma as she began to gather vegetables to chop for the stew.

Uma shrugged her shoulders and moved to the back door.

"How is our soldier?" she asked cheekily. Uma cracked the door enough to peer through. "Hmm?" she continued, "I don't see him. Wonder where he went?" she asked aloud, yet to herself, before going back into the main room to continue clearing the mid-day dishes from the tables.

Eliana heard Uma's comment and watched her friend go back to the main room before making her way discreetly to the opening to peer out for herself. She quietly pushed the door open a bit further, but Nazim was nowhere in sight. "I wonder," she said aloud, though quietly, then turned and began to busy herself as well.

Nazim kept still in his hiding place, against the wall right behind the door they had been looking through, completely hidden from their view. He had been heading to the stream behind the inn when he heard Grandfather's voice. He had hidden himself and listened to the entire exchange between Grandfather and Eliana.

"So, she wants to share her Jehovah with me," he thought to himself. *"Well, I shall do everything in my power to make sure she has exactly the opportunity she needs to do just that,"* he smirked quietly before carefully moving, undetected, back to his task.

Chapter Six

Nazim continued to work until the sun had moved across the sky. He assumed it was about an hour before the evening meal was scheduled to be served. He knew he would have to rectify the situation with Eliana, but he could do nothing in the condition he found himself in currently. He was hot, he was tired, and he was filthy, and adding to his exhaustion, his back screamed at him with every move he made. He decided a soak was in order before his nourishment.

The washhouse appeared unoccupied, so he made his way into the inn to order a bath. He knew that both Eliana and Uma would be busy preparing for the coming meal, so he would gladly draw the bath himself. However, he felt he should let someone know before he began his soak.

He entered through the front entrance of the inn, continued on through the central dining room, and peeked inside the cooking area. Seeing no one, he paused a moment until he heard movement further back. Nazim had not been in the back part of the inn. Before proceeding he knocked gently on the door frame, getting no response. Silently, he moved further into the cooking area.

"I'm telling you, Eliana," he heard Uma saying, "we have so many things in common. Ezra is so different than I expected! He is coming back tonight, so please, may I serve him?" she begged. "Do not take this small pleasure from your dearest friend," she pleaded. Nazim heard Eliana's laughter fill the small space, and he grinned slightly, enjoying the sound of it.

He continued further into the back room, knocking again as he went, both ladies now in his view.

"Excuse me," he spoke softly in an attempt not to frighten either of the women. They were clearly caught up in their private conversation and had yet to realize they were not alone.

"Women in Jericho were much more aware of their surroundings," he thought to himself. *"These two would not stand*

a chance in a big city." He stood behind them, though there remained a large space between them. Their backs to him, Eliana worked diligently as she talked, adding vegetables to a large, boiling pot while Uma continued her plea from her place beside her.

"You always serve the good ones," she pouted.

"I do not," Eliana argued with a chuckle, "I only strive to protect you from yourself by serving anyone who could potentially do you harm," she laughed. "You must take caution, Uma! You are far too careless with your obvious affection when it comes to men." Finally, she relinquished to Uma's pouting face. "Fine, you may serve the tentmaker's son. He seems harmless enough," she consented, laughing at her friend who jumped up and down beside her.

"Thank you, Eliana!" Uma giggled. "Ezra is harmless, and though I think he is *very* attractive, you have to admit he still isn't as handsome as our resident soldier," Uma crooned, snatching a carrot from the pile Eliana worked from. "But you go ahead, serve Mr. Handsome and his 'dangerous' self. It isn't like you are going to allow me to anyway," she laughed, "but I truly think it is because you believe he is extremely handsome as well," she smirked as she bit down hard on the raw carrot.

"Uma," Eliana began, and Nazim decided before the conversation continued he must make his presence known, regardless of frightening them or not. He cleared his throat loudly, provoking a small squeal from Uma, who spun around quickly, dropping her carrot to the floor and causing Eliana to drop the vegetables she held in her hand into the steaming pot with a plop. The boiling water sloshed up onto Eliana's hand, and at once, she grabbed it, rushing to a basin filled with water.

"I did not mean to frighten either of you," he apologized quickly, "but I had knocked twice in an effort to make my presence known," he defended himself, pointing back toward the door frame. He continued speaking quickly, explaining the purpose of his intrusion. "I realize the two of you are busy preparing for the evening meal, but I was hoping to have a bath before I dine if that is suitable. I am more than capable of drawing the water myself if that is allowed." As he finished, though her back was to him, he noticed Eliana had her hand submerged in the water basin.

"Of course," she stated, not looking back at him. Her hand felt as if a fire had been set to it, even as she kept it submerged in the cool water. "Uma, please show our guest the location of the bath pitcher and assist him with gathering the water," she instructed from her place. "And please make sure it is heated to his liking as well." She worked to control her voice as her hand continued throbbing, even submerged in the cool water.

Uma kept her place, watching silently as Nazim, unknowingly to Eliana, slowly made his way to the table where Eliana stood soaking her hand. Eliana did not notice his approach, but she felt his presence behind her as he reached the spot where she stood. She did not turn to face him but kept her head low, focusing on her hand. The fact that Uma had not jumped at the opportunity to assist him, although she had specifically been asked to, also guaranteed that something abnormal was happening.

Without a word, Nazim, now standing at her side, reached down touching her wrist gently as he lifted her hand out of the water. He did not miss the way she tensed at his touch or how rapid her breathing had become. Whether it was from the pain of the burn or the fact that he was so near to her, he was not sure. Her entire hand was bright red, and though the overall burn did not look severe, one small spot had already begun to blister where the scalding water had hit her skin.

"I have caused you to both flee my presence in fear and to harm yourself in but a few short hours," he spoke quietly as he looked at her hand. Eliana had yet to look in his direction. She kept her face downcast toward the water basin, reminding herself to breathe as he continued to hold her wrist. "If I am to continue working for you, we must work on your apprehension of my presence," he joked. "But first, I sincerely ask that you accept my apology for my reaction to our earlier conversation and for my causing you harm just now. I would never intentionally hurt you," he promised. "Please, forgive me," he paused, giving her lead to speak.

Eliana continued to remain silent as she stared at her hand hovering above the water. That his gentle hold lingered on her arm did not go unnoticed, and she could not have found her voice if she had wanted to. She could not even bring herself to turn her head to look at him.

"Secondly," he continued in her silence, "wait here and do not submerge your hand back in that water," he instructed as he moved to exit the back entrance.

As soon as he was gone through the back door, Uma was at her side.

"What was that????" she asked excitedly. "Eliana, what earlier conversation is he talking about? You have told me nothing of a conversation with him! And why is he apologizing? What did he say to you?"

"Not now, Uma," she begged, finally finding her voice, though it sounded broken even to her own ears. Eliana swallowed hard, trying to get past the lump in her throat. She did not feel near to tears, yet she wanted to sob. Her pulse was racing, but she didn't know if it was from the pain in her hand or the way her arm continued to tingle from where his touch had been. She was embarrassed and angry, but she wasn't sure why or at whom. Eliana couldn't define exactly which feelings were running through her just now or which of them was going to win the battle. She chewed her lower lip, attempting to control the whirlwind of emotions that rapidly coursed through her entire body, and startled when she heard his footsteps approaching once again. Uma backed away silently, watching as Nazim approached.

"This is a plant that was used in the palace for burns when I was a boy," he explained as he broke apart a tender branch. "I saw it growing by the stream behind your inn earlier. I have not seen it in years until now," he continued, and Eliana watched as smooth sap began to flow from the broken branch. "May I?" he asked, reaching for her injured hand.

Eliana hesitated for a moment but then, surprising even herself, relinquished her hand to him. Nazim held it gently as he began to coat the entire burn with the sap. Instantly, Eliana felt the effects of the application. It honestly felt as if ice had been applied to her scalded skin, and she was amazed that she had never known of the medicinal purposes of this plant before. Nazim then reached for a clean rag that lay folded nearby, stripping a section of material from it. The hands, which had effortlessly lifted masses of beams and stone all day, were gentle now as he carefully wrapped the cloth around her injured hand.

"It will be perfectly well by tomorrow," he assured her. Eliana could do nothing but breathe and had to remind herself to do even that. She pulled her hand back, cradling it with her other, as soon as he had tied a small knot in the cloth to keep the burn secured. Try as she might, she could not bring herself to lift her head to look at him. Nazim backed away, and it was Uma who broke the silence.

"I will get the water pitcher for your bath water," Uma spoke softly, moving to do just that.

"Keep that hand dry this evening," Nazim instructed Eliana before turning to follow Uma.

Eliana knew she would have no choice but to explain her actions, or the lack thereof, to her friend, but how could she explain something she did not understand herself? He had frightened her earlier, yes, but he had apologized for it. Was that what scared her so now? Obviously, despite his demeanor, there was a kindness in him that she had not witnessed until this moment, nor, if she were honest, had she wanted to.

Now alone in the cooking area, Eliana finally turned to look in the direction Nazim had gone. The cloth wrapped tenderly on her hand, and the way her arm continued to tingle where he had touched her was proof of what had happened, but it all had happened so quickly she almost thought it had been a dream. As she continued to gaze through the portal he had exited, Uma appeared. Her friend's face was solemn, and Eliana knew that though she was curious, Uma also realized that now was not the time for more questions.

Eliana swallowed and turned back to her task. "We should, um, finish our preparations," she began slowly. She took a deep breath and returned to the table of vegetables. "Guests will be arriving soon, and they will be eager for their meal."

"Of course," Uma agreed softly, moving into action.

The ladies finished preparing for the meal in silence. Uma automatically attended to anything that required placing her hands in water, and Eliana made sure the food was prepared and ready to be served. Finally, right before the guests began to arrive, Uma spoke.

"Is your hand okay," she asked her friend sincerely.

"It is," Eliana acknowledged.

"Are *you* okay?" Uma questioned hesitantly, watching her. Eliana appreciated her friend's concern and knew she was worried.

Eliana took a deep breath and exhaled slowly. She motioned for Uma to sit with her at the table in the cooking area where the two of them often sat to have their own meals. The ladies sat down, and Eliana told Uma of the earlier conversation she and Nazim had shared. She told her what she had said to him, how he had frightened her, and the conversation she and Grandfather had shared immediately after. Uma listened intently to her friend.

"I had no idea he was the soldier from Jericho that the entire town has been buzzing about," Uma acknowledged amazed. "I guess I really am naïve when it comes to men," she smirked. "So, he is the infamous Nazim we have heard of? He sure did not seem so rogue and ruthless as his reputation dictated when he tended to your hand," she said softly, reaching for her friend across the table.

"Which is why we must be careful," Eliana agreed, extending her hand to her dearest friend. "We do not know him at all. And now I am embarrassed for not even telling him thank you. That sap is a miracle straight from Jehovah," she laughed. "I tried to thank him, Uma, but I could not even acknowledge him!" she answered in complete honesty.

Uma sat back and looked at her friend, a quizzical look on her face.

"What is that look for," Eliana asked.

"Because, admit it or not, I believe my levelheaded best friend finally has a crush," she smirked.

"Uma! That is ridiculous! I just told you how dangerous of a person he is!" Eliana denied. "How could you even suggest such a thing?" she questioned as she jumped up from the table and began to gather bowls of stew to serve the guests who were beginning to file in.

"I cannot believe that you would not allow Kylus the time of day when he pursued you," Uma joked as she moved to assist Eliana, "but a dangerous, albeit handsome stranger wanders into town, and you forget to breathe and have butterflies in your stomach!"

Eliana shook her head and cast a playful glare in the direction of her friend. "This ridiculous conversation is over!" she whispered adamantly before moving into the main room to begin serving their guests.

"Good evening, Abner," Eliana stated more loudly than necessary as she set a steaming mug of stew in front of one of her favorite customers.

"It is about time you got out here," he grumbled. "I have been waitin' all day for this stew." Eliana bent down to kiss his withered cheek. "Sure does smell good," he grinned in his small, lopsided way. "I know it will be worth the wait."

Uma laughed at being so clearly ignored as she began to serve other patrons. Her hands were empty quickly, and she moved back to the cooking area to gather more bowls. Before she entered, she paused just out of sight of the others. In what had become "his spot" was their wandering soldier. Back corner, just in the shadows, almost undetectable. His gaze was careful yet clearly fixed on something across the room. Following his gaze, Uma wasn't surprised to catch him carefully watching Eliana, who had yet to spot him, as she served and spoke to the guests who now filled the inn.

Uma continued into the cooking area, and it was only a moment before she was joined by Eliana. Gathering more bowls of the steaming stew, Uma spoke quietly so as not to be overheard.

"The soldier waits in his corner," she spoke in low tones. "Would you rather I wait on him this evening?" Eliana recognized Uma's thoughtfulness and appreciated her kindness. She knew her offer to serve him this time was not because Uma sought his attention; the offer stemmed out of pure concern for her friend.

"No, I will see to him," Eliana conceded. "He did apologize, and I do need to thank him for his assistance earlier."

"Just do NOT bring up anything from his past," Uma reminded her, firmly speaking the words. "Remember what you told me Grandfather Eli has stressed to you."

"Never. Again." Eliana promised sternly. Both girls shared a grin as they exited the cooking area. True to her word, Eliana turned to the corner where Nazim sat patiently waiting. He watched as she approached him.

"I was about to worry that I would not be served this evening," he joked as she placed the stew in front of him.

"Do not be ridiculous," she answered softly, forcing herself to look at him. He met her gaze, and she cleared her throat before she continued. "I," she swallowed past the lump in her throat, "I want to thank you," she forced her voice to say, "for your assistance earlier. That sap was...a miracle." She looked at her hand still wrapped in the bandage he had prepared.

"So, it feels better then?" he asked. She nodded simply.

"Great!" he grinned at her, "because I was not sure that was going to work!" Eliana allowed a small laugh to escape at his jest. That he had made her laugh caused his grin to widen, and Eliana could not believe how much the gesture softened his face.

"This stew smells amazing," he continued, taking his spoon in one hand and a crust of bread in the other. "Join me?" he requested sincerely.

"I...I... cannot just now," Eliana declined. "I must see to the other guests, and Uma..." she looked around to see her friend now seated with Ezra, a smile stretching across her face from ear to ear as she held his complete attention, "is occupied," she shrugged with a sigh.

"Maybe next time," Nazim acknowledged.

Before she could answer, Reuben bounded to the table.

"Good afternoon, Sir!" he exclaimed, taking the seat Nazim had been hoping Eliana would occupy. "I just spent quite a bit of time with Ares, and he is desperate for a ride."

Eliana smiled softly at her brother, patting his head as she turned to tend to the other guests. Reuben had saved her, and she was so thankful for that innocent interruption that she would not care if he talked to the soldier all night. She chuckled to herself as she heard Reuben reminding Nazim and then praying himself over the meal their guest was about to enjoy.

Other guests were now filling the empty seats, and Eliana worked quickly to fill her tray and see to them. As she exited the cooking area, she took a moment to pause in the doorway as she looked back to the table where her brother sat still chatting away. She even went so far as to return a small smile when she noticed that the soldier he was talking to continued watching her.

Chapter Seven

The next morning, Nazim woke to the morning light shining brightly through his window. He had no idea what time it was, but he could tell the sun was higher in the sky than at his usual waking time. He had gone another night without the nightmares, and he assumed it was due to his body being utterly exhausted. If that's what it took, then so be it. Working hard was a small price to pay for a decent night's rest.

As he rolled over to rise, he felt his back protest in every possible way. The soak the night before had helped, but hiding out on the Jericho Road had done nothing for his physical or mental well-being. He had been "out of service" for too long, and now he was paying the price for his inactivity. Finally on his feet, he moved to the wash basin and splashed the cold water on his face. He stretched his back as he watched people going to and fro in the street below him.

He observed the scene for a moment before he altered his gaze to the stables behind the inn. Reuben had stated that Ares grew restless, and the lad was surely right. His horse was not used to being stabled, and some exercise would do him good. Nazim reminded himself to make it a point to check on his animal and to give him the needed exercise before the day was over.

As he continued to watch the villagers move about to begin their daily tasks, he thought back to the events of the day before. He had genuinely been concerned over Eliana's well-being yesterday. First, when he had frightened her, and then when she had burned her hand. Where that concern stemmed from, he was not sure, and it unnerved him slightly. He had come here with a clear mission and a clear plan. He could not allow himself to be distracted by a pretty face and alter his intentions. He had encounters with beautiful women on a regular basis and truth be told, he enjoyed them, but other than Rahab, none had ever intrigued him as this woman did.

Rahab. There she was wandering into his thoughts again. With a deep breath, he turned to ready himself before going about his day. Quickly, he tied his hair into a knot. *"Remember your plan,"* he reminded himself with his hand on his doorknob.

Moving downstairs, Nazim was surprised to see that the majority of the patrons had already broken their fast and gone about their way.

"Good morning, Nazim," he heard a raspy voice call from a table just below the stairs. Grandfather was seated there, a block of wood in one hand, his carving knife in the other. "Did you rest well?" he asked as Nazim approached.

"I did, thank you," he answered honestly. "Though I believe I had more than I deserved."

Eli shook his head in denial. "A man who works as hard as you did yesterday is deserving of an extra hour. Sit," he commanded, "and break your fast. Ellie!" he called toward the cooking area, "we have a guest," he stated simply.

"Ellie," Nazim grinned, repeating the name he had just heard her grandfather use for the first time.

"Only I can call her that," the old man said sternly, pointing his knife in Nazim's direction, a small smile playing on his lips. "She will not allow it from anyone else," he finished, as he went back to his carving.

Eliana came from the cooking area with figs, bread, and porridge. She paused when she realized it was Nazim whom her grandfather had summoned her for, and the shock that he was seated at her grandfather's table was evident on her face as she served him.

"Good morning," she spoke politely as she set the food in front of him.

"Thank you," he smiled in acknowledgment as Eliana quietly returned the gesture.

Nazim enjoyed his meal and conversed easily with the old man as he ate. Their conversation remained light, and they talked mostly of the inn and how Eli had acquired it. Careful not to linger on the battle of Heshbon between the Israelites and King Sihon's armies, Eli told Nazim of the way he, Eliana, and Reuben had repurposed the structure, which had once been used as a tavern, into this inn for those who needed a place to stay until they were settled.

Once the town had been rebuilt and the inhabitants had established homes of their own, the rooms in the inn remained open for travelers. Most of their daily patrons for meals continued to be those who had once lived here, returning often, some even daily, to enjoy the hot meals and to fellowship with friends.

Nazim soaked in the information and then voiced a question that continued to plague him. "This, Kylus, that Eliana seems so concerned over," Nazim asked as he continued to eat, "what is he all about?"

"Ah, so you are familiar with Kylus?" Eli asked.

"In name only," Nazim clarified.

Eli took a deep breath as if he were deciding carefully on his next words. Nazim continued his meal but watched the old man closely.

"Kylus was one of the men who was chosen by Joshua at a time when our people faced off against Amalek in Rephidim. Moses, our leader at that time, had instructed Joshua to choose the men who would go into battle and fight alongside him. Being a young man, full of life and full of energy, despite the fact that he had issues with authority, not caring for being told what to do and when to do it, Joshua recognized the fact that Kylus was eager and felt that would serve him well on the battlefield. Kylus was not pleased that Joshua had gained the attention of Moses in place of himself, but because he was among the men chosen by Joshua to fight, he fought hard during the battle regardless. Kylus failed to realize that Joshua, like Moses before him, had been hand-picked by Jehovah and that Moses' choice of Joshua was simply him following the orders he had been given from our God.

Nonetheless, the battle was not an easy one, and if it had not been for Moses carefully following the will of Jehovah, we would not have prevailed against the army of Amalek."

"How did your people prevail?" Nazim asked, laying aside his eating utensils and intertwining his fingers clearly engrossed in the story Eli told. *"Finally,"* Nazim thought to himself, *"we are getting somewhere."*

Eli continued, pleased with how intently Nazim was listening. "The battle was long, and our men grew weary. So, Moses, with the rod of God held tightly in his hand, moved to the top of a nearby hill. As long as his arms were extended toward

Heaven, with the rod of God high above us all," Eli demonstrated with his carving block and knife, "Israel prevailed. Yet as soon as Moses would lower his arms for a rest, Amalek would prevail. The battle raged on, and Moses kept his arms extended as high as he could for as long as he could, but eventually, he grew weary, and his arms became weak. Seeing his despair, two of his most trusted men, Aaron and Hur, raced to the top of the hill where Moses stood, and one standing on either side of him supported his arms, keeping the rod of God aimed high toward Heaven.

"We finally defeated Amalek," Eli finished, bringing his arms back to the table, "but Kylus was unhappy when Aaron and Hur received praise for their part in the battle. He did not feel it was fair that men who did not physically fight, but simply 'stood by' as he accused them of doing, would receive accolades for their actions, right along with the men who had physically engaged in the war."

"So how did he become, I believe Eliana called him, 'a self-appointed leader' among your people?" Nazim asked.

"Kylus has his strong points," Eli admitted. "As I said earlier, he proved himself a good fighter and defender, and he does well at keeping peace between large groups of people as long as he feels he is in complete control. He just has problems with those who rule in authority over him, and his ego often gets in his way, which makes him a poor soldier. When our people defeated King Og and took the city of Bashan, Joshua knew that a strong leader would need to be left behind to make sure any Amorites who had been outside the city would not return and try to overthrow our people who were to remain there to rebuild the city once our main company had moved on," he explained. "Kylus offered to stay, coveting a role in leadership, and he did well there at the job he was assigned to," Eli admitted. "No one else coveted his role, which meant that he felt no threat to his power. Once our men moved here, into Heshbon and overthrew King Sihon as well, Kylus assumed the same role here, traveling often between the two cities to make sure his task was carried out to perfection.

"It wasn't until recently, likely due to his continued station among our people, that his ego seems to have totally taken over and gotten the best of him. As of late, nearly nothing can please him other than growing the city treasury. It is as if he feels that growing the treasury grows our dependence upon him as well since he controls it all. He has ordained what he calls 'righteous tributes' and demands them freely, and often, from anyone he feels is necessary."

Nazim wanted to hear more about this Kylus, but even he could tell that the old man was growing tired. From the back, Eliana had been keeping a watchful eye over her grandfather. Sensing his exhaustion, she returned to their table, added more juice to Nazim's cup, and made sure the men had no need of anything further.

"Ellie, sit with us if you would," Grandfather instructed before she moved to return to the cooking area. Eliana opened her mouth to protest, but Grandfather cut her off before she could. "Chores can wait," he stated, and Eliana took the seat between her grandfather and Nazim, sliding her chair closer to her grandfather as she settled.

"Nazim, what do you think of the damage to our structure?" the old man asked, laying his carving knife and the block of wood on the table in front of him. Nazim drank from his cup before he spoke.

"The damage is extensive," he answered honestly. "But it can be repaired. Beams and roofs are easily replaced, but my main concern is with the earth beneath where the stoop had stood. It seems to have been giving way for some time, and finally enough so that the main beam collapsed. The collapse did not affect the structure of the inn itself, only the stoop. It is not absolutely necessary to replace it. I can continue clearing the debris and remove the remaining stoop and it will appear as if it was never there. However, if you require it to be replaced, a foundation will need to be laid under the stoop in order to keep the beams stationary. The thatch roof which covered the stoop will also need to be rebuilt if you desire one, but the structural roof over the main part of the inn itself remains very sound."

Eli listened intently, and Eliana found herself paying close attention as well. Now that she realized the conversation was not intended to be a personal one, she felt a little more at ease with her company, as much as she could in the presence of Nazim, at any rate.

"We cannot thank you enough for all you have already done in clearing the majority of the debris. Should we choose to rebuild the stoop, is that something you would be able to complete as well?" Eli asked outright.

"I can," Nazim answered honestly. "We kept a close eye and made any repairs necessary to the wall in Jericho, due to settling earth or to the natural breakdown of bricks and mortar, and that wall was nearly impenetrable..." Nazim's voice trailed off, and he appeared to be lost in thought for a moment. Eliana lowered her head, toying with the wrap around her hand from yesterday before forcing herself to look at Nazim once again. He was quiet for only a second before he blinked rapidly and began to speak again. Eliana did not miss the painful look that crossed his face at his mention of Jericho, and surprising even to herself, it hurt her for him. Nazim cleared his throat and began again.

"I am quite familiar with construction and will be happy to make any repairs necessary to ensure the integrity of your inn," he promised.

Eli nodded his head. "I believe you have already made a bargain with my granddaughter," he continued, looking first to Nazim and then to Eliana, who nodded in affirmation. "We will make sure you have any materials you need and will assist you in any way we can. Please do not hesitate to let us know whatever materials are necessary to complete the task."

"But, Grandfather," Eliana began, "how can we afford to replace..."

"I desire the stoop to be replaced, Eliana," he clarified kindly. "Many of our patrons enjoy it, and it provides temporary shelter to those passing by on a hot day or seeking shelter from an unexpected rain."

Nazim agreed, and Eli pushed back his chair to stand. The old man looked at his granddaughter and then at the soldier before him. He could not explain the peace he felt this morning, yet he must remain cautious. Just because he had enjoyed a conversation with Nazim did not counteract the things he had heard about him, though he believed the plan forming in his own head now was straight from Jehovah Himself.

"Ellie," he began as he started to ascend the small flight of stairs leading to his room, "make a list of anything Nazim needs straight away and have Reuben gather the items this afternoon. Better yet," he paused and turned back to look at the pair from the first landing, "take the coins, and all of you go to gather the materials. Kylus will be returning soon, and we do not want any righteous tribute penalties. No doubt he has already been informed of our misfortune. The sooner Nazim has what he needs to complete the project, the sooner all of this will be behind us."

Eli closed his door behind him, signaling he was finished with the conversation. The rest was up to Eliana and Nazim. Eliana looked at the closed door and felt her face begin to heat. There was no one in the room except the two of them, and Eliana was suddenly very warm.

Nazim sat back in his chair and looked at the woman beside him. Sensing her discomfort, he could barely keep the smile from his face. He knew he should not tease her, but it was just so hard not to. Still, he decided to refrain from that just now.

"How is your hand?" he asked sincerely as he leaned forward on the table.

"It is well, I believe," she answered curtly with only a glance in his direction. She almost seemed angry at him for her grandfather's suggestion. Nazim bit his lip to keep from smiling.

He reached across the table. "May I see?" he asked.

"There is really no need," she answered quickly.

"Eliana," calling her by her name for the first time. It surprised her so much that she looked directly at him. He held her gaze for a moment before she blinked and looked away.

"You do not have to be afraid of me," he stated sincerely.

"I am not afraid of you," she stated. In an effort to prove her point, she looked directly into his eyes as she spoke, though she, herself, knew she only spoke a half-truth. It had been different when someone else was in their presence. With only the two of them in such close proximity, the uneasy tension had returned. She held her breath as she looked at him and could only force herself to for a moment.

"Then let me see your hand," he laughed.

Stubbornly, she laid her hand on the table with more force than she intended. She grimaced as it hit the table with a thud.

"Why are you so angry?" he laughed again as he gently took her hand and began to carefully untie the knot that he had tied only yesterday.

Eliana scoffed. "I am not angry," she argued, and she could not help but chuckle herself as he arched his eyebrows in disagreement in her direction.

Nazim removed the bandage from her hand. Eliana could hardly believe it. The spot the blister had begun to form just yesterday was now only slightly red. She would hardly have known anything had happened.

"That really is amazing," she agreed, examining the wound. She secretly chided herself for being so childish at the thought of having to spend time with him. Grandfather would never intentionally put her in harm's way. More frustrated with herself and her own actions than at anything else, she quickly rose to retrieve a piece of parchment and a quill.

"What supplies do you require?" she asked, ready to make the list her grandfather had instructed her to.

"We do not need a list; I have the list," Nazim stated, rising and pushing his chair under the table.

"You already made a list?" she asked curiously.

Nazim pointed to his head. "It is all right here," he assured her.

Eliana laughed at his light banter.

"Where is Uma today?" Nazim asked, looking around the inn.

"Why do you seek Uma," she asked quickly, surprised and a little agitated that he would inquire after her friend.

"Because you and I are going to find materials, which means you will not be available for the mid-day meal," he stated plainly.

"Oh," Eliana was a little shocked at the relief she felt. "The inn is only open to overnight guests for the remainder of the day today," she explained, "and today, you are the only overnight guest," she finished.

Nazim nodded his head in approval. "And Reuben?" he asked.

"Reuben is in the stables with your Ares," Eliana answered. "Allow me to grab my wrap, and we will be on our way. Eliana

74

moved up the few steps to her grandfather's door. "Grandfather, we are heading for supplies now," she called through the closed portal.

"Mind yourself, Ellie," he instructed from behind the door as if she were still a little girl.

"I promise that I shall, Grandfather," she called back.

Eli leaned against the door and waited until he heard her footsteps descend the steps before he moved to his bed. He rarely slept well anymore, and he had risen well before sunrise. A short rest was in order. Stretching his tired body across his simple cot, he whispered a prayer to Jehovah.

"Please watch over my Ellie and keep her safe," he whispered. *"I am old, and I am worn. I do not know how many more sunrises I will get to witness. I pray that she will be cared for when I am gone, and if, by chance, this wandering soldier is the man you have sent to fill the void I shall leave when I go, then soften his heart and bring him into your favor, dear Jehovah. Help me, Father, and help Ellie to tell him of your love. Break down the walls around his heart, as you broke down the mighty walls of Jericho, and God, please, protect my Ellie's young heart and keep her free from harm."*

Eli fell into a peaceful slumber as he finished his prayer, resting in the knowledge that the faithful God who had brought his people out of the wilderness and led them into the Promised Land would remain faithful and would not forsake him now.

Chapter Eight

The streets were busy, but not overly so, as Eliana and Nazim made their way from the inn to the stables beyond. True to his word, Reuben was there, brushing Ares and speaking to the animal as they approached.

"I have told your master that you require exercise soon, Ares. It is not fitting for a fine beast such as yourself to be contained in a small stable such as this one for long periods of time. It will make you anxious," he explained, stroking the horse's side.

"Please let me know if that horse responds to you," Eliana joked her brother. Reuben spun around, embarrassed at being caught talking to the animal. Nazim chuckled and almost felt bad for Reuben's embarrassment. The lad had done an amazing job taking care of his horse.

"He *is* a wonderful listener," Nazim emphasized.

"You have talked to him too, then," Reuben smiled, not feeling quite so ridiculous.

"Oh yes," Nazim confirmed. "When you have been traveling as I have, the days and nights can become rather lonesome." At the sound of his voice, Ares grew excited and moved in an attempt to get a better view of his master. Nazim calmed the horse by moving into his sight and gently stroking the animal's broad neck.

"We will run soon," he promised, and immediately, the animal calmed.

Eliana was intrigued. "It almost seemed as if he understood you," she commented.

"He absolutely understands me," Nazim agreed. "Ares understands me better than most humans do. We have fought many battles together, and he has always done his part to keep me safe."

Nazim noticed her reluctance of the horse now, the way she stood back nervously, just barely inside the door. Ares was a large horse, and from the looks of the empty stables, she was not accustomed to being around very many animals.

"Come pet him, Eliana," Reuben encouraged, watching his sister where she stood.

"Oh, no, I do not believe I should," she began, but Nazim noticed the hesitant, though small step forward she took. Clearly, she wanted to; she was just afraid.

"He will not harm you," Nazim promised, coaxing her. "You have my word."

Eliana kept her position for a moment, and then Nazim watched as she slowly began to approach. He stood in front of Ares, holding his head and rubbing the sides of the horse's face. Eliana approached slowly before gently reaching out her hand to lightly touch the animal's neck. At her touch, Ares flinched, sending Eliana running to stand behind Nazim. Reuben doubled over in laughter at his sister's response.

"He only flinched because he was not expecting your touch," Nazim explained over his shoulder, where Eliana continued to stand. He enjoyed the fact that she had run behind him for protection. Just yesterday, she had fled from his presence, and today, in this particular instance, she sought it.

Nazim turned his body so that the horse could see Eliana clearly. Continuing to keep his hand on Ares, Nazim moved to the side, encouraging Eliana's movement to stand directly in front of the animal. Nazim, now beside her, moved gently, coaxing the horse to lower his head. Ares bowed his head low, and Eliana looked up into a pair of the most beautiful brown eyes she had ever seen. Slowly, she framed the animal's face with her hands as Nazim had been doing and laughed as Ares nuzzled against her head.

"See! He likes you, Eliana," Reuben cheered.

"I suppose he does," Eliana laughed, suddenly more at ease in the magnificent animal's presence as she continued to stroke his face.

"Though their eyes are on the side of their face," Nazim explained, "horses cannot see the sides of their bodies. Make sure he knows you are approaching, and he will always welcome your touch," he finished as he stroked his animal. "We will run," he promised again, speaking to Ares once more. "But first, I believe we have some errands to see to," he finished, turning his attention to Eliana.

"Yes," she agreed, moving from the horse and speaking directly to her brother. "Reuben, Grandfather has asked that you accompany me and Nazim to gather the supplies that Nazim will need to make repairs to the inn."

"Straight away," Reuben promised. "I will be right back," he assured them as he ran from the stables. Eliana turned back to Ares with a final pat and a promise that she would come again soon. The horse nuzzled her face once again, and Nazim contemplated how quickly she had conquered her fear of the animal.

"Have you ever ridden?" he asked as they made their way from the stables.

"I have not," she admitted with a light laugh. "I have been in a wagon pulled by donkeys, but I have never been on the back of an animal."

"Perhaps we can rectify that," he offered with a small smile, looking down at her.

Eliana did not confirm she would be willing, but she also did not deny that she would like to. Nazim watched her as she glanced back once again to where Ares stood. They remained in comfortable silence for only a moment before Reuben returned, ready to go.

The three of them made their way into the village in pleasant conversation. They talked of many things, not lingering on any particular subject during their short walk there. Nazim told them of how he had trained Ares from a colt and funny stories of things that had happened during that time.

Once they arrived in town, they took their time purchasing the materials that Nazim would need for the repairs. He tried to be frugal with the items he requested, but he also wanted to ensure the job was done correctly. The looks he had grown accustomed to when he was alone in the village failed in comparison to the looks he was receiving with Eliana by his side. That people were amazed, and even surprised, that she was in his company was an understatement.

Reuben remained between them much of the time as they shopped, but the lad ran back and forth visiting with friends, and more than once, Nazim and Eliana were alone as they walked from merchant to merchant. Eliana had decided to make the trip productive for them both and was also shopping for goods and food items for the inn as they went.

She seemed less than interested in the gawking stares from villagers and the not-so-quiet whispers being cast in their direction. She was almost ignorant to those coming and going around them, Nazim noticed. It was not until they were spotted by Uma, and she called for Eliana, that Eliana seemed even remotely uncomfortable.

"Eliana," her friend waved frantically as she called to her from across the street.

"I shall be only a moment," Eliana assured Nazim as she turned to cross the street to where Uma stood anxiously, beckoning for Eliana to come quickly. Nazim noticed Uma's eagerness but continued collecting materials.

Eliana approached Uma, then paused, noticing the strange look on her face.

"What are you doing?" Uma asked, grabbing Eliana's arms, pulling her to the corner, and emphasizing every word.

"We are purchasing the supplies Nazim will need to repair the inn, as well as some other supplies I need for cooking," she answered. "What are you so upset over?" Eliana asked, clearly confused at Uma's question.

"The whole town is buzzing about you being alone in the street with him," Uma explained. "Have you forgotten who he is and how frightened you were of him just yesterday?" she asked dramatically, convinced that Eliana had lost her senses.

"Of course, I have not," Eliana answered pulling her arm from Uma's embrace, her tone more than a little put out with her friend's insinuation. "Grandfather requested I accompany Nazim and pay for the materials he needs to make the repairs that he has so kindly agreed to see to for us. And we are hardly alone!" she continued. "The streets are full of people, and Reuben is also accompanying us," she emphasized, pointing at her brother, who was now back at Nazim's side.

Eliana paused as Ezra strolled up to the two of them, offering a piece of fresh fruit to Uma. Eliana looked at her friend, crossing her arms while tilting her head to the side. "And who is accompanying the two of you?" she asked pointedly, posing a question of her own. "This one certainly does not have a spotless reputation himself," she finished, glancing at Ezra.

Uma looked at Ezra in a huff.

"What?" Ezra asked, shrugging his shoulders, clearly at a loss as to the conversation which had ensued. Without another word, Eliana turned on her heel and moved back across the street to where Nazim and her brother were finishing their purchases. She paid the coins required and confirmed that the materials would be delivered to the inn by the end of the week, then refused to even glance in Uma's direction as they passed by where she and Ezra still stood.

Nazim took the bags of fresh vegetables Eliana had purchased, noticing her tension and her silence as they walked back to the inn. Reuben ran ahead as they drew close, and Nazim took the opportunity to question Eliana.

"Did something upset you in the village?" he asked, looking down at her, where she walked quietly by his side.

"Nothing of importance," she admitted with a small sigh, continuing to look straight ahead. "Sometimes I spend so much time inside the inn that I forget what it's like outside in the village. I enjoy my solitude and my home," she admitted, glancing up at him.

"The inn is a busy place," he argued. "I would hardly call it a place of solitude."

"At times, that is true," she agreed. "But it is home, and it just seems different. Plus, once meals are served, the people go on about their own business with very little interest in mine," she concluded with a second glance in his direction.

"Ah," Nazim shook his head as understanding dawned. "So should I assume then that the conversation you had with Uma could have possibly had something to do with me?" he asked sheepishly.

"One should never assume anything," Eliana smiled up at him now. She was a little surprised at how easily conversation came with him today when she could not even bring herself to look at him just yesterday. Using the back entrance directly into the cooking area, they took the vegetables inside. Eliana stored them properly and then moved back to the exit, turning to move farther behind the inn. Without waiting for an invitation, Nazim curiously followed her.

Quietly, she moved alongside the stream but did not go far before seating herself along the bank, leaning her back against a large tree.

"This," she said quietly to Nazim as she settled herself, "this is my solitude."

Nazim looked around them now surprised that she was sharing this place with him. He seated himself near her but was careful to leave plenty of distance between the two of them. Though they seemed to be in another world, they were not secluded at all, the inn still very much in view and able to be reached in only a few short steps. Trees were scattered about but far enough apart that one could not hide among them. The few windows on the back of the inn were in plain view so that anyone who happened by could easily see whoever lingered by the stream.

"Grandfather cleared this spot for me shortly after we arrived in Heshbon," she began to explain. "He wanted the inn. He hoped to be a help to others, but he knew that in my bashful moments, it would be hard for me to cope with having so many people in our home," she explained. "Sometimes even Uma," she laughed.

"She seems she could be a bit…much," Nazim grinned, looking for the right word.

"Uma has been through a lot," Eliana admitted. "She and her parents were residents of Heshbon when King Sihon forbade to allow us passage through the city. When the battle was over, Israel had won, and many had lost their lives or fled, but Joshua allowed some of the original citizens to remain. Uma and her parents were among those citizens. Her parents own the pottery shop, and together, they do wonderful work. Uma and I, being so close in age, formed a friendship, and after a time, she came to accept our God and our beliefs. She is now one of my truest friends, though there are times I need space from even her. She can be too trusting and is sometimes a poor judge of character. Her playful and silly attitude has often been misconstrued as something more by those who do not know her well," she explained. "She and I have had several conversations on the matter," she chuckled. "Grandfather wanted a place for me that I could feel alone and find the solace that I need yet remain perfectly safe," she went on, "so he created this oasis for me, and I still come here often when I need time to think, reflect, or pray."

"I can see why," Nazim admitted as he looked around. Though not completely blocked out, basic noise from the street was muffled by the gently flowing stream, and the singing of birds from the trees above them added to the tranquil setting. "Do you feel safe when you are here?" he asked.

"I do," she admitted as she relaxed and laid her head against the tree behind her.

"Even now," he asked quietly as he watched her, "in my presence?"

Eliana paused for a moment before she answered. "At the moment," she stated, turning to look at him. She allowed a small laugh as she continued. "*For* the moment," she continued smiling at him.

"Eliana, you must believe how deeply I regret my actions that frightened you so badly yesterday," he said once again. "I did not mean to get so angry when you mentioned Rahab," he said, being completely honest.

Eliana raised her head and turned to look at him. "Rahab?" she asked, confusion marking her voice. "My mention of Rahab is what made you so angry?" she questioned as she turned her body to better face him.

Nazim felt like being honest with her, though he was not sure why. "We were," he paused, searching for the words to explain his relationship with Rahab without being offensive to his present company, "very close," he decided. "I fell short in my protection of her, as well as the others of our city when your God destroyed *everything* I had by the hands of your people." Though admitting these things to Eliana was difficult, Nazim was confident that he could continue to control his temper just now. "The thought of Rahab being happier and more cared for in her present state than what she was when she was in Jericho under my protection," he paused and chuckled. "Well, it does not do much for the pride of the chief warrior and captain of the fallen city," he admitted, now looking at Eliana.

She smiled in understanding. "I am sorry, too. I should have been more sensitive in the words I chose," she apologized.

Unsure of why she felt so brave at the moment, she decided to continue giving voice to her thoughts. "But I do feel Jehovah has a plan for you, Nazim, else you too would have been inside those city walls when the city fell." She paused, waiting for his response and readying herself for whatever his reaction may be. Thankfully, he remained calm, though unknown to Eliana, it was due to no small amount of effort on his part. Though he kept his temper in check, the words still cut him. Deeply. He gazed at the water in front of them but said nothing.

"What really brought you to Heshbon," she finally asked, changing the subject somewhat.

"Boredom," he began, "and curiosity. I grew tired of wandering the Jericho Road, going from place to place fighting thieves and beggars for food and shelter."

"I do not see how that would be boring," she laughed, and Nazim enjoyed the sound.

"I decided that no amount of fighting or misery I evoked upon myself could change what had happened, what I had allowed to happen, and that I needed to move on." He paused for a moment but then continued. "I know you feel I am callous toward your God," he began, going back to the earlier conversation, "but you must understand that I am not one of His 'chosen people' as you alluded to earlier. Quite the opposite, in fact. I know nothing of Him except the loss and misery He has caused me."

"Nothing happens out of Jehovah's control, Nazim," she said carefully. "Everything that transpires is ordained, instituted, or allowed by God. You were chosen *not* to be killed in Jericho", she said as she watched his face.

Nazim looked away from her again and to the water.

"He would not choose me," he spoke certainly, his gaze directly in front of him. "You do not know the things I have done," he stated matter-of-factly, pulling a reed from the bank, breaking it into pieces, and casting it into the flowing stream.

"Our God is a forgiving God," Eliana assured him. "Even Moses sinned against Jehovah."

"Your Moses?" Nazim questioned, looking at her now, sure that she was jesting.

"Yes, *our* Moses," Eliana laughed quietly. "Among other things, I am sure, he murdered, and he questioned God's decision to use him to lead our people out of Egypt. And even though his disobedience cost him, Jehovah still went on to use him in mighty ways and forgave him of his trespasses."

Nazim moved now so that he could better face her.

"You are telling me that your Moses, who I have heard parted the waters of the Red Sea, the man who stood against Pharaoh and led your people out of the land of Egypt, *that* Moses was a murderer."

Eliana smiled at the pique in his curiosity.

"I told you," she chuckled again, "He is a forgiving God."

Nazim shook his head and settled once more against the trunk of the large tree.

"I do not understand the ways of your God," he admitted, settling against the tree once again. "Though I admit that I am curious about Him. How did your people end up captives in Egypt anyway?" he asked. Before Eliana had time to comment, sounds of commotion coming from the street interrupted them. Eliana was to her feet and heading toward the noise before Nazim could stop her.

"Eliana, wait!" he called as she moved quickly toward the direction of the commotion. *"She would not last a minute in Jericho,"* he thought to himself, moving rapidly to catch up to her. Her tenacity irritated him and intrigued him at the same time.

She stopped at the corner of the inn just as Nazim caught up to her. He noticed she purposely stayed out of view from those beyond them, and he remained behind her, doing the same. Peering around the corner of the building, they saw a man parading through the street on a horse almost the size of Ares. Women and children ran along beside him as he dropped coins time and again into their uplifted hands.

"It is Kylus," she whispered in disgust, just loud enough for Nazim to hear.

"The man you and your grandfather are so concerned about," Nazim clarified, continuing to peer around the corner to watch the commotion.

"Yes," Eliana confirmed. "Someone must have told him of our misfortune. See the way he 'pays off' his fanatics, those who are surrounding him so that he can barely get through the street. It is the way he gets by with demanding his righteous tributes. If someone from the town informs him of wrong being done or of something they feel is not honoring to Jehovah, he arrives with his handouts to reward them and those who 'honor him' and to execute his penalties on the offender."

Nazim watched from their hiding place as Kylus pulled his horse to a halt in front of the inn. Though they were not touching, he could feel the tension surrounding Eliana at the exchange she knew was coming.

"Fine patrons of Heshbon," the man spoke loudly from the back of his horse. "It appears misfortune has befallen your village," he stated in mock sympathy as he motioned toward the inn. "Someone fetch me Eli so that I may reveal his intentions on cleaning up the unsightly mess that has befallen his house," he instructed as he dismounted his horse.

Eliana turned to face Nazim and looked straight up into his face. He noticed as he looked down at her that there was no trace of a timid nature about her now.

"Do. Not. Move," she instructed forcefully, emphasizing each word. Nazim almost smiled at her assertiveness with him but instead held up his hands in submission. Once she was satisfied that he would stay put, she moved from her hiding place and into the street. Nazim did move, but only enough that he could keep her easily in his view while remaining out of sight by any onlookers.

"Eli is unavailable," Eliana answered as soon as she was in clear view of the street. "What is that you want, Kylus?" she asked pointedly, directing her words to the man across the street from her.

"Well, if it is not the lovely Eliana gracing me with her presence," he scoffed as he began to move in her direction.

"You wanted an audience with my grandfather; you have an audience with me. What is it that you need?" she asked again, her voice stern.

Nazim was impressed with her straightforward attitude. There was more to this woman than he had initially given her credit for. Kylus stood directly in front of her now, and folks began to once again move about their business now that his coins were pocketed and the fanfare had ceased.

"I need a great many things, Eliana," he spoke, a sickening grin crossing his face. "How many of those things are you willing to assist me with?" Nazim moved ever so slightly to clearly hear the conversation that was taking place not far from where he stood. Eliana did not even flinch at his question; she simply crossed her arms and stood her ground. Nazim instantly knew he detested the man just from the tone and the words he was using with Eliana. "To begin with," Kylus continued as Eliana stared at him with malice, "I want to know who exactly moved the giant boulders and beams that were once attached to your inn. It is clearly more than you or Eli are capable of."

"The beam collapsed, and the roof fell," she clarified, her voice monotone so as not to encourage his questioning. "The rubble has been cleared from the path, and the stoop will be rebuilt. There is no need for you to be here on our account," she finished.

"Who moved the boulders from the path?" he asked pointedly, and Nazim noticed the man's voice beginning to intensify.

"A stranger who was passing through," Eliana answered, shrugging her shoulders. "He offered to help for room and board until the task was done."

"I have heard of this *stranger*," Kylus emphasized. "This *stranger* who also accompanied you in town earlier today. Where is he?"

"I do not make it a habit to keep up with strangers, Kylus. I do know that he is not currently inside our inn," she spoke honestly, knowing Nazim continued to stand around the corner just behind her, "if that is what you are implying."

"I want to know who he is, Eliana," Kylus clarified, irritation beginning to sound in his voice. "There are rumors floating around that he is the wandering soldier who escaped the destruction of Jericho. He is dangerous, and he has no business in Heshbon. He must be dealt with before he causes problems in our village."

"Problems in our village or problems for you?" she questioned, allowing her own anger to show in her voice. "If you find this *dangerous* wandering soldier, be sure to let us know," she stated, turning on her heel. Kylus quickly grabbed her arm as she began to move away.

"Do not mock me again, Eliana," he spoke in low tones. Nazim took a step forward, witnessing Kylus take Eliana's arm, but was stopped by a hand quickly grasping his own just above his elbow. It was Eli, exiting from the back, shaking his head as he held tightly to Nazim's arm, motioning for him to remain quiet and in his place. Nazim fervently wanted to step out of hiding and give Kylus a greeting of his own, but for reasons he himself was unsure of, he succumbed to the old man's will. Clenching his teeth, he turned back to the street but remained in his hiding position to listen carefully as the conversation concluded. He would only tolerate so much, regardless of the old man's bidding.

"Let go of me, Kylus," Eliana spoke firmly.

"I tire of your stubborn will," Kylus spoke through clenched teeth of his own. "Tell me what you know of the stranger who came to your aid," he demanded.

"I cannot tell you that which I do not know," Eliana spit back at him. "Let go of me," she said loud enough to gain attention from anyone in close proximity. As Kylus looked about them to see if she had caused any unwanted attention with her demand, he released his grip enough to allow Eliana to free her arm from his grasp. As she did so, she turned and moved swiftly toward the front entrance of the inn.

"This mess will be completely cleared and rebuilt when I return," he yelled to her back so that all could hear, "or you will owe twice the tribute I normally require," he concluded.

Eliana slammed the door to the inn and leaned against the inside. It had taken everything she could muster to stand up to Kylus that way. Knowing that Nazim was close by had helped in some ways but had been agonizing in others. She continued to stand against the door, her breathing labored, and fought back the frustrated tears which threatened to come. She swallowed hard, working to gain control of herself before she dared move back outside, where she knew Nazim was waiting for her. She rubbed her forehead and neck in a desperate attempt to calm herself.

Eliana did not realize that Nazim had come in from the back as soon as she had fled Kylus or that he stood quietly in his corner even now. Nazim continued there in the shadows, watching her as she worked for composure, unsure of his own emotions at the moment. He had come to Heshbon with plans to divide and conquer these people after he had learned all he could of their God. Could this Kylus not be the aid he needed to do just that? He seemed to have abandoned his own assignment as a peacemaker among the people in order to fulfill his selfish desires for power. Together, they could make quite an alliance.

If Nazim discovered this God could not be destroyed, his plan had been to bring Him as much pain as possible by taking all the things from Him that had been taken from himself. Again, this man could be just the aid he needed, not only to gain the knowledge he desired but also to carry out his plan. He did not have to like someone to use them to accomplish his purpose, and once he had succeeded and used Kylus to his abilities, Nazim would have no problem finishing him off as well.

Yet, something about this family Nazim had found himself in the midst of intrigued him. He felt something stir as he continued to watch Eliana. For reasons he could not explain, he felt protective of her. As he kept his place in the corner, watching Eliana continuing to struggle with herself, he wanted nothing more than to comfort her. He wanted to tell her that he would take care of both the inn and the man who caused her so much distress. But why? Why had so little time in the presence of this family caused him to question his initial purpose for being here? Hiding in the shadows would not bring him answers, and he did not want Eliana to discover his presence.

As quietly as he entered, he turned, moving back through the cooking area to once again exit the back door. Eliana never even realized he had been there. Once she was satisfied that Kylus had gone on about his way and felt that she was again in full control of her emotions, she took another deep breath and then moved through the cooking area to join Nazim once again outside.

Chapter Nine

Nazim returned to the outside corner where Eliana had left him and where Grandfather still remained. It was only a moment before Eliana also came through the door.

"So that was Kylus," Nazim stated before she had a chance to say anything about her delayed return.

"That was Kylus," she confirmed.

"I do not understand," Nazim continued. "Why did the two of you insist on me remaining hidden? Which I did against my better judgment," he added before either of them had a chance to speak.

"Perhaps this conversation would be better had inside," Eli suggested, moving toward the doorway. Eliana and Nazim followed him through the door, and the trio made their way to a table inside. Eliana stopped in the cooking area long enough to gather a pitcher of juice, a bowl of fruit, and cups for the three of them before joining them in the center room.

"Thank you, Ellie," Eli spoke as he took the cup from his granddaughter. After a long drink, he began directing his comments to Nazim. "Kylus approached me six months ago requesting Eliana's hand," Eli began. Nazim caught himself right before he spit his juice across the table. Instead, he swallowed hard and sat back in his chair. He could not imagine her tied to a man anything like the one he had just seen. "I would not speak for my granddaughter but gave her leave to make her own decision. Marriage to Kylus would ensure Eliana a secure home, a profitable future, safety, and...." at Eli's pause, Eliana spoke up.

"A miserable life," she finished for him. "I cannot imagine being joined to someone like he has become," she said blatantly.

"Like he has become?" Nazim asked, curious as to the way she had phrased her comment.

"Kylus was not always the self-righteous, pious leader you saw today," Eliana explained. "Though he has always had issues with authority and pride, his spirit when he was among our people in the wilderness was much humbler than what he now exhibits as a leader."

"As I have told you before," Eli continued, "Kylus was appointed the position over Bashan because of his leadership abilities. The man he has become as of late is quite different than the man allowed by Joshua to look after our people."

"Joshua has no idea that Kylus has instituted righteous tributes or that he parades through our town promising coins to those who relay information to him," Eliana spoke again. "Joshua would never countenance the behavior Kylus exhibits now, especially the way he enjoys how some of our people idolize him."

"Some of your people?" Nazim questioned again.

"Many in our town do realize that Kylus has gone too far and are not accepting of his behavior," Eliana continued, "but there are those who seek his favor in any way possible. Those are the people who send for him at any given opportunity with the promise of knowing something that will require a penalty be paid."

"They covet the attention Kylus affords them," Eli spoke up, "and they covet the growth of the 'town treasury' because they feel the more in the treasury, the more chances they have with Kylus to line their own pockets."

"Though 'town treasury' is a phrase Kylus has instituted, the town never sees a dime of the money. Only what Kylus hands out to the people he feels are worthy of it," Eliana interjected.

Eli agreed with his granddaughter and spoke again, "Yes, and those are the people who continue to feed his power-driven ego."

"Kylus does not take well to anyone who can or would challenge his authority," Eliana continued. "That is why I asked you to remain out of sight. One look at you and he would have penalized us on the spot just for allowing you to remain inside our inn."

"He would consider you a challenge, Nazim," Eli looked at his granddaughter before speaking his next words carefully, "in several different ways." Eliana felt her face begin to heat and rose to get more juice from the cooking area. As she excused herself, Eli continued his conversation with Nazim, his face and attitude solemn. "Kylus did not take kindly to Eliana refusing his hand," he spoke honestly, "and he all but threatened to find a way to force her to wed him. No doubt, Kylus will eventually see you as you continue your work here, that is to be expected, but if he were to have seen you for the first time today, coming from behind the inn with my granddaughter…"

"He would have expected that my intentions were directed toward Eliana and not focused on the task at hand," Nazim finished as understanding dawned.

"Exactly," Eli emphasized, sitting back in his chair. "You are more wise than you are given credit for," the old man admitted.

"Do I have a reputation for being a fool?" Nazim asked light-heartedly, though his question was completely serious.

"Not a fool," Eli clarified, "but one who is prone to violence and a quick temper. Those attributes can be considered foolish," he smiled at his guest.

"That I will not deny," Nazim chuckled as Eliana returned with more juice. Sensing the conversation had turned away from embarrassing realizations, she spoke as she again filled the men's cups with juice.

"Kylus will return to make good on his promise sooner rather than later. The merchants are set to deliver the materials we purchased by the end of the week. Nazim, how long do you expect the repairs to take?" she asked sincerely.

"If the weather holds fair, I should be able to have the foundation repaired and the new stoop built within a couple of weeks," he answered thoughtfully.

"But if these old bones are any indication," Eli began as he slowly stretched his feeble arm out in front of him, "there is rain to be expected in the near future."

"Hopefully, the rain will hold off until after Nazim is finished with the repairs," Eliana admitted. "Grandfather, we really cannot afford a righteous tribute."

"I am aware, Ellie," the old man spoke pointedly. "Do not forget that Jehovah is in control of the weather, not Kylus, nor Nazim, nor you, nor any of us." Eli rose from his place, closing the conversation. "I am going to rest these weary bones. I will see you in several hours for the evening meal," he spoke over his shoulder as he began to make his way to his room.

"Rest well, Grandfather," Eliana called to him. "I will let you know when the meal is ready."

"Something light," he returned, and Eliana smiled softly as he closed his door behind himself. Nazim noticed the concern that crossed her face as she continued to stare at the closed portal.

"He really does quite well for his age," Nazim reassured her.

"He does," she agreed, looking at him and appreciating his concern. "But he has had a hard life. He is weary," she spoke honestly.

The two sat for a moment in comfortable silence before Nazim spoke again. "So, on the bank of the stream before, I had asked how your people became captives in Egypt," he reminded her as he leaned forward on the table. Eliana realized how much his current stance decreased the amount of space between them, and out of instinct, she sat back farther into her chair, folding her hands in her lap.

"Well," she began, "it is a long story and a lot of history which can all be rather confusing," she grinned. Nazim selected an apple from the bowl she had sat before him and, taking a large bite, settled himself, indicating he was in no hurry. Eliana chuckled. "I suppose it began with a man named Joseph. Joseph was a Hebrew, born of Jacob, who was born of Isaac, who was born of Abraham. Joseph's brothers sold him to a group of Midianites, who took him to Egypt, where he was sold into the house of Pharaoh's captain of the guard as a slave. But eventually, though he was wrongly accused and spent time in prison, he found favor with Pharaoh and became a ruler over Egypt himself."

Nazim crinkled his brow and stopped her with one simple word.

"What?" he said in shock, around another bite from the apple.

Eliana laughed out loud. "I warned you that it is very complicated," she laughed. "That is barely the beginning."

"Alright," Nazim conceded, holding his hand out in front of himself. "Skip ahead to Moses. Tell me of Moses," he requested instead.

"Very well," Eliana agreed. "Moses was born after the time of Joseph when there rose up a new king over Egypt. This king did not know Joseph or from where he had come. This new king only realized that the children of Israel, who continued to dwell in their land, were multiplying faster and growing stronger than the Egyptians. He began to fear that the Hebrew people would turn against Egypt in a time of war and fight against them. So, the king enslaved our people, giving them rigorous tasks that would, in some cases, be so intense that the work would take their lives, but eventually, he realized that his plan was not working and that our people continued to multiply. So, he then commanded the midwives of our people to kill any male babies who were born to the Hebrew women. But the midwives, fearing our God, refused to kill the sons born to the Hebrews. God had mercy on them for their obeisance to Him, and He blessed their families as well and continued to grow the Hebrew people among the Egyptian nation." Eliana paused but, seeing Nazim so carefully following her story, continued. "Finally, Pharaoh gave a charge to all his people commanding that any time they found out a son had been born to a Hebrew, they should cast the boy into the river and only allow their daughters to live."

"But somehow, your Moses survived this plan?" Nazim questioned. Eliana enjoyed telling the stories of her people, and it had been a long time since she had been able to tell the story to someone who had no knowledge of her history. She continued the story, becoming more excited about it herself.

"Yes!" she grinned. "A baby boy was born during that time to a Hebrew couple, Amram and Jochebed. He was not the first child born to them or even the first son. Aaron had been born three years prior to Moses, before the decree was made, and their daughter, Miriam, before Aaron. Jochebed knew that her baby son had a purpose, so she hid him for three months. Eventually, it became impossible for her to keep him in hiding, so with a heavy heart but a heart full of love for her son and for Jehovah, Jochebed constructed a basket of bulrushes, slime, and pitch and placed her son inside of it. Then she took the basket and put it in the river where she knew that the daughter of Pharaoh would come to wash herself."

"That sounds risky," Nazim interjected, totally engrossed in the story Eliana was telling. "How did she know that Pharaoh's daughter would not demand his death."

"It does sound risky," Eliana agreed. "But Jochebed trusted that Jehovah would protect her son and intercede where she could not. So, Miriam, Jochebed's firstborn, stood in the flags by the river to see what would become of her baby brother. When Pharaoh's daughter and her maidens walked along the river's edge, she saw the basket among the flags and sent one of her maids to fetch it. As soon as her maiden returned with the basket and she opened it, the baby inside began to cry. She knew the boy belonged to a Hebrew woman, but Pharaoh's daughter had such compassion on the child that she chose to raise him as her own.

Miriam saw that Pharaoh's daughter had compassion on the baby and ran to her offering to go and find a nurse among the Hebrew women who could nurse the child for her until the time came that he should be weaned. So, Pharaoh's daughter agreed, and Miriam returned the child to Jochebed, under the protection of Pharaoh's daughter."

"So, this Jochebed got her son back," Nazim grinned.

"For a time," Eliana continued. "Once the time had come, and the child was weaned, Jochebed had to say goodbye for a second time when the boy was sent to live in the palace with Pharaoh's daughter. His name was given to him at that time."

"Moses," both Nazim and Eliana said together.

"Yes, Moses," Eliana laughed.

"So, hold on." Nazim sat back in his chair, taking in all he had learned. "So, this princess just happened to have compassion on this boy that she knew was of the people her father wanted dead. So, the boy was returned to his biological mother, who raised him until he was what. Four, maybe five years old, then sent him back to the palace to the people who wanted to kill him, but now protected him, and then he rose up to overthrow all of them and lead your people out of Egypt and into the desert. Did I follow all of that? Is that about right?"

"Well, close," Eliana agreed, "but a lot of events transpired in between all of those."

"So, in your opinion, your God...Jehovah," Nazim looked to her to make sure he was pronouncing the name correctly. Eliana nodded and urged him to continue, "protected Moses from infancy to get him to where he needed to be to eventually free your people."

"It is not only my opinion, Nazim; it is, in fact, exactly how it happened," Eliana agreed. "Jehovah has a plan in every situation and in every circumstance," she explained. "Just as He had a plan for Joseph when his brothers sold him into slavery, as I was speaking of earlier. We may not understand it, but nothing happens that is outside of His divine intentions." She was trying to be careful in her words, fear of offending him once again creeping into her mind. She decided to push past that fear with a quick prayer for wisdom in her words as she continued. "Nothing surprises Him, nothing causes Him fear, nothing is beyond His realm of control. That is why I am adamant that you have a purpose, Nazim. He intentionally spared you from destruction in Jericho." Though her heart was pounding at the mention of that city, her composure remained calm, and thankfully, so did his.

Nazim thought about his next question carefully. Finally, he decided to follow through with the question. "So where exactly did your God...Jehovah, come from?" he asked. "Who created Him?"

Eliana smiled at him as she answered. "Jehovah God was not created," she answered as sincerely as she knew how. "He created all things. He came from nowhere. He has always been."

"That seems rather impossible," Nazim spoke plainly, again sitting back in his chair.

"We cannot understand all there is to know about our God, Nazim," Eliana continued unthreatened. "We can attempt to grow in grace, knowledge, and truth in order to understand Him better, but to know all there is to know of Him, to be able to think as He does, to be able to see and feel things as He does, that would be a useless attempt to make ourselves equal with Him. That is what is impossible. That is why He is our God, and that is why we worship Him," she finished quietly.

Eliana did not realize it, but in her excitement of her explanation, she herself had leaned in closer to Nazim. The soldier noticed her presence, but he did not care at the moment. He was honestly intrigued by all he had heard and found himself more curious than he was when she had begun.

He looked at the wall beside him, chewing on his lip and wrestling with the many thoughts inside his head. A God that has always been? An all-knowing, all-powerful, uncreated, unseen being? Just the little bit Eliana and her family had shared in the short time he was here was enough to conclude there was no destroying a being such as that. And it angered him more that he was not even sure he still wanted to. What was wrong with him?

Eliana was concerned with his silence, afraid that she had gone too far, and wondered if she should make her exit before his temper flared. Their individual thoughts were interrupted as Reuben bounded through the door.

"Oh! There you are!" he began enthusiastically. "Sir, if you run Ares, may I accompany you?" he asked outright. Nazim broke his trance into nowhere and looked at the lad in front of him. He would sort through the turmoil in his soul at a later time.

"I tell you what," he began, clearing his throat and turning his chair to face the boy. He moved to lean his elbows on his knees. "To begin with, you call me Nazim, and I shall call you Reuben."

Reuben looked to his sister for approval, who shrugged her shoulders in an unconcerned way. "Certainly, Nazim!" Reuben answered excitedly.

"Second, you shall accompany me as I give Ares some exercise, if…" he paused and looked to Eliana, "your sister will accompany us as well."

His look was gentle, and Eliana recognized it as being so. She knew he was not offended by the conversation they had just had and thought that with more time, she may be able to teach him more of the God she so loved. That thought intrigued her, and in truth, so did his invitation.

"Please, Eliana," Reuben begged. "I will stay with you so the villagers will not be prone to gossip," he reasoned with her.

Eliana chuckled and looked to Reuben in surprise, "And what do you know of the villagers' gossip?" she asked pointedly.

"Enough to know that you are concerned about what others will think if they see you alone with a practical stranger," Reuben answered honestly.

Nazim now laughed himself at the lad's blatant response. Eliana took a deep breath before finally conceding to her brother's pleading eyes.

"Very well, I suppose a walk would do us good," she agreed. "I will just let Grandfather know that we will be quick. The day grows long, and we must be home before darkness falls," she told them as she moved to do just that.

"Thank you, Eliana!" Reuben shouted as he ran back toward the exit.

"Do not unleash Ares before I get there," Nazim called to him.

"Perhaps you should go ahead with him," Eliana suggested. "I shall only be a moment," she promised.

With a simple nod, Nazim turned to follow the direction Reuben had gone. Eliana paused outside her grandfather's door, hoping she had made the right decision. She raised her hand, but before she could knock, Grandfather's gentle voice met her ears through the closed door.

"Mind yourself, Ellie. And be careful," he instructed. She smiled, knowing now that he had been listening and had approved of the entire conversation that had just taken place between her and their wandering soldier.

"I promise, Grandfather," she returned. "We shall not be long."

Chapter Ten

Eliana moved to quickly join Nazim and Reuben in the stable where Ares impatiently waited. Reuben had brushed the majestic horse until his black coat was shining. His mane was long and thick, and it was evident that the horse adored Reuben and the attention he had been shown. He now stomped his hoof, a clear indication that the animal was ready to move. Nazim led Ares from the stables into the open area, his coat glistening in the late afternoon sunlight.

"He is a beautiful animal," Eliana commented as she stood in front of him, offering an apple. She held it up to the horse but was surprised when it was Nazim who quickly, though gently, grabbed the apple from her hand. "I am sorry!" she apologized. "Is he not allowed apples?" she questioned.

"Oh, he is allowed," Nazim answered. "I am just saving your fingers from being part of his treat," he explained. "Hold the fruit like this," he instructed placing the apple in the palm of his hand and extending his fingers out flat. "Horses cannot see your hand when it is placed at that angle beneath their nose. Ares would not be able to distinguish the food you offer him from your fingers. And you do not want that."

Nazim offered the apple back to her, and she placed it on her hand as he instructed. Eliana laughed as the horse's giant lips took the apple from her hand and gasped when she caught sight of his giant teeth. "I had no idea his teeth were so large," she laughed aloud. Nazim looked around.

"Where is the best place to run him?" he asked innocently.

"By the pools!" Reuben answered enthusiastically. "There is plenty of room, and it is doubtful anyone will be there at this hour!"

"He is right," Eliana agreed.

Nazim thought back to his first full day in Heshbon. "I believe I have seen these pools. They are located on the outskirts of town?" he asked. Eliana nodded. "We will have to go directly through town to get there," he mentioned, directing his comment to Eliana. "Everyone will see us," he said hesitantly with his sideways grin.

"We shall go my way," Eliana remarked with a small grin of her own.

"Reuben," Nazim called. "Come to me." The lad instantly obeyed. "Have you ever been on the back of a horse?" Nazim asked.

"No, sir...I mean Nazim. I have not," he answered honestly. Nazim motioned for the boy to stand between himself and Ares. "Relax your body, and trust me," he instructed, turning Reuben's back to him and positioning the boy to face the animal. Nazim placed both hands on either of Reuben's sides, effortlessly lifting him to perch him directly on the back of Ares. Reuben's eyes were almost as wide as Ares' which caused Eliana to laugh at the sight.

"Hold tight to the reigns, but relax your arms," Nazim instructed again. "I will lead you. Just focus on maintaining your balance and keeping your body centered over his back. You will have to move with him slightly, as he moves, in order to keep your balance. Do you understand?" he asked, looking up at the lad atop his horse.

"Yes, sir! I believe so," Reuben answered, a little overwhelmed but mostly excited at his position on the back of such an animal.

Nazim took the rope attached to the horse and began to lead Ares in a slow and steady walk. "Lead the way," he motioned to Eliana.

The trio made their way behind the inn along the path Nazim and Eliana had been on just a couple of hours before. They moved beyond the bank they had sat on, moving further into the forest. The evening was warm but not overly so as they began their short journey to the pools. Nazim could sense the anxiety in Ares over being stabled for several days straight, but he also knew the animal needed time to stretch his legs and warm up before he allowed him the satisfaction of a run. Reuben took to riding quickly and was soon comfortable being led along the path on the back of Ares. He was so overtaken by the sense of riding the animal that his constant chatter ceased entirely as he took in the familiar path from a brand-new vantage point.

"Did your grandfather create this path as well?" Nazim asked as they continued deeper into the woods. The path was narrow, but there was room for the two of them to walk side by side, with Ares being led behind them.

"No, Garrick made this path," Eliana answered as they walked.

"Garrick?" Nazim questioned. "How do I know that name?"

"He is my grandfather's oldest brother's son," Eliana clarified. "His parents perished in the wilderness, as did mine, and when we first arrived in Heshbon, Garrick stayed with us for a little time until he moved back to the Israeli camp to join the soldiers in battle. He loved the pools, and he insisted on a route to them without having to go through town each time he wished to visit. He created this path to take us there."

Nazim remembered the first conversation he had with Eli then and why the name was familiar to him. Grandfather had said that he had come to visit them after the walls had fallen and the Israelites had overtaken Jericho. This Garrick had a direct part in the destruction of the city. The name left a putrid taste in Nazim's mouth.

They had not walked long before the clearing came into view. Though they approached now from a different angle, it was the same as Nazim remembered from just a few days before.

"This place is amazing," he said softly.

"It is," Eliana agreed as she stepped into the clearing. True to their assumption, the pools were secluded, not a soul in sight other than themselves. The sunshine danced across the pools, making the water sparkle in the afternoon light. The air seemed clearer without the dust of the street lingering within, and the low tree branches swayed gently in the evening breeze. It was such a serene setting that Nazim hated to disrupt it, but a promise was a promise, even for a soldier such as himself.

Nazim turned and reached for Reuben, who obediently and without complaint allowed himself to be helped down from the back of the horse. "When you are more familiar and have more skill, I will allow you to run Ares, but this time, I need to do this alone," he explained.

"Of course!" Reuben agreed. With no effort whatsoever, Nazim mounted himself on the back of his animal. Ares seemed to know what was coming and began to prance around in anticipation.

"I will be right back," he promised Eliana and Reuben with a big smile as he spurred his animal into action. Ares took off like a flash as Nazim lowered his own body, giving the animal the freedom to run as fast as he desired. Reuben yelled from the sideline, spurring him on as the horse ran faster and faster around the tree line surrounding the pools. He made one complete lap, going out of sight for only a moment before reappearing and then continuing to make another, and then another.

A little over halfway through the third lap, Ares began to slow, and Nazim straightened himself, pulling the animal gently into a slow gallop, then slower still to walking, and eventually to a complete stop in front of Eliana and Reuben once again. The horse was labored and breathing heavily, but there was a sense of peace about him now that even Eliana could detect.

"May he drink from the pools?" Nazim asked, sliding off the animal's back. He paused as he pondered on the thought which crossed his mind. Never before would he have cared what anyone else considered sacred or holy. His own question even surprised himself.

"Of course, he may drink," Eliana answered. "These pools are not sacred. They are just beautiful." She began walking toward the closest pool.

"May I?" Reuben asked, requesting the reigns. Nazim handed them off to him without a verbal answer and then followed as Reuben led his animal to the pool. As Ares drank his fill, Nazim approached where Eliana waited, gazing into the water. He watched her as she stared into the pool, wondering what she was thinking. She was quite beautiful, the way the wind slightly stirred her veil and the way one whisp of hair blew across her face. He almost reached to tuck it behind her ear but caught himself just in time. She was not like the women of Jericho. She respected her personal space and would not appreciate him infringing upon it.

Nazim looked away quickly, concerned at his current state of mind. Why did he care what she thought or how attractive she was? He was here for a purpose, and again, he seemed to be forgetting what that purpose was. Yet, at the same time, he could not deny how intriguing this God of hers sounded. It was no wonder Rahab had been so caught up in the things she had been told of this Jehovah if the Israeli soldier had shared the same stories with her. He, himself, wanted to hear more. Nazim rubbed his forehead to clear his mind. This place was obviously getting to him. He had to remember his plan and stop being distracted by a pretty face and interesting stories.

"So where is Garrick now?" Nazim asked, looking again at Eliana and breaking the solitude of the moment. Even he thought his question sounded a bit forceful.

"Garrick?" Eliana questioned, breaking her trance, confused as to why her cousin was coming back up in their conversation and why Nazim had asked so harshly. "He remains with our people, aiding in the conquest of the remainder of the land promised us," she answered, turning to look at him.

Nazim did not answer but turned away. Of course, he fought; why else would he not remain in the inn with them now, then he remembered Grandfather Eli mentioned the same thing during their conversation. Nazim could feel his blood pressure rising and his heartbeat began to increase. He needed to get control of himself. He needed to change the subject before he allowed his temper to rage again.

"Are there more paths beyond the pools?" he asked, pointing to a particular spot through the trees across the meadow, distracting himself from his current thoughts.

"There are, though I have not explored many of them," she spoke honestly. "Grandfather would not rest easy if he thought I was out and about wandering the woods alone. Plus, it would not be proper."

"Many of them?" Nazim asked with a smirk. "That makes it sound as if you have explored at least a few," he smiled.

"Perhaps," she admitted, "one in particular. But you cannot expect me to confess to you all of my sins. We only met a few days ago," she chided. Nazim laughed aloud at her halfhearted confession. Eliana enjoyed the sound of his laughter, and it brought her own to her ears. Her laughter was a balm to his troubled soul.

Nazim realized he had to come to terms with these feelings of unrest: this confusion over the feelings that wrestled within him as he learned more about this God and more about these people. But for now, he would innocently enjoy the presence of a beautiful woman in a beautiful location.

Reuben had led Ares to a different area of the pool, and as Nazim watched him, something beyond the tree line caught his attention. Out of instinct, he grabbed Eliana by the waist, moving her quickly behind him, placing his body between her and whatever, or whoever, had caught his attention. His touch surprised her so much that she steadied herself by holding to his arm even after he had released her and turned his back to her. He recognized that her hand lingered on his arm, but Nazim was presently more concerned with the movement in the woods beyond them. Reuben was several feet away, his view blocked from whoever it was by Ares' body.

"Do not move, Reuben," Nazim instructed loud enough to be heard by the boy but not loud enough that their uninvited guest would hear. "Stay behind Ares."

Eliana looked to Reuben, who obediently nodded his acknowledgment.

"Who goes there?" Nazim spoke loudly, and Eliana recognized a sound in his voice she had not noticed before. The voice he used now was the voice of a warrior. It was terrifying.

To her shock and terror, it was Kylus who stepped out of the wood line. "I suppose it is I who should be asking the same question," Kylus yelled back in return. "Although I am not certain of who you are, I am quite sure of the female in your presence," he spat, "though I must admit I am utterly disappointed in what I have witnessed," he continued, slowly coming closer.

Eliana remained in her position behind Nazim but dropped her hand from his arm. Nazim kept his stance in front of Eliana. "You have witnessed nothing, and you have not answered me," Nazim called again to him. "Who are you, and what do you require."

Kylus continued to slowly come near but was still far enough away that the men had to raise their voices to be heard by one another.

"It is Kylus," Eliana whispered so only Nazim could hear.

"I know who he is, but he does not know that," Nazim clarified quietly. "Keep your place, and do exactly as I say," he instructed her.

"I know there is a female in your presence; she cowers behind you now," Kylus stated, hatred dripping from his voice. "I heard her laughter. Who are you, and why have you lured her here, to a secluded place, alone?"

Eliana knew exactly where this was going and what accusation was about to be made. And she cowered from no one, especially not Kylus.

"I came on my own, Kylus," she called out, stepping from behind Nazim.

"Eliana," Nazim stated so harshly that she jumped. "Get behind me, now," he commanded her.

"It is alright, Nazim," she answered quietly, though the glare she received from him said otherwise. In other circumstances, that glare may have caused her to flee. Turning back to Kylus, she continued. "I am not alone with him; Reuben is with us," she answered, motioning for Reuben to come out of hiding.

"Do not move, Reuben," Nazim instructed harshly. Reuben quickly decided he would obey Nazim and apologized on the spot if he was doing wrong by his sister. Kylus continued to come closer to them and only then did Eliana notice his hand already grasping the sword at his side. Eliana stopped in her tracks, Nazim moving now to stand beside her. Kylus stopped out of reach but close enough that the malice was easy to read on his face.

"So, you are the so-called 'wandering soldier' who escaped the destruction of Jericho. Did you finally decide to come out of hiding and face the people who took your city?" Kylus teased, his fingers playing on his sword. "The *stranger* Eliana knows nothing about, yet who she now finds herself with by the pools. Alone," he said slowly, while shooting daggers in Eliana's direction with his eyes.

"I suppose I am the soldier you speak of, though I hide from no one. What is that to you?" Nazim asked never taking his eyes from Kylus's face.

"I will be your worst nightmare if you have not cleared this town before sunrise," Kylus answered, his hand gripping the hilt of his weapon.

"I have already encountered my worst nightmare, and you pale in comparison," Nazim returned. "I will leave this town as soon as I have kept the promise I made to Eliana and her grandfather and not one second before."

Eliana felt smothered by the tension she felt. She did not miss the fact that Ares had moved on his own volition to be closer to Nazim and that Reuben still kept himself hidden behind the animal as Nazim had instructed him to. It was Kylus who broke the gaze with Nazim when he again turned his glare to focus on Eliana.

"And you," he spat as he stepped forward, reaching out suddenly to grab her arm, "will return to the village with me."

"I will not!" she yelled back at him, jerking her arm from his grasp. Nazim moved forward, but Eliana stopped him by stepping between him and Kylus. "Kylus, you are not the same man you were when Joshua appointed you as peacekeeper," Eliana accused him. "He will learn of your treachery, and you will pay for it," she promised.

Kylus spat on the ground at Eliana's feet. "Your word is nothing now, Eliana. Once I report that I caught you, alone, with him, your reputation will be worse than that whore from Jericho who deceived Salmon into marriage!"

Nazim felt a rage course through his body that he could no longer control. He rushed around Eliana, grabbing Kylus by the throat in one fluid motion so powerful and so fast that Kylus had no time to react. Before Kylus could blink, he was on the ground with such force that the land beneath him began to sink and give way.

"Nazim, stop!" Eliana cried as Kylus's face began to darken. Shades of red and purple began to color his cheeks and forehead as Nazim continued pressing his body into the earth. Kylus's eyes began to bulge, his legs and arms flailing uselessly about him as Eliana continued her cry for Nazim to stop. Finally, something beyond Nazim's control forced him to loosen his grip. Looking from the face of the man he held and into Eliana's, he saw the fear in her eyes, and he realized that Eliana was about to witness a murder at his hands.

Nazim completely removed his hand from the neck of the enemy before him and stood over Kylus as he lay on the ground, now gasping for air. In only a second, his natural color began rushing back to his face and head. Reuben was still sheltered by Ares and had witnessed nothing visually, only verbally. Eliana stepped to where Nazim stood, still towering over Kylus, and without thinking or even questioning herself, placed one hand on his arm and her other on his chest.

Nazim looked into her face and felt his own breathing begin to calm. The fear he saw in her eyes hurt him. He had caused part of that fear, and the weasel in front of him had caused the rest of it. Looking back to Kylus, he spoke once again. "You will say nothing to harm her reputation, as you have nothing to report," Nazim demanded in a tone so sinister that Eliana felt chills run up her spine. "Do I make myself clear?" he asked plainly.

Kylus stared up at him, struggling to sit up. "And you will not return to this village for at least a month, at which time the repairs to the inn will be completed, and I will be gone. Do you understand me?" Nazim finished.

Kylus was in a partially upright position now, though he still remained seated on the ground. Eliana blinked as she noticed the imprint of where his body had laid on the land in the ground beside him. With her hands still on Nazim's arm and chest, she began to pressure Nazim to retreat. She knew she could not move him and that any movement would be of his own volition.

Her encouragement was all he needed. Nazim turned as Eliana continued to hold to his arm and moved with her toward Ares and Reuben. She looked back only once to make sure Kylus would not attempt an attack on Nazim from behind.

"He will not," Nazim scoffed, realizing her fear. "He cannot at the moment," he clarified as they approached Ares. Nazim lifted Reuben back onto Ares, then took the lead to escort the trio out of the clearing and back to the path from where they had come.

Chapter Eleven

It was a somber group that made their way back over the narrow path toward the inn. As they approached the barn, Reuben was met by his friend Thomas, who requested that he be allowed to join his family for their evening meal.

Before agreeing to his request, Eliana pulled Reuben to the side. "Nothing is to be said about what happened this afternoon," she instructed him quietly.

"I promise, Eliana," Reuben assured her.

"Then you may go, but do not be out late," she reminded him as he ran to join his friend. Nazim made sure Ares was comfortable and fed him well. A word had not been spoken between the two of them, and Eliana decided to face her fear head-on.

"Are you angry with me?" she asked sincerely, watching as he brushed his animal.

He turned from Ares to look at her. "Why would I be angry with you?" he returned, just as sincere.

"Because you asked me to stay behind you in the meadow, and I did not, but I knew that Kylus was about to accuse you of luring me there against my will, and I will not allow you to be accused of something you did not do," she defended herself.

The shock at her confession showed on his face as he stared at her. That she was willing to risk her own reputation just to keep him from a wrongful accusation was amazing to him.

He moved closer to her and looked down into her face. When she looked to the ground, he used one finger to lift her chin, forcing her to look at him. He held her chin gently as he spoke. "I am not angry with you," he answered honestly. "I knew Kylus would try to provoke me to lose my temper, and I knew if he saw you, it would fuel his anger and that I would retaliate. Which he did, and in turn it did, and then I did," he smiled. "I am sorry that you witnessed that side of me," he apologized, releasing her face and turning back to Ares.

"It was Rahab again, wasn't it? The mention of her name." Nazim realized it was as much a statement as a question, but he also felt that Eliana deserved an honest answer just the same.

"No," Nazim said truthfully. He turned to look at her again and then clarified the reason for his anger. "It was his comparison of you to what she used to be."

"Oh," Eliana stated simply. Nazim turned his body completely to face her now, crossing his arms and leaning his back against Ares.

"It was really rather strange," he stated.

"What was strange?" she asked.

"Well, normally, when I go into fight mode, I hear nothing except the sound of my own blood coursing through my veins," he began to explain. "It is a kind of a survival tactic I guess, to being in battle. You have to learn to tune out the cries and the agony of everything going on around you. There are so many distractions. But allowing only one distraction to pull you from the moment can mean the difference in life or death. So, I have taught myself to hear nothing except the sound of my own body. But today, when I was holding Kylus to the ground, listening to my heart pounding in my ears, there was something more."

"Me begging you to stop?" Eliana asked with a small chuckle.

"Not at first," he said honestly. "It was not something audible; it was something I honestly cannot explain. Something was compelling me to stop choking him. To let him go and to look at you," Nazim looked directly at her now. "I eased my grip on him before I let go completely, and when I finally did look at you, I had no choice but to let him go."

Eliana looked at him and tried to find the words to say. "Perhaps Heshbon is having an effect on you," she smiled softly.

"Perhaps it is Heshbon," he said thoughtfully, continuing to watch her. He paused for a moment more before turning back to his care of Ares. "You really are something," he half grinned at her over his shoulder.

"How do you mean," Eliana grinned back at him.

"You come across as a humble, fearful female, then surprise me by running headfirst into a dust storm in the middle of the street, approach Kylus knowing he would demand a tribute, then risking your own reputation in an attempt to save mine," he laughed. "What will be next?" he asked jokingly, laying aside his brush, now satisfied that he had cared for his horse.

"It depends on what comes up," she answered truthfully, gaining a laugh from Nazim. "I need to get inside and prepare our evening meal," she said around her own chuckle as she turned to go, "Grandfather will be famished."

"Could you use some help?" he asked, following her.

"In the cooking area?" she laughed out loud.

"I was on my own for quite some time, and I did not starve," he defended himself.

"True enough, I suppose," she relinquished as they entered the inn.

Entering through the main dining room, Eliana gasped at the sight she beheld.

"AVI!" she almost screamed, causing Nazim to stop in his tracks. He knew the surprise had to show on his face when a man almost as tall as himself rushed over and grabbed Eliana in a fierce hug, lifting her off the floor. Eli did not miss the look on Nazim's face as he witnessed the surprise clearly written all over the soldier's features.

"What are you doing here?" Eliana asked with a laugh as the man called Avi returned her to her standing position and took a step back.

"Let me look at you," he demanded. "Eliana, you are simply beautiful," he announced. "You have not changed a bit. How is it that you remain unattached?"

"It is not due to none showing a lack of interest, I assure you," Grandfather smiled, complimenting his granddaughter.

Eliana ignored the jest. "And you have gotten taller, and so handsome," she laughed. "What brings you back to us?" she asked, and suddenly the smile on her face vanished. "It is good news, I hope."

"Joshua sent me. He wanted me to bring an update on the progress of our people and our continued quest for the Promised Land. We have just been catching up," he motioned to Eli. "And

113

you must be Nazim," he stated turning to the man who was continuing to stare at him with a cynical glare. He offered his hand. Nazim hesitantly extended his own, though his face remained stern. He was not clear if he should consider this man a friend or a foe.

"I am so sorry," Eliana apologized. "Nazim, this is Avi. Avi, please meet Nazim, our…" she paused.

"Ah, the wandering soldier I have heard so much about," Avi finished in her pause. He did not miss the fact that Nazim's hand continued to swallow his own in a firm grasp. "Grandfather was just telling me the help you have been since the misfortune with the outer structure. I know your presence is appreciated."

"And we are so thankful for yours!" Eliana continued directing her comment back to Avi. "Sit, talk with Grandfather! Nazim and I were just about to prepare something for our evening meal, and we will join you."

"Where is Reuben?" Avi called as she began to move to the cooking area.

"He was just invited to eat with Thomas and his family, but he will join us soon. I trust you will be with us for a while?" she asked, stopping and turning to face him once again. Nazim did not miss the hopeful expression in her tone. Nor did he care for it.

"For a little while, and then I must return to aid our people," Avi admitted honestly.

"Well, we shall be thankful for the time we have with you. Regardless of how long or short," Eliana returned as she again moved toward the cooking area.

Nazim had stood back but began to follow her now, a hard expression continuing to mark his features.

Once the pair had left their presence, Eli allowed a small chuckle to exit his throat.

"What amuses you?" Avi asked, a confused smile on his face.

"Nazim's response to you," Eli admitted. "I am not clear on his original intentions for coming to Heshbon, but I am fairly certain that his interests have changed since his arrival here."

"And you are amused by that? He is not one to be trifled with," Avi reminded the old man. "Rahab has spoken of him on more than one occasion."

"Tell me," Eli requested, his interest piqued.

"Salmon was quite concerned for some time after Rahab's family joined us," Avi began. "He was quite certain that Nazim would seek them out. Apparently, he and Rahab were very close while in Jericho, and Salmon felt that Nazim would attempt to come for her. He is not a warrior you want to have at your back from all she has shared with us," Avi looked again in the direction he had gone, then turned back to Eli as he spoke once again. "And you are certain that you feel at peace with having him here?"

Eli nodded his head as he, too, gazed at the cooking area door Nazim had just gone through. "I do. I feel Jehovah directed him to us for our own good, as well as his. He has already been quite a help, as you can see, and he is showing an interest in Jehovah, though he still harbors many reservations. I feel with time, with Jehovah's help and intervention, we can break down his resolve and that he will be quite an asset to our people."

Avi shook his head. "I fear it is not only Jehovah he has gained an interest in," he admitted. "Though I trust you and Jehovah completely, do be careful, Grandfather." He directed his attention completely to the man in front of him now and changed the subject. "It is good to see you fare so well," he smiled.

"I am well," Eli confirmed. "Now, tell me of our people," he requested.

"Things are, better," Avi hesitated, "now."

"Now?" Eli questioned.

"We had an instance shortly after Jericho was defeated. We continued on to Ai," Avi explained. "Joshua granted Salmon time with his new bride as was commanded in the law, and sent myself and Garrick into the land to spy it out, the same as he had done when Salmon and Garrick had gone first into Jericho. The men of Ai were so few in number, Grandfather, that we should have had no issue overcoming them. We told Joshua he needed to only send in two or three thousand men. We should have easily conquered the city." Avi paused, his mind traveling to another place.

"Should have?" Grandfather asked, encouraging him to continue.

"We were defeated," he answered honestly, "badly. Joshua discovered during his pleas and petitions to Jehovah afterward that someone in our camp had sorely sinned. In the end, it was Achan."

"What had he done?" Grandfather asked plainly.

"We had been instructed that all of the spoils of Jericho were to go into the Lord's treasury. Achan had taken a garment, two hundred shekels of silver, and a wedge of gold from the spoils for himself. He had hidden the treasures beneath the earth under his tent. God brought judgment upon our people for Achan's sin through our defeat in Ai," Avi finished.

"What has become of Achan now?" Grandfather asked with sorrow in his voice.

"The valley of Achor now marks the place where his body and those of his family are laid," Avi stated sadly. "We had to restore our people, Grandfather. Joshua had no choice," Avi defended.

"Of course, he did not," Grandfather stated with understanding. "It just breaks this old heart that our people have come through so much yet can still be so blinded."

"With the death of Achan and his family, God's favor returned to our people," Avi explained. "With careful instruction from Joshua, on a second attempt, we were able to take the city of Ai."

"Does Kylus know of the demise of Achan?" Grandfather asked carefully.

"Not that I am aware of, though I cannot see how it would overly concern Kylus. He had no direct dealings with Achan that I am aware of," Avi answered. "They were not family," he concluded thoughtfully.

"Maybe not," Grandfather began, "but perhaps it would enlighten him how greed can consume one so completely."

"Why so?" Avi asked curiously.

Before Eli could answer, Eliana and Nazim returned with trays laden with food. Meats and cheeses, olives, dates, pomegranates, and fresh vegetables were loaded on the trays. They set the food on a larger table, where Eli and Avi moved to join them. Eliana completed the fare by bringing a large loaf of bread and vessels of various beverages. Eliana's face seemed a bit more somber than before, and her grandfather could sense a slight tension in her that he had not noticed earlier.

"I thought our fare was to be light this evening," her grandfather teased her.

"It is not every day that Avi is present with us," she explained as the group gathered together around the larger table. Nazim noticed that each of them instinctively bowed their heads once they had taken their places, and he followed suit, though his desire was to keep his eyes locked on the stranger before him.

Nazim realized that his demeanor had changed and that he had been quiet during the time he assisted Eliana with the preparations. He could tell she wanted to question him about the sudden change in his mood, but he was glad she had refrained. He could only assume the man before him now was a suitor, and he was angry with himself for allowing the thought to bother him more than a little.

Eli began the prayer by thanking their God for His provisions and safe keeping, then asked for blessings on the food they were about to partake of before ending with yet another prayer of thanksgiving for bringing Avi once again into their presence. Nazim allowed himself a look at Eli as he prayed and noticed how he seemed to be speaking directly to someone. Nazim looked around himself, searching for an aura or a spirit, anything unusual, but he saw nothing. Yet, he had never heard anyone pray so fervently and seem so in touch with an unseen, spiritual being before.

As soon as Eli concluded his petition, Avi spoke again, his remarks directed toward Nazim. "I trust your time in Heshbon has been enjoyable." Nazim recognized the statement for the question it was intended to be.

"It has been interesting," Nazim answered, a serious look on his face.

Eliana made sure everyone's needs were met before seeing to her own fare. Nazim noticed her selflessness and admired her for it. Finally, she took her place and saw to her own meal, settling herself between him and the man Avi. Nazim was quiet as they ate, and the conversation remained mostly about specific people that Eli and Eliana asked about. Avi answered each question, and it sounded as if their people were faring pretty well.

"And what of the destruction to the front of the inn, what are your plans for that?" Avi asked, changing the subject.

"Nazim has been kind enough to agree to repair the stoop and the roof for us," Eliana answered. "The materials for the repairs are to be delivered later this week," she continued. "And they cannot be here quickly enough. We have very little time for the repairs to be completed."

"Why so?" Avi asked curiously.

Eliana looked to her grandfather for direction. She was not sure how he wished to explain Kylus's recent change in behavior.

Her Grandfather took over the conversation then, wisely and calmly explaining how Kylus now ruled over their people. He told Avi of the righteous tributes, how and when people benefitted from them, the way many now seemed to seek Kylus's favor in exchange for money, and how they felt someone in Heshbon constantly reported to Kylus. He continued by telling of Kylus's request for Eliana's hand, the rage he had shown at her refusal, and finally, the encounter Eliana had had with Kylus in the street earlier.

Avi took in all the information given him without a word, and Nazim took in Avi's reaction to the information. The man was terribly calm and that unnerved him more than a little. He would have expected more anger from him based on the welcome he had been afforded by Eliana. Avi seemed unbothered that Eliana's hand had been requested even though she had denied the proposal.

"I am pleased with you for denying him," Avi said speaking directly to Eliana. "Most young women would jump at the chance to marry a man of his stature regardless of his character."

"You know me better than that, Avi," she spoke as she laid another piece of meat on Nazim's plate and moved to add more cheese to Avi's.

"Has Joshua been told of this change in Kylus's attitude?" Avi asked.

"We did not know how to send word," Grandfather admitted. "Joshua has a lot on his shoulders already with the conquest of the Promised Land."

"This is true, but Joshua has trusted Kylus to govern in Jehovah's will here, not in his own as it appears he has now taken to. I will make sure that Joshua hears of his actions," Avi promised. "In the meantime, I will stay until Nazim has finished the repairs, to keep any further misfortune from coming to you from the hand of Kylus."

"That would be wonderful, Avi!" Eliana exclaimed. "Are you sure Joshua can spare you for that long?"

"I planned on being here a few weeks at the least. And in the meantime, I can assist Nazim in anyway necessary with the repairs. Is that suitable with you, Nazim?" he asked looking around Eliana to the man on the opposite side of her who continued to eat in silence.

Nazim was surprised that he was even being consulted on the matter. He had just taken a bite, so he politely nodded his head that he agreed. Did he have a choice in the matter? Besides, he was one who chose to keep his enemies close. Before he could speak, Reuben bounded through the door.

"AVI!" he yelled as he threw himself in the arms of the man he was so delighted to see. Nazim almost rolled his eyes. Even the lad was overcome with joy at the arrival of this man. "Brother! You are home!" Reuben cried, excitedly.

Nazim could not help himself now and swallowed the food in his mouth hard. "Brother?" he asked aloud.

"Yes!" Eliana explained, surprised that she had left that out of her introductions. "I apologize, Nazim, I thought I had told you when I introduced the two of you! Avi is our older brother."

Nazim surprised himself again as he realized the feeling of relief that washed over him. Why he cared of Avi's relation to Eliana, he did not want to admit, but the fact that he did was evident. The relief he felt that this man was not a welcome suitor but was, in fact, her brother, caused him to feel as if a weight had literally been lifted from his shoulders. Why did he care?

He continued to sit there as the conversation continued around him, though he heard little of it. He may be able to lie to others, but he could not lie to himself. Nazim knew that his ideals were changing. He realized quickly, in that moment, that his entire thought process concerning this place and these people had begun to change. He still had questions which he longed to find answers for. He still wanted to learn the secrets of this God they served and what allowed Him to be so victorious, but perhaps destroying these people in the process, in particular this family, was not the answer.

Chapter Twelve

Nazim finished his meal in silence, content in the conversation that continued around him. Soon enough the lively chatter began to wane as the participants began to tire. Reuben had fallen asleep in the chair where he sat beside his older brother.

"There is a lot to catch up on, but thankfully, we do not have to do it all in one night," Grandfather said finally. "I am weary, and my bed is calling to me," he laughed as he slowly began to rise.

"I will see you to your room, Grandfather," Avi offered as he stood to offer his assistance. "Then retire to my former room?" he asked looking to Eliana for confirmation.

"Of course," she smiled. "Top of the second flight of stairs to the right," she clarified.

"Do you plan to continue work on the inn tomorrow?" Avi asked now directing his question to Nazim.

"I do," he acknowledged. "There is a bit more clearing to do before the materials arrive and the rebuilding can begin."

"Until morning then," Avi concluded with a nod in their direction as he assisted his grandfather up the stairs.

Eliana moved to rouse her younger brother and directed him to his room, then began clearing the table. Nazim moved to assist her. With the two of them working, the chore went quickly. Eliana remained quiet as they worked, unsure of the change in Nazim's mood and how exactly to approach him. It was Nazim who broke the silence as they finished.

"I did not realize you had a brother other than Reuben," he spoke with his familiar sideways grin. "How many are in your family?" he asked leaning against a counter now and facing Eliana.

"Only the three of us and Grandfather are left," she smiled back, relieved that he did not seem angry now, only confused. "There are no more surprises," she chuckled.

"That, you should not be so quick to promise," he smiled back at her. Eliana could not get over how much the small gesture softened his face. "You, Eliana, are full of surprises," he accused.

She laughed quietly as she pulled out a chair at the nearby table and sat. Nazim followed suit, sitting across from her.

"As you know, my parents passed in the wilderness, as did my grandmother," she began to explain. "She passed early in the wandering before even Avi was born, my parents, obviously, years later. Avi is four years older than myself, so he and I remember our parents very well. Being the youngest, Reuben remembers them, but not as clearly as we do."

"I am sure you miss them," Nazim spoke truthfully.

"I do," she answered as she looked away. "But Jehovah had a plan and a purpose for their passing. I am thankful for Grandfather and his presence in our lives. I am not sure what I would ever do without him."

"I am sure your Jehovah has a plan when that time comes as well," Nazim reminded her with a grin.

Eliana looked at him with a sideways glare. "I am sure He does," she agreed. "What about you, Nazim?" she asked after a moment had passed. "What of your parents? What was it like growing up in Jericho?"

Nazim thought for a moment before he spoke.

"I do not remember my parents," he said honestly. "I was orphaned, as far as I know, when I was very young. The closest person I had to a parent would have been a man named Malik. I suppose he took me in; I do not remember a time before he was in my life. I often wondered if he could have been my brother, though he never said as much. I just remember that he moved me onto the grounds of the palace with him when he became a soldier. I remember little of our life before that time."

"Nazim, I am so sorry," Eliana spoke sincerely.

"Do not be sorry," he chided her. "I was the youngest in the history of Jericho to begin training for the king's army, and I was determined to make Malik proud of me. Though he showed little kindness, he cared for me when no one else would. They had no pity on my age or my size and trained me as if I were one of the older boys. It was beneficial to me at a time when I had nothing else. Otherwise, I would have had no one to provide for me and nowhere to live. It was the only life I have ever known, and it served me well. I became the man I am now because of that training."

"What became of Malik?" Eliana asked quietly.

"He went to battle and never returned," Nazim answered nonchalantly. "I assume he was killed, but I never really heard. By then I was moving quickly through the ranks and was on a path to becoming the captain of the guard of the city. No other soldier could match my abilities. Little else mattered."

"And you had no one else? No family of any kind?" Eliana could not fathom having no one. Without a thought otherwise, she placed her hand on top of his where he rested them in the center of the table.

"I had my brothers in arms," he answered as he watched her face, surprised by the amount of concern she so openly showed. "And I had Rahab," he said carefully. "She was the closest thing to family I ever allowed myself to have."

"You must have been very close to her," Eliana admitted, her eyes brimming with tears. "I am thankful Jehovah saw fit to save her from the destruction of the city." Eliana wiped a tear that had escaped her eye. She did not know why his story affected her so. It must be a combination of her being tired and the events of the day.

Nazim looked to his hands where her hands continued to rest, then to her face. He did not want to be the first to move, but he knew she was exhausted. He, himself, needed time to sort through the emotions stirring within him.

"I feel rest is in order, for both of us," he admitted still, maintaining his posture and position.

"I feel you are correct," she said then, pulling back her hands and moving to rise. They moved from the cooking area in silence, walking side by side to the stairs. As Eliana turned to enter her room, Nazim continued to ascend the stairs. She turned to watch Nazim now approaching the door to his room.

"Nazim." He stopped, turning to face her as he heard her quietly call his name. "Thank you for sharing your story with me tonight," she said sincerely.

He nodded speaking a simple, "Goodnight," then continued into his room.

Nazim did not know why he was being so honest with her. She was practically a stranger. A pretty face. An Israelite. An innocent woman. Her people had destroyed everything. She was genuinely kind. She believed in a ridiculous notion of an unseen God. She was openly and honestly sharing her history with him. A history of imperfect people, but a people who continued to prosper because of their worship of an unseen God. A forgiving God, Eliana had said, and He must be very forgiving after the few stories she had shared. And she said that He had always been that way. She also claimed that He created and constructed everything, and it did not seem as if He only sought perfect people to do His will.

He lay across the cot in the far corner of the room, staring at the ceiling above him and continuing to argue with himself. His mind was a jumble of frustrated thoughts and ideas. He was frustrated that he could not understand himself. He had come here with one thought, one plan, one idea, and he was finding the more he learned of these Israelites, the more confused he became. Not only about their God, he was certain he would never fully understand their beliefs, but he was more confused about his own feelings. His feelings toward these people, his feelings toward Eliana, his feelings regarding her well-being and that of her family, but mostly his feelings of interest toward the God he had been so determined to destroy.

He heard her laughter just around the corner from where he stood. She sounded so happy, so content. As he rounded the corner, he watched as the alley directly in front of him split into two separate paths. To the right of the fork, he saw her, Rahab, beckoning him to come to her. She looked just as she had the day he had seen her on the bank of the river. She was beautiful, yet different. He was not looking at the same Rahab he had last seen in Jericho. Their last conversation came back to him in a wave of unrest and regret.

To the left of the fork stood Eliana, looking first to him, then to Rahab, and then back to him again. The confusion on her face was as evident as the confusion he felt in his gut.

Nazim stood at the fork, looking back and forth between the two women, unsure of which way to go. Suddenly, he heard horsemen approaching. He could hear the angry shouts of the men and the sounds of the horses' hooves as they stormed closer kicking up dust and debris all around them. He could tell from where he stood it was enemies who approached, enemies sent to seek and destroy everything in their path. Nazim looked behind himself but saw nothing; he just continued to hear the sickening sound of their approach until, finally, in a frantic search, he saw them. They were approaching on either side of the fork, not coming from behind himself, but coming up behind the two women.

He called out both their names, but neither woman would move. Rahab continued to look at him, smiling and waving for him to join her completely oblivious to the danger rapidly approaching behind her. Eliana continued looking first at him, and then at Rahab, in sheer confusion, also unaware of the danger pressing upon her too, from behind.

Nazim knew he had a decision to make and fast. He could not save them both from the stampede pressing down so quickly upon them. He looked from one to the other trying to deduce how he could possibly save them both, but there was simply no way. He had to make a choice.

Finally, another set of hooves was heard, these coming from behind himself. He turned quickly to see Salmon, the Israelite, on his own horse thundering past him. Salmon did not pose a threat to Nazim as he passed, he did not even seem to notice him as he raced toward Rahab. Reaching her, he reached down in one swift motion and grabbed her, landing her safely on the back of his steed.

As he turned racing her toward safety, Nazim lurched into motion, racing as fast as he could down the path to the left toward Eliana. The harder he ran toward her, the farther away she seemed to be. She was not backing away, the path seemed to be growing longer. The horses were advancing on her, the men on them shouting and screaming their battle cry. They lowered their swords as they approached her. Nazim ran harder and faster in an attempt to reach her. He reached for her, and as he did, she began reaching for him. Finally, she was just within reach before suddenly she disappeared into a cloud of dust as the horses fully descended upon her.

His own tortured cry woke him, but he quickly muffled his own face. He was on his feet in a split second, realizing this was yet another very real, yet very new, nightmare. He moved quickly to the wash basin, his pulse racing, and splashed the water on his face, knocking the basin to the floor in the process. Water poured onto his feet, but he did not even notice. He took several deep breaths as he felt the cool water roll along his neck before he moved to look out the window willing his heart to slow. He did not know if it was the confrontation with Kylus, or the story of his past that he had shared with Eliana, but something had caused his nightmares to return.

After a few moments of pacing between the bed and the window, willing his heartbeat to slow, he finally relaxed enough to achieve the satisfying deep breath he had been waiting for. After cleaning the spilled water from the floor, he slowly returned to his bed. He lay in the quiet, hearing nothing except the sound of his own breathing, calmer now, though still somewhat labored as he stared at the roof above him.

Tonight's dream was different, he realized again. Rahab had been saved. He had not been the one who saved her, but her hero had been no threat to him. It was Eliana who had needed him, and it was Eliana whom he had failed. He had heard of men who could interpret dreams, but Nazim was wise enough to realize he had no need of an interpreter.

If the stories he had recently been told were true, and if the God Eliana believed in so fervently was real, perhaps He had sent the Israelite to Jericho in order to save Rahab when Nazim could not. If it were not for Salmon, Rahab would not have been told of Jehovah. She may have never fully believed in the God of Israel, and she, too, would have perished in the city. And he had seen with his own eyes that Rahab was happy and, even more importantly, that she was safe.

Turning onto his side, he stared into the darkness. Nazim did not fully understand what was going on inside his mind and heart. He still could not completely comprehend their notions and their beliefs in this unseen, all-powerful God. But he did know that Kylus was flesh and blood, and he knew that men like him did not

126

back down easily. Eliana had told Nazim that their Jehovah still had a use for him, that he still had a purpose. Nazim accepted that he may have failed Rahab, but he determined now, in this moment, that he would not fail Eliana.

Eliana sat upright in her bed. Something had awoken her. She was certain she had heard someone yell or heard something fall… she went quietly to her door laying her head against the closed portal to see if she could hear movement from Reuben's room across the hall from her. Complete silence. Perhaps she was dreaming she thought as she moved back to her bed.

Eliana lay on her back staring at the ceiling. She thought over the radical changes of the past few days, and she had to be honest with herself. She had met Nazim. She had feared Nazim. She had sought safety behind Nazim. She had felt jealousy when she thought he was seeking for Uma. She had worried for his reputation when they were in the meadow, and if she were completely honest, she secretly enjoyed his company.

"He is dangerous," she whispered into the darkness. "He is temperamental; he is violent," she continued listing his faults to no one. "And most importantly," she whispered as she sat up and threw her legs over the side of the cot, "he is not a believer." She sighed and buried her face in her hands. With a deep breath, she moved from her bed once again. It was still earlier than normal, but she felt that morning was not far away, and she knew without a doubt, that no more sleep would be had this night.

Coming to terms that her rest for now had ended, she dressed and readied herself for her morning chores. Patrons would begin to arrive sooner rather than later. Uma would arrive late, as usual, and Eliana decided she would have things ready ahead of time. She was surprised when she entered the cooking area and saw her older brother had beaten her there, sitting at the table alone in silence.

"Avi," she asked quietly. "What are you doing up at this early hour?"

"I could ask the same of you, Sister," he returned.

"Could not sleep?" she asked, ignoring his question.

"I suppose the change in my location has upset my internal clock," he grinned. "Or, I am just used to my tent," he admitted, laughing softly.

Eliana sat a pitcher of juice and two mugs in front of him on the table.

"I could use some company," he grinned as she pulled out a chair to join him. "How are things here, really?" he asked as she sat.

"Things are fine," she answered honestly, settling herself. "Other than our little setback out there," she motioned to the front of the inn, "I have no real complaints…"

"Other than Kylus," he finished for her.

"Kylus is a whole other story," she huffed, pouring juice into their mugs. "I will admit, I was concerned when Nazim first came into our inn…"

"As you should have been," Avi politely interrupted.

"But now, I think he was sent here for a purpose," she continued absolutely. Avi nodded his head and took a drink of the juice she offered, weighing his next words carefully.

"You know I trust you, Sister," he finally spoke directly. "But do be careful of Nazim. He is not an everyday, common soldier."

"How so?" she asked as she, too, drank from her mug.

"Nazim was the chief captain of the entire army in Jericho. No one could match his strength or his abilities. He did not get to his station by being a humble soldier. He was fearless, and mighty, and he uses those same characteristics in his everyday life. He is an aggressive leader and an aggressive man. You know that it is simply by the grace of God that we took the city of Jericho. Without the miracle straight from Jehovah, Himself, we never could have breached those walls, and," he continued matter-of-factly, "Nazim was not present when we fought once those walls were breached. It was all orchestrated by Jehovah."

"As we have been told," she agreed. "And I assume it is Rahab who has divulged all of the information regarding Nazim to you," she stated, sitting back in her chair.

Avi could not help himself and laughed out loud before catching himself. He must be quiet as the others were still sleeping at this early hour.

"Is there a hint of jealousy I hear in that statement from my baby sister?" he asked quietly now, around a chuckle.

"Absolutely not!" Eliana defended herself. "How could you even accuse me of such? Nazim has simply shared part of his story with me, and I can tell from all he has said that the two of them were close."

"They were *very* close," Avi emphasized.

"*Very* close," she mocked setting down her mug. "Avi, I am not ignorant, nor do I need to know the sins of others. I have never even met the woman, but I do know that Rahab is married to Salmon, and that union would never have happened were she the same woman she was while in Jericho."

"Rahab is not the same, you are correct. She is far from it, a different woman completely. But it is because she now believes in Jehovah and worships as we do. And it is because..." he continued.

"Because she was told of Jehovah by Salmon," Eliana interrupted him. "So, what makes you think that Nazim cannot also be changed by my telling him of the same great God?" she asked.

"I am just requesting that you be careful. You are not familiar with the ways of men, Eliana. And Nazim is not your typical village boy looking for a suitable companion..."

"Avi, I know the ways of our people. I would never enter into a union that grandfather, or you, did not approve of for a just cause. I have admitted, I was fearful of Nazim at first, and I found out quickly that he is not, as you say, a typical village boy, BUT," she continued before he could interrupt her again, "he does need to know of our God. He was spared in Jericho for a reason, Avi, and he deserves an opportunity to learn of Jehovah and to fulfill that purpose."

"Be that as it may, I just do not wish to see my baby sister hurt, physically or emotionally, in any way," he answered pointedly.

"I feel safe with Nazim," she began, "most of the time," she laughed honestly. The thought crossed her mind to tell Avi of the encounter they had just had with Kylus in the meadow. However, she dismissed the thought quickly, deciding it would only worry her brother further. "And I would not be so careless as to put myself in a compromising situation," she promised, "with

129

anyone," she added for emphasis. Avi held up his hands in mock surrender. "Plus, it is not like my big brother will not be present for the next few weeks to keep his eye on things," she finished.

"The arrival of my timing was of Jehovah," he agreed. "I am glad that I will be present to help with the repairs of the inn, as well as be present to learn more of this wandering soldier who has found himself among my family. For example, what exactly were his intentions for coming to Heshbon to begin with?" he stated plainly.

Eliana rolled her eyes playfully at her brother and then rose to look out the window. The stars were growing faint which meant that sunrise was indeed approaching.

"I must prepare for our morning guests. Draw me some water?" she asked holding a bucket in his direction.

"Yes, dear sister," he mocked as he rose to take the bucket from her hand. "Promise me," he stated sincerely, looking into her eyes as he took the bucket from her, "that you will guard yourself."

"I promise, Avi," she smiled. "Now go get my water," she demanded playfully.

Chapter Thirteen

Eliana was only slightly surprised when she entered the main dining area close to an hour later to see that Nazim was already there, seated in his usual spot. What surprised her most, however, was seeing his elbows propped on the table and his head resting in his hands. His hair was not in the knot at the back of his head that she had gotten accustomed to but instead lay about his shoulders in reckless curls.

"Nazim?" she asked quietly as she approached. Quickly, he looked up at her, wiping his eyes and blinking rapidly. "Are you well?" she asked setting a mug and pitcher of juice on the table before taking a seat across from him.

"Yes, yes," he stammered, as he began smoothing his hair into the familiar knot. "I did not realize anyone was in here yet," he answered.

"I woke early and found Avi already in the cooking area when I arrived." She poured juice into his mug. "Did you not sleep well?" she asked as her mind wandered back to the sounds that had awoken her, though she dared not voice the thoughts aloud.

"I have nights when sleep eludes me for one reason or another," he answered honestly. "Last night was one of those nights." He tied his hair with a leather strap and then wiped his eyes once again.

"Perhaps you should return to your room for a bit and gain more rest," she suggested. Nazim appreciated her concern, but returning to that room was the last thing he needed. What he needed was hard work to clear his head.

"I will be fine," he assured her attempting a smile while taking the mug she had placed before him.

"I thought I heard voices," Avi exclaimed as he exited the cooking area. "The porridge is boiling," he directed to Eliana.

"Thank you, Avi. I will be right back with food for the both of you to break your fast," she stated as she moved away.

"Rough night?" Avi asked as he took the seat his sister had vacated.

"I have had better," Nazim answered honestly watching the man who now sat across from him.

"I found little rest myself," Avi continued. "Perhaps after a full day of work, we will both rest better this night. What are your plans for the day?" he asked as Eliana returned placing food in front of both of them.

Nazim waited until she had finished before speaking again, and his first comment was directed toward her.

"Thank you," he stated kindly. "It looks delicious."

"You are most welcome," she smiled at him. "Do not forget to pray over it," she leaned toward him and whispered with a smile as she left. She heard him chuckle as she entered the cooking area.

Avi prayed for the both of them, asking for blessings on the food and safety for their day. Nazim noticed that Avi's prayer was as respectful and as fervent as Eli's.

"May I ask you a question before we form our plan?" Nazim asked openly.

"Of course," Avi stated as he broke the loaf of bread before them in two offering one half to his companion.

"Your younger brother, as well as your grandfather, are very adamant about praying. Are mealtimes the only times you speak to your God?" he asked sincerely.

"Not at all," Avi answered honestly. "We pray to Him when we rise up, when we lie down, and before every meal, yes, but we also take any cares and concerns to Him as the need arises."

"And He always responds?" Nazim asked.

"Not audibly. But He accepts our prayers of gratitude and thankfulness if we have been forgiven of the sins in our heart, and He answers our petitions according to His will and in His time."

"Do you think He always hears? What if He is away, or is sleeping when you talk to Him?" Nazim asked curiously.

Avi chuckled, not in mockery, but in admiration of the God of Whom he spoke. "He never sleeps, Nazim. He never tires; He never wanders away. He is always here, always present, and always aware of His children and their needs. He longs to hear from us."

"So as long as you are in His favor, He grants your desires?" Avi knew that Nazim was not being callous but could tell that he was curious.

"No. He does not always give us what we want. But He does give us what is best for us, whether we can understand it or agree with it or not. Jehovah's will is perfect. Our will is flawed," Avi answered as he took a bite.

Nazim followed suit and processed the information he had received as the two ate in silence. Finally, now that his questions had ceased, Avi continued their earlier conversation.

"So, plans for today?" he asked again.

Nazim nodded, as he swallowed, remembering the earlier question.

The men talked over the remainder of their meal and made their plan as to how they would proceed. They had just finished when Reuben shot through the door and pulled up a chair between them. Elaina heard her younger brother arrive and met him with juice, a piece of bread, and a plate of figs.

"Eat quickly, Reuben," she instructed him. "You cannot be late again for your studies." More guests were arriving, and Eliana moved quickly to accommodate them.

Reuben quickly bowed his head to pray and then began speaking as quickly as he could around large bites of food. Once his plate was empty and his mug was dry, he said his goodbyes as he ran out the door. Avi watched him go and then turned to Nazim.

"Did you understand a word of what he said?" he asked.

Nazim smirked. "About as much as any other morning," he grinned. The men rose then to go about their day, Avi telling Eliana she could find him outside if she needed him. She acknowledged him with a wave, the room now crowded with guests. The men moved to exit the front door as Uma was arriving.

She barely spoke as she brushed by them but then paused and turned to look in the direction they had gone as they departed. Moving on to the cooking area, Eliana could tell her friend was mulling something around in her mind.

"Finally, Uma! You are here! The people are hungry this morning," she laughed, deciding her patrons needed to be tended to before she questioned Uma's mood.

"Who was that man?" Uma asked, looking again toward the door the men had just exited. "The one with our soldier?" she continued when Eliana looked puzzled over the question.

"Nazim is not *our* soldier," Eliana corrected her.

"Should I have said *your* soldier, then?" Uma asked with a smirk.

Eliana did not appreciate her friend's attitude this morning but decided that now was not the time to press the issue.

"Avi?" Eliana asked. "Is he who you are speaking of?"

"That was Avi!" Uma stated in shock. "Your brother! I have not seen him in ages!" Uma took the wooden slab Eliana held loaded with plates of fruit and bowls of porridge.

"He arrived just last night," she answered as she added bread to more baskets. "He will be with us for yet a little while, and he will be hungry after the work he is about to put in today. Help me serve this morning meal so we can prepare another for tonight," she smiled over her shoulder as she moved back into the main area.

The ladies worked quickly together, and soon the morning rush was over, the cleaning was done, and they sat together in the cooking area catching their breath before beginning preparations for the evening. Patrons who came for the midday meal today would be served a simple fare of nuts and fruit, left over from the morning rush. Eliana was thankful she had purchased so much at the market just yesterday.

"So, Avi has returned," Uma spoke in interest, regarding their earlier conversation.

"Yes, he brought news from Joshua and has agreed to stay and help Nazim with the majority of the repairs to the inn," she answered. "It will be good to have him here," she continued. "With Kylus breathing down our neck about righteous tributes and timely completion, I do not know how Nazim would accomplish the task without him."

"I wonder if they are thirsty?" Uma asked craning her neck toward the door to see if she could catch sight of them.

Eliana laughed out loud at the not-so-subtle remark from her friend, then moved to fill a flask with water. She handed the flask and two mugs to Uma, then filled a sack with apples and a handful of nuts.

"By all means," she laughed again, "let us go find out," she remarked exiting the back door. Eliana was surprised at the progress the two men had made. The remainder of the stoop had been removed back to the original roof of the inn, and the debris that had remained was completely cleared. Nazim and Avi stood together, covered in dust, discussing the eroding earth that had been beneath the structure.

"I believe Ares would be capable of pulling the stones you spoke of if we are able to acquire them. We could smooth the earth here," he pointed as he spoke, "lay the stones flat and then build the pillars up to meet the floor."

"That sounds like a good plan," Avi agreed as he studied the area.

"Anyone interested in some nourishment?" Eliana commented as they approached the men from behind.

"You read my mind, Sister," Avi exclaimed, turning to face them and then reaching for the sack she extended.

"Avi, you remember Uma," she stated directing his attention to her friend.

"Uma?" he asked, amazement marking his tone. "I would not have recognized you!" he answered honestly. "You look well."

"Hello, Avi!" she smiled sweetly. "It has been a long time."

"Save at least one of those apples for Nazim," Eliana instructed her brother as he began digging through the bag.

Eliana moved to look around at the work they had already completed. Nazim moved to accompany Eliana.

"I cannot believe how much you have accomplished in such a short span of time," she remarked as he approached her. "At this rate, you will be finished in no time."

"There is still much to be done," he responded honestly. "You will not be rid of me that quickly," he smiled. Eliana looked up at him, a small smile playing about her lips.

"HELP ME! SOMEONE, PLEASE! HELP ME!"

Eliana turned quickly to see Sarah racing toward them. Uma met the older woman before she did, who collapsed into her arms.

"Sarah, whatever is the matter?" Uma asked frantically, trying to brace the older woman before she finally sank to the ground along with her. Uma remained in her position, cradling the

135

elderly lady as best she could. Eliana, Nazim and Avi were at her side in only a second.

"It is Jasaphar," she cried. She paused and tried to catch her breath and calm herself so she could be understood. "He is trapped under a beam on our farm! He cannot free himself! I fear…" She could say no more.

"How far?" Nazim asked, lurching into motion and racing toward the stables, Avi close behind him.

"Not very," he responded as Nazim worked to free Ares from where he was tied. "Follow me," he instructed, mounting his own horse. In less than a minute, the two men shot past the women, where they remained seated on the ground, continuing to comfort the elderly woman so overtaken with grief.

Finally, Uma and Eliana had Sarah on her feet and moved her inside the inn where Eliana quickly offered her water. The distance from Sarah and Jasaphar's home was not great, but Sarah had run the entire way, and now that she had secured help for her husband, exhaustion was overtaking her. Once Sarah had caught her breath, and calmed her nerves, she explained to the two women how Jasaphar had been adding hay to the loft in their barn when the loft had given way. The fall he experienced was not terribly far, but the beams that collapsed on top of him were too heavy for either of them to remove, and he was trapped beneath them.

"He was responsive when I left him promising I would find help," Sarah continued, "but he was weak and in agony from the beams that had fallen on top of him." Her voice broke and Eliana moved to hold the woman as she cried. The sound of a wagon arriving outside interrupted them. Eliana left Sarah in Uma's care to find Abner waiting outside.

"I saw the commotion in the street and have come to offer my assistance if needed," Abner called to her from the wagon seat. "When she is ready, Sarah should not return to her homestead alone," he spoke frankly. Eliana agreed and quickly moved to her grandfather's room to explain to him what was happening.

"I will remain here to care for any guests who arrive for the mid-day meal," Uma offered. Eliana agreed expecting their noon crowd to be sparse. Uma could easily handle them on her own. After finding Reuben and instructing him to find Asa, the closest thing their town had to a doctor, Sarah, Eliana, and Eli were all seated in Abner's wagon heading back toward Sarah's. home.

Sarah was most appreciative of all the help and attention she had received, but the ride was quiet as the party moved toward the farm, each of them uncertain of what they would find once they got there.

Nazim and Avi had not ridden far when Avi veered off the main road and headed toward a small house with a barn beyond. The men approached, dismounted, and ran quickly into the barn, Avi calling for Jasaphar as the entered. They immediately saw the problem, noticing the fallen loft and seeing the man lying still underneath it.

Nazim reached him first, leaning down and reaching to feel for a pulse.

"His heart beats," Nazim spoke quickly to Avi who now approached them. Jasaphar was lying on his back, completely still, with not one, but two large beams pinning him to the ground beneath, one beam over his torso area, the other across his legs. Nazim knew with little observation that at least one of the man's legs was most certainly broken. Avi began to call to Jasaphar who moaned something at the sound of his name.

"Do not move," Avi instructed him. "We are here to help you." He spoke calmly, but Nazim knew that Avi also observed the severity of the situation. The men quickly came up with a plan to free Jasaphar from his trap. It would not be ideal, but they had to get the beams off of Jasaphar, and sooner rather than later. The beams were pressing hard on his body, but the remainder of the loft overhead continued to creak under the weight it now held with little support. They had to get Jasaphar, and themselves, out of harm's way before what remained of the loft fell on them all.

Together, the men worked to move the first beam from off Jasaphar's legs. As they expected, his left leg was twisted underneath in an unnatural way. Other than some cuts and bruises, his right leg looked to be intact. The larger beam was next, and the only option they had was for Nazim to lift the beam and for Avi to pull Jasaphar free. The massive beam was heavy, and Nazim summoned all of his energy to be able to lift the beam high enough on his own for Avi to be able to pull Jasaphar from beneath it.

Jasaphar was not a small man, and Avi had his work cut out for him as well, to pull Jasaphar's weight by himself. As soon as he had pulled him clear of the beam, Nazim released his load, then moved to help Avi quickly pull Jasaphar outside of the barn. The move was not an easy one on the injured man, and Jasaphar cried out in pain as the men pulled him, as gently as possible, to safety. They had just exited through the back door when the remainder of the loft gave way and crashed to the earth beneath.

They heard Sarah's scream as the wagon approached. The team arriving was coming from the front and had no indication that the men were safely behind the barn before the collapse. Avi ran around the collapsed structure to meet them, while Nazim stayed behind with Jasaphar. He lay on the ground, but Nazim had lifted his head and was attempting to get some water in him that he had retrieved from the nearby well when Sarah approached. Collapsing on the ground beside him she quickly began examining her husband from top to bottom.

Reuben had been successful in his quest to find Asa, and they arrived quickly behind the wagon driven by Abner. Nazim moved, giving the doctor room to work, moving now to help Eliana and Eli from the wagon.

Carefully he assisted Eli as he climbed down from the seat of the wagon before moving to help Eliana.

"How is he?" Eliana asked as Nazim gently assisted her from the back of the wagon.

"He is alive, but I am no doctor. I cannot be sure of the seriousness of his injuries, other than a broken leg at least," Nazim answered honestly. The pair walked slowly toward the barn. "We were just able to pull him to safety before the remaining structure collapsed," he finished.

"Thank God that the three of you were not under that structure when it collapsed," Eliana spoke genuinely. Nazim stopped looking down at her.

"Do you really believe He had something to do with that?" Nazim asked sincerely.

"Absolutely," she answered without hesitation.

"But your friend was hurt. Do you feel Your God has had a hand in that as well?" he asked staring down at her, his face a mask of confusion.

"Nazim, bad things happen to good people. Wars are fought, people perish, sickness comes, accidents occur. I am not implying that our God causes those things, but I am saying that He is in control even when those incidents occur. And do I believe that He protected you from harm once again? Yes, I do," she spoke sincerely. "Jehovah allowed you and Avi to get to Jasaphar just in time to pull him from that barn before the final collapse. I do not know if Jasaphar will live, but there is a reason that all of this happened. And there is a reason that you were a part of that rescue."

Nazim continued to look at her for a moment before turning to continue their short walk to the others. Eliana surprised him when she reached out to place her hand on his arm. He stopped in his tracks, looking down at her.

"And the reason I believe he has spared your life once again, Nazim is for a higher purpose. He has a plan for you." He watched her for a moment and looked to where her hand still lingered on his arm. Not a word was spoken as he placed his hand on top of hers for only a moment before she pulled it away and the two continued to join the others.

Chapter Fourteen

It took both Nazim and Avi to lift Jasaphar and carry him into the house close to an hour later. Asa had assessed the situation before they moved him further and had determined that other than a badly broken leg and some serious bruising to his abdomen, Jasaphar's injuries seemed to be minor. The men helped Sarah get him as comfortable as possible and made sure the couple had any provisions they needed for the next few days. Asa had agreed to stay on the property through the night in case anything unforeseen occurred, with Avi, Eliana, and Reuben all promising to keep a close check on their neighbors in the coming days.

Tears of gratitude and thankfulness were shared by Sarah and Eliana. Eli led them in a prayer of gratitude and request for healing over Jasaphar. What Nazim did not expect was Sarah's attention turning to him before they departed.

"I cannot thank you enough for your assistance today," she cried as she spoke directly to him. "Without you, my Jasaphar would be beneath the rubble out there," her voice broke as she tried to continue.

"It was not all me," Nazim spoke. "Avi..." he began but stopped as she held up her hand.

"I was wrong about you," she continued. "I judged you from gossip I had heard and from my own prejudices. I have asked for Jehovah's forgiveness, and now I ask for yours."

Nazim stared at the elderly woman in front of him now, unsure of what to say or how to react. He simply shook his head and leaned into the hug she offered him.

Avi had moved to assist his grandfather back into Abner's wagon, Eliana waiting behind to give Sarah one more hug before she took her leave as well. As soon as Sarah released Nazim, she turned to Eliana, thanking her once more for her comfort, assistance, and prayers.

Before she climbed onto the back of Abner's wagon, Eliana stopped, another thought crossing her mind.

"Grandfather, I think I should like to walk back to the inn," she began. "It is such a fine day, and we are not in quite the hurry we were to arrive here."

"I will make sure she arrives safely back to town," Nazim interrupted coming along beside her. Before anyone could object, Nazim continued. "Reuben," he called. "Feel like riding Ares?"

"Do I!" the lad called excitedly, running toward the horse. Nazim lifted him into place, keeping the lead in his own hand. "Remember to keep your balance," he reminded him as he began to lead Ares behind himself and Eliana. Grandfather nodded his approval, and Abner lurched his team into motion, followed by Avi on his own horse, Eliana, Nazim, and Reuben coming along slowly behind them.

It was a beautiful day, and Eliana's heart felt light now that it appeared Jasaphar would make a complete recovery.

"I hope I am not imposing on your solitude," Nazim stated as they walked slowly.

"Not at all," Eliana responded honestly. "I am not certain Grandfather would have appreciated me walking alone, though I believe he would have allowed it. I know that his heart is lighter due to your kind offer to accompany me."

The wind stirred softly as the pair quietly made their way down the dusty street. Eliana looked at the sky as they walked in comfortable silence, nothing but the sound of Ares' hoofs behind them. Nazim had given one set of the reins to Reuben, to allow him to learn the feel of guiding the animal, though he held tightly to the other set, still in control of each move Ares made. Reuben was using full concentration, which assured his solitude as well.

It was Eliana who first spoke. "I did not realize how beautiful the view is from this path. I suppose I have not taken the time to look around me lately," she admitted.

"The view is quite lovely," Nazim agreed looking down at her with a smile. Eliana glanced in his direction and realized the view he was speaking of was his view of herself. She rolled her eyes playfully, causing him to chuckle.

"You will not accept a compliment?" he asked honestly. Eliana took a deep breath and shook her head.

"Thank you," she managed. They were approaching another home now, and movement on Nazim's right caught Eliana's eye. Seeing her crane her neck to look around him, Nazim instructed Reuben to pull on the reigns in his hands indicating he desired Ares to stop. The boy did as he was told, and the horse came to a halt. Eliana moved past Nazim and into the yard of the home they approached. Nazim followed suit, leading Reuben and Ares along with him. He watched as Eliana knelt down in front of a small girl as he tied Ares to a nearby post, instructing Reuben to wait for them there.

"It is my doll," the little girl cried to Eliana. "She fell into the cavern, and I cannot go in after her. She was a gift from father, and I love her so much." At her confession, the little girl burst into tears and fell into Eliana's arms. Eliana allowed her to cry for a moment and then pushed the little girl away from her neck, though not releasing her from her grip.

"Can you show me where your doll is now, Ada?" she asked calmly. The little girl nodded her head and moved toward the back of their house. They had not walked far into the shallow woods behind the structure before the earth seemed to stop, opening up right in front of them. Though no water stood in the hole now, it was evident that the natural washing of the earth had caused a deep cavern to form. At the bottom of the deep hole lay a small handmade doll. The sight of her doll caused Ada to burst into tears once again.

The hole was deep, too deep for them to attempt to climb into, or so Eliana thought. Nazim knelt down in front of the child now.

"Wait right here," he instructed her. "And I will retrieve your doll for you," he promised.

"Nazim, you cannot! Do not make promises to her that you are not able to keep," Eliana quietly scolded him.

"You do not know me well, Eliana," he returned. "I will be right back."

Eliana stood with Ada until Nazim returned with both Ares and Reuben behind him. He pulled a long rope from the bag he carried on Ares' side, securing the rope to the horse.

"When I instruct you to," he explained to Reuben, "pull back on the reins as hard as you can, but not before."

"You mean as if I am wishing for him to stop?" Reuben questioned.

"Precisely," Nazim agreed securing the opposite end of the rope to his own waist.

"Nazim! What are you doing?" Eliana asked as he began leading Ares to the edge of the cavern, Reuben high atop his back.

"My second rescue of the day," he smiled at her as he carefully sat himself down and began to climb over the edge.

"You are going to get yourself killed!" she accused.

Nazim stopped and looked up at her briefly before he continued to climb deep into the pit.

"Is that worry I detect in your voice, Eliana?" he chided. She stepped back from the cavern, but only for a moment before allowing herself to look over the edge once again. She watched as he continued to carefully lower himself deeper and deeper into the gully. Once or twice, Ares would begin to inch forward, and Nazim would call up for him to be still and instruct Reuben to tighten the reigns. At his commands, the horse would plant his hooves firmly on the ground beneath him.

Eliana breathed a sigh of relief as Nazim finally made it safely to the bottom of the cavern and retrieved the doll. He placed her safely in the inside pocket of his vest, then moved to begin his ascent back to the top of the gulley. Twice his footing gave way on the loose earth beneath him, and twice, the rope connecting him to Ares would tense. Eliana felt her own breath catch in her throat each time, and her heart pounded as if she were being chased.

"Pull back!" Nazim called to Reuben when his footing lost hold once again. Reuben did as he was commanded, and Ares followed suit, beginning to back away from the cavern, pulling on the rope that was attached to Nazim's waist, and pulling him up with it. It seemed as if an eternity passed before Nazim finally made his way back to the top of the cavern, climbing out and onto solid ground once more.

"Praise Jehovah!" Eliana exclaimed as Nazim stood firmly before her once again. He untied himself from the rope and untied the rope from Ares.

"Well done, Reuben," he smiled up to the lad. Reuben beamed in light of the praise he received. Nazim then turned to the little girl staring anxiously up at him. He reached into his vest and removed the small doll she so adored, then knelt down, handing the doll to her owner.

Ada hugged the doll with all her might and then, to his surprise, flung herself into his arms throwing her small arms around his neck. Eliana smiled at the sight, confused at the tears which filled her eyes, threatening to spill over. She blinked them away quickly as the little girl released her grip on Nazim and then came to stand before her. Then, something on the ground where Nazim had knelt claimed Eliana's attention, and she moved to collect it.

"Thank you both, so much," Ada smiled, and Eliana could not stop herself from directing her attention back to the girl and hugging the little one herself. Without thought, Eliana pushed the item she had collected into her own pocket.

"I cannot help but wonder how that beautiful little doll ended up at the bottom of such a deep hole," Nazim began. "Perhaps someone had gotten a bit closer than she should have?" he questioned.

"Perhaps," Ada admitted looking down at the ground in front of her in shame. "But it will never happen again," she promised as she looked up at the giant in front of her.

"See that it does not," he instructed tapping her nose with his finger. "That is definitely not a safe place for you to be."

"I promise!" she called as she happily ran back toward her home. Nazim, Eliana, Reuben, and Ares had just come from the woods when Ada's mother appeared.

"Ada Elizabeth!" she called as she fell to her knees hugging the child. "Where on earth have you been? I have been looking all over for you!"

The little girl told her mother everything that had happened and how Nazim had rescued her dolly from the giant hole. After a brief scolding for being too close to a forbidden area, her mother ordered her inside and turned her attention to her guests.

"I am sorry Ada has troubled you," she began, and Eliana noticed how worn she appeared. "I confess with Heshputh out of town and the talk of the rains that are to come, my mind has been preoccupied. I was attempting to mend the fence and had not noticed that Ada had wandered so far away."

"Is there anything we can help you with?" Eliana asked sincerely.

Elizabeth shook her head. "You have both done quite enough already. Thank you for all you have done for my Ada. Heshputh has been meaning to secure the area around that gulley for some time, but with everything else going on I am afraid it has not been a priority."

"What fence are you mending?" Nazim asked as he walked toward the area from where Elizabeth had come.

"It is nothing really," she confessed. "Our goat continues to butt her way out and until Heshputh returns, patching it is all I can really do. Kylus has already required one penalty because he feels the goat could cause destruction in the community."

"That is preposterous!" Eliana stormed. Nazim continued to investigate the area Elizabeth had mentioned.

"This area?" Nazim asked looking at a particular area of the fence.

Elizabeth nodded, embarrassed at how he was investigating her work. She was a housewife, not a carpenter, and even her best was a feeble attempt.

"You have done a fine job," Nazim smiled, "but if you ladies would enjoy a visit for just a few moments, I can have this repaired for you in no time. Then neither you nor your husband will have to bother with it."

At his offer, Elizabeth let out the sigh she had been holding. It felt as if a weight had been lifted from her shoulders. "That would be wonderful," she admitted, "but I do hate to detain the three of you further."

"It is no trouble," he assured her. "Reuben can help me, and we will make short work of this task." Reuben climbed down from the back of Ares and ran quickly to Nazim's side waiting for any instructions he would be given. Eliana took Sarah's arm and turned her toward the house.

"I am dying to see the new addition to your family," Eliana smiled.

"And I would love some female companionship," Sarah commented as she led the way. "It has been too long," she laughed, and Eliana caught the tear Elizabeth quickly wiped from the corner of her eye.

"Has Heshputh been gone long?" Eliana asked moments later as the ladies were seated at a small table enjoying a cup of milk, Eliana soaking in the newborn cradled in her arms. Elizabeth sat her mug down thoughtfully.

"He has been gone for about a week," she admitted shrugging her shoulders. "I confess we had words before he left. I know that he must travel occasionally, but with Ada so young and the baby so small and the household to maintain, I just do not understand why he had to go away now."

"When do you expect his return?" Eliana asked, taking her eyes off the baby and looking to her friend.

"He had planned to be gone for a week, maybe two," she shrugged. "He had told Kylus that he would be leaving the last time he came through, and Heshputh asked him to keep a check on us. I was hoping he would return, and I could ask for his assistance with the fence, but…" she shook her head.

"Well, who needs Kylus?" Eliana grinned. "Nazim will have your fence repaired in no time."

"Speaking of Nazim," Elizabeth began, cutting her eyes toward her friend. "I had heard of the wandering soldier in town. I must admit he is nothing like I expected. He is quite handsome…" she teased.

"I have far too much to do at the inn to have even noticed," Eliana laughed. "But may I ask you a personal favor?" Eliana asked her friend. "Help me pray that Nazim will come to believe in our Jehovah. I see the interest there. I do not know why he came to Heshbon to begin with, but I feel like Jehovah has given him a second chance at life in order to learn of Him and to serve Him." They were interrupted by a knock on the door. Eliana was somewhat thankful for the interruption. Elizabeth rose to answer, and Reuben stepped inside, announcing that the repairs had been completed.

"I cannot thank you enough," Elizabeth continued after seeing the fine work the men had done. "Are you sure there is nothing I can offer for your trouble?"

"It was no trouble," Nazim argued. "But we must be on our way before Eli and Avi fear I have run off with Eliana and Reuben," he joked.

"Elizabeth, if you need anything at all, please feel free to come into town and ask," Eliana insisted, handing the baby in her arms to his mother. "Better yet, I will send Reuben to check on you periodically until Heshputh returns," she offered.

"That would be wonderful," Elizabeth conceded. "Kylus never seems to come around unless a tribute is to be paid," she admitted quietly. She hugged Eliana once more and whispered into her ear. "Jehovah will hear our prayers," she whispered. "Thank you again, all of you," she waved as the trio departed.

Their banter was light as they returned to the inn. Once there, they discovered that the materials Nazim had ordered from town to repair the stoop had arrived and had been left by the side of the inn. Reuben led Ares to the stables as Eliana and Nazim went in around the back to let the others know they had returned. Avi and Uma were seated at the table in the cooking area when they arrived.

"Grandfather has gone to his room for a rest," Avi informed them. "That was quite a bit of excitement for him this afternoon," he added thoughtfully.

"And the materials arrived to repair the stoop while you were away," Uma continued. "I hope the location where they left them is suitable?" she asked, directing her question to Nazim.

"I believe it will be sufficient," he answered honestly. "Feel like getting to it?" he asked, looking to Avi.

"Nazim, are you sure?" Eliana interrupted. "You have had quite an eventful day yourself." Eliana sat a bowl of apples, nuts, and a pitcher of juice in the center of the table, telling the others of the additional rescues Nazim had made on their way back from the farm of Jasaphar and Sarah.

"I do not understand," Avi began after her story. "Where is Kylus during all of this? Joshua left him here not only to guide our people but to be a help to you all as well."

"I told you, Avi, Kylus always shows up as soon as something goes wrong, but instead of aiding our people, he only comes to penalize us for not acting quickly enough to remedy the situation. He penalized Elizabeth just because their goat butted through their fence, and he threatened a penalty on us if we do not have the stoop repaired when he returns."

"It appears Kylus has a spy," Nazim spoke around a bite of an apple.

"A spy? What does Kylus need spies for?" Avi asked, frustrated. For the next half hour, Eliana told him everything, adding more specific details to the information Eli had shared with him earlier.

Finally, the men moved outside to their work and left the women to meal preparations for the evening. They worked the remainder of the afternoon with Reuben's assistance organizing the materials Nazim had purchased for the repairs. Once things were situated and a plan had formed, they ceased their outdoor activity as patrons began to arrive for the evening meal.

The area was already bustling with more activity than usual, most folks coming to hear news of the incident with Jasaphar earlier in the day. Nazim did not feel like sitting in his normal spot, instead moving back to the cooking area. Eliana and Uma worked feverishly, cooking additional food due to the crowd continuing to arrive, dishing up meals, moving to serve their customers, then returning to prepare more plates. Nazim watched for only a moment before he stepped in front of Eliana just as she was turning to hoist a wooden tray heavily laden with food up on her shoulder.

She stopped in her tracks at his sudden appearance.

"Show me where this goes," he instructed, taking the load from her.

"Nazim, I cannot allow..."

"There was no question as to if you would allow anything," he interrupted her with a small smirk. "You have worked as hard as I have today. You have assisted people both inside and outside of this inn, and there are more people here tonight than I have seen since I arrived. You take that pitcher of juice," he instructed, pointing to a pitcher behind her, "and I will follow you," he finished, adding a small smile to soften his words. Eliana knew the matter was closed.

Slowly, she turned, looking to her friend, only to see that Avi had followed Nazim's cue and had taken the wooden tray Uma had been filling as well. Her friend watched to see what she would do as Eliana moved to fill the pitchers with juice before turning to go back into the main dining area, Nazim close behind her.

He worked alongside her all evening, serving the food as she filled the cups with juice. Avi and Uma worked together as well, and time and again as a table would empty of its occupants, more people would come to fill the spot. Nazim endured a few stares and whispers at first, but soon the patrons appeared comfortable in his presence. Finally, Nazim and Avi continued serving as Eliana and Uma worked to prepare more food inside the cooking area and to keep the serving pitchers filled.

At last, the patrons ceased to come and the last of their guests finished their meal, bidding their hosts goodnight and commenting on the good service and delicious food.

"That was quite an evening," Eliana commented, falling into a chair at their table in the center of the room. Uma set their own meals in front of them as Avi blessed the food they were about to partake of. They enjoyed their meal quickly before moving to clean the dishes and the room from the busy evening. All of them were exhausted by the time the chores were finished.

Uma bid them goodnight and moved to make her way home.

"Do be careful, Uma, it is quite a bit later than normal," Eliana insisted.

"I will be fine, my friend," she promised with a quick hug.

"She certainly will," Avi commented, stepping up beside her. "For I will be her escort home."

"Avi, is that quite proper?" Eliana whispered, taking her brother's sleeve and pulling him to the side.

"It is most certainly the right thing to do this evening," he spoke plainly. "It is far too late for her to be walking across town alone. Plus, Uma is like family."

Eliana cut her eyes at her brother, bringing a chuckle from him.

"Fine, I will insist Reuben accompany us," he conceded. A few moments later the three of them left the inn. Nazim and Eliana walked them outside, and Eliana did not miss the giddy attitude that had overtaken her dearest friend. Rolling her eyes, she turned to go back inside, Nazim close behind her.

"Do I detect apprehension?" Nazim smiled as he held the door for her to enter.

"Uma is innocent, do not misunderstand my concern, but as I have said, she can be careless when it comes to her affections. I do not wish for either of them to hurt the other."

Nazim nodded his head in understanding.

"You never know," he teased, "perhaps theirs could be a lasting union."

"Miracles do happen," she laughed. "It is growing late, and tomorrow will be a full day I am sure," she smiled up at him.

"Goodnight, Eliana," he grinned down at her as she turned to retire to her room. Suddenly she stopped remembering the trinket in her pocket. "Nazim, with everything that happened I almost forgot," she began, turning back to him and pulling what she now realized was a beautiful pendant from her pocket. She held it up in front of them both and watched the small ruby and diamonds glisten in the light.

"Where did you get that?" he asked moving quickly.

"It was on the ground after you helped Ada rescue her doll. I retrieved it and meant to return it to you earlier, but I honestly forgot."

Nazim took the pendant she offered him without a word.

"Thank you," he said after a moment of just staring at the pendant he now held in his hands. "It must have fallen from my vest when I returned the doll to Ada."

"It is quite exquisite," she commented looking at the pendant as he turned it over and over in his massive hands.

"It belonged to someone very special to me," he finally stated. "I cannot believe how careless I was to lose it."

"Well then, I am glad that I found it and returned it to you. Sleep well tonight," she smiled again as she turned to go.

"Eliana," he said quietly as she approached her door. She stopped and looked back at him before pushing her door open. "Thank you," he finished.

With a smile and a nod, she entered her room and closed the door softly behind herself. Nazim stared at the closed portal for a moment before looking again at the pendant in his hands, then slowly made his way to his own room.

Stretching out on the cot he now considered his own, he held the pendant up and watched as the ruby swayed slowly back and forth. He thought back to when he had first given the pendant to Rahab. He remembered the argument they had engaged in leading up to his reason for purchasing such an exquisite gift. He had told her that if circumstances were different, he would declare his love for her from the rooftops, and she had countered that love was too strong of a word.

"Was love too strong of a word?" he thought now to himself, the pendant still swinging in front of him, catching the light from a single lamp still burning by his cot. *"And what are these feelings I am experiencing now? Toward this family, toward their God?"* Nazim continued to ponder on the thought until sleep finally overcame him. He woke later, long enough to lay the pendant on the table by his cot and to blow out the lantern before turning to his side and falling into a deep, yet troubled sleep.

Chapter Fifteen

Nazim and Avi worked tirelessly the next few days, moving rocks and large stones into place to create a firm foundation for the new stoop to rest on. On one occasion, they used their horses to pull an exceptionally large stone from the branch behind the inn into place. Reuben was a great help in the afternoons once he had finished his schooling for the day, and he enjoyed the time he worked alongside his older brother and Nazim. Even more, he enjoyed his time with Nazim and Ares once their work for the day was done. Reuben was becoming very comfortable atop Ares.

Avi also worried they were fighting to beat the oncoming weather. Several of the elders continued to claim their achy joints and pains indicated a significant rain was coming, and as the rainy season was quickly approaching, it was only to be expected. The men worked hard to get the stones into place to prohibit more of the ground from washing away when the rains did fall. Smooth stones would be placed on top of the uneven ones, creating the foundation they required. Finally, the stones were in place, and they were ready to begin rebuilding the stoop.

The men decided that in order to continue the restoration process, they would need a few days without patron interruptions. Folks coming and going created a problem. After much debate, they decided they would talk with Eliana and Grandfather once this evening's meal was finished.

As had become habitual, Nazim and Avi assisted the ladies in serving. Nazim had become such a novelty in the inn that many of the regular patrons now laughed and joked with him as he worked alongside Eliana. Abner had asked for his assistance in rebuilding a small barn on his property once he was finished here, and more than once, he had left quickly to aid a widow or elderly patron with a small repair or emergency project.

Oftentimes, after the rush, Nazim, Eliana, Uma, and Avi would sit and enjoy their own meal with Eliana and Avi recounting stories of their wanderings in the desert or stories of their ancestors that had been told to them by their family. Grandfather had become a regular at their late meals as well. Oftentimes, he had already eaten, but he would join them for a late cup of milk and crust of bread or a piece of fruit before he retired for the evening.

Nazim soaked in every story, but not with the same intentions he had when he had first arrived. He was growing more fond of this family and of these people by the day, and he was becoming more and more interested in the God they served but no longer with an intent to destroy or harm any of them in any way. He experienced a sense of peace when he was with them unlike any he had ever experienced before, even when he had been with Rahab.

As Avi and Nazim discussed, Avi had proposed tonight that they close the inn for a week in order to rebuild the stoop, and though hesitant, Eliana agreed at her grandfather's suggestion that they do so. Finally, she persuaded them to give her the rest of this week to inform her regular guests of their temporary closing before shutting the doors to them.

The decision was made. Grandfather had retired to his room, seeming a bit more tired than usual, and Reuben had accompanied Avi and Uma on her walk home. Eliana and Nazim remained in the cooking area when she decided to bring up something that had been plaguing her thoughts over the past few days.

"Nazim, it has been weeks since your encounter with Kylus at the pools. Do you worry that he will return before the restorations are complete?" she asked, toying with the mug in front of her. "I am slightly surprised he has not shown his face since… well… that he has not already returned."

"I care not when he returns," Nazim answered plainly. "Are you concerned of his return?" he asked, taking a drink from his mug.

"Only that…" she paused and took a deep breath. Nazim recognized that she was about to share something with him that she was quite uncomfortable bringing up.

"What is it?" he asked, leaning on the table.

"I am only concerned that he will cause trouble for you," she continued quickly. "Nazim, you have become so comfortable here, and our patrons have come to adore you. I just do not want Kylus to… upset you and force you to…" she paused looking down at the table in front of her. "I do not know how our people would react to…" she continued to stumble over her words and his heart ached at the turmoil he saw on her face.

Nazim reached across the table and took her hands in his. His hands swallowed hers. "Eliana, I am sorry I scared you that day by the pools," he began. "I have a hard time with my temper, in case you have not noticed," he smiled. She chuckled, but he could tell her concerns ran deep. "I will do my best never to cause you fear again," he promised.

Nazim had no idea how quickly his temper would be put to the test. Eliana began telling patrons the next day that at the end of the week, the inn would close for one week for Avi and Nazim to finish the restoration to the front of the building. The men would work the remaining of this week only between the morning and the evening rush.

This morning, the rush was over, and the men were attempting to set the posts that would hold the cover over the stoop. Suddenly familiar fanfare began to fill the street around them.

"What is going on?" Avi asked as his sister and Uma appeared in the doorway of the inn.

"Not again, already," Eliana said quietly. Nazim saw the concern on her face before turning to see the man who was now in the street across from them. Kylus was still seated on his horse, two other men, each on opposite sides of him atop their own horses.

"Avi!" he stated, his surprise at seeing the man evident on his face. "What brings you to our lowly Heshbon from the battlefields just beyond *Jericho*?" he emphasized, his eyes shooting daggers in Nazim's direction.

"It is good to see you too, Kylus," Avi remarked with a smirk. He had truthfully never cared for the man and was secretly thankful Joshua had chosen to leave him behind when their troops had advanced beyond Heshbon. He was now anxious to return to his leader in order to relay how Kylus had begun to misuse the authority that had been granted him. "Is there something we can do for you?"

Kylus waved the patrons away, who were still gathered around his small entourage. "I was just coming to see if myself or my men could be a help to your family, but it appears that you have already employed a servant for the task," he remarked again. "However, it is my duty to inform you that this man has no place in our fair city, and for the betterment of our people, I must require you to relieve him of his duties and send him immediately about his way."

"Nazim has proven nothing but helpful to us, Kylus. I require his assistance. I will be responsible for his presence here. He will remain in Heshbon under my direction."

Nazim rolled his eyes as both of these men spoke of him as though they controlled him. No one controlled him. One glance at Eliana, however, reminded him of his promise to her, a promise that he was determined to keep. Quickly and silently, he checked his pride and attempted to control the acceleration of his temper. Eliana did not miss the way his jawline clenched beneath the small beard that rested there. She knew his temper was being pushed to the limit.

"Kylus, Nazim has caused no problems here. You must be reasonable…" she began as she stepped forward.

"Silence yourself, woman!" Kylus commanded. Eliana knew her eyebrows met her hairline as she began to move forward. Her brother moved to block her and held his hand out to her ceasing her from going any further. Nazim stepped up beside her now and she could feel the tension radiating from his body.

Kylus chuckled. "So, this is the path *you* have chosen, Eliana," he accused. "How does your grandfather feel about your decision to align yourself with such as this?" he asked motioning with disgust toward Nazim. Though he spoke as if he were fearless, Kylus had yet to dismount his steed.

"My path is the same as it has been, Kylus. To follow the Lord God Jehovah. Your path seems to be the one which has been redirected. What path is it that you now tread?"

Kylus glared at her in pure hatred as he directed his remarks back to Avi.

"As ruler over Heshbon and Bashan, I command you to release this man to me at once," Kylus demanded, drawing his sword and pointing it in the direction of Nazim.

"And as an *active* soldier under the direct command of *your* ruler, Joshua, I do not answer to you, Kylus," Avi retaliated. "You have forgotten your place. I suggest you take your minions and direct yourself back to Bashan. I will care for the people of Heshbon while I am here," he finished.

The color in Kylus's face reminded Eliana of the day Nazim had strangled him by the pools of Heshbon. She quickly glanced up at the wandering soldier close beside her to gauge his reaction. Nazim never took his eyes from Kylus and the men that were with him, and though his facial expression failed to change, she knew from where his hand rested on the dagger in his belt that he longed to launch it directly into the chest of the man before him.

"This is not finished," Kylus spat in their direction as he urged his steed forward. Avi and Nazim watched as the men quickly rode through the street back toward the gates of the city. Once they were out of sight, Avi turned to Nazim.

"I did not intend to speak of you as if you do not control your own actions, Nazim," Avi defended himself, "but Kylus is..."

"I have met the man," Nazim stated, interrupting him. He turned back to his work, signifying the conversation was closed.

Uma and Eliana returned inside, all of them working independently and without the confrontation being brought up amongst them again. Eliana had spent time with her grandfather, checking on his well-being and filling him in on the morning events. He was very tired and had developed a cough, but he refused to allow her to call for Asa.

"I do not wish to rush Avi back to the battlefield, yet I will be glad once Joshua is informed of Kylus' actions," Eli admitted. Eliana informed him of her plans for the remainder of the day then moved to carry them out.

She compiled a list with directions to Uma of the provisions they needed from town. Eliana gathered a few baskets and would collect the berries she wished to have for the evening meal. She was trying to make these last few meals before their temporary closure extra special for their regular patrons.

As they departed the inn, Eliana produced bags of figs and cheese as well as fresh water for Nazim and Avi.

"Wait for us," Avi requested. "Give us a moment to enjoy this nourishment, and one of us shall accompany each of you," he suggested. The men had come to a good stopping point for the day, though there were still several hours before the evening rush would begin. With the events of the morning, Avi admitted that he would feel more comfortable for the ladies to be accompanied on their outings, especially Eliana as she planned to pick wild berries that grew behind the inn. Though she would remain in close proximity to their home, he did not trust Kylus in the least, and though he did not voice his thoughts aloud, he met Nazim's approving glare at his suggestion.

The ladies sat alongside the men in the warm sunshine as they ate. "Notice the clouds building just there," Nazim pointed out. "I have seen that many times in my journeys," he admitted. "I feel the elders are correct in their predictions that the rains will return soon."

Avi looked at the sky above them. "I agree. I feel we may be delayed in our work at some point," he agreed.

"I do hope it does not prolong our closure," Uma spoke up.

"The foundation is secure," Avi remarked. "Maybe Jehovah will rule in our favor. The rains could come the remainder of this week, and good weather could be in our favor during the closing."

"Well, I must get my berries before the rains come," Eliana remarked rising. "And Uma, you must get to town. I need those items!"

"Let us be on our way! Avi, you are with me?" Uma asked hopefully, casting a smile in his direction.

Avi looked to his sister, who smiled and rolled her eyes. He took the mocking gesture as lightly as it was intended.

"My lady," he motioned as Uma moved to begin the walk to town. He quickly moved up beside her as they began the short journey, her laughter trailing behind her at some joke he had already made.

Eliana looked to Nazim who stood smiling at her. She adored the smile on his face though she knew what he was thinking.

"Lead the way," he stated simply, and she turned to move behind the inn.

"I did not notice wild berries growing back here before," he admitted.

"They are off the beaten path," she admitted. "Luckily, no one else knows exactly where these berries grow. Grandfather found them shortly after we arrived in Heshbon, and we vowed to keep it a family secret," she laughed.

"You mean I am going to be let in on a *family* secret?" he joked.

"I suppose you are," she agreed. They moved off the path and just beyond a small grove of trees before a hedge line appeared laden with beautiful berries. Eliana focused on her task, and Nazim followed suit. Quickly her baskets were full. She continued then, with Nazim easily handling the baskets, to pull her apron into a pouch in which she also collected several handfuls of the delicate fruit. She then moved back onto the path, choosing the same tree she had before to nestle herself against. As she sat, she patted the ground beside herself, inviting Nazim to join her. He sat close to her, leaning against the same tree, their shoulders barely touching.

"Thank you for these delicious berries, dear Jehovah. Bless them now as we partake of this delectable treat. And thank you for the new friend you have blessed us with in Nazim," she finished. Nazim looked down at her, smiling slightly as she offered him a handful of the berries she had nestled in her apron.

"I know what you are thinking," she scoffed.

"Do tell," he encouraged, knowing she had no clue as to what was on his mind.

"You are thinking," she continued in a deep voice to mock his, "that these people really do pray over everything."

Her imitation of himself caused him to laugh out loud, which brought her own laughter.

"That was a pitiful imitation of me," he chuckled. "And you are not correct in your attempt to read my mind," he accused once his laughter had subsided.

"Then do tell, wandering soldier," she demanded, popping a berry in her mouth. "What was that quizzical look for?"

Nazim looked at the stream in front of them before he admitted his thoughts. "I am amazed at your kindness, and the kindness of most of your people," he began. "And I am amazed you pray for me, knowing so little about me, other than how utterly imperfect I am."

"Jehovah does not search for perfection," she stated simply, as she watched Nazim as he watched the stream. "He does not call people who are qualified to do His will. He qualifies those whom He calls. And you, Nazim, have a purpose, which He is preparing you for, and He has been, I feel, for longer than I have known you," she admitted softly.

"Rahab tried to tell me of this God you all serve," he confessed, looking toward her and then toying with the berries she had handed him. "I would hear none of it. I was cruel in my last words to her. Much more so than I care to remember. The things I said to her, and the way I reacted, it is an action that haunts me to this day. Your God would never forgive me for the things I said to her the last time I saw her, and neither, I regret, would she." Nazim looked at the flowing stream before them as he popped a berry into his mouth. Eliana watched him in silence. He had been wandering, because he was broken. He had so many regrets in his past. What could she ever say to help him as she so desperately wanted to?

She thought carefully over her next words, and as she was accustomed to, she said a quick and silent prayer for God to give her wisdom. Finally, she turned her head to face him, looking up into his face.

"Nazim, I have not been told of all the sins of Rahab, nor do I care to, but I have been told of the change in her since she accepted Jehovah. I was not raised as you were so I cannot pretend that I can understand all you speak of. But you have no idea what my God is capable of. He takes our sins that are as deep as the color of scarlet and washes us white as snow."

Nazim closed his eyes, the scarlet cord that hung from Rahab's window now in full view of his mind's eye. His past was so painful for him. He pinched the corner of his eyes.

"What makes you think that a God such as that cannot forgive you for whatever wrongs you have done?" she continued. "And for whatever it is worth, from the change I have heard that was made in Rahab, she would have no problem in forgiving you for your trespasses against her. After all, her own trespasses have been forgiven."

Nazim could not stop himself as he turned to look at her. He was ready to relieve the burdens from his chest, no matter the consequences.

"Eliana, I came to Heshbon with my mind set on destroying this God you speak of and all that He holds dear, even if it meant destroying His people." He could not stop the honesty that suddenly spewed from his mouth. "I intended to hurt you, Eliana, to hurt all of you. If I could not get to Him, to this Jehovah that you people worship and so admire, then my intention was to take everything from Him that He had stripped from me. My home, the woman I loved, my career, everyone and anyone that I had considered my family. I wanted to leave Him in exactly the same place He had left me. With nothing." He expected Eliana to bolt then at his open confession. He could almost see her fleeing, leaving her baskets of berries and running as hard as she could without looking back, but when she did not move, he continued.

"And then I met you and your brothers and your grandfather. And you all opened your home to me, knowing what I had been. You told me stories of your ancestors and of the path that had led you to Heshbon, and I realized," he paused, "I realized then that all Rahab had been trying to tell me, could possibly be real. Maybe it was not just a story, and all we had heard was true. Now, I could not hurt you or your family if my life depended on it." He stopped and took a deep breath. "That was a heavy confession," he said calmly, turning again at the water before them.

Surprising them both, Eliana reached for his hand. Nazim cradled her small hand in his own. "You are not the man you were when you first arrived here, Nazim," she began.

"But I am, Eliana. I still have this anger raging inside of me. Anger that Rahab chose Salmon over me after all we had been through. Anger that it was my own fault for not loving her as she desired and deserved to be loved. Anger that I was not present in Jericho to protect my city and my king when my city fell, and anger that your God took everything and everyone I had ever known, for His own purposes," he admitted. "A purpose I cannot even understand." His touch remained gentle, but the passion in his confession was real. "How can I ever surrender to a God like that as long as this anger boils inside of me?"

"Believing in Jehovah does not make you perfect, Nazim. Nor will it correct all the wrongs you have done or will ever do," she replied. "We struggle with our flesh, our emotions, our frustrations, every single day. We can never uphold the law fully.

That is why we must daily repent and offer sacrifices for our transgressions. We are all broken vessels, repaired and restored by our God alone. But, Nazim, you must not allow your anger to stand in the way of becoming what Jehovah desires you to become. Turn to Him, and let the anger go," she advised.

"I wish it were that simple," he said, clearing his throat.

"You are making great headway," she encouraged. He turned his face toward hers once again, confusion on his face.

"The incident with Kylus this morning," she reminded him, "were that to have happened a few weeks ago, neither he nor my brother would have been standing now, much less have been able to walk away on their own accord," she admitted freely, bringing a smile from Nazim.

"You are correct about that," he smirked. She smiled, facing him once again.

"And a few weeks ago, you and I could never have had the conversation we just had without you frightening me and me fleeing, not even giving a thought to all of these delicious berries," she continued to jest.

"Eliana, I apologized!" he argued with a laugh. Finally, they turned and sat, just gazing at one another. Nazim realized how close their faces were and fought every urge inside his body to keep from kissing the beautiful woman in front of him now. *"Another sure sign that something has changed inside of me,"* he thought silently as he continued to hold her hand. *"If this scene would have played out a few weeks ago, I would have resisted nothing I desired from her, but Eliana is different,"* he continued to ponder as he sat staring at her, *"everything about her feels different,"* he thought.

"Since I am making confessions," he began softly, finally giving a voice to his thoughts, "I must confess that I am growing very fond of you, Eliana."

Her heart thundered inside her chest. "I am fond of you as well, Nazim," she smiled to him. She turned her face from his and withdrew her hand to pop a berry in her mouth. She knew that she was allowing herself to get too close to this wandering soldier who had wandered into her life. "In fact, I am almost as fond of you as Reuben is," she scoffed, attempting to lighten the moment. Nazim laughed out loud at her jest. She did love to hear him laugh, and she, truthfully, loved his company.

"And he has loved the company of many others before you," flitted through her mind. The thought brought her back to reality. How could she allow herself to become so comfortable with him? *"Stop it, Eliana,"* she silently reminded herself. *"He is a wanderer, he will not stay in Heshbon, and he has yet to confess that Jehovah is God."* Eliana continued to list all of the things that were wrong with him in her mind. She stirred but remained seated.

"What are your plans, once the restorations are finished?" she asked, watching the water and changing the subject. "Will you move on to Bashan or choose another course?" she asked. Eliana dared look at him again, but he did not utter a sound. He just sat, watching her face.

"I suppose that depends..." he began and then stopped as their gazes met. Their eyes locked, and Eliana could not look away from him this time, no matter how hard she tried. Suddenly, a noise behind them broke their trance, both of them jumping at the sound.

"There you are!" Avi exclaimed. "I thought you were picking berries," he accused.

"We picked them!" Eliana stated, jumping to her feet a little too forcefully, embarrassed at being caught gazing at Nazim by her brother. She stumbled, the berries in her apron scattering across the ground. Nazim caught her quickly to keep her from hitting the ground as forcefully as the berries.

"We were just enjoying some of our findings," Nazim stated, popping another berry in his mouth once Eliana was steady again on her feet.

"Make sure that is all you were enjoying," he scoffed, as he bent to pick a wayward berry from off the ground. He popped it into his mouth, noticing how red his sister's face had become. "These are good," Avi grinned.

"Delicious," Nazim agreed.

The three stood awkwardly, looking from one to the other until Eliana moved to go inside and help Uma put away the goods from the market. Nazim followed close but paused as Avi clasped him on the shoulder as he passed. His grip was firm as he began to speak.

"That," he spoke slowly, "is my sister," he reminded Nazim quietly, "and, she is very special."

"That she is," Nazim agreed.

"And, though I now consider you an ally more than an enemy do not forget that," Avi warned, releasing his grip and patting Nazim's face.

Nazim recognized the gesture as the "gentle" warning it was implied to be. He held up his hands in surrender.

"You have my word," he promised.

With another clap to Nazim's back, the men moved inside.

Chapter Sixteen

Grandfather did not join them after the rush that evening, preferring to remain in his quarters. Eliana visited with him there for a short while before moving into the cooking area with the others, relaying the conversation she and Nazim had shared on the bank of the stream that afternoon.

"I feel he is coming around, Grandfather, and the truths he shared with me today were so open and so honest. I never felt threatened, his whole demeanor has changed, but I admit I cannot comprehend an anger such as he harbors."

"You have never experienced such loss all at once, Ellie," he answered once she had finished. "The truths he shared with you are commendable. His honesty with you is a big step in the right direction, but remember that our actions, or confessions to one another, do not win Jehovah's favors. It is our belief and acceptance of Him that is required for salvation."

"Will he ever reach that point, Grandfather?" she asked sincerely. Tears threatened to spill from her eyes, and Eli realized that her affection of Nazim was growing into something more than wishing only for his salvation. On one hand he had feared as much, on the other he had hoped for as much.

"With fervent prayer, I believe he will, but only Jehovah knows the outcome, my dear child," he said honestly reaching up to brush a tear from her face. He loved this child as much as if she had been born directly from his Anna. Eli recognized the tug playing on his heart. "Ellie, send Nazim in. I wish to speak to him myself," Eli instructed finally.

"Right away, Grandfather," Eliana rose, bending to kiss his forehead as she was prone to do. "I will see you in the morning," she promised as she exited.

Eliana moved to join the others now seated in the cooking area. "Nazim, Grandfather has asked to see you," she smiled.

"Me?" he asked pointing to himself. Eliana chuckled at his expression.

"Yes, there is no other called Nazim in our inn," she laughed.

Nazim quietly and carefully made his way to the door of the room the old man occupied. He knocked quietly and entered reverently when he was bid to do so.

Eli was stretched on a cot, a thin blanket covering his body. Nazim had not noticed how frail the man had become until seeing him like this.

"You sent for me?" he asked quietly.

"Please, come sit by me," Eli invited motioning to the chair Eliana had vacated by the cot. Nazim moved to do as he was asked.

"I cannot thank you enough for all the help you have been to us since you arrived here. I daresay the work you have done and continue to do far outweighs the cost of your room and meals," he began.

"The payment for my work is fair. It is all I requested, and the company even more so," he acknowledged with a sincere smile. He breathed a little easier now that he felt he wasn't about to be reprimanded for breaking some covenant he was unaware of.

"I will be honest with you, Nazim," the old man continued. "I want to know your heart now that you have spent several weeks in our company. I understand that you hail from Jericho and that the gods and beliefs of your people are nothing like ours. You were born into, and have protected all your life, a people quite different from us. Do you still feel as most of the Canaanites did toward our God and our people?"

Nazim took a deep breath, the conversation he had just shared with Eliana coming back to him. "I do not know where I stand," Nazim spoke honestly. He sat forward in the chair to be closer to the old man. "My thoughts have softened somewhat both toward your people and toward your God. The stories all of you have shared with me cause both understanding and confusion regarding the thoughts I had and the things I have always believed. Yet, I still harbor so much anger and confusion and have so little understanding of the ways of your God that I do not feel I could ever truly know Him. And the things I have done, along with the things I had planned to do, if He knows those things as you all proclaim, I do not feel He would ever care to know me," Nazim spoke as sincerely as he knew how.

"He should care to know none of us, Nazim, but *He created* each of us for a specific purpose. And He does not want you to only *know* Him, His desire is for you to *love* Him as you love no other," Eli continued. "The enemy will fight to keep you from ever surrendering your heart to the Almighty. He will offer you every excuse, he will remind you of every sin, every thought, everything you have done or would ever desire to do, in an attempt to keep you from our God. But if you call out to Him, Jehovah is faithful to listen. He is faithful and just to forgive.

"Moses wrote during our wanderings, *Know therefore that the Lord thy God, **he is God**, the faithful God, which keepeth covenant and mercy with them that love him and keep his commandments to a thousand generations*. He is God over the just and the unjust. He only requires that we love Him and do our best to keep His commandments, Nazim," Eli paused as a coughing fit overcome him. Nazim did not miss the small spot of blood on the cloth as he removed it from his mouth.

The old man breathed deeply before he continued. "I need for you to know this," Eli began again. "Nazim, you have regrets over past actions, as we all do, but Jehovah has a way of working all things together, for His own good. He can weave our tattered lives and sinful past, into a beautiful tapestry." Nazim could not get over, even in this weakened condition, how alive Eli seemed when he spoke of his God. Nazim listened intently as the old man continued. "We have told you much of Jehovah, but these are the things I want you to remember. Jehovah God is omniscient, knowing everything that has ever happened and all that will ever happen. Everything we have done that we should not have, and everything we will do that we should not. He knows every thought we have, every desire we harbor, every situation that we will find ourselves in both present and future, yet He still desires our fellowship. He cannot be surprised or shocked by our actions for He knew they were to come. He knew you would be outside those city walls when they fell, and it is my most sincere belief that He orchestrated it to be that way. He has a purpose and a plan for you, Nazim." Nazim smiled, remembering the same words coming from Eliana on so many occasions.

"He is also omnipotent," Eli continued. "There is nothing too hard for Jehovah. You have witnessed that for yourself as you saw in Jericho upon your return to the city. There is nothing that can stop Him. He is omnipresent, never beyond our reach, always available to us when we call out for Him. He never tires, He never sleeps, He never *wanders* off," he smiled, laughing softly. The soldier before him smiled broadly at the old man's lighthearted jab.

"He is also unchanging Nazim, which means in order for us to live eternally with Him, we have to be the ones to change. We cannot change ourselves; we have to be transformed in a way that can only happen through belief and acceptance of Him." He finished speaking just as another coughing fit racked his body. Nazim rose to pour fresh water from the pitcher at his bedside and offered it to him now. Eli sipped the water, thanking Nazim for the drink.

"There is one thing God cannot do," Eli continued with another deep breath. Nazim tilted his head completely curious as to what it was this God was incapable of. "He cannot lie," Eli stated simply. "The Ten Commandments state that to tell an untruth is a sin, and Jehovah simply cannot sin."

"I will think on all you have said," Nazim promised as he turned to go, knowing the man was worn and tired and realizing now that he was very, very sick.

"Do, my son," he advised, "and then pray to our God. Ask Him to come into your heart, to help you surrender your anger and to rule over your life," he finished, laying his head back on his cot and closing his eyes. "You will never know true peace, Nazim, until you accept Him." Nazim felt as if he had been dismissed. He began to open the door, but stopped suddenly when Eli called his name.

"And Nazim, do be careful with my Ellie. Her heart is young and tender," he finished. "She will be needing you very soon in a way she has yet to experience."

"I promise," he stated with a small smile, but his smile faded as the realization of what the old man said sank in. "Thank you, Eli," he said from his place. "Thank you for everything you shared with me tonight. It will not go unheeded."

With that, he turned and exited the door. Before he returned to the others, Nazim stood outside the closed portal. There was so much more wisdom he would have loved to have gained from this old man. He had given him much to think on. Perhaps on the morrow, he could speak with him again, or perhaps he had only been given this short amount of time. Whichever the case, Nazim was thankful for it.

Eliana and Nazim sat on the bank of the river, the water flowing somewhat faster than before due to the rains that had recently fallen. Eliana had spread out a blanket and packed a small lunch for the two of them. Their stomachs content, they now laughed and talked of nothing in particular. Nazim stretched himself out, propped on his elbow, Eliana sitting close beside him. He could not get over how beautiful she looked today.

A wisp of her hair had escaped her veil as she looked down at him. He did not hesitate, and she did not flinch, as he lifted his hand to tuck it gently behind her ear. As he did so, he cupped her face, pulling her toward him. She did not retreat as his lips gently touched hers in a simple kiss.

Pulling back, she looked at him for only a moment before she smiled gently and leaned in for another kiss, more passionate yet still completely innocent. They went no further, for she would remain an innocent until the day they were wed as per the commandment of her people. For now, the kiss was enough. She nestled against him now, in perfect peace and contentment.

Suddenly, Nazim heard something, or someone, coming up quickly behind himself. He moved to rise to a standing position, but before he could get on his feet, four men advanced from behind him with staves and nets. Before he could react, they had bound him on the ground. Kylus approached from behind Eliana now, grabbing her with such force that he knocked the breath from her lungs. She lay limp in his arms as he lifted and carried her deep into the woods, laughing as he fled with her.

Nazim kicked at the nets, struggling to free himself from the ties that bound him. Finally... he awoke, literally tearing the covers from his bed into two perfectly separate pieces. He caught himself before the emotions inside him erupted from his mouth but leaped so quickly from the cot that he landed on the floor with a thud.

He had barely gained his footing when he heard a light knock on his door. "Nazim," he heard Avi whisper through the closed portal, "is everything alright?" Nazim moved to the door and pulled it open. Avi couldn't help but gawk at what he beheld. His new friend was a sight. His hair, always so neatly pulled behind his head, now lay in wild ringlets around his face and shoulders. His eyes were bloodshot, and his face was ashen in color. "Are you well, my friend?" he asked, pushing his way inside the room and shutting the door behind himself.

Nazim walked to the wash basin and splashed the cold water over his face, pulling his hair behind his head. He stood for a minute gazing into the darkness beyond the window. "I struggle with sleep," he admitted finally, his voice broken from waking so abruptly.

"As it would seem," Avi admitted. "How long has this been going on?"

"I often dream… less than pleasant things. I have always felt that was just something that occurs due to the things I have witnessed in the battles I have fought."

"As most soldiers do," Avi agreed, "but I cannot help but feel there is more to this than that."

Nazim still stood looking out the window. Today had been a day full of confessions. First to Eliana, then in his conversation with their grandfather. Why not bear the remainder of his soul to Avi, his newest friend? He turned to face him. "I have had countless dreams, nightmares actually, since the destruction of Jericho," he began. "Up until recently, they all included Rahab and my inability to rescue her from one exaggerated situation after another. Since my time in Heshbon, however, the nightmares have changed somewhat."

"Let me guess," Avi interrupted him. "Rahab has been replaced by my sister."

"Somewhat," Nazim admitted, looking to his friend. "Do not be misguided, the dreams are never…inappropriate," he explained. "First, it was always Rahab who was in danger, just out of reach of my rescue. In those dreams, the 'danger' was always enhanced. Flames, or massive earthquakes, but tonight, and a few before, it was Eliana, and now the dreams are more realistic. Tonight, she was being taken by Kylus while I struggled to free myself from a net that bound me, keeping me from her. Before it was implied that Rahab was injured, she would disappear in a cloud of smoke, or I could hear her voice but not find her, but tonight I watched as Kylus took Eliana by force. She was unconscious, and all I could do was struggle to free myself, unable to protect her." Nazim paced the floor, playing the dream again in his mind.

His frustration suddenly became replaced by fear. "Go, check on her, Avi. It would be inappropriate for me to do so, please, make sure she is safe," he insisted suddenly.

"She is fine, Nazim," Avi moved close enough to his friend to touch his shoulder, attempting to calm him. He led Nazim to his cot, encouraging him to sit. It was then that he noticed the quilt on the bed had been torn in two.

"I will replace the quilt," Nazim promised, rubbing his face with his hands.

"I am not worried about the quilt, Nazim," Avi laughed. "But you, my friend, need some serious rest. I have heard of dreams before that plague men as they sleep, but I know little about them. What I do know is that dreams are not reality and that the dream has passed. Morning will be upon us soon, and we both need rest. Return to bed, and we will discuss this more at length on the morrow," Avi instructed as he moved to go. "I will pray for peace to come to you," he stated just before he left the room.

Nazim lay back on the cot but knew he would not rest until he had assurance that Eliana was safe. He realized that to approach her in her room at this hour would be forbidden, but he also knew that he had to assure her safety. Knowing that Avi was now back in his own room, Nazim crept down the stairs and stood outside Eliana's door. Laying his ear to the door he listened for any sound of movement on the inside. He heard nothing. He checked the central room, the cooking area, and the back entrance; everything inside the inn looked to be secure. Nothing was moved or out of place. Quietly he exited the establishment to move around the outside of the building. The moon was bright overhead, the breeze slightly stirring through the trees. All seemed peaceful.

He rounded the inn, moving to the back and checked the entrance from the outside that they often used into the cooking area. He was thankful, realizing now that the only access to Eliana's room was from inside the inn itself. There was no way to access her room from outside the inn. Content with this realization, he went back to his room now satisfied that she slept peacefully and in safety.

Nazim lay back down, though sleep still would not claim him. His mind and his heart were troubled, and he could not get the conversation with Eli out of his head. This God they served, He was nothing like Nazim had imagined. He remembered Rahab telling him before, when she tried to speak to him of this God, that He was not an idol made of stone, not something you could manipulate or conform to an image. She had been so open to their beliefs, and so quickly receptive to them, but she had also struggled for years with the gods served by the people of Jericho.

Being completely honest with himself, he began to examine his own heart. Nazim had truthfully never struggled with the gods of Jericho; he had no real allegiance to them at all. He had never understood the need to worship pieces of stone that had been formed by the men who then worshipped what they themselves had created. He had always gone through his life alone, making his own way by doing what was right or wrong in his own eyes, or so he had thought.

He turned to his side and saw the pendant lying on the table by his bed. He had showered Rahab with gifts and trinkets all the years he had known her, when all she had really wanted was a life in the open with him. He had encouraged her to *employ* only him, but all she really desired was a life that she could *share* with only him. How thoughtless and selfish he had been.

He realized now that though he did love her, his love had been born purely of his physical attraction to her. The physical passion they had shared had been shared with many before, but after their physical needs were met the two of them had also formed a relationship. He could not deny the mental connection he had to her as well. He had loved her in the only way he knew how, preferring her company over any other, but he had not loved her enough to sacrifice anything for her other than a week's pay from time to time.

His heart broke again for the way he had spoken to her when she tried to tell him of her new relationship, a relationship with the God of Israel. He knew he had hurt her in ways he would never be able to forgive himself for.

If he had listened to her, would he have saved himself the years of torment he had experienced since the walls fell? Would things have been any different at all? Grandfather had said that Jehovah could work all things together for good. Could this God really bring something good out of all the wrongs Nazim had done?

He picked up the pendant, turning again to his back. Nazim remembered the tears Rahab had shed the last time they had spoken, the tears that he had caused. He remembered how broken she had been as he had left her that day, he had seen it all over her face, and yet, he had chosen to leave her there. He remembered when he had returned to the fallen city and found the pendant, this pendant that she had once cherished, broken and rejected in the ruins of Jericho.

Yet, when he had seen her on that riverbank a year later, the look of brokenness he remembered on her face had been replaced with a look of utter contentment and peace, a peace she would never have found with him. Nazim realized that Rahab was happier with Salmon than she could ever have been with him. She had given her life to the God of Israel before she had joined Salmon, and it was that God Who had taken a broken prostitute and created a beautiful, safe, and pure life for her and her new family. Could this God do the same for a broken, wandering soldier?

Nazim lay the pendant on his chest and stared overhead at the ceiling. Had the God of the Israelites been at work in his life all along? How was it, after years of wanderings, that he had arrived in Heshbon just before misfortune would fall upon this place, and Eliana would need his assistance? His own evil plan had brought him to Heshbon, a plan of revenge and pure retribution, but the information he had sought for his wicked desires had transformed him into someone different.

Something inside of him had definitely changed since he had arrived here. The same peace he had witnessed on Rahab's face existed in this place. A peace unlike any he had experienced, and he knew that, honestly, he longed to continue to experience that peace. He knew these people still had troubles, Kylus being a main player in that, but even so, there was still a contentment about these people that he desired for himself.

And then there was Eliana. He smiled as she came to his mind. So beautiful, so pure, so innocent, though she had quite a passion about her. He chuckled as he remembered the look on her face when she attempted to charge Kylus yesterday, only to be stopped by her brother.

Eliana is a beautiful soul, he thought. As beautiful on the inside as she is physically. He had once believed there would never be a woman he could desire as much as he had once desired Rahab, but this, along with so many other things he had once believed, had been proven wrong over the past few weeks. Eliana deserved so much more than he had ever offered to Rahab. She deserved a man who would love and cherish her, for all her attributes. A man like Rahab had now in Salmon. Could he, Nazim, ever be a man like that? A man worthy of such a woman?

For the first time in his life, Nazim thought of attempting a prayer to this Jehovah God they served, the God they had been telling him of for so many weeks, the God Rahab had tried to tell him of years ago. *"He will not hear from the likes of you,"* flitted through his mind.

"So, what if He will not listen," Nazim whispered, arguing with the darkness that surrounded him. "Eli just told me that He is always available when we call out to Him. At least I can attempt an audience with Him." He lay on his cot, continuing to listen to the sound of the silence around him.

"I do not know You," he finally found the courage to whisper. "I do not even know how to pray to you. Yet, from what I have been told, there is nothing You do not know of me. They tell me that You will still listen, regardless of my past, and that You could still use me if I am willing to surrender to You. If that be so, show me what it is that You want from me. I cannot deny that something inside of me has changed. I no longer wish to destroy these people, and I know that I cannot destroy You. I am still angry and confused about why You took so much from me, why I had to lose everything...." Nazim stopped, sitting upright on his cot. The answer had come as audible to him as if it had been

174

spoken aloud, though he knew was still alone in the complete darkness that surrounded him.

"Because you had to lose everything in order to find Me," he had heard in his heart. He swallowed hard and looked around himself. He lay back slowly on his cot, pondering on that sentence that would not leave his mind. He knew exactly what he had to do.

"I cannot deny that the God of Israel is the one true God," he continued a few moments later. "I cannot understand many things, but I am willing to try. I cannot change my past, but I can ask Your forgiveness for all the ways I have wronged You, for all of the ways I have wronged Rahab, and for all of the wrongs I had sought upon these, Your, people."

He whispered his simple prayer into the darkness, but he felt a light igniting in his very soul as he continued. "I am sorry for all of my wrongs. I cannot understand why You would, but if You still want me, I am willing to serve You. Use me to aid these people in whatever way You deem worthy, and teach me to serve You, the One True God, the living God of Israel."

Nazim could not remember the last time he had shed a tear, but he could not stop the lone tear that crept from the corner of his eye and slid down his cheek. For the first time in his life, he felt a peace consume him that he had only recently realized he was missing. He had found the God that he had searched for, the God he had once sought in an attempt to destroy, whom he would now attempt to serve all the days of his life.

Chapter Seventeen

Nazim was the first one downstairs the next morning. Quietly, he moved to Grandfather's door listening for any sign of movement on the inside. The coughing coming from within concerned him, but he realized that Eli was awake. Without hesitation or time to change his mind, he knocked gently on the door.

"Enter," the old man said simply. That simple word even sounded painful for the man. "Nazim, it is good to see you," he said slowly and weakly. Crossing to his bedside, Nazim did not spend time on pleasantries.

"I had to lose everything in order to find Him," Nazim said plainly, looking down at the man before him, who he now admired so much. "If Jericho were still standing, I would still be there. I would still be patrolling the streets, lost in that life. Rahab would not have been rescued by Salmon and now share a life with him that she can live freely out of the darkness. I would never have come to Heshbon, I never would have found Eliana, and I never would have been open to hearing of your God. I came to find out all I could in order to destroy Him, but instead, I found that I cannot continue my life without Him."

Eli smiled and laughed with all the strength he had left. "Praise be to Jehovah, my son," he slowly clapped his hands together then motioned for Nazim to come closer to him. As Nazim bent down to meet him, Eli pulled him to his cot and wrapped his frail arms around Nazim's neck to embrace him.

"Care for my Ellie, Nazim," he instructed as he released him. "Watch over her. Love her, and she will be good to you all the days of her life. Guide my Reuben," he continued weakly. "He looks up to you in so many ways. Teach him to continue in the ways of Jehovah," he whispered.

"But there is so much I do not know," Nazim began interrupting the old man.

"Hush, now," he instructed, waving his doubt away. "I do not have much time."

"I promise," Nazim stated. Even on his deathbed, Eli was looking out for those he loved the most.

"I need to see Avi. Bring him to me," he requested now.

Nazim moved quickly, meeting Avi as he came down the stairs. He sent him straight in to see his grandfather. Nazim remained outside the door, though he heard Eliana moving about the cooking area. He could not go to her just now. In only a few moments, Avi summoned them all to his grandfather's room.

Eliana, Nazim, Reuben, and Avi all stood by Eli's bedside. Eliana held her grandfather's hand, silent tears sliding along her face. Nazim stood behind her reverently. Reuben was on the other side, Avi beside him.

"I love you, Grandfather," she whispered, stroking his face. "Thank you for always loving and directing us." He smiled up at her once more, reaching to touch her face.

"I love you, my Ellie. I am going to see my Anna now," he mouthed to her, "and the Jehovah God Whom I have served for so long." He closed his eyes, a small smile lighting his face, and took his final breath. Eliana bent down once more, kissing his forehead as her own tears spilled in a torrent across his face. Her heart felt as if it had broken in two, and she turned as she released his frail hand, collapsing into the strong arms of the man behind her. Nazim held her as she cried. Reuben threw himself across his grandfather, his own tears flowing freely. Avi stayed close to his little brother, allowing him time to grieve, his own heart being twisted inside him as silent tears wet his face.

Nazim continued to hold Eliana as tightly, yet as gently as he could. She wet his vest with her tears, staying wrapped in his arms for several minutes before she finally had control of herself and pulled away. She looked up at him, her tears still streaming.

"I am sorry," she began. He wiped the tears from her face and bent to softly kiss her head.

"You do not owe me an apology," he said gently. "You do not owe me anything." He began to lead her from the room, shielding the body of her grandfather from her view were she to look back. Once they were in the central room, she broke down again at the sight of the table where her grandfather often sat, and Nazim was there to hold her again as she cried. His arms were still around her when Reuben and Avi exited their grandfather's room a few minutes later. Reuben clung to his older brother, then ran across the room to Nazim. He threw his arms around Nazim's waist, holding on to the soldier with all the strength he had left. Nazim held the lad, allowing him the time he needed.

The next few hours went by in a flourish of activity. Uma arrived shortly after Eli's passing, and after a few minutes of grieving with the family, she went to tell the village of his death. Many arrived for their morning meal, only to find out then that Eli had passed. They offered their condolences then some moved on their way, while Abner and several others sat with them in an effort to grieve with and console the family.

Eliana had changed into mourning clothes, but Nazim thought she had never looked more beautiful. He stayed close by, watching for any sign that she had a need of him. Reuben had requested to go to the barn for solitude, and Eliana had granted his request. His friend, Thomas, had arrived soon after and gone to be with his friend.

Soon, ladies began to arrive to prepare Eli's body for burial. Avi busied himself making the necessary arrangements, and it was decided that Eli would be buried the next day. Nazim had given Eliana space, moving outside to speak with some of the men who had come by, and checking on Reuben, still in the barn with his friend.

Uma worked in the cooking area, offering small meals to those who came to visit, refusing Eliana when she tried to help. Uma attempted to feed her, but Eliana waved away anything she offered. She was trying to be strong and was talking with her visitors, but Uma began to grow concerned. Even Reuben had come to her requesting nourishment for himself and Thomas before retreating back outdoors. Finally, as the day grew long, Uma waved Nazim to a corner.

"Eliana has not eaten nor drank anything all day," she confided in him. "I know she is trying to be strong for those around her, but I am concerned for her well-being." Nazim realized that Eliana was in deep mourning, and though it was not uncommon for her to see to everyone else's needs first, it was time for him to intervene.

"Put some things in a sack for me. I will take care of it. If you see Avi, please tell him we are just behind the inn," he requested, thanking her for her concern.

"Thank you, Nazim," Uma breathed. He returned a small smile as he moved to seek out Eliana in the crowded room. Soon he found her sitting at a table with Sarah and a few other ladies he did not know. Approaching the table, he stood behind Eliana and spoke softly to the ladies around her.

"How is your husband?" he asked, directing his question to Sarah.

"He is improving every day," she smiled up to him. "I am still so thankful for all you did, Nazim. If it were not for you, I may have been in mourning over my husband today," she stated, wiping, a tear from the corner of her eye.

"You are most welcome," he smiled to her. "I need to steal Eliana from you for a moment," he continued. He touched Eliana's shoulder requesting her to accompany him to the cooking area. She stood and Nazim could tell by her movements that she felt as if weights sat upon her shoulders. Though she continually forced a smile to her guests, her weary eyes brimmed with tears and her face was pale. Uma had left a sack filled with food, as well as a vessel of juice, on the table in the cooking area, and as they moved through, Nazim picked them up.

"Nazim…" Eliana began to protest as he ushered her to the back door.

"You are coming with me," he instructed, opening the door for her to exit. Reluctantly, she gave in with a sigh. He led her behind the inn to the tree she often sat by. They sat, and before he had gotten comfortable beside her, she began to weep once again, releasing the sobs she had been holding in for most of the day. He held her as she cried against his chest.

"I feel so weak," she cried. "I thought I would be stronger than this. I feel like all the strength I had died with Grandfather," she sobbed. It broke Nazim's heart that she hurt so deeply, and it hurt him that he could do nothing to fix it. Then he remembered that he could. He began to pray aloud.

"Jehovah, I am still new at this, but I pray for peace now, for Eliana and for her brothers, and for each of us who loved Eli. As Eliana has often reminded me, You have a plan and a purpose for everything, even in his passing. I thank You that his passing was peaceful, and I thank You for bringing me to this place and for the wisdom that Eli shared with me. I thank You for Eliana and for what she means to me, and I pray now that You will grant us peace and lead us as we begin to navigate life without him."

As he expected, Eliana rose from his chest and looked into his face. "You prayed to Jehovah?" she asked, tears flowing once again, but this time different. She had a weak smile on her face.

"I had a long conversation with your grandfather last night, and afterward, I had a lengthy conversation with your God. Our God," he emphasized. "Among other things, I told Him that if He still wanted me, I was willing to serve Him," Nazim smiled, brushing her hair from her face.

"Did Grandfather know?" she asked simply.

"He did," Nazim confirmed. "I told him this morning before he called for all of you."

Eliana stared at the man beside her. Her heart was still broken, but she felt such relief over what Nazim had just shared with her that she was able to achieve the deep breath she had longed for all day. "Thank you for telling him before he passed, and thank you for telling me. It has brought joy to an otherwise mournful day."

Nazim pulled her back to his chest and settled his arms around her. "I will need help, Eliana," he said honestly above her head, "and I will need someone to guide me. I am hoping you will continue to teach me of your ways and the ways of Jehovah. I would like to spend more time with you as well...and...Eliana?"

The peace of the moment, the beating of his heart, and the soft rumble of his voice coming from his chest was more than she could bear. Exhaustion had won, and Eliana had quickly fallen into an exhausted slumber as he held her. He sat completely still, allowing her time to rest as he thought upon all the miraculous transformations he himself had endured since coming to Heshbon. The tranquil setting and the quiet stream in front of him, along with the restless night he had experienced, began to weigh on him as well. He had almost dozed off himself when she stirred.

"I am so sorry," she spoke as she jumped, realizing she had fallen asleep.

"Will you stop apologizing to me?" he grinned. He then remembered the supplies Uma had sent, and reached for the sack and juice, offering them both to her. "What I need you to do, is eat. Uma said you have touched nothing all day."

Eliana took another breath and accepted the sack. "Nazim, I am just not hungry," she said honestly.

"Regardless, we will not return to the inn until you have eaten something from that sack," he informed her. "Is there an apple in there?" he joked.

Eliana pulled out an apple, handing it to Nazim with a smile. She also pulled out berries and cheese, a small bowl of olives, and a fig cake. Uma had packed all of her favorites.

They spent a few moments more by the stream, Eliana nibbling on a few berries and a small bite of the fig cake before moving back to the inn. Though she was still exhausted, she did feel some better. She stopped him just before they entered and stood looking up to Nazim.

"Thank you," she spoke softly, "for looking after me today. I could not have gotten through this day without your strength and support." Her eyes filled with tears once again, and Nazim gently framed her face with his hands. He brushed a tear that had escaped her eye.

"Thank you," he returned, "for your patience and persistence. I never would have known this peace in my soul were it not for you and your family." Gently he bent to kiss her forehead. She closed her eyes, the simple kiss sending chills throughout her body.

A noise from inside the cooking area broke their serene moment. It was Avi approaching the back door where they stood.

"I was about to come looking for you," he stated, and Nazim noticed the stern look on his friend's face.

"I had asked Uma to alert you as to where we were," he defended them both, thinking that Avi was angry with him.

"No, she did, and I thank you for that," Avi clarified. "It is Kylus. He has arrived," he spoke firmly, "to pay his respects," he stated smugly as he opened the door wide, encouraging them to come inside. The trio moved to the main room. Kylus stood in the center of the room, along with two men who were with him that Eliana did not recognize. No one else remained, their friends finally retiring to their own homes for the evening. Reuben had been invited by Thomas's family to stay the night with them, and he had accepted with Avi's approval, who realized his younger brother needed a break from the sadness encompassing the inn.

"Thank you for coming, Kylus," Eliana began, Nazim and Avi both close behind her. "I trust Uma offered you and your men some refreshment?" she asked.

"She did," he confirmed. "I wanted to pay my respects to your family, Eliana, and to inform you that my men will carry Eli's body to the tomb tomorrow that you have chosen," he informed her.

"Thank you, but that will not be necessary," she spoke kindly yet firmly. "My brother, Avi, and Nazim will transport my grandfather to his final resting place."

"Nazim?" he questioned harshly; shock evident on his face.

"Yes, Nazim," she reiterated.

"He is not a member of your family! He is not even a member of this village! He is a stranger, a vagabond who has found his worthless way into your good graces for some unknown reason." Kylus stated, raising his voice. "I forbid it!"

Nazim remained calm and silently prayed for strength from the God he now served. Yet, he could not help but clench his teeth together as he felt his blood begin to thicken inside his veins.

"First of all, neither you nor your men are members of my family or patrons of Heshbon," she clarified, "and it is ultimately my oldest brother's decision as to how my grandfather's burial is handled, Kylus. Frankly, Nazim has done more for this village in the few weeks he has been here than you have done in your lifetime," she answered, her anger evident on her face.

Kylus placed his hand on his sword, and the men beside him sprang to attention. Nazim took a step closer to Eliana, his temper rising quickly to the boiling point.

"Eliana," Avi spoke firmly. Immediately she dropped her head and took a step back, allowing her older brother to position himself in front of her.

"The arrangements for my grandfather have been made, Kylus," Avi spoke firmly. "I thank you for your offer of assistance though we respectfully decline it. Nazim will assist me with my grandfather's burial. I politely ask that you exit my home now to allow my family the time of mourning that we require. We appreciate your concern, but your presence, or that of your men, is no longer necessary."

"You are on dangerous ground, Eliana," Kylus spoke through clenched teeth, looking around Avi to his sister, pointing a finger directly in her direction. It was more than he could take. Nazim stepped in front of Eliana and Kylus quickly lowered the finger he was so bold and quick to point.

"You are the one on dangerous ground," Nazim stated plainly, glaring straight into the soul of the man before him. Kylus nervously looked to the men on either side of him, quietly instructing them to exit the establishment.

"I will give you the time required for mourning," he spat, directing his attention to Avi. "But this is not over," he glared back at Nazim. Nazim watched him until the door was closed behind him. The trio then waited until they heard the horses' hooves outside the inn before moving. Eliana sunk into the chair nearest her. Uma peeked in from the cooking area with a small tray of meat, bread, and olives.

"Is he gone?" she asked, peering through a small opening in the door. Avi chuckled and bade her to come.

Uma was content with the small bite of bread and few olives that Eliana ate. They talked of the coming days and what that would mean to the inn. They decided that after the seven days required for mourning, the inn would remain closed for two additional weeks in order to allow Nazim and Avi to finish the stoop.

Nazim told Uma and Avi of the decision he had made to serve the God of Israel that he had shared with Eliana earlier, resulting in praise, hugs, and thankfulness from them both. Before they retired for the evening, Avi offered special thanks to Jehovah for bringing Nazim to them, for Nazim's acceptance of Him, and for the friendship they now shared. He also prayed for guidance over the coming days, and for peace to come to their weary souls as they adjusted to the passing of the man they had all clung to for so long.

Chapter Eighteen

The burial of Eli was peaceful the next day. The weather could not have been more beautiful, but their souls were heavy as they laid him in his final resting place in the company of most of the village. Kylus made his appearance, flanked by four of his men this time, standing far back from the rest of the entourage of mourners. Eli had been a very respected and a very loved member of Heshbon. His passing would be felt by all.

Citizen after citizen moved to pay their condolences to Avi, Eliana, and Reuben as they filed past the family after the burial had taken place. Even Nazim was offered condolences as they left the scene, most everyone now accepting, and appreciating, his presence in their small town. Kylus watched the display of empathy taking place around him, fuming at how accepted Nazim had become among the people. This man was a direct threat to him, to his position, and to his power. And how he had won the affection of Eliana, Kylus would never know. He would put a stop to this, he vowed, he just had to figure out how he would do it while maintaining what popularity he had left among the citizens of Heshbon.

The seven days of mourning ensued, and during those seven days, the rain the elders had been predicting came. The weather was as dreary as Eliana's soul. She rejoiced in Nazim's acceptance of Jehovah and drew strength from his presence, but the inn felt empty without her grandfather. Reuben spent most of his time in the barn with Ares, and Nazim used the time between the rains to work with Reuben, his riding skills now nearly perfected. Avi had promised his brother a foal of his own once the mares had birthed in the spring, and Reuben was beyond excited with the promise.

Finally, the rain subsided, and the skies cleared. The mourning period now complete, Eliana tucked away her mourning clothes, dreading the day she ever had to wear them again. The mourning period may have passed, but her heart remained heavy. She could not remember when she had achieved a decent amount of sleep. She had tried, as she had been taught, to seek Jehovah in her despair, but her soul was so exceedingly sorrowful that she could do nothing but cry.

She would drift into a fitful sleep at each attempt, but then she would snap awake feeling as if the world had been ripped out from under her, and the tears would begin again. Eliana did not recognize the depression that had consumed her. If she were not thinking of her grandfather, she worried about what was to come once Avi returned to the battlefield. She could accept his departure, she was accustomed to her brother's absence, but she had come to depend on Nazim far more than she was comfortable with, especially now that he had claimed Jehovah. She appreciated both his attention to her and the strength she drew from him. She longed for his company while he was here, but she feared that once the restorations were complete, he would be gone, and honestly, she could not bear the thought of his departure. The thought troubled her more than a little.

"I must speak with Grandfather," she would decide out of habit. Then the tears would begin again as she was reminded that he was no longer here to seek out for advice and counsel. It was a vicious cycle she repeated night, after night, after night.

No number of tears would bring her grandfather back, and knowing he was now complete and in the presence of her grandmother, her parents, and their Lord, she honestly would not bring him back to the cares of this world even if she could. Still, that did not make her miss him any less.

Her family did not recognize that she had not been sleeping. Even Nazim, with his watchful eye, had been fooled, secretly accusing her swollen, bloodshot eyes on excessive mourning. He had no idea of the feelings she had for him, and she planned to keep it that way. It would be less embarrassing when he moved on.

She exited her room this morning, her heart heavy, only to find Nazim already waiting for her. He was at his table in the corner, a couple of sacks on the table before him.

"Good morning," he spoke, standing as he saw her.

"Good morning," she returned, as she tied her apron around her waist.

"How do you feel this morning," he asked as he moved closer to her.

Eliana took a deep breath before she spoke. "Hollow," was the only word she could find that explained the sinking feeling inside her heart. "But I am trying," she admitted, attempting a smile.

"Come with me," he informed her. "We are going on a journey," he informed her.

"A journey?" she asked puzzled. "I thought you and Avi would begin working on the repairs again today."

"We shall take care of that tomorrow," he continued, picking up the sacks. "We have an extra week than what we had originally planned, and the weather has cleared. Today, we celebrate the end of the mourning period and my new life in Jehovah. I have already received Avi's approval. You are to come with me. He knows exactly where we are going, and once Uma arrives, they will join us there."

Eliana's heart remained heavy in her chest, but she could not help but chuckle at the gleam of excitement dancing in his eyes.

"Reuben?" she asked, looking around for her younger brother.

"Already with Thomas," he informed her.

Eliana remembered, nodding her head, but truthfully, she did not feel like going anywhere. She felt like crawling back into bed and attempting to sleep once again, but she also recognized the look on Nazim's face. He was determined, and her brother had already approved of his plan. She would not be allowed to wallow in self-pity today.

"Very well," she conceded. "I suppose I can spare a few hours." She removed the apron she had just put on, laid it to the side, and stood before him. "Where are we going?" she asked with a deep breath as he ushered her through the cooking area toward the back entrance of the inn.

"To the paths beyond the pools of Heshbon," he said excitedly as they exited. "You must show me where you 'have not' explored!" he joked.

Eliana could not stop the chuckle that bubbled inside of her at the comical look that crossed his face. That sound was balm for Nazim's soul. They moved slowly down the path behind the inn that led to the pools, talking of many things as they walked, many things except her grandfather. Nazim shared more with her about his life and what his profession had consisted of while in Jericho. They talked of specific people he had come to know in Heshbon, the relationship they both anticipated blooming between Uma and Avi, and about how Nazim's life had changed since he had arrived here.

Finally, they were beyond the pools and on the same path Eliana had "secretly explored" in her younger days.

"You will not believe what is right around the bend," she commented as they continued on. She had decided to embrace the time she had with him and was trying hard to be cheerful, though he could still sense the sadness in her voice. Nazim suddenly heard the sound of rushing water but had no idea of the sight that was in store. The stream they were walking alongside continued to widen as they walked and suddenly Nazim realized they were now following a river. They did not have to go much further before he beheld a sight such as he had never imagined. Water rushed from above their heads crashing forcefully into the river below. In all his travels, he had never seen anything like this.

"These waters fill our pools," Eliana explained, having to raise her voice to be heard over the falls. "I admitted both my disobedience to him and that I had explored this path when I asked Grandfather about the 'falling water' I had found," she chuckled. "He scolded me, refusing to allow me to leave the inn for a solid week. Afterward, he accompanied me here and explained how beautiful and how spiritual a waterfall can be, as well as how dangerous. He was in much better health then, obviously. It is symbolic to me now," she admitted looking up at the falls. The spray of the water hit their face as they watched it fall, crashing into the rocks below. "The water never stops flowing," she explained, "constantly changing, to follow the course laid out by the Father. Much the same as our life," she admitted as a tear made a slow trek down her cheek. "We have no real control over what life hands us, but we have no choice but to keep going." She wiped her face and blinked rapidly to clear her eyes. He knew she still hurt, but he almost detected something more. Was grief all that consumed her now?

Nazim watched her closely. Just a few days ago, he had held her as she collapsed into his arms, broken to pieces, drawing from his strength. Today she stood on her own strength, yet something still seemed wrong. Her face was ashen, and there was an edge about her usually pleasant disposition. It was not the words she said that bothered him, it was the attitude with which she said them.

A thought came to his mind that scared him more than a little. He had seen what depression could do to a person. He had watched as it had turned his toughest warriors into mere schoolboys who made foolish decisions when it came to matters of life or death. It had turned his strongest soldiers into weaklings, as they turned away meals having no concern for their own wellbeing. He had to intervene to keep this from happening to Eliana.

"I think we need a break," he advised setting down the sacks he carried onto a large, flat rock that was positioned nearby. "Avi and Uma should be joining us soon," he promised. "I do not think they will mind if we start without them." Eliana moved to sit beside him as he blessed the food.

They settled on the rock, and Eliana pulled olives, cheese, berries, and bread from the sack. "Did you pack these?" she asked, watching him as he watched her.

"I did," he acknowledged. "All by myself," he grinned.

"He has been paying attention," she thought as she pulled all of her favorites from inside the bag. She offered a small smile acknowledging as much to him. "No apples?" she asked, looking deeper inside the sack.

"I fear we are out of apples," he said sorrowfully, a comical look on his face. His attempt at humor brought the chuckle from her that he desired, and he smiled broadly at her in return.

"Then we shall go to market this afternoon," she promised, amazed at his thoughtfulness. *"Better enjoy it while you can,"* the thought flitted through her mind. *"Then he will disappear as surely as your grandfather did."* Nazim did not miss the tears she blinked rapidly away, and though he was unsure of what caused them, he kept his peace.

189

They enjoyed their meager lunch on the rocks, very little being said between them. Nazim stretched out on the rock as Eliana placed their belongings back into the sack. Once finished, she sat quietly, resting her chin on her knees, watching the water that seemed to fall directly from the sky from this vantage point. She had been unusually quiet, even for herself.

Nazim watched her for only a moment before he turned to his side to better see her. "What is on your mind, Eliana?" he asked sincerely. She looked at him, attempting a smile, but he saw the tears brimming in her eyes once again. He assumed she was about to speak of her grandfather, but he was surprised when the conversation turned in another direction.

She thought for a moment before she spoke, deciding then to be completely honest with him. "In all sincerity," she replied, looking again toward the falls, "I am fearful of what will happen once you and Avi have completed the repairs to the inn."

"Meaning?" he asked, puzzled.

Her voice trembled, and she cleared her throat as she attempted to continue speaking. "It does not matter," she said, blinking rapidly and waving her comment away, suddenly embarrassed and ashamed of herself for her honesty. "In truth, I am just very tired," she admitted. "I have not been sleeping, and things always seem much worse when you are weary," she admitted, the pain evident on her face. Nazim rose, closing the distance between them and sitting directly next to her, their shoulders touching.

"Why are you not sleeping?" he asked, truly concerned. He knew what it was like to have interrupted sleep. It was not something he wished for anyone, especially for her.

"I do not know," she admitted. "I have tried to rest in Jehovah, but sleep continues to elude me. I just keep thinking of how life will change now that grandfather is gone, and I am fearful of what will happen when Avi returns to the battlefield, and Reuben and I remain here, alone," she continued being only partially honest.

Nazim spoke softly, taking her hands in his. "Eliana, Avi will have to return to the battlefield eventually, but you will not be alone. I am not planning to go anywhere," he promised. The gesture was more than she could bear, and her tears began to flow freely.

"No, you will leave too," she stated with assurance. "Though I will miss my brother, I can bear his absence, but yours… honestly, I fear I have become too dependent on your strength and your presence at the inn," she admitted truthfully. "You have been so strong for us since grandfather passed. I could not have gotten through it without you. I am just not certain what Reuben and I will do when the two of you are gone." She glanced in his direction but could not bear to look at him directly. She had not meant to be so open with him and was embarrassed that she had been so transparent.

He positioned himself in front of her, looking into her face as he continued. "Eliana, my entire life has changed since I came to Heshbon. I have admitted to you that I came here looking for vengeance, but what I found is something far more wonderful than retribution. I found a peace here that I did not even realize I longed for. How could I leave all of this behind?" He paused before he continued. *"How could I leave you behind,"* he thought to himself. As he took in her features, he realized she could not mentally handle any personal declarations this day. He would keep that thought to himself for now.

As he closely took in her appearance, he realized that her lack of sleep was clearly affecting her health. Her eyes were sunken into her head, and dark circles pooled beneath them. Her face seemed hollow and was ashen in color. "How long has it been since you slept?" he asked aloud, now changing the subject.

"I have no idea," she answered honestly.

"The problem now is that you are worn, and you are weary. You need rest. Have you not continually told me that Jehovah has a plan for each of us? Trust in the Jehovah you taught me of, Eliana."

"I know that Jehovah has a plan," she agreed, "but sometimes it is hard to convince yourself of the words you speak so easily to others. I will admit that when it directly concerns myself and those I love, it would be helpful to know what that plan is," she chuckled as she wiped the tears from her face.

"Well, do not concern yourself with my leaving," he promised again, looking directly into her face. "You will have to run me from this town," he smiled.

"It may only be temporary," she thought to herself, *"but for now, I will take what I can get."*

Nazim looked into her weary eyes and caressed her face with his hand. He almost succumbed and pulled her face to his for a gentle kiss but stopped himself as memories of the last nightmare he had endured came swiftly to his mind. The look that crossed his face brought confusion to Eliana, but only for a moment before they heard rustling coming from behind them.

Nazim turned, his sword drawn, ready to attack who or whatever was about to appear. It was Avi who stepped out, Uma close behind him. Her laughter abruptly ceased when she saw Nazim standing with his sword in hand.

"Did we miss lunch?" Avi joked, never even hesitating. Nazim sheathed his sword as his friend moved toward the sack that his sister now held out to him. Nazim was thankful it was Avi and Uma who had appeared, but something about him now did not feel settled. Perhaps it was simply his concern over Eliana.

He attempted to join in conversation, laughing at all the appropriate times, but there was an unsettledness in him that he could not identify. He continually looked around them all and was constantly on edge.

Avi recognized the tension in Nazim and moved to ask him about it as the women packed up their belongings. "Thank you for all you have done for my sister," he began. "Though I still worry over her wellbeing…".

"I would like to speak with you about that," Nazim interrupted.

"I was hoping so," Avi answered with a smile clasping his friend on the shoulder once again. "We will talk about your intentions concerning my sister later, but I do not believe that is what troubles you at the moment," he spoke honestly. "What is it?" he asked.

"I cannot say," Nazim answered, looking around once again. "I was rarely surprised in battle because I always had a sense when someone unwelcome was approaching. That sense protected me and saved my life on more than one occasion," he explained.

"I feel it now. We need to get these ladies back to safety," he instructed.

"Relax, my friend," Avi suggested. "You have been through quite a lot of changes of your own over the past few weeks. It is only natural that you would experience some anxiety. Our ladies are well protected and completely safe with us nearby," he bragged as he flexed his muscles. Nazim laughed and rolled his eyes. "Now, regarding my sister…my grandfather and I shared a very important conversation just before he passed that we need to discuss," Avi continued quietly, speaking only loud enough for Nazim to hear. Together, they fell behind the women who were now moving to begin their journey back to the inn.

Neither of the men noticed the man who had been hiding in the thicket, even when they walked directly past his hiding place. Kylus had heard more than he had bargained for. Nazim had confirmed his intention to remain in Heshbon, and it was more important than ever that Kylus stop that from happening. He pondered on an idea that had just occurred to him as he remained in his hiding place.

"Kylus, you are brilliant!" he chuckled to himself as the plan continued to form in his mind. The mourning period had passed, and it was entirely appropriate for him to now pay one more visit to the family. A visit he decided he would pay sooner rather than later.

Chapter Nineteen

Later that afternoon, Avi, Eliana, Nazim, and Uma all made their way into town. Reuben accompanied them as well, proudly seated on the back of Ares, the reins in his own hands as he independently steered the animal. Nazim had tried to convince Eliana to remain at the inn, but she insisted that she would rest better if she waited until night to attempt sleep again. It was their first public appearance since the burial of Eli, and many of the townsfolk welcomed them with warm embraces and extended sympathies.

It was not an easy trip for Eliana, but the weight in her chest did seem lighter than she imagined it would have been, likely due to her outing that morning with Nazim and the promise he had made to remain in Heshbon.

They made the purchases they needed, including apples, and assured their beloved town folk that the inn would open again in only two weeks.

They were just leaving the main street when Kylus appeared, his now usual entourage flanking him on either side. Never before Nazim arrived had Kylus felt the need for protection, but now at least two, if not four, of his soldiers accompanied him each time he came into town.

"Well, if it is not the family of Eli returning to society," he mocked as he dismounted his horse. "I trust you all are faring well?" he asked, though he really could not care less. Though his question was directed to Avi, he did not take his eyes from Eliana. She recognized it as a tactic to make her feel uncomfortable, and perhaps it was the emotional turmoil she had been in over the past few days, but this time he was easily succeeding. Though her heart had felt lighter, the weight began to return under his pathetic gaze. She had no fire left in her today. Nazim noticed her discomfort and moved closer to her.

"We are well, Kylus. Thank you for your concern," Avi acknowledged as they continued to pass by the man. Kylus' soldiers came up on either side of him, blocking their way through the street. "Is there something else?" Avi asked, his own patience growing thin.

"I wonder of your future plans, Avi. Specifically, when you will be returning to the battlefield," Kylus continued, pulling a piece of parchment from his vest pocket.

"My exact return has not been scheduled at present, but will occur sooner or later," Avi responded. "May I ask why that concerns you, Kylus?" Avi was attempting to be respectful and to keep the peace, but he was losing the battle with his temper, his own emotions running the gamut over the past week.

"I am simply curious," Kylus began. "The passing of your grandfather's lands and property should fall to you, of course, Avi, but with you being unable to assume that responsibility due to your enlistment in the armies of Israel, and Reuben being too young to acquire such responsibility, our rules state that the property will be left to the town of Heshbon. Including," he continued, "the care of any widowed or unwed maidens who reside in that establishment. We cannot allow such fine 'responsibilities' to become neglected now, can we?" Kylus continued, cutting his eyes toward Eliana once again. She moved further behind Nazim. Kylus smiled a disgusting smile as he continued, relishing in how easy it was today to make her squirm. "Being the just man that I am," he began again, "and understanding what the inn means to the fine patrons of Heshbon, I have decided to endure the sacrifice myself," he declared, signaling toward his own body and speaking loud enough for all to hear. "I will move my primary residence to Heshbon, I will assume control and the responsibility of the inn, and I will wed the damsel who resides therein," he smirked, looking around Nazim to Eliana. The look on his face was sickening, and the public scene he was making made Eliana want to vomit. Her heart began to thunder in her chest, and tears of anger burned her eyes.

"You, sir, have a death wish," Nazim spoke slow and firm, attempting a losing battle at controlling his temper. His teeth clenched together, his heart pounded in his head, and though he stood his ground, in his mind this man was already in pieces at his feet.

Eliana felt her knees begin to weaken as she fought to remain on her feet. Reuben distracted her from her present state, as he fled passed them all on Ares after hearing the proclamation Kylus had made.

Avi slowly approached Kylus now, who began to look slightly nervous at his approach. "May I see that parchment?" Avi asked calmly, reaching for the paper in Kylus's hand.

"Read it for yourself," Kylus agreed, relinquishing the paper. "As a founding member of Heshbon, Eli himself agreed to these terms," he stated absolutely, continuing his attempt to see Eliana. He made no secret of seeking her out. She stood completely behind Nazim now, looking directly at the ground, unable to bear the sight of the sickening man before her. Nazim maintained his position. Kylus would get no closer to Eliana than what he was now, and he was about to find himself blind if he continued to attempt sight of her.

Avi looked over the parchment before turning to Nazim.

"Our agreement stands as we discussed?" he questioned Nazim.

"Emphatically," Nazim agreed, his eyes never leaving Kylus's face.

Eliana had no idea what agreement Avi spoke of, but in truth, she heard nothing, the words Kylus had just spoken continuing to radiate through her mind striking unbelievable fear in her heart. Eliana tried to silently pray for Jehovah's intervention, but her troubled soul continued to interrupt her prayer as the words radiated through her mind again and again. *"I will assume control and the responsibility of the inn, and I will wed the damsel who resides therein."*

Avi handed the parchment back to Kylus. "You did not read the amendment at the bottom of this parchment," he stated, pointing to a paragraph at the bottom of the page. "My grandfather, in his infinite wisdom, expected you to act as such and made sure that I was aware of what the ENTIRE document states before he passed." Kylus looked quickly at the paragraph Avi had pointed to. "

Let me help you since you seem to have trouble reading," Avi smirked. It states," he said, now raising his own voice to be heard by all, " ' that the terms stated above will be null and void IF the original heir to the property', which is me," he pointed out for clarity, " ' is able to propose an agreement with a man of his choosing who is willing to assume the role as caregiver of the property, as well as willing to provide safety and security to the widow' or in this case, 'to the maiden, who resides in the establishment, so long as the arrangement is agreeable to the living widow or maiden.' "

"Preposterous!" Kylus stormed, scanning the document.

"This document, Kylus," Avi continued to explain, "was created to *protect* any widow or damsel who was left with nothing, not to force them into a union out of desperation for their survival. Furthermore," Avi continued, "it was my grandfather's wish, when I return to the battlefield, that Nazim will assume the role as caregiver of the inn, as well as assume the care of Eliana, so long as she is agreeable. Nazim will be allowed to remain on the property until the time comes that Eliana weds a husband capable of providing for her. At that time, she and her husband will decide who is, or who is not, allowed to remain on the premises, and the care of the *entire* establishment will fall to the man whom Eliana weds," he finished. "And I wonder who that could possibly be?" he asked, turning with a smirk in Nazim's direction. Nazim's face continued to appear as if it were set in stone as he stared at Kylus, who was clearly in shock before him.

"You have no proof!" Kylus stormed.

"Actually," Avi spoke once more as he pulled his own neatly folded document from his vest, "I do." Carefully he held the document up for Kylus to view, the entirety of what he had declared written out plainly with his grandfather's signature across the bottom of the parchment.

"Kylus, why do you not put an end to your foolish attempts to run Nazim out of our town," Abner spoke up from where he had been listening. "This family has done nothing to you, yet you continue to torment them!"

"Yes, where were YOU, Kylus," Sarah called out now, "when Jasaphar lay pinned beneath our barn? It was Nazim and Avi who rescued him, and he is alive today because of them!"

"And where were you when my husband was away, and our goat continued to break through the fence?" Elizabeth said next. "It was Nazim who repaired it, and it was Reuben who checked on us daily until Heshputh returned."

"And Nazim saved my dolly from the giant hole," little Ada piped up from beside her mother.

"He drew water for my family until my arm healed," one man yelled.

"And he assisted me when my ox was stuck in a ditch," another man called out.

"You were here for none of that," someone yelled.

"You are never here unless it is to accept our penalties!" someone else called out.

"ENOUGH," Kylus yelled, furious at the outpour of community support this man had gained. "You are all fools for trusting in a man such as this! He is not of our people! He is not even Jewish! What he is, is a wandering vagabond who fights against the God of Israel! Do you know all the wrongs he has done? The sins of his past are too many to count!" he continued.

"His sins are *in* his past," Avi spoke up loud enough for any and all to hear. "Nazim no longer stands *against* the God of Israel, Kylus. He now stands *with* Him, and he *stands* with all of us, which is more than you have done in all the years the care of this city was left to you. And what of *your* past sins, Kylus? Do you need to be reminded of why you are here and not on the battlefield as was originally intended?"

Kylus looked around himself at the few men who stood with him. He then looked at the entire town standing with this family, this family he had grown to hate, with Nazim standing firm in the center of them all. Nazim did not smirk, he did not scoff, he just glared directly at Kylus with Eliana concealed discreetly behind him.

"This. Is. NOT OVER!" he stormed, mounting his horse. "All of you who speak against me will be penalized for your treachery!" He jerked his horse into motion as he and his men rode quickly toward the city gates.

Once they were out of sight, Nazim turned to see the town which had stood rallying behind himself and these people he now considered his friends. He smiled, nodding to all of them in gratitude for their support. He then turned his attention to Eliana, who stood visibly trembling behind him. "Do not make me go with him," she begged quietly. In her weariness and distress, she had missed the entirety of the conversation.

Nazim noticed how weak she suddenly appeared. Without hesitation, he put his arm around her, supporting her and urging her forward as they began their trek back to the inn. He felt her body continuing to tremble as he led her.

None of them spoke a word as they walked. They were within sight of the inn when Eliana tripped, her exhaustion allowing her to go no further. Nazim caught her, lifting her effortlessly into his arms. The day was not yet over, but he took her straight to her room, laying her carefully on her cot. Gently, he pulled the covers over her worn body, then knelt by her bed, praying for perfect peace and rest to come to her. He then rose, brushing the hair from her face and gently kissing her forehead before turning to go.

"Nazim," she whispered softly. He turned to see her, one lone tear seeping from her eye. "Do not let him come for me," she begged.

"Sleep now," he commanded her softly. "I will be right out here if you need anything," he assured her, moving toward the door. "I will not leave you, and he will get nowhere near you," he promised.

"Is she ok?" Uma asked, approaching him quickly as he moved back through the main room, where she and Avi waited.

"She confided to me at the falls this morning that she has not slept in days," he revealed to them. "She is utterly exhausted, both physically and mentally, and I do not believe she heard anything after Kylus made his ridiculous proclamation." Both Uma and Avi noticed the clenching in Nazim's jawline, a sign of how desperately Nazim was attempting to control his anger even now.

"Thank you for caring for her, Nazim," Avi spoke. "When will you reveal to her all we have discussed?" he asked.

"As soon as she has had some rest," he decided. "She is not in any condition for declarations of any kind. I would ask that no one speak to her again of the document or our arrangements. I want to make sure she is emotionally able to handle our proposition before she hears it again. Both Uma and Avi agreed, promising him their discretion. "Reuben?" he questioned, remembering how he fled from the scene.

"With Ares in the barn," Avi answered. "I will check on him now that Eliana is settled."

"May I?" Nazim asked.

"Of course, and I will walk Uma home when you return. Take your time with my brother," he encouraged.

"We will remain in here to make sure Eliana does not need anything until you return," Uma promised.

Nazim nodded his thanks as he exited the inn and moved to the barn. He approached quietly, seeing Reuben sitting in a corner, his head buried in his arms across his knees. Ares stood by him, moving only when he saw his master approach.

Nazim quieted the animal before he moved to settle on the hay beside the boy. Feeling his presence beside him, Reuben looked up at Nazim, his face wet with tears.

"It is not fair," the lad spoke, wiping his face, embarrassed at being caught crying by his hero.

"What is not fair?" Nazim asked.

Reuben looked away before he spoke, trying with all his might to control the tears continuing to force their way down his face. "First, we lost Grandfather, and now Kylus will take over everything. He will force Eliana to wed him. Avi will return to the battlefield, and you and Ares will leave Heshbon," he finished, burying his face in his arms once again. Nazim looked around the barn, wondering how much he should share with the lad before speaking to his sister. Finally, he decided that complete honesty was always better than half-truths.

"You are correct in what you say on portions of that, and incorrect on others. You see, you left the scene before we got to the good part with Kylus," Nazim began, gaining the boy's attention.

"What good part?" Reuben asked, turning again to look at Nazim. "What good could there possibly be?" he asked, sniffling and wiping his face again.

"Well, you are correct that your grandfather is no longer with us, and though that does not feel very good, the good part of that is that we have not 'lost' him. According to what your family has taught me, we know exactly where he is," Nazim pointed out.

Reuben continued to watch him as he continued. "And Avi will return to the battlefield as you stated, but the good part of that is that Avi is doing what Jehovah requires of him, it is his sworn duty, and he fights for the God we serve," Nazim continued. "But you are terribly incorrect that Kylus will take over everything and force Eliana to wed him."

"But Kylus had a document that stated," Reuben began, interrupting him.

"But, you see," Nazim continued, "there was an additional paragraph on that document that Kylus had failed to read, as well as a parchment Avi had that had been signed by your grandfather, and that is the really good part," Nazim continued. Reuben watched him intently. "You see, that paragraph gives ME the right to remain at the inn, to become caretaker of it, and the right to take care of both you and your sister."

Reuben began to breathe quickly, wondering if he had heard Nazim correctly. The look on Nazim's face confirmed that he had. Reuben bolted up straight, looking at Nazim in amazement. Before he could speak, Nazim held up his hand. "I did not say any of that would happen," he clarified, "I have not yet spoken to your sister about it. She has to agree to the arrangement. She is very tired and is resting now, but if she will allow me, Reuben, I would be honored to remain here and take care of things."

Reuben threw himself into Nazim's arms. "Praise be to Jehovah!" the boy cried out. "I am so thankful for you, Nazim," he cried, unashamed now of his tears. "I know Eliana will allow you to remain with us!" he stated excitedly. "She is *very* fond of you, you know."

"Did Eliana tell you that?" Nazim asked with a laugh.

"She did not have to. She has never been good at hiding from her face what is inside her heart," he whispered quietly. Nazim laughed at Reuben's observation of his sister. Suddenly the boy pulled back, wiping what remained of the tears from his face with his tunic. "May I please know when you and Eliana are to wed so that I can tell Thomas that you are to be my brother?" he requested. "I have prayed for you to be my brother since I have known you!"

Nazim could not help himself and laughed at the boy's excitement. "Slow down, Reuben!" he advised, quietly. "Your sister and I have never spoken of marriage." The boy's face fell.

"But if you remain, I am sure…" Reuben began.

"I promise, *IF* that time comes," Nazim interrupted him, "you will be among the first to know," he promised, a wide smile stretching across his face.

Before they departed the barn, Nazim had one final request. "Reuben, your sister is very tired, and though she was present for the entire conversation with Kylus, I do not believe she understood the 'really good part' that Avi shared. Please do not mention anything I have told you until I give you the freedom to do so."

"I will not," the lad promised, "but please do not wait too long," he pled, bringing laughter from Nazim.

Reuben paused once more as they approached the door to the inn, turning back to Nazim.

"Nazim, what did Kylus say about that 'really good' part?" he asked.

"He was not happy about it, that is for certain," Nazim admitted. "But there is nothing he can do about it," he leaned in and whispered with a grin.

"I sure wish I would have remained there to see his face," the boy laughed. Reuben hugged Nazim once more before they moved inside. Avi and Uma could tell that the boy's demeanor had changed as he bid them all goodnight and bounded to his room, a smile still on his young face.

"That must have gone well," Avi commented as Nazim entered. "I suppose I will walk you home alone this evening," he laughed, looking at Uma.

"I suppose that will have to be alright," she agreed, snickering. "The sun is low, but it is not dark out yet, I can be home before dark," she offered.

"Not after the day we have had," Avi informed her, rising.

Nazim bid them goodnight, then moved to check on Eliana again. It may not have been entirely proper, but God in Heaven knew that he meant no disrespect to Him or to Eliana as he crept quietly into her room. She lay quietly, sleeping in perfect peace for the first time in days. Nazim finally realized how exhausted he was himself. Content that she rested, he moved to his own room, but only long enough to retrieve a blanket. He then moved back downstairs, just outside her door, quietly pulling three chairs together, creating a makeshift cot for himself for the night. Leaving her door open, he sat just out of sight, two chairs holding his weight, and the other his legs.

Avi took in the sight of the giant outside his sister's room when he returned from escorting Uma home and could barely contain the chuckle that attempted to escape his throat. He popped the soldier's foot to wake him.

"What?" Nazim asked, with a smirk.

"Eliana is fine, Nazim," Avi whispered. "She has been asleep for hours now."

"I promised her I would be here while she sleeps, and this is where I am going to be," Nazim argued quietly.

"At least take Grandfather's room across the hall," Avi insisted.

"I will not," Nazim stated. "I will be fine here. I have slept in much less favorable conditions," he stated honestly, "as have you."

"Suit yourself," Avi laughed, moving to ascend the stairs.

"If she continues to sleep, you can start without me in the morning," he joked as Avi continued up the steps.

"You only hope that is the case," Avi whispered back quietly as he entered his room.

Nazim rose from his chair far enough to peek in at Eliana once more. She was in the same position as when he had first laid her down, but more importantly, she slept. Nazim rearranged his chairs and blanket before settling himself once again. Surprisingly, though his "cot" was not as comfortable as the empty one upstairs, he was able to rest quite content, knowing that he was exactly where he needed to be.

Chapter Twenty

Eliana opened her eyes and stretched her back. She was not sure how long she had been asleep, but despite her aching joints from maintaining the same position all night, she already knew that she felt better this morning than she had in over a week. She sat up slowly, trying to remember the events of yesterday. It was then that she recognized she was wearing the same clothing now that she had worn before she slept.

She remained on her cot, trying to focus on the hours before nightfall. She remembered going to the falls with Nazim, Uma, and Avi and she remembered sharing with Nazim that she had not been sleeping. She smiled as she remembered all he had said to her. He did not plan to leave Heshbon. She took a deep breath, knowing that it was that assurance that had helped her achieve what she had needed most, a decent night's sleep. Even if his promise had spurred from his concern over her wellbeing, at this time, he had no plans to leave their city.

She bowed her head and prayed for Jehovah to forgive her for her forlorn attitude over the past few days. She had allowed her worries and fears to consume her. It was only expected that she would mourn and grieve, but her life had not stopped because her grandfather had passed. God still had plans and a purpose for her, and she would do her best to trust those plans and to fulfill that purpose.

She also prayed, if it was Jehovah's will, that His plans for her would include Nazim. She realized she had fallen for the wandering soldier, and she prayed he would choose to remain in Heshbon, just as he had said, even after she achieved the courage to release him from the promise he had made out of concern for her. Though she knew he cared for her, she felt his heart remained with Rahab, and that he could never love another as he had once loved her. As she ended her prayer, she felt peace knowing that if Nazim did choose to leave in the future, God would see her through that as well. *"It still would not be easy, but Jehovah will see me through. It is amazing how a good night's sleep can change your entire frame of mind,"* she thought.

She readied herself for a new day and moved to exit her room, surprised that her door was already open. Thinking back again to yesterday, she vaguely remembered Nazim carrying her into her room. She had fallen, or tripped... and he caught her, she remembered. *"We had been to the market,"* she remembered now, *"and Kylus had shown up."* She closed her eyes, her stomach clenching. Quickly, she moved back to her cot, sitting down as her head whirled.

"There was a document," she whispered, rubbing her head, trying to remember more details. "What had Kylus said?" she asked aloud, but for the life of her she could not remember the details. She just remembered a disgusting look plastered across his face as she attempted to hide behind Nazim.

She had to find someone to tell her about that conversation. Moving quickly toward the main room, she exited abruptly and almost fell over... Nazim!

"What are you doing?" she asked, taking in his makeshift cot. "How long have you been here?" she asked as he popped awake and slowly began to lower his legs from the chair that she had almost knocked out from under him.

"Give me just a second," he requested, attempting to smile as he worked to lower his legs which protested every movement. His feet finally on the floor, he shifted, scooting his body up in the chair that had been his bed all night. His back protested more so than his legs had, popping loudly as he slowly rose to a sitting position. "I promised I would be here when you awoke," he explained arching his back, "so here I am," he smiled, pushing through stiffness and pain.

Eliana watched him in awe, realizing that he had stayed outside her door all night. "Can I get you anything?" she asked, wondering how he had managed any rest at all.

He took a moment more, stretching his back, then reached for her hands as she took the seat his legs had just vacated. "How do *you* feel?" he asked.

"I think much better," she acknowledged. "I slept finally, all night long," she said thankfully. "Though, I must be honest,

Nazim, I only remember bits and pieces of anything that happened yesterday," she admitted.

"You were utterly exhausted," he explained. "Sleep is exactly what you needed." Gently he kissed the backs of her hands before she stood. The gentle gesture sent chills up her spine.

"Let me get you something to break your fast," she offered.

"That would be amazing!" Avi called, bounding down the stairs from his room. "That was the best night's sleep I have had in weeks!" he stated enthusiastically.

"Good morning, family!" Reuben announced, now exiting his own quarters.

"Well, everyone is certainly cheerful this morning," Eliana commented with a smile.

"After the news yesterday, how could we not be," Reuben began but stopped quickly as both Nazim and Avi shot him a look.

"News, what news?" Eliana asked, looking at the men before her.

Reuben thought of something quickly. It was the truth, though not what he had intended to speak of. "The...news... that," he stated slowly, "Thomas's father's mare will give birth soon, and Avi is to obtain the foal for me!" he finished quickly with a wide grin.

"That is not in stone," Avi reminded his younger brother, "but we shall see. You must first work to pay the debt," he reminded him, "and you can begin today by helping Nazim and I work on the stoop."

It was enough for Eliana to be satisfied, and she moved toward the cooking area to begin a meal for her brothers and Nazim. The shock of finding Nazim outside her door had caused her to temporarily forget about Kylus and his document.

Her heart much lighter today, she threw herself into her work preparing a heavier meal than usual for the morning. Porridge, dates, fig cakes, grapes, and small pieces of meat adorned the table in only a little while. It had been ages since she had prepared such a meal.

Nazim looked around as he spoke. "Am I back in the palace?" he teased as she continued setting food before the men. "This meal is fit for a king!" he grinned up at her.

"Oh," she said, turning to retrieve the items she had almost forgotten, "apples, from the market yesterday," she smiled, setting the fruit directly in front of Nazim. It was then that she remembered that Kylus had been at the market with some sort of document. She did not wish to dampen the fair mood of the group just now and decided to ask her older brother about it a little later.

She made sure the men had their fill and then sat between Nazim and Avi to eat as well. For the first time in over a week, she was famished and ate heartily. The men devised their plan for the day, appreciating the sunshine and cooler temperatures. If nothing unexpected occurred, they should be able to get much accomplished. Eliana promised to have a light fare for them around mid-day as she began to clear the table.

"Avi," she called to her brother as the men began to move outdoors to begin their day. He turned back to her as Nazim and Reuben continued to move outside. "I do not remember much about yesterday," she admitted, "I guess I was more exhausted emotionally and physically than what even I realized, but I do remember some sort of parchment that Kylus presented to us at the market. What was in that document?" she asked, her stomach lurching again at the thought of it.

"Nothing you need to worry about just now, dear sister," he explained. "Just legalities," he assured, waving away her concern and patting her arm as he turned to go.

"What sort of legalities?" she asked.

"We shall talk about it later," he promised. "There is much to do," he stated with a grin as he moved through the door.

Uma arrived soon after to assist Eliana with some extensive cleaning they had planned to do while the inn was closed. As the ladies worked, Eliana quizzed her friend.

"Uma, do you remember the document Kylus presented to us at the market yesterday," she asked directly.

Uma paused briefly, remembering Nazim's request that they not divulge any information. She could not look at her friend just now, though Eliana waited for an answer. She busied herself running a cloth over the furniture on the opposite side of the room they were cleaning, pretending she had not heard the question.

"Uma," Eliana tried again. Her friend paused, now turning to her. "What was on the document?" she asked.

"Eliana, you know how ignorant I am of legal matters. Most of it sounded as if it was in another language," she laughed, turning back to her work.

"Eliana," a voice sounded below them, calling up the stairs before Eliana could press the issue. "Are you here?"

"Thanks be to Jehovah," Uma thought to herself, breathing a visible sigh of relief. "Hello, we are here," she called quickly, moving to the stairs to see who had come. It was Sarah and Jasaphar coming to check on the well-being of their friends.

The ladies moved down the steps, and as Eliana visited with her guests, Uma provided juice and fig cakes left over from Eliana's morning meal. They enjoyed one another's company and talked of many things, including Jasaphar's leg, which was healing nicely, though he still walked with a cane.

"Asa has said I may never get away from this cane," Jasaphar grimaced, thumping the stick on the floor.

"But at least you are able to walk, dear husband," Sarah reminded him. He agreed with a snarl, bringing a laugh from the ladies. Jasaphar had another reason for their visit and had requested Nazim's assistance in rebuilding his own barn once repairs to the inn were complete. Nazim had agreed and had even offered to do portions of the job for nothing.

Eliana smiled to herself, thankful for the work he had been offered. The people of Heshbon had come to accept Nazim as one of their own, and he had come to adore them. His acceptance of the job also assured his plan not to depart the city anytime soon. Eliana could not help but feel almost giddy and silently thanked Jehovah immediately. The friends enjoyed a nice visit and stayed longer than they intended.

As their friends prepared to go, Sarah looked to Eliana.

"You look much better today," she began patting the young girl's face.

"I was very concerned about you at the market yesterday," she admitted.

"You were at the market?" Eliana asked. "Sarah, do you remember…"

"Thank you both so much for coming," Uma interrupted enthusiastically. "We are so appreciative of your friendship. Do be careful on your way home," she smiled, ushering the group toward the door.

Finally, they moved outside and said their goodbyes to the men, Jasaphar commenting as they left once again on the fine job they were doing on the stoop. Nazim helped the older man back onto his wagon as they bid their goodbyes. Eliana took water, meat, and cheese to her brothers and Nazim as their neighbors left. The ladies sat and admired the work that had been completed as they all took a break to eat together. They did not pause for long, eager to get as much done as possible.

The men worked hard and accomplished much in just one day despite the number of on-lookers who stopped to comment on their work all throughout the day. Reuben was such a help to them that Avi agreed he could remain with them the remainder of the week and resume his studies once the inn re-opened. Things were right on schedule for that to transpire the following week.

At the evening meal, Avi took extra time to thank Jehovah for all He had provided and for his noticeable presence continually in their lives. He thanked Him especially for His peace and comfort over the past week, for restoring Eliana, and then for bringing Nazim into their lives, and for bringing Nazim to Himself. Avi then asked for continued guidance as they continued their lives without the wisdom of his grandfather, and for Jehovah's blessings on all that was to come.

Eliana kept her peace until Reuben retired to his room for the night much earlier than usual, the physical work he had put in that day having a toll on his young body.

"He worked as hard as we did," Nazim commented. "He is a fine lad," he finished.

"He is working for that foal," Avi laughed, "but he is becoming a fine young man," he agreed.

Eliana finally voiced the question that lingered in her mind. "I know you all are withholding information from me," she accused with a grin. "I wish to know, and I am certain I can handle whatever it is. What was on the document that Kylus presented yesterday at the market?" she asked the group. Each of them looked to the other before Nazim rose from his seat.

"Come with me, Eliana, and I will tell you," he promised. She looked very confused, wondering why it was Nazim who would divulge the information, but at her brother's nod of approval, she moved to begin clearing the table so she could join him.

"I will clear the table," Uma announced, placing her hand on her friend's stopping her from retrieving a bowl.

"And I will help," Avi promised.

Nazim moved toward the back entrance and Eliana knew where he planned to go. Together they silently made their way to her favorite place and settled by the trunk of the tree overlooking the stream. The sun was just beginning to set, and the last of the rays danced across the water.

"So, how bad is it?" she asked as he sat down beside her.

He paused before he began, searching her face.

"Nazim, I can handle it," she promised. "I just need to know."

He hesitated only a moment more before he began to speak.

"What do you remember?" he asked first.

Eliana looked to the stream and focused. "I remember Kylus appearing in the market seemingly out of thin air," she began. "And I remember the look on his face, so cynical and cruel, as he continually sought me out. And then I remember hiding behind you," she admitted as she reached for his hand. "Thank you for offering me that shelter," she said softly as he took her hand in his. "I know it was something unpleasant, otherwise my stomach would not lurch every time I think of it. I just cannot remember what."

Nazim took a deep breath as he caressed her hand. He looked to the stream as he spoke. "Kylus came to us with a document stating that the entirety of this inn and surrounding property is to fall to Avi since the passing of your grandfather. He also proclaimed, however, that because Avi is unable to care for it due to his assignment in the Israeli army and because Reuben is not yet of the proper age, that the inn will go to the town of Heshbon." Eliana closed her eyes and laid her head on the trunk of the tree.

"Give me peace to endure this," she prayed silently to Jehovah. "Please continue," she encouraged aloud.

Nazim did so, though he was reluctant. "Kylus went on to proclaim that because there is no one to care for the inn or the inhabitant of it," Eliana's head jerked upright, and she looked to him as he continued, "that he will move to Heshbon and assume the care of both the inn and of you." Eliana jumped up as her stomach lurched. She was about to lose the meal she had just consumed. It was worse than she had imagined.

"But there is more," he assured her, rising to stand behind her, taking her by her shoulders. She quickly shook her head, attempting to regain control of her stomach.

"I do not think I can handle anymore," she began as a tear ran down her face. "I was wrong," she stated as she held her breath, desperately trying to keep her meal in place.

"It gets better," he assured her as he turned her to face himself. "At least, I feel it does. There was another paragraph at the end of the document that Kylus had tried to hide, but your grandfather, before he passed, made sure Avi was aware of what it read in its entirety. The document states that if there is a man of the original heir's choosing, who is willing to step into the role of caregiver of the property, and if that man is agreeable to the widow or maiden who resides on the property, that he may take control of the property and the care of the widow or maiden until she be wed. Avi then produced his own document, signed by your grandfather before he passed, declaring his wish that I assume that role."

Eliana searched his face. "Nazim, what are you saying?" she asked brushing a tear that had escaped as it rolled down her face.

"I am saying, Eliana," he said softly as he took her hands in his once again. "That if you will allow me, I would be honored to assume the role as caregiver of this inn and to provide safety and security for you until you wed." He searched her eyes as she watched his face. Eliana could not help herself; she fell into his arms, sobbing uncontrollably. He held her allowing her to cry. Finally, her sobs abated, and she stood looking at him once again.

"Nazim, you are an answer to prayer that I did not even know had been prayed," she spoke honestly. "If I thought I had to spend my life with Kylus," she paused as her voice broke, unable to continue the statement.

"You will never be forced into a union with anyone as long as I am living," he promised her. His face was completely serious as she hugged him once again.

"If he only knew how secure I feel in his arms," she thought to herself. *"I could face anything so long as I am with you."*

"So, I take it that you are in agreement with my becoming caretaker of Avi's inheritance?" he asked with a grin. "You may have me around for quite some time," he warned her, "unless there are more surprises and an unknown suitor awaits our return," he chuckled.

Eliana looked up at his face, "Do not tease me, Nazim," she accused him with a smile as she began to walk away. *"If you only knew that the only man I would request to pursue me, is you,"* she thought.

"Eliana, there is something else," he began. She stopped and turned to face him once more. He settled against the tree, motioning for her to sit next to him again. As she settled, he began. "I have shared more of my past with you than I have with anyone else, other than Rahab," he said honestly, "I have told you things that I thought I would never speak of to anyone else. I not only feel drawn to this place, but I also feel drawn to you. I would be lying if I pretended that my agreeing to stay here was solely because Avi had requested me to and because of my growing attachment to Heshbon." He looked to her to make sure she was understanding him clearly. "I want to learn more of Jehovah, Eliana, but I also want to take care of you," he said, taking her hand. "I want to protect you, to look after you, and to continue spending time with you, in an effort to come to know more about you as well."

"I would love nothing more, Nazim," she said truthfully, looking into his eyes, "but if the time comes that you are no longer content here, please do not feel bound to any promise that you have made to Avi or to myself," she continued. "You know my wish for you to remain in Heshbon, I have already confessed as much to you, but I do not want you to be unhappy here," she reasoned with him.

He turned to frame her face in his hands. "I have already told you, I am not going anywhere," he promised again. He continued to search her eyes when she did not pull away. Slowly he began to lower his face toward hers but released her quickly as the sound of someone approaching met his ears.

"Everything okay out here?" It was Avi. Nazim chuckled to himself at her brother's always perfect timing.

"Yes, we are well," Eliana spoke first. "Nazim has filled me in on everything I had forgotten, as well as the arrangement the two of you have made," she informed him as they stood.

"And you are in accord?" Avi asked.

"Most certainly," she answered.

Eliana was the first to begin moving back toward the inn.

"It is settled then," Avi proclaimed, slapping Nazim on the back a little harder than necessary. The solider laughed out loud at his friend's clear message.

"What did Kylus say once Avi pointed out what grandfather had told him?" she asked as they walked side by side.

"There was little he could say," Nazim smiled. "Kylus made his proclamation in front of most of the town. Avi corrected him in the same fashion."

"I cannot believe that I remember none of that," Eliana stated as they approached the door to the back entrance.

"You were mentally exhausted," Avi reminded her. "Much has happened in a short amount of time. It is a lot for anyone to deal with. I interrupted the two of you because I knew you would be anxious to see our visitor," Avi grinned, holding the door open for his sister and Nazim to enter.

"More surprises," Nazim chuckled to himself as he breathed deeply.

"Garrick!" she yelled, running to her cousin, who embraced her in a fierce hug.

"Eliana!" he returned. "It is so good to see you. I am so sorry to hear about the passing of Uncle Eli. I requested leave as soon as the news arrived at our camp."

Suddenly, he forcefully pushed her behind himself, drawing his sword as Nazim entered the room. The soldier stopped in his tracks and held his hands up before himself.

"Garrick, put your sword away," Eliana urged. "This is Nazim, and..."

"Then my assumptions are correct," he spat. "He looks exactly like the man who has been described to us. The wandering soldier from Jericho who searches for Salmon's wife, a continuing threat to all of us."

Avi moved in front of his cousin and pushed his sword toward the ground. "Nazim is no longer a threat to our people,

Garrick. He *was* exactly as you accused; however, he is now our brother in Jehovah and a dear friend to our family," he smiled over his shoulder.

Garrick was not immediately accepting of Nazim's newfound faith, after all, they had been warned of this wandering soldier for years. Yet, after he was filled in on all of the events of the past few months, though still somewhat hesitant, he relinquished his doubts and accepted, on Avi's word, all that he had been told. It was decided that Garrick and the soldier who accompanied him, Hallel, would assist the men with finishing the stoop while they remained in Heshbon. Once the restorations were complete and the inn successfully reopened, Avi would return to the battlefield along with Garrick and Hallel.

"I suppose since the inn is temporarily closed, we should be in search of a place to pitch our tents, Hallel," Garrick joked.

"Do not be ridiculous, Garrick. You are family! You both will reside with us," Eliana informed them as she moved up the stairs to show the men to their rooms.

"I was hoping that was the case," Hallel spoke for the first time, gaining laughter from all of them. Soon the men were settled in their rooms, and everyone began to bid one another goodnight. Tomorrow would be another full day. Avi left to take Uma home, Garrick accompanying them due to the complete darkness now upon them and to spend time catching up with his cousin regarding things on the battlefield.

Nazim and Eliana were left alone in the dining area where they finished cleaning up from the refreshments that were served to their most recent guests. The full day began to catch up to both of them before they finally moved to retire to their own quarters.

Nazim paused as he stood outside the door to her room. "Would you like to me stay outside your room again?" he offered.

"There is no need," she answered with a smile. "I will sleep in perfect peace this night," she assured him with a smile as she entered her chambers.

"Goodnight, Nazim," she said softly as she gently pushed the door closed.

"Goodnight, Eliana," he returned. Nazim ascended the stairs, ready for his cot. For the first time in years, he slept that night in perfect peace.

Chapter Twenty-One

The next few days passed by uneventfully. Garrick and Hallel learned more of Nazim and his conversion to the ways of the Israelis, and both agreed that they genuinely liked the man and were relieved to have him on their side. Uma and Eliana worked inside the inn finishing the extensive cleaning they had begun. Everything was on schedule for the inn to reopen in just a few days, and the stoop looked wonderful. The men had done an outstanding job, adding their own touches to the structure.

Eliana and Uma, longing for sunshine, had joined them outside this morning. The ladies worked sweeping the porch, the structure now completed, while the men were adding more nails to loose boards here and there.

"What do you think, Eliana," Avi called to her. "Do you see anything else that needs extra attention?"

Eliana moved from beneath the stoop now standing in the street admiring their work. "I think it looks just perfect!" she praised them.

Avi had been in battle many times, but never would he forget the sounds of the next few moments. Everything happened quickly, though it seemed it was occurring in slow motion. A horse approached, moving much faster than what was necessary in their small town. Avi and Nazim turned together, attempting to see who was riding so recklessly. Suddenly, Avi heard the swoosh of an arrow flying directly past his head, just before it grazed Nazim's left shoulder, ripping through flesh and muscle, the surprise knocking him off balance before landing in the wall just behind him.

A second arrow followed immediately, this one hitting its target, plunging into Nazim's chest, just below where the first arrow had grazed his shoulder. A third arrow barely missed his body as Nazim stumbled into the wall directly behind him. The cloaked attacker never faltered and quickly reached where Eliana stood frozen in horror, dipping his body from his horse in an attempt to grab her as he passed. He caught her arm with force, pulling her toward him, then reached to secure her waist. Nazim's warrior instincts overrode the pain he endured. He quickly recovered, grabbing the dagger always at his side, and with all of his force, launched the dagger through the air in the direction of his attacker. The dagger lodged in the cloaked man's back, just as Nazim intended for it to. The shock of the blow knocked him off course, and though he managed to stay on his horse, he released Eliana, sending her crashing to the ground. The animal ran faster now, carrying the man swiftly toward the city gate, the dagger planted firmly in his back.

Nazim heard the scream he had so often heard in his nightmares as Eliana recovered and realized all that had happened. Seeing that she was free from the attack, he allowed himself now to slide along the wall which held him as he sank slowly to the ground. Blood from the gash in his shoulder, as well as from where the arrow continued to be lodged into his chest, began to pool around him.

More hooves approached and Avi realized that this rider was Reuben on Ares, in perfect pursuit of Nazim's attacker.

"GET ASA!" Eliana screamed as loud as she possibly could as she finally reached where Nazim sat against the wall, breathing heavily as blood streamed from the gash in his shoulder and from where one arrow still rested in his chest. Uma sprang into action at Eliana's command, tripping in her haste, then regaining her footing as she fled toward town, screaming for Asa as she went.

"Nazim!" Eliana screamed as she quickly jerked off the veil that covered her head. She began wrapping it around the gash in his shoulder to attempt to slow the bleeding while being careful not to disturb the arrow still stuck in his body.

"Your... face," he said slowly. "You are bleeding!" He attempted to reach out to her, but the arrow protruding from his chest hindered his movement.

"I am fine," she spoke quickly. "It is just a scratch," she promised as she worked to control the blood pouring from the gash in his shoulder.

Nazim could not take his eyes from the blood that eased from under her hair line and along her jaw. "I will kill whoever did this to you," he promised, his heart racing.

"Nazim, you must calm your heart rate," Avi instructed him. "Eliana is fine, I promise, but you must slow the pumping of blood through your veins," Avi applied pressure to the veil Eliana had wrapped around his shoulder.

"How bad is it?" Nazim asked, now looking to Avi. He knew he was losing blood quickly, and he worked hard to concentrate on his body and judge the severity of the situation he was in.

"You have a terrible gash across your shoulder, and one arrow remains lodged in your chest," Avi spoke firmly.

Nazim realized if any major organs had been hit, he would have been dead already.

He continued to try to breathe through the confusion that was attempting to come. "I will avenge her," he swore to Avi.

"You must live in order to do so, my brother," Avi reminded him.

Nazim swallowed hard, trying to control his breathing.

"The arrow needs to come out," he managed, reaching up to the shaft.

"Not, yet," Avi instructed, forcefully grabbing his hand. "Pulling it out may cause more damage depending on the type of arrowhead that was used."

Avi quickly moved to the arrow that had missed Nazim, still lodged in the wall. He pulled it free, bringing it to where Nazim sat.

"It appears to be a simple design, one that was intended to be lethal, but should be able to be removed without causing much further damage," Avi began. "However, to do so now would increase the amount of blood that you're already losing. We will need to quickly staunch the bleeding once the arrow is free," he explained. "And we must do the same to the gash in your shoulder."

Nazim knew exactly what he meant. He had never had the practice performed on himself, but he had seen the act of "searing a wound" painfully performed on other soldiers who were bleeding profusely on the battlefield.

"Can you help me inside?" Nazim asked, preferring not to have an audience for what needed to happen.

"Eliana," Avi spoke quickly to his sister. "Are you certain you are okay?"

"Yes, I am fine," she promised. "What can I do?" she asked, desperate to do something to help Nazim.

"I need you to gather some supplies. We need a bowl of warm water and several fresh cloths," he began. "I also need something very hard that Nazim can bite down on, and the knife that you use for carving vegetables. Place those items in the cooking area, and make sure the fire is hot in the hearth," he instructed.

She had no idea what was going to happen, but she understood her assignment and moved quickly to perform the task asked of her. Avi assisted Nazim to his feet, and though the world attempted to spin, Nazim was able to regain his balance and assist Avi in getting himself inside.

Asa arrived quickly and assessed the situation.

"Avi is correct," he agreed. "Removing the arrow and then searing the wound by burning is the best option we have. We have to stop the bleeding from the gash in your shoulder as well," he finished.

"Then let us get it over with," Nazim insisted.

Eliana had gathered all the supplies Avi had requested and stood watching as the men assisted Nazim in lying on the table, which she normally used to prepare meals. It was not an ideal situation, but they had to use what was available.

"Eliana, I need for you and Uma to wait in the main room," Avi instructed her. "And regardless of what you hear, you are not to enter this room again until I come for you," he stated firmly.

Eliana nodded her understanding, but before she left, she moved to Nazim's side once more. He tried to put on a brave face for her, but she could see the pain in his eyes as she bent to kiss his forehead. "My prayers are with you," she said softly as tears rolled along her face.

"I told you, I am not going to leave you," he reminded her as he attempted a grin.

"You promised," she reiterated, as she bent to kiss his forehead once more. She then moved quickly toward the door, looking back only once before she exited into the main room as she had been instructed.

Reuben did not have to go far before he came upon the man who had attacked both Nazim and Eliana, now lying by the side of the road. His horse had continued to flee though his rider had fallen from his back. Reuben pulled the hood from the man's head in an attempt to recognize the face that met him. The man winced at the motion, and Reuben noticed that although he looked vaguely familiar, he could not place where he had seen him.

As he stood trying to remember the man, Reuben knew exactly what he would do with his life. He would work to rid the world of men like this one. He would be a warrior like his brother before him and like the man he hoped he would be able to one day call brother.

He had only been standing there a moment before both Garrick and Hallel caught up to him. They dismounted quickly and moved to where Reuben stood.

"I found him this way," Reuben stated. "The dagger rests in his back exactly where Nazim intended for it to be." Reuben spat on the ground in disrespect beside the man who lay before him. He was not dead, but he was dying.

Garrick observed the situation carefully. "Who are you?" he asked forcefully, kicking the man's foot to gain his attention. The man winced and looked at him but said nothing. "Who do you ride with?" he asked now. "You have no hope of life. You are not known by this boy who is a citizen of this town. Who was it that orchestrated your attack on this family and ultimately sent you to your own demise?" he stated plainly.

The man began to stutter, blood now coming from his mouth. "K... K... K... K... Kylus," he finally managed just before he drew his last breath.

"Kylus!" Reuben yelled to his cousin. "Kylus did this?"

"Silence yourself, Reuben," Garrick instructed him firmly, his hands going to the boy's shoulders. "We will deal with this, and justice will come, but we must deal with this carefully. We only have this man's word that it was Kylus who is behind this, and now our one witness is dead. Do not speak what we have heard to anyone just now," he instructed. "If it was indeed Kylus who sent him, I will find out," he promised.

"This man suffered from internal injuries, no doubt from the fall from his horse," Hallel commented as he pulled the dagger from its place in his back. Hallel moved to a nearby stream, rinsing the blood from it before handing it to Reuben. "You pursued the attacker with courage," he praised the young boy. "You should be the one to deliver this dagger back to its rightful owner." Reuben appreciated the compliment, then looked quickly to Garrick.

"Nazim! Is he…" he could not even form the word.

"He was living when we left to follow you, but that is all I know," Garrick answered honestly. Together, Garrick and Hallel lifted the man, slinging him across the back of Garrick's horse.

"Hallel," he instructed. "Return to our camp. Our leaders must know what has happened and what accusation has been made. Spare no detail in your story but tell only who you must. We will wait for your return before we retaliate," he finished. Hallel nodded his head in understanding, then urged his steed quickly to head in the opposite direction of where they had come.

Reuben had ridden Ares hard and realized he had pushed the animal faster than he should have. He now led the horse, along with Garrick and the attacker's body, back toward the inn.

Before they stabled their animals, they moved inside to check on the status of Nazim. They were met with the tear-stained faces of Uma and Eliana, clutching to one another as they prayed for the man in the room just beyond them.

"Nazim, you know this will not be easy to endure," Asa spoke honestly.

"I am aware," he answered. "Make it as quick as you can," he requested.

"Avi, prepare the knife," Asa instructed as he placed a thick stick between Nazim's teeth. Bite down on this," he instructed.

Avi held the knife directly into the flames. Soon the dark blade changed to red, the extreme heat now distributed throughout the steel. "It is ready, Asa," he informed him.

Asa knew the arrow would have to be removed, but Nazim was currently losing the most blood from the gash in his shoulder. Quickly but carefully, he began to unwrap Eliana's veil from where it was tied around the wound, exposing the torn flesh once again. As he finished, he looked to Avi, who removed the blade from the fire and then quickly moved to Nazim's side.

"Dear God, be with him," Avi stated as he touched the glowing knife to Nazim's flesh. Nazim refused to scream, knowing that the women waited on the other side of the thin door, but he could not stifle the groans that left his body. He clenched the thick stick between his teeth as Avi continued to draw the glowing knife across the gash on his shoulder. The smell of burning skin and torched blood filled the room as the knife seared the edges of the wound together, successfully stopping the bleeding immediately.

Nazim breathed quickly, as Avi pulled the knife away. The pain was intense, but he had made it through the first of the procedure. Eliana's face swam through his memory, the cuts on her head and jaw being the fuel he needed to push through the pain. Asa gave him a moment, carefully watching Nazim's face as his eyes remained fixed on the ceiling above him. The pause was also allowing Avi time to place the knife back into the flame, where it quickly began to glow red once again.

"Just do it," he instructed, appreciating the man's consideration but anxious to get it over with.

Asa took hold of the shaft, still sticking from Nazim's chest. It took both hands, and with all of his might, he began to pull the arrow from its lodging place. The arrow moved slowly at first but began to gain momentum once Asa had freed it from the thick muscle in which it had been resting.

Finally, the arrow free, Asa looked to Avi for the knife. When he laid the red-hot blade once again against his skin, the stick in Nazim's mouth broke into two pieces. The pain from the hole left in his chest, along with the pain so fresh from the arrow being pulled free and the gash in his shoulder that continued to smolder was more than Nazim could quietly handle. He could not stifle one small yell that escaped his lips, just before he lost consciousness.

Eliana and Uma sat at a table, neither of them speaking to the other, spending their time instead speaking to the Father. It seemed like hours passed before the men reentered the dining area. Eliana jumped each time she heard the low groans coming from beyond the door and then sprang to her feet at the sound of his yell. Instinct pushed her toward the door, but Uma stood to stop her before she reached it.

Garrick sat quietly with Reuben, who was thankful for the noises coming from the other room. The sounds signified that at least Nazim lived.

Finally, the door opened, and Asa moved directly to Eliana, who kept her place and waited.

"I will not pretend his wounds are not serious, but Jehovah was certainly with him," Asa spoke honestly. "The arrows seemed to have missed their initial target. If the arrow which grazed his shoulder would have been just a bit higher, it would have struck his neck and a major artery. If the arrow to his chest a bit lower, his heart could have been directly hit. If either of those arrows had landed where they were intended to, Nazim would no longer be with us. It is my most sincere belief that Jehovah directed those arrows. Had Nazim not already become a believer, this would have been sure to make him one," Asa said plainly.

Eliana swayed on her feet and used the table to balance herself. "But he will recover?" she asked.

"Now that we have stopped the bleeding, his afflictions are not life-threatening, though I feel certain that they were intended to be. However, I will not lie, Eliana, he has lost a lot of blood," Asa answered honestly, "and, the burns he had to undergo in order for us to sear the afflictions closed are severe. I admit, I have never witnessed a man endure pain like that as well as he did. Make sure to keep the wounds clean, and his bandages will need to be changed, often. He will need rest over the next couple of days. Let him sleep as long as he can," he advised.

"May we move him to a room?" Avi asked. Asa nodded his head in acknowledgment, and Garrick and Avi moved to carry Nazim to the room Eli had once used. Once he was placed on the cot and settled, Asa prepared to leave.

"I have left plenty of clean cloths for you by the bedside," he told Eliana a few minutes later. "He is strong," he assured her, clasping her hand. Eliana turned her head slightly, and Asa noticed the bright blood that tinged her hairline. "Eliana, I need to look at your head," he stated sincerely.

"No, I, I am fine," she stammered, reaching up to touch the spot he looked to. She winced from the pain she felt as she pressed it. She had been so concerned with Nazim that she had forgotten that she had been injured. "He protected me," she remembered now, her voice catching.

Avi instructed her to sit so that Asa could examine her head. Asa then asked her some questions and cleaned the wound on her head and the scratches on her face. In only a few moments, other than a headache, a small gash above her temple, and a scratch along her jaw, she appeared to be okay. "I will return in the morning to check on him," Asa promised, "as well as you. In the meantime, my prayers will be with you all. Again, do not try to wake him until I return, and he will most likely sleep. However if he does happen to wake, try to get some water and broth in him," he finished patting her arm.

Eliana thanked him and then moved toward her grandfather's room where Nazim lay. Her family gave her solitude as she entered the room almost reverently. Nazim was still unconscious and lay completely still; only the rise and fall of his chest as he breathed indicated that he lived. She crossed slowly to his bedside, her heart breaking at the sight of him lying there, so strong, yet now, so helpless. His frame swallowed the cot.

His vest had been removed, and large white cloths covered his left shoulder and chest. His left arm lay by his side, his right resting across his torso. Nazim had been her strength for weeks; now, she would be his. She did the only thing she knew to do. She knelt by his bedside and cried out to her Lord.

"Father God, Master of the Universe, Ruler of All," she began. Her tears flowed peacefully as she cried out to her God. "I have been broken, and I have failed to trust you in recent days as I should have. Help me not to falter in my faith once again. Help me to trust Nazim to You. Please heal him," she begged. "Please touch his body and bring him back to full health. I need him, Father," she cried. "But I thank you for the assurance that I have now, that if he does not pull through this, that he will be with You," she paused to catch her breath as the realization of what she prayed occurred to her yet scared her to death at the same time. "But, Dear Lord, please, please, hear my humble plea," she cried, realizing what she had said. "Please bring him back to me," she prayed. She did not bother to close her prayer, knowing that she would petition her God throughout the night. She rose then, standing over the soldier once more. Gently, she brushed the hair from his face before leaning down to tenderly kiss his forehead.

"I will be right here," she whispered into his ear before she turned to go. She looked back at him once more before she exited the room. No movement, no indication at all that he knew she had been there, but she prayed that he knew.

She walked silently back into the dining area where her family waited for her. "Thank you all for all you have already done," she stated quietly. "He continues to sleep as Asa expected," she finished.

"May I go to him?" Reuben asked now.

"Yes, but do not disturb him," Eliana instructed quietly, hugging her younger brother as he passed. "He will be in a great deal of pain when he wakes." Reuben obeyed his sister and moved silently into the room. As he entered and closed the door, Eliana turned to Avi and Garrick.

"Do we know who did this?" she asked. "Someone from his past, perhaps? It is evident that this was a clear attempt on Nazim's life," she stated plainly.

Avi moved to his sister's side. "It appears it was both an attempt on his life and an attempt to capture you," he reminded her tilting her face to look at the small gash in her head and the scratches on her face.

Garrick stepped forward. "I do not recognize the man, but whoever he is, he has paid the ultimate price," he stated.

Eliana sat down quickly. "What do you mean?" she asked.

"Reuben followed the man who attacked the two of you," Garrick informed her. "He had fallen from his horse as he rode away, and I expect sustained internal injuries as well, though the dagger Nazim threw was planted firmly in his back."

"May I see the body?" she finally asked.

"I do not believe that will be appropriate," Garrick advised.

"I may be able to identify him, I know the people of this town better than either of you do," she argued, "and we also have come to know the inhabitants who were spared in our conquest of the land."

Garrick looked to Avi. "She has a point," Avi admitted.

"Take me to see who attempted to kill Nazim," she begged. "He attacked me as well, Garrick," she reasoned. "Do I not deserve to see my attacker?"

Garrick considered all she had said before he finally conceded, although it remained against his better judgment.

Avi led his sister to the barn where Garrick had placed the body in a vacant stall near the back, well out of sight of anyone who happened by. Eliana approached the stall with a fierce courage neither of the men expected. Upon sight of his face, she gasped and turned back to the men.

"Was it too much?" Avi asked, assuming her reaction was from viewing the body.

"No," she stated firmly. "I recognize him," she stated in shock, looking again at the face of the man. "I do not know his name, but he has accompanied Kylus each time he has come to Heshbon since Nazim arrived."

"It is true," Avi confirmed. "This man has been with Kylus every time I have seen him."

Garrick nodded his head, the affirmation he needed now complete. "This man had not yet died when we found him, and when I asked, he stated that it was Kylus who had sent him. But, Eliana, you said this man accompanied Kylus only since Nazim arrived. Why would that be?" Garrick questioned.

"I know the answer to that as well," Eliana admitted continuing to tell the men of the first time Nazim had come face to face with Kylus by the pools of Heshbon. "Kylus attempted to force me to return to the village with him, and when I refused, he made very rude remarks about my credibility. Nazim could have killed him then with his bare hands, but he withdrew."

"Kylus was too much of a coward to attempt an attack against Nazim himself," Avi accused. "So, he sent his minion in his place, no doubt promising a large amount from the town treasury once his evil plan was carried out."

"Town treasury?" Garrick asked, utterly confused.

"That is another conversation entirely," Eliana stated "but, Garrick, it is only a matter of time before Kylus realizes this man has failed in his attempt to kill Nazim. What are we going to do?"

"We wait," Garrick instructed them both. "I have sent Hallel with instructions to report to the leaders in our camp." Garrick continued. "Joshua must know of Kylus's treachery."

"It is impossible to keep anything quiet in our small town, especially something of this magnitude," Avi began.

"No one besides the two of you and Reuben know that Kylus has been tied to this, and I have already instructed Reuben to keep the accusation to himself. We will not speak of it outside ourselves until Hallel returns," he instructed.

"So, we are to plead ignorance if Kylus shows his face?" Eliana questioned.

"We will," Garrick acknowledged. "He is still considered a leader in this area, and we will continue to allow him to act as such until I hear from our leaders. I will act as if I do not know the two are associated. He does not know that the two of you have been able to identify him as one of his men, or that Reuben heard him proclaim that Kylus is who sent him."

They all agreed to keep quiet as they returned to the inn. Eliana moved behind the building to the stream before going back inside. Avi followed close behind her, Garrick continuing his path inside.

"What are you doing, sister?" he asked as she bent, picking plants by the stream.

"I burned my hand while cooking shortly after Nazim had first arrived, and he used the salve from these plants to cure the burn. It is amazing," she smiled. "I will use them on him now," she informed her brother.

"Eliana, the burns Nazim has suffered are not in the same league as burning your hand on a pot," he began, "and changing his bandages will not be for the weak of heart," he continued.

"Avi, I just identified a dead body and witnessed an arrow protruding through the body of a man I have grown very fond of. I will care for him as he would care for me. And I will do so using every plant on this bank if I need to," she said plainly.

Avi knew better than to argue with his sister, and he had not missed the declaration she had made without thought. He moved to the side, offering to hold the plants as she continued to gather more. Soon, she had as many as she desired, and together they moved back inside just as Reuben was exiting Nazim's room.

Reuben's face was firm as he approached Garrick.

"When you return to the battlefield, I wish to go back with you. I want to serve the Lord our God by destroying men who seek to destroy others unjustly," he stated plainly. "I want to be a warrior, like Avi and Nazim," he finished.

Garrick knew the lad in front of him was hurting and angry, but he also knew that he himself had determined at a young age to become an Israeli soldier. "You are too young just yet, cousin, but in another few years, if you still feel that way, I know our men will welcome you to our camp," he assured him.

Avi moved to him, clasping his shoulder. "You have shown yourself more than worthy over the past few days, my brother. Your work ethic on the stoop and your courage in pursuing Nazim's attacker, not even realizing who it was you were after, is commendable. In the meantime, you will remain here and assist your sister and Nazim as he heals. They will need you."

The assignment was enough for Reuben. "And train my horse?" he asked with a sideways glance to his older brother. Avi snickered at how quickly his younger brother went from a man of war to a fourteen-year-old boy.

"I suppose, as long as the foal is born healthy," he conceded. The prospect brought a smile to Reuben's face.

"Did you know the man?" Uma whispered to Eliana as she stood by her friend.

"I did not know his name," she spoke truthfully before she moved back to the room Nazim now occupied. She approached his bedside gently, looking to where this man, larger than life, now lay. The cloths Asa had applied were already beginning to show stains. Eliana wondered now exactly how she would go about changing the bandages, realizing she could not do it alone.

She summoned Avi to assist her. Eliana had never had a weak stomach before, but as she removed the soiled bandages, seeing the fresh burns across the wounds on Nazim's body it was almost more than she could stand. However, she continued her task, Avi moving Nazim as gently as he could while she carefully applied a generous portion of salve to the burns, then reapplied clean cloth to his chest and shoulder. He stirred as they completed the task, even the slightest movement and touch causing him extreme discomfort.

Eliana stayed with him, rubbing his forehead and praying for his comfort.

"The salve you taught me of will soothe the burn," she whispered to him. She knew he did not hear her quiet whispers, but it helped her to speak to him. "You are going to be completely well very soon," she continued.

The men and Uma decided that Uma would stay at the inn for the time being, preparing meals for the family and speaking to guests who arrived to check on Nazim. She had prepared a light meal for all of them to end their day, and Eliana had put broth on to stay warm in case Nazim woke. Though she could not stomach much, Eliana determined not to allow herself to sink into another depression. She nibbled on cheese and olives and then excused herself once again to sit with Nazim. He continued to sleep.

Eliana did not move throughout the night, except to kneel by his bed in prayer for his healing. She slept as best she could in a chair close to his cot, and though it was not the most comfortable position, she refused to leave his side.

Asa arrived the next morning, pleased with how well Eliana had done in caring for his patient. He was interested in the salve that she had applied to the burns and encouraged her to continue doing just as she had done. He was not concerned that Nazim continued in his sleep and continued to be encouraging to Eliana. "Jehovah's mercy is upon him by allowing him to sleep through the pain. He is strong," Asa reminded her again.

He then checked her head once more, pleased that the bleeding had completely ceased, with only some significant bruising to her face and the small gash on her head indicating where she had been injured.

Eliana prayed that Jehovah's mercy would continue with them all, thanking Him that her injuries were not serious and praying that he would allow her wandering soldier a complete recovery.

Chapter Twenty-Two

Soon, twenty-four hours had passed since the attack had occurred, and Nazim still had not stirred. Avi and Eliana continued to change his bandages as needed, Eliana applying more of the salve with each application of clean cloth. Even Avi was convinced the salve was straight from Jehovah as he saw the amazing effect it had on the burns after only one day.

Eliana left Nazim's bedside only long enough to pick more of the plants, pick at whatever food Uma provided, and to put on fresh broth for Nazim were he to awaken. It was almost noon of the second day when the visitor they had all been dreading appeared in the doorway of the inn.

"Family," he began sadly as he entered. "I have heard that more tragedy has befallen your household." Eliana could hear the sarcasm in his voice from where she sat by Nazim's bedside. Slowly she moved from her station and approached the main dining area where Kylus stood before her family.

"Jehovah was with us," she announced, coming through the door and pulling it closed behind her, "and He continues to be. Nazim is resting, but Asa expects him to make a full recovery," she stated as she moved to stand beside her oldest brother.

Kylus approached her, taking her by the shoulders and looking into her face. He masked his anger, until then not realizing that Nazim still lived. In truth, he had been told of the attack in Heshbon, but his man had not returned to update him on the situation. He had come hoping to find news of his whereabouts. "We can all hope, dear Eliana," he stated, patting her shoulders before she moved out of his reach. "Eliana, what is this?" he asked in surprise, looking at the side of her face.

"The man who attacked Nazim attempted to grab me," she informed him. "Nazim stopped him, but I fell," she finished.

Avi stepped closer to his sister.

"Is there something else, Kylus?" he asked, his face very serious.

Kylus looked shocked over the realization that Eliana had been injured in the attack.

"Praise be to Jehovah that you were not hurt more severely," he stated, sincerely. "God had mercy on you," he smiled.

"The man who orchestrated this attack best hope that God has mercy on his soul once Nazim is recovered," she spoke, staring directly into his eyes.

Kylus's smile faded, and he cleared his throat, clearly uncomfortable as Avi now stepped in front of Eliana, blocking his view of his sister.

"Avi," he stated as if he had forgotten that man was in the room, "now that Nazim has regretfully fallen to his prey," he began.

"Nazim has fallen to no one," Avi interrupted him.

"Of course," he corrected himself. "Now that he is unwell, he is unable to care for this inn…"

"And as long as I am here, I remain caretaker," he reminded Kylus, interrupting him again. "Of the inn and everything in it," he finished sternly.

Kylus exhaled the breath he was holding. "So, it would seem, yet your absence is surely felt by Joshua and the men you fight beside. I cannot imagine they will accept your absence for much longer," he stated taking a bite of an apple he had confiscated from a nearby table.

Before Avi could retaliate, Garrick appeared from the back. "Ah, Kylus," he spoke in greeting. "Just the man I was expecting to see," he stated as he approached.

"Garrick! When did you arrive?" Kylus asked, noticeably shaken that yet another soldier had arrived in his town unannounced. He choked on the apple before recovering quickly and continuing. "Things must be very quiet on the battlefront for Joshua to extend leave to so many of his fine soldiers at once," he assumed.

"Eli was my uncle, and I was granted leave out of respect for his passing and to check on my family," Garrick reminded him. "And now that I am here, there is some urgent business I need to share with you as leader of this area," Garrick announced, moving toward the door and leading him back outside.

"Of course, of course," Kylus agreed. Garrick led him to the barn, eager to see Kylus's response to the body he was about to show him. As they entered the barn, a less-than-pleasant stench met their nostrils.

"I ran across this man shortly after the attack on Nazim," he stated. Garrick had moved the body from the original location it had been placed so he could speak in full truth to any questions Kylus may present.

Kylus appeared to be completely astounded, and in actuality, he was, though not for the reasons he pretended. "I recognize this man," he admitted, "though I know little about him," he lied. "Other than he was an original citizen of Bashan. Who else is aware that this body is here," he asked, knowing that if Eliana or Avi saw the man, now dead before them, they would recognize him as one of his own.

"To the best of my knowledge, no one knows the body is here. I assume this is the man who attacked both Nazim and Eliana. It seems as if he fell from his horse as he fled."

"It would appear," Kylus pondered, "and Eliana commented that Nazim had stopped the attack being attempted against her. How did that happen exactly?" he asked, clearly curious as to how the events unfolded.

"Three arrows were fired at Nazim by a man on horseback, one grazing his shoulder, one hitting him in the chest, and the other missing him completely. The rider then proceeded to grab Eliana as he passed, but he failed when Nazim's dagger met his back," Garrick continued.

"So Nazim's injuries are life-threatening?" Kylus asked with hope.

"I can tell from your tone, Kylus, that you care little for Nazim. May I ask why that is so? Has he wronged you in some way?" Garrick questioned him.

"It shows?" Kylus scoffed. "Come, Garrick do not be naïve. He has wronged us all. Do not tell me you have become as forgiving as your family. You know that man is the wandering soldier from Jericho that we have been warned of," he pointed in frustration in the direction of the inn. "A wandering, reckless vagabond, seeking nothing but the destruction of our people. He is dangerous and a menace to our society," Kylus proclaimed.

"Yet, he is the one laying afflicted in his bed," Garrick pointed out.

"Surprisingly, yes," Kylus pondered, "and it is such a pity that Eliana was harmed in the process. A sure indication of how foolish any alliance with him would be. I am amazed the surprise attack on his life failed," he stated staring again at the body in front of himself.

Garrick's eyebrows raised in curiosity at Kylus's proclamation. He kept silent but marked the fact that Kylus knew it was a surprise attack. That information had never left Garrick's mouth. "Of course, I am alarmed that someone in our fair city would stoop to such lows, even for the likes of him," Kylus interjected, realizing he was speaking too freely. "Tell me," he quickly continued, changing the subject somewhat, "are you aware of when Avi is expected to return to the battlefield?" he asked, curiosity evident in his voice.

"What? Why does that concern you, Kylus?" Garrick asked, growing more disgusted with this ridiculous man by the minute.

"Well, with the absence of your grandfather and now that Nazim has fallen, he will be unable to care for the inn and the inhabitants of it, and I just wondered when I might…"

"Assume control?" Garrick interrupted him. "Kylus, I do not believe this is a conversation we should be having currently," he spoke plainly.

"True. Of course," he backed down. "How insensitive of me. With all of the chaos and discord recently due to Nazim's presence in our town, I have not been myself. Forgive me," he begged. "I will have some of my men come straight way and take care of this, Garrick," he continued motioning to the body. "Thank you for your discretion. I would hate to alarm the rest of the family knowing that Nazim's assailant is under their roof."

"See to it," Garrick instructed as he turned to leave. "Good day, Kylus," he said over his shoulder as he walked away.

"Kylus stated one truth during that entire conversation," Garrick thought as he moved. *"Nazim's assailant is under their roof, but he lives."* Garett knew with every fiber of his being that

Kylus was behind the attack on Nazim. He was eager for Hallel's return, ready to see this man hanged for the grief he had brought upon Heshbon.

Kylus watched Garrick walk away, wishing he had an arrow of his own at this moment. Then he stood glaring at the fool dead on the ground before him. *"How could you have messed this up!"* he demanded in his mind. *"You had one assignment. To kill Nazim and capture Eliana. She would have had no choice once in Bashan but to come crawling to me! You idiot!"* He kicked the foot of the man before him, furious that his plan had been foiled, then turned, storming from the barn.

"He is as guilty as Achan when he took the spoils of Jericho," Garrick confided to Avi once he had returned inside the inn. Garrick paused, as a thought began to form in his mind. "I am going to follow Kylus back to Bashan. I want to see where he goes and who he goes to. I shall return in a few days," he promised. "I should be back before Hallel returns."

"Do you need assistance?" Avi offered.

"I feel you would be better off here in case another attack is made. Kylus is now aware that Nazim lives," he advised. "And pay close attention to the whereabouts of the women," he finished looking around. He knew that Eliana remained with Nazim, but he did not see Uma. "Where is Uma?" he asked now.

"She is out back gathering herbs," Avi answered.

"Make sure to keep a close eye," Garrick reminded him.

"Of course," Avi agreed. "I still have a hard time believing that even a man such as Kylus is capable of this," he sighed. "Though we were never close to him, we *fought* alongside him."

"He is not the first man whose head has been turned by power and greed," Garrick reminded him.

"Be careful, cousin," Avi ended.

"I shall," Garrick promised, now slipping from the room.

Once Garrick had gone, Avi moved to find Uma, who was just then entering the kitchen. The sun was down, and he spoke quietly, the second day since the attack now drawing to a close.

"The inn is set to reopen in only a few more days," he began. "The stoop is all but finished, but I am most certain we should prolong the opening. Eliana will barely leave Nazim's side long enough to tend to her own needs, much less to those of anyone else," he said, confused about what to do.

"We should wait another day," Uma suggested. "If Nazim does not improve, then we will talk to Eliana. You all have taught me that we serve a God of miracles," she reminded him. "If He can part the waters of the Red Sea, and the waters of the Jordan River..." she let the sentence hang with a smile, shrugging her shoulders.

"Oh yes, I am aware," he chuckled. Uma had a way of making tense situations much lighter, and Avi appreciated that about her personality. "In truth, I am almost fearful of what will ensue once Nazim does awaken," he chuckled, before becoming completely serious once again. "When he learns that it was Kylus who was behind all of this...," he let the sentence hang between them.

Chapter Twenty-Three

Eliana spent another night by Nazim's bedside. She knelt beside him off and on throughout the night, pleading with Jehovah for his healing. During her last petition, she had laid her head on the side of his bed as she knelt. That was when exhaustion finally caught up to her, and she fell into a hard sleep on her knees. It was the wee hours of the morning when she felt his hand slowly searching across the top of the blanket before resting on hers. She snapped awake, moving quickly to look at his face.

His eyes were weak, but they were open. Immediately, she smiled as tears filled her eyes. She bent to kiss his forehead, and then his jawline, and then his forehead again. He laughed weakly at her display of affection.

"Easy," he finally managed though his voice was weak. "I feel as if I have been asleep for days," he admitted.

"You have," she confirmed, wiping the tears from her face. "I am sorry for my forwardness, but I was beginning to worry that you were not going to wake."

"I will sleep again if I get to awaken to that," he joked quietly.

Quickly she moved to fill a cup with water from the pitcher near his bed. Holding his head up, she encouraged him to drink. "Small sips," she instructed as he tried to gulp the liquid.

"So, it was not another nightmare," he confirmed as he tried to move.

"It was no dream," she acknowledged sadly. "You were attacked. One arrow sliced through your shoulder, the other lodged in your chest."

"That explains the excruciating pain," he stated, trying to move again. She offered him more water, which he accepted gratefully. "How is your head," he asked, reaching to turn her face to see more clearly. His face tightened as he noticed the bruising still present.

"I am fine," she promised him. "Only scrapes and bruises. Do not move," she instructed. "I am going to get you some broth and will be right back. She was only gone for a moment before she returned, a steaming bowl of broth in her hand. She gasped as she saw Nazim now sitting, instead of lying, on his cot.

"What are you doing," she rebuked him quietly. She did not want to rouse the entire house just yet.

"Only sitting," he promised. Even his slight movements had caused massive pain on his left side, and Eliana noticed new stains marking his bandages. "Nazim!" she quietly rebuked him shaking her head. "Well, while you are sitting, I need to change these bandages again," she informed him as she moved to collect fresh cloth and the plants she had come to cherish.

"Again?" he questioned.

"Yes, again," she grinned, touching his shoulder as she began to unwind the mass of cloth. *"Her gentle touch is worth the pain,"* he thought to himself.

"Does it look bad?" he asked as she removed the last of the soiled cloth.

"It looks beautiful," she said softly, beginning to carefully clean around the wounds. "These wounds will forever be a sign of the time Jehovah heard my plea and healed you," she continued. Nazim reached out with his uninjured arm to caress her face, gently touching the bruises and scratches as he brushed a tear that had escaped her eye.

"I cause you far too many tears," he confessed.

"These are happy ones," she argued, smiling at him. He thought she had to be the most beautiful sight he had ever seen. Her touch was soft as she applied more salve to his burns.

"Is that the salve I showed you," he laughed softly.

"Yes!" she smiled. "Remember that I told you that everything happens for a reason and that Jehovah can work all situations for good? If I had not burned my hand when you first arrived in Heshbon, you would not have used this salve on me, and I would not have known of its medicinal properties," she said excitedly.

Slowly, she began applying new cloths to his injuries. It was much easier now that he was sitting and not having to be held up by Avi. She managed to get about half of the bowl of broth into him before he waved it away.

"I am good for now," he assured her, lying back slowly on the bed. "Are you well," he asked of her taking her hand and holding it in his own.

"I am now," she smiled to him, "but you need more rest. You have lost a lot of blood, and you have endured much pain. Sleep now, and regain your strength. I will be here when you wake," she promised.

"Wake me the same way again," he teased, closing his eyes.

He was asleep before she finished brushing the wayward ringlets from his face. Eliana slept no more this night; she continued her night in prayer thanking Jehovah for unending grace and mercy at hearing her petition and answering her prayers.

Nazim did not wake again until the sun streamed in through his window. Eliana was still there, still holding his hand. He lifted her hand, kissing it gently. With her help, he moved to a sitting position once again.

"You know I cannot remain much longer in this bed," he informed her.

"Asa will be here soon to check on you," she stated.

"Do I hear voices?" Avi called, coming into the room. "My brother! You are awake!" he grinned, moving to Nazim and clasping his uninjured hand. "Praise be to Jehovah!" he rejoiced.

Soon, they were joined by Reuben, who could not contain his tears, as well as Uma. Reuben simply lay across Nazim's legs crying and thanking God for healing this man he loved as a brother. His praise brought tears to all their eyes, even Nazim's. After a few moments, Reuben contained himself and ran to his room, returning quickly.

"I followed your attacker and found him on the side of the road," Reuben announced proudly. "Hallel retrieved your weapon from the man's back, but he allowed me to return it to you," he smiled, handing Nazim his dagger.

"You pursued the man who attacked me?" Nazim asked. Reuben affirmed by shaking his head. "You could have put yourself in a lot of danger," he continued, "but I thank you, and I admire your courage."

The boy beamed at the praise lavished on him by his hero.

Soon after, Asa arrived, checking his wounds and asking Nazim questions about how he felt. Satisfied with all he heard and with how well his chest and shoulder were healing, he succumbed to Nazim's request to move about. Slowly and carefully, they helped him out of bed and to a table in the main dining area, where he sat and broke the fast with all of them. Uma had outdone herself with the meal. Eliana could not remember when she had felt such joy.

Once they had their fill, Eliana moved to assist Uma with clearing the table, leaving the men to talk.

"Has Garrick returned to the battlefield," Nazim asked, noticing his absence.

"Garrick is in pursuit of another man who we feel certain orchestrated this attack against you and my sister," Avi answered honestly. Nazim turned to better face him.

"I am listening," Nazim encouraged.

"Nazim, there is nothing you can do in this condition, and if I reveal too much just now," Avi paused but continued at Nazim's glare. "What do you remember of the attack?" he asked.

"Everything," he said honestly. "I have full memory up until the last time *you* touched a red-hot knife to the hole in my chest," he said slowly.

"I did not enjoy that," Avi promised, bringing a smile to Nazim's face. Avi then began to tell Nazim about the body that Garrick and Reuben had recovered. He told him of Eliana identifying the man and of Kylus's visit and his reaction to the body that was hidden in their barn. He also told him that Hallel had been sent back to their camp and that he would return soon with more soldiers to aid them in their accusation against Kylus.

"You cannot expect me not to avenge Eliana," Nazim remarked. "If Garrick returns with the news we expect, I will not rest while Kylus walks this earth," he promised.

Before Avi could continue, the women joined them once again, and their talk changed to a more pleasant conversation. Eliana noticed how quiet Uma had become, but when she asked her about it, she blamed it on being tired from all the work she had been doing during Nazim's ailment.

"Perhaps the conversation we could overhear the men having was disturbing to her," Eliana thought.

"I think I should like to go to my own home this evening if you think you can spare me," she said to Eliana later in the day. "I have not seen my parents or my bed in days," she laughed.

"Of course, Uma. You have been such a help," she hugged her friend. "I will have Avi walk you home," she offered.

"No, no, that is not necessary," Uma quickly declined. "There is plenty of time before nightfall, and I am utterly drained," she laughed. "Besides, Avi is busy catching up with Nazim. I will see you tomorrow. After a good night's rest in my own bed, I will be better than ever," she assured her friend with a hug.

Uma departed with a wave and smile over her shoulder.

"Where is she going?" Avi asked as he entered the kitchen.

"Home to rest," Eliana confirmed, a puzzled expression on her face. "Speaking of rest," she continued looking now to Nazim and dismissing her foolish notions, "you are going back to bed," she informed him.

"And this night, you will return to yours," he instructed. "I will not have lack of rest bringing you down again," he informed her.

"I promise," she smiled at him, "but first, your bandages," she said, motioning for him to sit.

Gently, she cleaned his wounds, applied the salve, and applied clean clothes once again. "Is there anything I can get you before I retire?" she asked sincerely as she finished.

"Nothing that you have not already done," he answered as he stood now, looking down at her.

"Eliana, thank you for your tender care of me," he spoke sincerely.

"The way you looked after me when Grandfather passed," she smiled. "It is the least I could do," she said softly.

"I have grown quite fond of you," he admitted, brushing a stray hair from her forehead and tucking it behind her ear.

"That is fortunate," she smiled to him. "The feeling is mutual," she whispered. Nazim gently kissed her hand before she turned to enter her room.

Retreating to his own room, he lay on the cot that had been his sick bed for the past few days thinking back over everything that had happened since he had arrived in Heshbon. He realized how rarely Rahab occupied his thoughts anymore. Eliana had replaced the emptiness he had felt when he had thought of her in the past. The bruises on Eliana's face came to his mind, and he felt anger surge through his body as aggressively as when he had discovered the scarlet cord hanging from Rahab's tower.

Nazim prayed now, for peace to get him through the night. Without Jehovah, he knew that he would not rest, and that was what he needed most right now. Finally, he drifted into sleep, Eliana on his mind and in his heart.

The next two days consisted of preparation for the grand re-opening. Nazim assisted as he could, weary from all the rest Eliana insisted he needed. Uma came each day and things quickly returned to normal. Nazim continued healing well, and quickly, and though he still experienced some tenderness at the site of the wounds, his routine was almost normal once again.

Today they were behind the inn picking berries for the special morning meal Eliana planned to prepare the next day. Nazim held the basket, eating as many of the berries as Eliana picked. She continued to scold him as she laughed. The basket was nearly full when they heard the sounds of hooves approaching in the street. Moving back inside, it was Garrick who met them.

Garrick was ecstatic to see Nazim not only awake but also almost his normal self once again. Finally, he sat famished and tired from his ride back from Bashan. Uma had food before him promptly.

"What did you discover, cousin?" Avi wasted no time in asking.

"Exactly what I had hoped," he confirmed as he ate. "Kylus had no clue I followed him. He went straight to his men, and he was very unhappy." Garrick paused as Nazim spoke up.

"So, Kylus *is* assuredly responsible for this," Nazim spoke, his question more of a statement.

"When I left, we were not sure you were going to make it," Garrick admitted honestly,

"And it was apparent once Eliana informed him that you had, that Kylus was very disappointed," Avi interrupted.

"It is clear that Kylus did not physically attack the two of you," Garrick informed them, but there was no doubt in my mind after his visit here that he had orchestrated the entire affair. Now, I am certain he had designed what he considered a perfect plan, and I have proof of it. When he left, I followed him all the way to Bashan. He met his men in an abandoned barn, right outside the city gates. I easily hid and was able to hear the entire conversation. He has no idea that we have tied him to the attack," Garrick clarified as he continued. "He admitted that he had hired the man to take out Nazim and that though his first attempt had failed, 'he will not stop until you are out of his way,' " he quoted. "He also mentioned that he had not intended for Eliana to be hurt, going on to say that she was only to be captured and taken to Bashan. Once there, he expected it would be him who she would seek out for rescue, seeing as how she knows very few people in that town, and then be indebted to him."

A bowl shattered as it hit the floor. "I am so sorry," Uma began kneeling to begin cleaning the berries and broken pottery from the floor.

"Uma, are you well?" Eliana asked, concerned as she moved to help her friend.

"I am; I am just clumsy today," she apologized. "I will have father replace this piece," she promised as they continued to clean up the debris. With the broken pieces cleared away and the scattered berries contained, Eliana moved back to the previous conversation.

"Kylus has lost his mind! Why is he doing all of this?" Eliana asked.

"Out of greed," Avi guessed. "A greed for power, a greed for control? With men like Kylus, you never know what their underlying motive may be."

"I never imagined him turning into this kind of person when Joshua approved his request to lead in Bashan," she admitted.

"None of us did," Garrick agreed, "especially Joshua. Kylus has aligned himself with survivors of the original Bashan and allowed them to influence his decisions. The very thing he was to prevent happening to our people, he has succumbed to."

"So, what now?" Eliana asked.

"Hallel should be returning from the Israeli camp at any moment," Garrick began. "He will bring others with him, the number depending on the situation there. Once they arrive, we will travel to Bashan together to act against Kylus and his men."

Nazim stood slowly. He had been quiet for the majority of the conversation, but he could stay silent no longer. "I have learned that of all the battles I have fought, never once did I achieve victory due to my own abilities as I had once believed," he admitted. "However, if you all expect me to sit here knowing that this man still walks the streets after what he has already done and plans to attempt again, you are sorely mistaken."

"Of course," Garrick agreed as he rose and clasped Nazim's uninjured shoulder, "but though you have healed remarkably, you are in no condition to take them on alone. I ask that you give yourself time to continue healing and give us time to plan our retaliation and assist you when you go," he acknowledged.

Even with his newfound faith, Nazim continued to struggle with his temper, and right now, every fiber of his being longed to go after that ridiculous coward immediately, alone or not. He had been a warrior much longer than he had been a believer in Jehovah, and his warrior instincts continued to run deep in his veins. He had never feared going to battle with anyone, and he would not begin to now just because he had aligned himself with these people.

"I will wait," Nazim spoke finally, "for three more days. If your men are in Heshbon to accompany me, then so be it, but if they are not, then I will set out on my own. It is enough that Kylus has continued to bring pain and unrest to the citizens of this town, but now, he has afflicted *MY* family. I will not rest until he has paid for what he has done."

As thrilled as Eliana was with Nazim's recovery, the thought of him going off to fight Kylus alone scared her to no end. She knew that Nazim had seen and done things far more than she could ever imagine, and she knew the warrior he had been rumored to be, but the thought of him facing Kylus and his entourage of soldiers alone was not something she could easily stomach.

The inn reopened, and the outpour of support for their family continued to astound them all. Nazim had been the topic of much of the conversation as their friends returned, each of them lavishing well-wishes and thankfulness regarding his recovery. Though he was ever polite and kind, Eliana sensed a tension around him that never wavered.

Nazim had promised to wait three more days. The end of the second day was now upon them. The evening rush had passed, the sun now low in the sky, and Eliana, Nazim, Avi, Uma, Garrick, and Reuben had just finished their own meals when they heard the sound of horses approaching. Garrick rose and went to the door, anxious to see who was arriving. He was more than pleased and slightly apprehensive with who he saw dismounting in front of the inn.

He backed away from the door, allowing entrance to the men who approached. Hallel entered first, followed by a man that Nazim had never expected and had honestly hoped he would never see again. Avi rose out of respect, Reuben out of admiration and Nazim out of expectation, as Salmon entered the room.

Chapter Twenty-Four

Introductions were kept to a minimum as the remainder of the men who had returned with Hallel made their way inside. Along with Salmon, three other soldiers, Asher, Zebulun, and Azariah had also returned from the Israeli camp. After brief introductions, Hallel informed Garrick that he had told the men of Nazim and his recent conversion to the beliefs of their people, now serving Jehovah and aligning with Israel. Eliana and Uma quickly prepared food for their guests while the men got directly to business.

Avi filled them in on everything Eliana and his grandfather had shared with him upon his return to Heshbon, as well as the things that he had observed regarding the many ways Kylus had changed since assuming control of both Heshbon and Bashan. Nazim was silent during the conversation, but everyone could sense his discomfort. Finally aware of the entire situation, Salmon stood, requesting a private audience with Nazim, who reluctantly agreed.

The two men walked silently to the edge of the stream behind the inn. It was Salmon who spoke first.

"The last time I saw you across the river, I feared for the safety of my family," he began, "but I also developed a newfound respect for you when you turned silently and walked away," he continued. "I want to thank you for that and for ending your pursuit of my wife."

"She is well, I assume," Nazim spoke finally, his voice sounding weak to his own ears.

"She is," Salmon assured him. "She and our son remain in good health." He paused before continuing. Finally, he spoke again. "I was quite surprised when Hallel arrived at our camp with your name on his lips. Especially when he secretly informed us of all that had transpired and asked that we return with him to fight alongside you and not against you."

Nazim looked at the ground in front of his feet. He knew the peace he was experiencing now was straight from Jehovah. There was no other way he could be as calm as he was, standing side by side with the man he had considered his sworn enemy, the man who was responsible for ending the life he had known in Jericho. Though he was calm, his pride remained hard to swallow. He clenched his teeth as he turned to face him as he spoke.

"All of the loss I experienced in Jericho came from your hand," Nazim said plainly. "My entire life. Everything I loved, taken from me." He stopped speaking as quickly as he began, and after a moment he continued, his voice now controlled and even. "I will not thank you for destroying my home and my life, I cannot," he said honestly, "but I can thank you for sparing Rahab and for leading her to safety when I could not. I can thank you for giving her the truth about your God, and I can thank you for the life you continue to give her now. My search to destroy your God eventually led me straight to Him. I have found a peace here that I did not know I needed," he admitted. "A peace I would never have found in Jericho. Yet, to say that my heart is at peace in your presence would be a lie," he said honestly.

"Nazim, we do not have to be friends to be allies," Salmon continued.

Nazim slowly shook his head in agreement, a small smile lifting one side of his mouth. "I suppose that is true," he conceded.

"We fight for the same thing in this regard: the safety of Heshbon and the people in it. Can we lay our past aside in this fight? Can you fight alongside me then, to rid this place of the man who is attempting to corrupt it?" Salmon asked.

"With no issue," Nazim confirmed. Satisfied with his answer, Salmon turned, moving back toward the inn.

The men made their way back inside in silence until Salmon spoke to the others with clear instructions. Himself, Nazim, Garrick, and Asher would depart for Bashan the following day. Because Avi was most familiar with the people of the region and could quickly identify anyone who arrived and was out of place, he, along with Hallel, Azariah, and Zebulun, would remain in Heshbon in case another attack was made.

As the men continued to make their plan, Uma slipped from the room, Eliana noticed and moved to catch up to her.

"Uma?" she questioned as Uma continued out the back entrance.

"I must get home before darkness falls," she informed her friend. Eliana noticed the tension on her face.

"I will get Avi," she promised, moving to go back inside.

"No," Uma said plainly. "He has much to catch up on with your guests," she stated, continuing to leave. "I will see you tomorrow," she promised over her shoulder.

Eliana watched her depart, slightly curious at her friend's poor attitude. Finally, she shrugged her shoulders, deciding she, too, needed some solitude. Nazim found her on the bank of the stream only a few moments later.

Moving quietly, he approached the bank he had become so familiar with. Eliana's back rested once again against the trunk of her favorite tree. He settled himself beside her before he spoke.

"Well, that was more than a little awkward," he chuckled, gaining a smile from Eliana. "I knew Salmon as soon as he entered the room," he admitted.

"I sensed as much from the tension I detected, but I was not sure how you could have known him before the introductions were made," she stated clearly confused.

"I had tracked them," he told her. "Him and Rahab, after the fall of Jericho, and I found them on the banks of a river," he informed her. "To my knowledge, Rahab never knew I was there, but Salmon knew. He and I made eye contact. Before I turned and walked away," he admitted focusing on the water.

"So, you did find her?" Eliana asked, the surprise evident in her voice. "But you did not make yourself known? I do not understand," she stated honestly.

"My bow was ready. I had a perfect shot at Salmon," he continued as he watched the water in front of them. "I could have ended his life and taken what I felt was rightfully mine. But," he continued after a brief pause, "she held their child. I have taken many men's lives, no doubt many of them fathers, but Rahab looked so happy and so content. She was at peace, and I could not bring myself to end her happiness."

"I know you love her, Nazim. And though I am not apologizing for the works of our God, I am sorry for the pain you have experienced," she answered sincerely.

"Do not be," he assured her. "That pain is what eventually led me to this place. To Heshbon, to the God you taught me of, to the peace and utter contentment I did not know I needed, and to you," he said looking at her again. "I will admit, however," he chuckled, "seeing Salmon again and not attempting to kill him…" he let the sentence hang as he joined Eliana in soft laughter.

They sat in comfortable silence for a moment before she spoke.

"I can imagine how painful it must be to love someone who is tied to another," she said quietly as she looked to the stream.

Nazim watched her for a moment before he stood, offering her his hand as an unspoken request that she stand as well. She accepted and stood, but he could tell she silently refused eye contact with him. He moved in front of her, blocking her view of the water and forcing her to look at him.

"You said that you *know that I love* Rahab, but you are wrong," he said honestly. "Eliana, I no longer love Rahab in that regard. She and I shared a sinful relationship, in a sinful time, in a sinful place. The love I had for her was built on sinful desires. We were very different people in Jericho. What we shared was destroyed as surely as the walls of that great city. And though I will never forgive myself for the way I treated her over the years and the things I said to her the last time we spoke, I can honestly say that I no longer desire to have a relationship with her. What I desire is a relationship with you," he said, taking her hands.

Eliana blinked away tears at his declaration, but she could not bring herself to believe his words. "Nazim, I do not desire your affection out of obligation and pity…" she began. He stopped her by placing his hands on either side of her face and speaking as he looked directly into her eyes.

"Eliana, stop lying to yourself. I do not love you out of pity for the situation you are in or out of any obligation. I love you for teaching me of your God. I love you for the fire I see inside of you. I love you for your stubborn tenacity. I love you for the care and concern you show to all those around you. I love you for what you have come to mean to me." He continued to search her face watching for any indication that she felt the same way about him. Perhaps it was too much, but he had to know.

Slowly he pulled her face to his, their lips finally meeting. He kissed her softly at first, then lifted his face. When she did not pull away from him, he pulled her lips back to his, kissing her again. It was an innocent kiss, not as passionately as he desired, that would be saved for a later time, but passionate enough that she would have no doubts as to how he felt about her. He pulled away searching her face, wiping away the tears that lingered on her cheeks. Her smile was the answer he needed.

"Eliana, I love you," he began again, "but before further declarations and plans can be made, there is something I must do."

"You are leaving with the others," she spoke with certainty, still breathless over the kiss they had just shared.

"I will not rest until Kylus has paid for what he has done. The reign he holds over these people and the threat he continues to be to you will end at my hand," he spoke with surety. "Jehovah Himself will have to intervene to keep me from you, Eliana. I will return to you," he promised.

Eliana shook her head in understanding and acceptance of his promise, but she could not help the fear that welled up inside her chest at the thought of him going after Kylus. Not because she doubted his abilities, but because of the evil Kylus had turned to.

She pulled away from him and turned toward the stream, watching the ever-changing water as it flowed across the rocks.

"I remember being afraid in the desert, just before the men would go into battle for whatever city it was that would not allow us passage. I feared that our men would not return. I feared that we all would perish at the hands of our enemy. But the day that Moses charged Joshua with the care of our people, he called us all together, and though I cannot remember everything that was said, I do remember this." She turned, reaching up to take Nazim's face in her hands this time as she continued. "Moses told us to be strong and of good courage…. the Lord, He it is that doth go before thee; He will be with thee, He will not fail thee, neither forsake thee: fear not, neither be dismayed.

"I am afraid for you, Nazim, but I am trusting that Jehovah will bring you back to me," she smiled. "I love you as well," she admitted before pulling his lips to hers once again. After a moment, she pulled back but continued in his embrace, resting her head on his chest as they watched the water. She felt secure in this moment as she listened to the beat of his heart beneath her ear, but she also knew that until Kylus was stopped, he would remain a threat to everyone in their city, including Nazim. They stood and embraced for only a few moments, both trusting their unknown future to their all-knowing God, before they turned hand in hand to return to the inn.

Chapter Twenty-Four

The clouds that hung over the town the next morning matched the dreary disposition that hung over Eliana's heart as she prepared to tell Nazim goodbye. She had worked into the night, preparing sacks of food and individual vessels of water for each of the soldiers who would be departing for Bashan. The ride to the neighboring town would take at least two full days, and the men would have to be alert along the way.

Reuben would not accompany the soldiers as he had hoped, instead being tasked with the assignment of an emissary. Salmon made certain the young boy knew the course they planned to take, and if anything happened in Heshbon before the soldiers returned, he was to bring the information to them immediately. The assignment was enough for the lad, especially when he learned that the foal he was promised had arrived and would be his as soon as it had been weaned from his mother.

Eliana quickly tucked more apples into Nazim's bag as the men secured the provisions she had so generously supplied onto their horses. It was evident that Ares was quite anxious to begin the journey he could sense approaching. Reuben had done well in his care of the animal, and Nazim stated as much. Eliana stood before Ares, offering him an apple and nuzzling his face.

"Take care of him for me," she instructed the majestic horse, quietly stroking his long nose.

Finally, the men were ready to depart. Nazim took a moment before he mounted Ares to speak quietly to Eliana. They stood between the horses, protected from view of the others. The small gash on her head was nearly undetectable now, and only a slight tinge of discoloration remained where bruises had once stained her cheek. Nazim bent to gently kiss the area, whispering his love and his promise to return in her ear before turning to mount Ares.

"Please be careful," she begged, holding his hand as he sat atop his horse. Carefully, he bent to kiss her hand before releasing it, then with a simple smile and a wink, he turned, steering Ares in the direction of Bashan.

His gentle action did not go unnoticed by Salmon, nor did the tear that escaped Eliana's eye as she watched him depart. Salmon decided he would approach the subject with Nazim at a later time as he hurried to ride alongside him.

"There is a force to be reckoned with," Eliana thought as she watched the backs of Nazim and Salmon as they departed. The men so alike in height and build, looked massive on the backs of their stallions. *"I am thankful they are now on the same side,"* she thought to herself.

She stood in the street, watching them leave, surrounded by a small entourage of her own. Avi, Hallel, Azariah, and Zebulun stood behind her, arms crossed, their faces stern, daring anyone to come anywhere close. Her surprise was evident as she turned around to return inside. She stood looking from man to man before speaking to her brother.

"Is this the way it is to be?" she asked, wiping her face. "Am I to have no privacy?"

"We cannot be too careful," Avi informed her. "We want to keep Nazim on *our* side," he grinned, teasing his sister.

Avi then instructed the men as to which stations they would occupy until the other soldiers returned with news that their mission had been accomplished. Zebulun, Hallel and Azariah would take turns watching the city gate, keeping it under close supervision at all times, knowing who entered and being aware of any suspicious activity. Avi would remain close to his sister and Uma, making sure they remained protected. The thought of Uma brought to their attention that she had not yet arrived.

"She has been acting rather strange," Eliana admitted shortly after as she sat at a table with her brother.

"I have noticed it too," Avi agreed. "Yet, she is a woman," he joked.

"Really, Avi," she argued rolling her eyes.

Avi took his sister's hand across the table from where she sat.

"Relax, Eliana. Nazim will be fine. He may be a different man than when he arrived in Heshbon, but he remains a warrior just the same. Those instincts run deep within him."

Their first patron of the morning arrived, interrupting them, and Eliana moved to gather the small meal she had prepared for the morning. As she stood looking at the steaming pot of porridge, she thought of the first morning Nazim had entered the inn. She longed for the day this would all be behind them and prayed her wandering soldier would return to her soon.

The men rode in silence for the first half of the day before Salmon, now in the lead, raised his hand, motioning for them to stop and gather around him. He dismounted to give his horse a rest and a much-needed drink at a nearby stream, the others doing the same.

"Make sure to keep your mind sharp as we travel," Salmon began. "If Garrick is correct, and Kylus has no indication we have tied him to the attack, we should have no issues, but we must not be taken off guard by an ambush now that Kylus is aware that Nazim lives."

He knelt as he continued to speak, using his knife to draw his plan into the dry earth.

"We will continue today until we reach Succoth. We should be able to make camp there for the night. Tomorrow, my plan is to reach the area close to Beth-Shan. We will then push on to Golan and then into the city of Bashan. We will confront Kylus and any men he has brought together, and then return to Heshbon. Does anyone have a better plan?" he asked, looking to the men around him for advice. At their silence, he instructed them to mount up and to continue. Salmon's plan now clear, the men moved quickly, each of them eager to reach their destination.

"You are certain they have tied me to the attack?" Kylus asked, furious. "How is that possible?" he asked, demanding an answer.

"I am not aware of how, sir, but I am most certain that an entourage of soldiers are now heading to Bashan, Nazim among them." The man stood in front of Kylus, exhausted from his journey. He had ridden straight from Heshbon, stopping only once to rest his animal and to provide the mare water. The horse stood beside him, more exhausted than he was. He rested his hand on her neck, attempting to calm her.

Kylus nodded his head in affirmation as another plot began to form in his mind. "You have done well, Oren. Return to your post in Heshbon, and remain there until I send word," he instructed as he began to form a plan.

The man did not move other than to look at the ground beneath his feet.

"Is there something else?" Kylus asked, his patience waning.

"My penalty?" he asked quietly. "Has my obligation to you been fulfilled?" he asked hesitantly.

Kylus snickered. This man was hilarious. Kylus's humor was quickly replaced by anger.

"Your obligation will be fulfilled when I say it is fulfilled," he spoke through clenched teeth. "You will return to Heshbon, and you will remain there until I send you word, do you understand?" he asked, quickly moving closer to him.

"I do, but you said…" Oren began.

"I know what I said, but things have changed," Kylus stormed. "Melech failed! Once Heshbon is free of that 'wandering soldier,'" he mocked, "I will then decide when and IF you will be free from your penalty and your occupation as my spy. Until that time, make sure your pathetic daughter continues to provide every detail necessary to both aid me in my quest to be rid of him and to continue growing the town treasury. Do you understand me?" he yelled into Oren's face.

Oren closed his eyes to the spit that sprayed across his face. He understood perfectly. He would be bound to this man forever, and even then, there was no guarantee that his daughter's reputation would be saved.

"I understand," he said plainly, and Kylus saw the hate for himself that radiated in Oren's eyes. Kylus backed away, a cynical smile playing on his lips.

"Do not tempt me," Kylus reminded him slowly. "You original citizens of Heshbon are fortunate that we allowed you to live at all, much less continue to dwell among us. It is no fault of my own that your daughter so enjoys the company of our Israeli people that she continues to be so careless with her affections. Especially when it comes to the men of the area."

"My daughter is innocent," Oren defended.

"Perhaps," he conceded, "but how easy it would be to convince the patrons of Heshbon otherwise," he smirked. "Everyone has seen her around town with multiple suitors. And how would your sweet little wife feel if her daughter were to come to be regarded as nothing more than the town harlot? None of you could ever show your face in public again. Your business would fail; your entire family would be ruined; you would lose *every*thing. And forget ever finding anyone suitable who would be willing to marry her."

Oren bowed his head defeated. Kylus chuckled as he turned away, dismissing him once again from his presence. He had work to do, and he was done with this wretched man.

Oren turned to go, his heart breaking in two. How had he allowed himself to get into this mess? His mind went to his daughter, and he closed his eyes once again. There was simply no other solution. He knew she was innocent, but her playful disposition and coy attitude toward men that they had always found so harmless, had now allowed room for questions regarding her integrity. He had told her that she could discontinue the charade, that she could be the friend to the people of Heshbon that they believed she was, but Uma had no choice. She would have to continue bringing him any information he could use that would be beneficial to Kylus.

The night was pleasant, but Nazim could not shake the feeling of apprehension that remained lodged in his chest. He sat alone by the fire, assuming the rest of his party had retired for the night. He had offered to take the first watch, coveting the time alone to collect his thoughts. He could not fathom the plan that had been orchestrated, by none other than Jehovah, that had brought him to this place and this time. Never in a million lives would he have imagined he would be riding alongside Salmon. As if he had been summoned, that man seated himself now beside Nazim.

"I cannot imagine what must be in your head tonight," Salmon chuckled quietly. Nazim continued to stare into the night, allowing a small smile to lift one corner of his mouth. "Seeing as how we are not friends, but only in a temporary alliance, feel free to share your thoughts," Salmon spoke again, "especially if they concern my wife," he finished plainly. Nazim turned his head to look at the man beside him but still did not speak. He looked at him for only a moment before he directed his gaze into the darkness once again. The men were silent for several moments before Nazim finally gave voice to the thoughts that consumed him.

"I should be dead right now," Nazim began. "Eliana continually told me that Jehovah had a purpose in sparing my life. From many battles, from the destruction of Jericho, from the attack in Heshbon, the list goes on and on," he paused briefly before he continued. "I am still learning of the ways of Jehovah and how to honor Him, but I will do my best to serve Him for the rest of my days," he stated plainly, "to fulfill whatever purpose He has for me, but I harbor so many regrets." He paused for another moment before he could continue, "Yet, nothing so great as the careless way I treated Rahab. Especially my treatment of her during the last conversation we shared," he admitted.

Salmon looked at Nazim's profile as he continued staring into the darkness, wondering himself how he could sit so close to this man yet be filled with such peace. He took a deep breath before he spoke. "I know my wife's former lifestyle does not match up to the woman that she is now," he began, "but I also know that she continues to pray for you every night." Nazim turned his face to him, shame and regret marking his features. "Rahab spared little from me of the life the two of you shared in Jericho," Salmon said honestly, "including the last conversation you spoke of. And though I regret the pain your words caused her; I feel they were necessary for her to hear. I feel that without that conversation, I may have never convinced her to leave with me," he said honestly. Nazim closed his eyes at the painful memory and of Salmon's perception of it. "In fact, she has told me as much," Salmon continued. "She feels it was Jehovah's way of clarifying the choice she was to make, and because of that, she has forgiven you for the hurt you caused her, and she prays every night that you would somehow come to find our God."

Nazim could not hide the relief that he felt lift from his shoulders at Salmon's words. He breathed deeply as he opened his eyes to look at Salmon once again. Salmon smiled at the man across from him. A true warrior who, at this moment, looked as innocent as a mere boy who had been forgiven of a grievous wrong.

"I am not foolish enough to welcome you into our camp and to tell her yourself," Salmon laughed, "but I am eager to report to her that I feel sure from the witness I have heard and from what I have seen for myself that her prayers have been answered."

Nazim looked at him, unable to speak, only acknowledging with a shake of his head how much that would mean to him. Finally, he swallowed hard as he looked back into the darkness. "Can I assume that another damsel has now captured your attention?" Salmon asked plainly.

Nazim scoffed as he looked from Salmon past the fire once more.

"Eliana is quite a woman," he admitted clearing his throat, "and one I would be honored to have as my wife if she will have me once this is over," he confirmed. Salmon slapped his shoulder, laughing with him. "Easy," Nazim joked, "that is almost a friendly gesture."

"Perhaps someday we may consider ourselves as such," Salmon agreed.

Chapter Twenty-Five

The rest of the journey was spent with one target in mind. Kylus. The men arrived in Bashan two days later, just as Salmon had planned. They could sense the tension among the people as they rode into town. Nazim recognized no one, though his presence was the most heeded as the men dismounted. Salmon whispered to him as they tied their horses. "It appears they are not terribly surprised at our arrival. That concerns me somewhat," he confided over his shoulder as he moved toward an inn. "Let me do the talking," he instructed his men before they entered. "We must be discreet to gain the information we seek."

As they moved inside, memories flooded back into Nazim's mind from the last time he was in this very place. He had not recognized it until now as the same establishment he had visited on his former trip to Bashan when he was trying to discover information on the Israelis who threatened Jericho.

A cluster of activity caught their attention as a portly man jumped up from his place at a table, knocking his chair over in the process. He stared at Nazim, never taking his eyes from him, as he ran over patrons and tripped over his own feet in his haste to leave.

"A friend of yours?" Salmon asked with little concern. Nazim shrugged his shoulders, recognizing him now as the man who had fed him the information that the Israelis had advanced and that Jericho had been placed under lockdown. Their last meeting had been a bit hostile.

"Salmon!" an older gentleman smiled in mock surprise. "What brings you back to Bashan?" he asked as he approached, embracing his friend.

"It is good to see you, Edom," Salmon returned. "You remember Garrick and Asher," he motioned to his men.

"Of course! The finest of men," Edom returned before directing his attention nervously to Nazim.

"We could use a meal," Salmon continued ignoring his discomfort. Edom continued to stare at Nazim who stood firmly beside Salmon with his face set and his hand resting on the dagger by his belt. Salmon cleared his throat, attempting to gain the innkeeper's attention. Quickly, Edom snapped from his trance and pointed to an unoccupied table.

"Of course, of course. You must be famished and eager to get on your way," he spoke as he invited them to sit.

The men enjoyed a hot meal and small talk with the patrons of Bashan who passed by their table, many of them commenting on how good it was to see them again. It was evident that their presence made the citizens extremely uncomfortable. Many of them left quickly after the soldier's arrival. Nazim remained silent throughout the meal. Finally, Salmon posed the question they had been waiting on.

"Edom, we come in search of Kylus," he said finally. "Do you know his whereabouts?" Edom cleared his throat and looked to another man. Salmon recognized him as well. "Jeroboam?" Salmon questioned, raising his eyebrows as he directed his attention to the man who had stood quietly by.

"Salmon, we are not looking for any trouble," Jeroboam answered quietly.

"Trouble? Why would you think I was seeking out Kylus due to a problem?" Salmon asked.

"Well," Edom began, "neither of us can rightfully say exactly where he may or may not be… Bashan is not exactly what you would consider a small town, and although he typically dwells…"

"Enough!" Nazim spoke loudly as he stood, pulling his dagger from the sheath at his side. "I seek no quarrel with any of you, but we demand to know the location of Kylus," he finished.

Salmon stood slowly, laying his hand on Nazim's shoulder with a sigh. "That is not exactly discreet," he informed him. Nazim clenched his teeth and returned his dagger to his side. Salmon stepped around him, speaking with authority but without hostility.

"Edom. Jeroboam. If you know the whereabouts of Kylus, I need you to inform me immediately. No trouble will come to you," he assured them.

It was Jeroboam who finally spoke. "Salmon, none of us can afford a penalty to come down on us," he said honestly, "but I have always trusted you." Salmon approached him, his hands on his hips, firm but disarming. Jeroboam spoke only loud enough for those nearest him to hear. "Word came to Kylus that an entourage of soldiers were coming for him, accompanied by the wandering soldier we have all been warned of," he continued, glancing toward Nazim. "We were not sure why; we assume it is because of the righteous tributes and penalties he has been executing on all of us. But at any rate, Kylus assembled his men quickly, original patrons of Bashan most of them, and they have fled the city. He threatened any of us who breathed a word of his exit."

"Who brought the information to Kylus?" Garrick asked.

"That I do not know," Jeroboam answered honestly. "They have all been gone for a couple of days," he informed them.

"Do you know where they went or even which way they headed?" Salmon asked.

"Heshbon," Nazim guessed, moving quickly toward the door. If Kylus suspected an entourage approached, including myself, he would assume the town was unprotected."

"I fear you may be correct," Salmon agreed.

Asher spoke next. "Would we not have passed them on the way here?" he asked. "We came straight from that very city."

"Not if they went through Ramoth-Gilead and Rabbah," Garrick confirmed. "They would have rather gone the long way around than take the risk of running into us," he stated directly to Salmon, "even though that route would take at least one, maybe two more days' time to travel."

"Asher, Garrick, remain here in Bashan until you hear from me," Salmon instructed as he left a handful of coins on the table and moved toward the door. "If Kylus returns, these people will need protection. Protect them at any cost," he spoke plainly. "Nazim, you are with me," he finished as he mounted his horse.

Nazim was already atop Ares, turning him back in the direction they had come. The feeling of dread he had experienced at his descent from Bashan before descended upon him again now. This time, he knew Jehovah was on his side, yet he could not stop the sense of fear that enveloped every portion of his being at the thought of potentially losing everything he loved once again.

The men had only been gone for four days, but Eliana felt as if it had been months since they had left. She remained in a constant state of prayer for each of them, and her heart ached at the thought of the danger they were potentially in. Avi continued to encourage her, reminding her of the warrior Nazim was, and he was even more protected now that he served their God and was in the company of their Israeli soldiers.

Uma had sent word that she was unwell and had not returned to the inn since before the men had left for Bashan. Eliana had decided that after the morning rush today, she would go to Uma's house to make sure she was okay. She missed her friend and could use her company to distract her mind from tireless wondering.

Though all of their patrons remained positive, the unrest that lingered since the attack on Nazim and Eliana was hard to ignore. Eliana tried hard to be uplifting to their friends who visited on a daily basis, and Avi was a constant help, but Nazim's absence was a reminder that things remained unsettled.

Finally, the morning rush was over, and the last of their visitors had exited. Eliana gathered fresh bread, berries, and a small fig cake into a basket in preparation to take to Uma.

"Where are you going?" Avi asked as she moved to exit the inn.

"I am going to check on Uma. Something is not right," she informed him.

"Give me a moment, and I will accompany you," he instructed.

"Avi, honestly," Eliana pleaded. "Perhaps she needs to speak with me, maybe even about you," she continued. "It would be rather difficult if you are present."

Avi looked at her, a puzzled expression on his handsome face. "What could she possibly have to say about me that she could not divulge in my presence?" he asked.

Eliana rolled her eyes. "If I must be accompanied, allow Reuben to go," she begged. Avi was not pleased with the idea, but he also knew that his sister could be very stubborn. There was a chance were he not to concede, that she would sneak away on her own.

"Fine, though mark my words that I am not at peace with it," he informed her. Zebulun will also follow close behind, remain in the area of Uma's residence, and then follow as you return. Do you understand?" he asked.

"Yes, fine," Eliana agreed with a sigh. "But I must go quickly, I have the evening meal to prepare. I thought you could possibly handle the mid-day fare," she suggested with a sly smile.

"I suppose," he agreed, "but return quickly," he instructed.

In less than an hour, Eliana stood on the steps that led into Uma's home. Reuben was beside her, Zebulun making himself scarce behind the barn. Uma's mother answered the door.

"Hello, Talia," Eliana smiled as the door slowly began to crack open. "I came to check on Uma."

Talia looked to the ground in front of Eliana, never opening the door wide enough for Eliana to see inside. "I am afraid she continues to feel poorly," Talia answered, still refusing to look at Eliana's face. "I will let her know that you came by to check on her," she promised as she began to push the door closed.

Eliana reached out, placing her hand on the door. "I brought her some things to make her feel better," Eliana insisted. "May I see her?" she asked.

"I do not think that is a good idea," Talia spoke quietly, reaching through the opening to take the basket Eliana held out to her, "but I will certainly give her these things and let her know you were inquiring as to her well-being. Thank you for your visit, Eliana," she continued as she closed the door completely.

Eliana stood staring at the closed portal, unsure of what to make of the entire affair.

"Perhaps she was afraid Uma had something that is contagious," Reuben spoke, attempting to comfort his older sister.

Eliana shook her head as they turned to go. "I do not believe that is it," she answered him. "I feel that something is very wrong here," she continued. They made their way silently back toward the inn, Zebulun close behind them.

Upon their return, Eliana described the entirety of the visit to Avi. "Talia has always been extremely kind," Eliana explained.

"She has never been so unwelcoming before. Something is not right," she concluded.

"If Uma has not returned by the end of the week, I will go to their home myself," Avi decided. "She has been acting very strange lately."

"Avi," Eliana began deciding to voice the question that had been plaguing her thoughts, "forgive me for being impertinent, but did something happen between the two of you?" she asked carefully.

Avi looked at his sister thoughtfully. "You are not being impertinent, sister," he began, "you are concerned for your friend. Uma and I have grown close as of late," he confirmed, "but we did so with the understanding that I will be returning to the battlefield. We have made no promises, no declarations, she was not misled. Nor was I," he stated with a chuckle. "Uma has made it quite clear that she is not fond of the idea of 'waiting for a wayward soldier to return home,'" he quoted.

Eliana did not find the humor in the statement that Avi appeared to. Though she loved Uma, she knew her friend could be callous when it came to others' feelings at times, especially when it came to men. She did not mean to mislead them; she was just careless with her attitude and her actions. It was a conversation the two of them had shared on several occasions.

Though her brother seemed comfortable with the conversation they were sharing, Eliana could sense a slight apprehension in his admission. She wondered if he really believed the understanding he and Uma had, or if he was simply trying to protect his own heart.

Chapter Twenty-Six

"Nazim!" Salmon called to the man riding steadily in front of him. "Nazim, stop!" he yelled louder this time. They had been traveling at a quick pace since they had left Bashan. Their animals were exhausted.

Nazim pulled Ares to a stop, turning him to face Salmon who quickly caught up to him. He understood Nazim's haste, this instance no doubt filling his mind with memories of the not-so-distant past. The look on his face said as much as he turned to look at the man who had broken his pace.

"I know you are eager to return to Heshbon," Salmon spoke from his horse beside Nazim now, "as am I, but arriving worn to nothing with your horse dead on his feet will be of no help to anyone. The sun has almost set, we must make camp, give our animals rest and water, and nourish ourselves," he requested.

Nazim clenched his teeth together, frustration over the current situation radiating in his eyes. He worked to control his temper, knowing deep inside that Salmon was right. The first thing he was taught as a child when training to become the warrior he had succeeded in becoming was that, first and foremost, you must take care of yourself and your animal. Nazim looked around, noticing a small bank to the left of their current location, with a small stream trickling just beyond it.

"There," he pointed. "We will rest there, but only for a little while," he agreed spurring Ares slowly in that direction. The men watered their animals and built a small fire, eating the remainder of the apples and nuts that Eliana had packed for them almost a week before. Both were thankful for the large meal they had consumed in Bashan. The night was cool and quiet, only the crackling of the fire breaking their silence. It was Nazim who spoke first.

"You were correct that we should rest," he acknowledged. "I had foolishly focused on my mission and was giving no thought

267

to the stress I was putting my horse through. I just cannot face losing everything that I have come to cherish. Not again," he admitted. He rested his elbows on his knees and his head in his hands, working to dispel the images of Jericho that lingered there.

"I understand," Salmon said quietly, with sincere empathy.

"May I ask you something?" Nazim now questioned, mild irritation marking his voice.

"I suppose," Salmon answered, not sure which direction his question would go.

"I understand that Jehovah was behind the defeat of Jericho, and though I am at peace with that now, there is still a question that burns to my very soul. How *did* your men take our city? Those walls, once believed to be impenetrable, ended up as nothing more than piles of stone." Though it was a question that had plagued him for years, Nazim was almost afraid to finally gain the answer.

Salmon stoked the fire as he continued. He had never expected to speak of Jericho to Nazim, preferring to let the sleeping giant lie, but he had asked the question, and he deserved the answer. "The walls fell simply by Jehovah's will; we had no hand in it other than to follow His direct orders," Salmon said truthfully. "Joshua was visited by a Captain of the Host of the Lord, who had instructed him specifically on our part in the battle. After we crossed the river on dry land, we were given the instructions to march around the city. We followed those instructions perfectly, and on the seventh day and on the seventh march around the walls, we gave a mighty shout. At that sound, the walls came down," he stated.

"So, it took a miracle to bring them down," Nazim thought aloud. Salmon smiled as he nodded in agreement.

"We could have breached them no other way," he said honestly.

"Though, Rahab's wall did not," Nazim remembered. "It stood perfectly sound."

Salmon recognized his statement as the question it was intended to be. "Rahab had aided myself and Garrick when we had spied upon the city. Because of her assistance, Joshua gave strict instructions that no one in her household would be harmed. We got them to safety, but it was simply by Jehovah's will that her tower was not destroyed."

"The scarlet cord that hung from her window, is that how she escaped?" Nazim asked now.

"Not exactly," Salmon began. "I rescued her from her rooms," he acknowledged. "Other soldiers aided her family members, but the scarlet cord marked her tower for the soldiers who would not have known where her rooms were located."

"That scarlet cord," Nazim thought back, a small smile forming on his lips as he put everything together. "I found that cord hanging from her window before I departed Jericho in search for answers. I lost my temper with her then, realizing that in some way she had assisted you."

"She used that cord to help us escape through that window from you," he admitted as he took a drink of water from his flask.

Nazim turned to him, shock on his face. "You were in her home when I searched?" he asked in shock, a small smile playing on his lips. "I searched all over that inn!" he stated, amazed.

"And you almost found us," Salmon admitted with a chuckle. "Garrick and I were concealed under the reeds of flax drying on her rooftop when you came kicking and stomping through," he stated adamantly. "I felt the wind off of your boot on one occasion," he confessed. "It was simply by the grace of God that you did not discover us."

"Unbelievable," Nazim scoffed, shaking his head. "I remember Rahab distracting me, and I see now that it was simply in order to get me away from those reeds," he admitted. "I thought it was because I was ruining her hard work," he chuckled.

"You were. She had worked very hard at concealing us beneath them," Salmon agreed. The men shared a small laugh and then remained lost in their own thoughts for a few moments before Nazim spoke again.

"She had cherished that scarlet fabric so much," he remembered. "What happened to it?" he asked.

"After she wound it into the lifeline it had become?" Salmon questioned.

Nazim nodded his affirmation. "I noticed that it had been cut away when I explored the remnants of Jericho."

"I salvaged it for her," Salmon confirmed, "knowing how much she had adored that fabric, I could not leave without it. She unwound it and created a beautiful garment. She wore that garment at our marriage," Salmon smiled. "I have yet to see a more beautiful sight than what she portrayed that day," he finished as he stared into the darkness above the flames.

"I can only imagine," Nazim said softly.

They sat in silence for a moment longer before Salmon stretched out, propping his body on a large rock behind him. He closed his eyes, giving Nazim the only amount of privacy he could really offer in their current situation, feeling the man needed a bit of space. Nazim continued to stare into the night as the flames danced in front of him for a few moments before he reached into his vest pocket, pulling the pendant from it that he had treasured for so long.

He toyed with it for a moment, turning it this way and that in his hands as he watched the light from the fire catch the jewels causing them to glow and dance in the darkness. He remembered the joy it had brought to Rahab when he had given it to her, and he remembered the pain he felt when he discovered it rejected in the ruins of the city. He recognized it as the token it had become for her. A token she used to indicate she had chosen to separate herself from one life to another. Slowly he stood, making his way quietly to the stream just beyond the camp.

Holding the pendant over the water, he felt it was time that he, too, release himself from the guilt he had harbored for so long. His memories of his life before Heshbon were marred by sadness and despair. It was time that he released those memories, that life, and everything that tied him to them. Slowly, he opened his hand, allowing the pendant to slip from his grasp and fall into the water below. It only took a second in the darkness for it to be gone from his view, and at that time, he turned, moving slowly back to the fire. He was surprised to see Salmon sitting upright, watching him as he approached.

"Are you well?" Salmon asked from his seated position.

"I am well, Nazim confirmed thoughtfully.

"The moon is very bright tonight," Salmon mentioned, looking to the sky where the full moon stood positioned right above them. Nothing else would be said of the separation Nazim had just made. "We could travel quickly in the darkness," Salmon suggested. Before the words were out of his mouth, Nazim was moving toward his horse, preparing to mount Ares once again.

Eliana moved from her chambers to begin her day. It was early, but she had much to do in preparation for their coming guests. She had just entered the cooking area to stoke the fire when she heard pounding on the outer door of the inn. The pounding was relentless and soon she heard Avi descending the stairs from his room. Reuben stood outside his own door; a questioning look on his face. Hallel and Zebulun stood on the landing watching as Avi moved quickly through the dining area.

"It is too soon for guests," Eliana commented softly, exiting the cooking area.

Avi glanced over his shoulder to where she stood as he approached the door. "Stay there," he instructed her. "Who is it?" he shouted through the closed portal.

"Avi, it is me, Azariah," the man called to him. Quickly, Avi opened the door allowing him entrance.

"A band of soldiers just approached the city gates," he spoke between breaths. "Kylus is among them," he finished.

"Kylus?" Eliana spoke in shock and fear. "But if Kylus is here…" her voice trembled, and she braced herself on the table nearest her. Avi moved closer to his sister.

"Do not assume anything, sister," he reminded her.

"What is our plan, Avi?" Hallel asked from his place.

"To act as normal as possible. To our knowledge, Kylus does not know that we have tied him to the attack. We will not go to him, but we will be ready when he comes to us," he confirmed.

Suddenly, they heard the back door open, and Avi rushed from his place to see who was there.

"Do not try to stop me, Avi," Reuben spoke to his brother as he hurried out the door and toward the barn. "If Nazim had failed, I would know it. I do not believe they have encountered Kylus at all. I have to get to our soldiers and tell them that Kylus has returned to Heshbon."

Avi watched as his younger brother began to saddle his horse. Reuben abruptly stopped as he remembered his place. "May I use your horse, brother?" he asked before he continued.

Avi nodded his consent, and Reuben immediately mounted him with ease. Avi kept the fear to himself that Kylus had somehow ambushed the soldiers on their way to Bashan. Perhaps the boy was right. He had grown very close to Nazim during his time in Heshbon, and the two had formed quite a bond.

"Go with God, Reuben," he said as he patted his brother's leg. Reuben nodded as he turned the horse in the direction of the city gates.

Chapter Twenty-Seven

It was not long before patrons began to fill the dining area for their morning meals. The soldiers acted as normal as possible, and though Eliana was quieter than usual, her smile was ever as pleasant and her demeanor more than kind. It was late that afternoon before the altercation they had all been dreading finally occurred. Eliana had been petitioning Jehovah all day, and though she felt His presence near, the pit of her stomach tightened at the sight of Kylus outside their door.

Avi walked to the stoop before Kylus or his men could enter. The townspeople could sense the tension among them all and gathered around, curious as to the encounter that was about to take place.

"More soldiers from the battlefield?" Kylus questioned as Hallel, Azariah, and Zebulun stood behind Avi. Eliana stood just out of sight around the back corner of the inn.

"Is there something we can help you with, Kylus?" Avi asked.

"Never before have I been greeted in this way," Kylus smirked. "Is there a problem I am unaware of?" he asked, mock concern dripping from his voice.

"Never before have you shown up on my doorstep with a whole squadron of men who look ready for battle. You tell me," Avi questioned, "what exactly is it that you seek?" he asked.

Kylus tired of his own charade. Patience had never been a virtue of his. Losing his temper at the site of these imbeciles, he decided to get straight to the point.

"Retribution," he answered with malice. "You will give me what I want for the wrongful accusations you have made against me."

"Accusations? What accusations?" Avi asked, leading Kylus directly into the confession he intended.

"What accusations?" Kylus mocked him. He scoffed. "Your accusations that I orchestrated the attack against Nazim and Eliana. That I am the person who instructed Melech to kill Nazim and to capture your sister. Your accusation that sent that wretched street urchin with his band of misfits to Bashan to find me," he screamed. "I am ruler of this town, and I will say who lives or dies," he yelled.

The townspeople began to back away in fear as Kylus continued his rant.

"We shared no accusations with anyone, Kylus," Eliana spoke as she moved from her hiding place, "but you know an awful lot about things that no one else seems to know," she charged.

Kylus looked around himself at the townspeople, who glared at him in fear and shock. "How do you always seem to know exactly when something happens that deserves a penalty to be paid?" Eliana continued, "And how is that you knew more of our soldiers had arrived, or that Nazim accompanied them to Bashan? You even knew the name of the man who attempted to kill Nazim, which is more than even I knew."

Kylus reached around, pulling a figure from behind him that had been well hidden behind a small group of his men. He jerked off the hood that covered her head, revealing that it was Uma who had been his spy.

"Does this harlot look familiar to you?" he seethed as he looked at Eliana.

"Eliana, I am so sorry," Uma began to cry. "He gave me no choice!"

Eliana stood in shock and disbelief, trying to breathe. Kylus' surprise announcement was like a punch to her gut. Avi's mouth hung open as he, too, attempted to recover from the shock Uma's appearance had caused.

"Uma, why? How could you?" Eliana finally managed.

Kylus laughed a sickening laugh. "Why she did it or how she did it matters not. The fact is that she has been feeding me reports on this town for months attempting to save her reputation and that of her family! She did not want me to call her out for the harlot she is!"

"I never knew his intentions were to hurt any of you! And I am no harlot!" she cried.

"None of that matters now," he laughed wickedly. "She has been exposed for her sins, but because of your treachery," he pointed to Eliana, "I will no longer be needing her services of deceit! Hiram, be rid of her!" he instructed. An overweight man lurched forward, grabbing hold of Uma as if she were a rag doll.

"NO!" Eliana screamed. Avi, and the other soldiers jumped immediately into action. They were severely outnumbered, but more than one townsman came to their aid. Kylus avoided their advance, mounting his horse once again and shouting out his final orders to his men as they began to fight. Townspeople who were not aiding in the fight began to flee from the area as swords and staves continued to fly all around them.

"You will pay for what you have done!" Kylus yelled over the chaos. He grabbed a torch one of his men held high, throwing it into the barn as he rode past. Immediately, the dry hay caught fire, and flames began to fill the empty stalls. Eliana screamed in horror as she not only witnessed the barn catching fire but also as the man called Hiram continued to stalk through the crowd with Uma thrown over his shoulder.

Eliana ran toward him, throwing herself to the ground and grabbing at his feet, attempting to trip him. He fell hard, dropping Uma in the process, but quickly recovered and reached out to grab her by her ankle as she tried to regain her footing, successfully pulling her back to him. At the same time, he kicked fiercely, catching Eliana on her shoulder and sending her sprawling across the dirt. She screamed for her brother as he drew his sword from another man's chest. He rushed to her side, helping her to stand and sending her to safety before focusing his attention on the man who continued to flee with Uma.

Nazim and Salmon had just moved beyond the borders of Rabbah when they noticed another rider swiftly approaching. Both men were on guard as the rider drew near. "Wait!" Salmon called out as Nazim reached for the bow strapped to his back. "That is Avi's horse!" Both men felt fear rush through their bodies when they realized it was Reuben on Avi's horse rushing toward them.

"Praise Jehovah, I found you! I feared…" his voice broke. Reuben breathed deeply, gathering himself, and then continued. "Kylus has returned to Heshbon!"

"We feared as much. He had fled Bashan before we arrived," Salmon informed him.

"We should waste no time," Nazim shouted as he hastened Ares once again. They had not gone far before Nazim saw the smoke begin to rise across the plain. Again, fear gripped his heart as he realized it was coming from the direction of Heshbon. Ares sensing the tension that rose in his master's body, immediately lowered his head, running as fast as he possibly could toward the town.

Avi reached the man, Hiram, in only a few strides as he limped away with Uma, stopping him by running his sword deep into his gut. Uma fell to the ground, crawling as quickly as she could back toward Eliana, who motioned for her and then pulled her quickly behind the inn.

Uma immediately began defending herself. "Eliana, you must believe me; I had no choice, he threatened me, my whole family…" she cried.

Eliana placed her hands on Uma's shoulders as she spoke firmly. "Uma, now is not the time. We will discuss this later; right now, we have to figure out what to do," she stated looking around for something, for anything that would give her an idea.

"I know exactly what you will do," Kylus spoke as he grabbed Eliana from behind. "You will come with me!" he ordered forcefully.

"I will not!" she screamed as she kicked and struggled to free herself from his grasp as he continued pulling her toward the wooded area.

"Stop fighting me, Eliana! You are nothing, and you have nothing!" he spoke through clenched teeth. "You will pay for your preference of him over me!" he continued, tiring of her struggle. Uma stood frozen in fear over all that was transpiring. She tried to scream, but nothing would come out. Eliana continued to struggle, attempting to free herself from his grasp, successfully moving them inch by inch back into view of the street. Kylus was stronger than she by far, but she was determined not to go down without a fight. He had one arm around her waist and the other around her shoulders, catching the one that had been injured by Hiram's kick. She felt the pain but refused to give up.

Nazim arrived just in time, barely catching a glimpse of Eliana as she struggled, just before she was hastily pulled back beyond the corner of the inn. Ares had not even stopped before Nazim dismounted, sprinting to the corner and reaching them just as Kylus drew back his hand.

"ENOUGH," Kylus yelled as he drew his arm back preparing to forcefully strike Eliana. What he did not expect was the larger hand that wrapped around his wrist just before he released his fury on her. Nazim stood behind him, his face a mask of anger and rage. He firmly held Kylus's wrist over his head as his other hand wrapped tightly around his throat. Kylus released Eliana, struggling to no avail to pry the fingers loose that continued to tighten around his neck.

"I should have finished this the first time," Nazim spoke through clenched teeth as he backed Kylus against the side of the inn. "This time, you will not walk away. Your torment of this town and of these people ends now," he seethed as he released Kylus's wrist long enough to draw his own dagger from the sheath at his side. Eliana and Uma fled inside the inn and did not witness the dagger as it sunk and then twisted deep into Kylus's stomach. Nazim breathed through the rage continuing to boil inside him, knowing the job was done, but wanting to mutilate the coward in his hands even more. Finally, he pulled away, watching as Kylus's body slid into a heap along the wall.

Nazim turned, ordering Reuben inside to wait with the women as he moved into the street, drawing his sword, ready to fight anyone who stood in his path. He joined Salmon, unleashing months of pent-up anger and aggression as the two of them fought side-by-side and back-to-back. Together, they plowed through the men who had pledged their support to Kylus. Finally, none of Kylus's men stood before them.

Avi, Zebulun, Azariah, and Hallel had joined people from the town who were working to form a water brigade in an attempt to extinguish the flames as the barn continued to burn. The flames had consumed it quickly, and the barn could not be saved. Thankfully, the inn was kept free from any harm.

The sounds of battle finally ceased as Nazim and Salmon stood in the midst of the bodies of men who had chosen to fight. Several had run upon seeing that Kylus was dead. Women of the town began to make their way from their hiding places, quietly at first, before several began thanking the Israeli soldiers and Nazim for their protection during the battle.

Eliana listened carefully and, hearing nothing, peeked through the one window at the front of the inn. It was then that she saw townsfolk as they began to emerge from their hiding places. Slowly, she pulled the door open to see Nazim, who was now standing on the stoop. He was splattered with blood, but she did not care. She moved toward him slowly but did not hesitate as he opened his arms to her. She fell into the strong arms of the man she loved, thanking Jehovah that he was alive, safe, and back with her once again.

Chapter Twenty-Eight

The dead had been buried, the debris removed, and the barn had begun to be cleared away. The entire town had pitched in, everyone in shock over the recent events, confused as to how things had taken such a turn, and surprised at themselves for allowing it to happen. There had been a subtle change in Kylus, many had remarked, while others claimed to have noticed a change in his demeanor as soon as Joshua had granted his request to care for the town. Regardless, the weight of righteous penalties and unfair treatment had been removed.

Oren and his family went before the town, seeking forgiveness for the part they had played in the whole affair. As patrons of Heshbon before the acquisition of the city by the Israelites, they had been targets of Kylus from the beginning of his leadership. They told of the threats Kylus had made to them about how easily he could ruin their family's reputation, especially Uma's, and in turn, their business, but they still took ownership for the wrongs they had committed against the Israeli people. Though it would take time to regain their trust, the town chose not to exile or punish them, choosing instead to forgive them as Jehovah had forgiven their own trespasses time and time again.

Uma had spoken specifically to Eliana, Avi, Reuben, and Nazim, giving them more specific details on Kylus's accusations and claims against her. She had no idea just how ruthless Kylus was willing to be with the information she was feeding him through her father, promising again that she had no indication of the attack that had been planned against Nazim or Eliana.

She also recognized how her former behavior could have been misconstrued with only a few exaggerated tales from Kylus or any of his men. Though she remained an innocent, she repented for her actions that would have made such allegations believable, with the promise to more carefully watch her behavior. Eliana embraced Uma with assurance that Jehovah would forgive her for her wrongs and that their own relationship could be restored. Avi had been less forgiving initially but promised his sister that he would attempt to get his relationship with Uma back to the close friendship they had shared before her treachery had been revealed.

The people of Heshbon had not realized until it had been removed, just how heavy the yoke of Kylus had been weighing upon them. Few remained in the town that had originally pledged their allegiance to him, and those who felt his death was unjustified packed their belongings immediately and removed themselves from the town.

Business resumed once again at the inn, the patrons of Heshbon supporting the family more than ever. Uma continued to work with Eliana, though her demeanor was not quite the same. Initially, she was much quieter, almost reclusive, preferring to do most of her work in the back, requesting that Eliana do the majority of the serving. Finally, she began to grow more comfortable, and though still not the same, Eliana could see glimpses of the cheery disposition they had missed beginning to shine through once again.

Soon a month had passed, and the debris from the barn had been completely cleared away. Salmon and his men, including Avi, had announced that it was past time for them to return to the Israeli camp. Eliana and Nazim had continued to grow closer. Daily, she shared stories of her people, and in doing so, she taught Nazim more about Jehovah, and Nazim continued to work at letting go of his past. Today they sat in comfortable silence, listening to the stream as it crossed over the rocks and the birds as they sang in the trees overhead. Finally, Eliana broke the silence.

"I believe I will need to employ your services once again," she joked. "You see I have a barn that will need to be rebuilt, and you did such a wonderful job on the stoop..." she let the sentence hang as she turned her head to smile at him.

He chuckled at her sheepish grin. "I suppose we could come to some sort of arrangement," he agreed, placing his arm around her gently.

"I can offer you room and board," she spoke, as if she were trying to convince him, "and the meals here are fabulous," she added, getting the laugh from him she had hoped.

"I have an idea," he mentioned, moving his arm to turn her to look at him.

"I am listening," she smiled.

"Marry me," he stated, looking into her eyes.

"What?" she asked with a chuckle as a smile began to light her face.

Nazim turned to face her, taking her face in his hands. "Eliana, I love you. I love you for the woman you are, and I love you for the woman you will be if you agree to become my wife," he promised. "Avi has given his blessing to our union," he added. "Would you do me the highest honor of becoming my wife?" he asked, looking at her intently as he waited for her answer. She continued to stare at him in shock. He was a warrior. He had loved someone else deeply and had lost her. Though Eliana knew that she herself loved him, and she did not doubt that he cared for her, she had never allowed herself to believe that he would ever come to the point that he would ask for her hand. "I will repair the barn," he bargained at her continued silence.

Her chuckle was enough to break the lump that had formed in her throat.

Eliana could not stop the tears that wet her cheeks. "Yes," she whispered as a smile spread across her face. "Yes," she said excitedly as Nazim pulled her face to his for a firm, yet sincere kiss. Pulling away, he embraced her as they stood by the bank of the stream for several moments, each of them relishing the moment. It was Nazim who spoke first.

"You had me a little worried there for a moment," he admitted with a chuckle. "I did not think I was nearly as irresistible as I thought." Eliana busted out laughing.

She hugged him again as she spoke. "Well, when you threw in that you would rebuild the barn…" she laughed. He pushed her away casting a skeptical look at her that she adored. "You have been nearly irresistible since the day I met you," she laughed, laying her head on his chest.

Nazim stood as he held her looking across the stream before him. *"I do not deserve any of this,"* he thought. *"I can never repay You for the favor you have bestowed upon me,"* he silently prayed, *"but I will live the rest of my days doing my best to serve You,"* he vowed again.

"How quickly can you be ready for our union?" he asked, suddenly breaking the embrace to look at her. "The men will be leaving in only a few more days. Let us wed before they leave," he requested.

Eliana's smile stretched across her face. "That is a wonderful idea!" she grinned.

They walked back to the inn, hand in hand, each talking about future ideas for the inn that would now be theirs. As they approached the door, Nazim pulled Eliana to himself once again for another kiss.

"I will never tire of that," she smiled at him as he pulled away.

"Good, because I will never tire of doing it," he assured her.

Nazim paused and called for Reuben to come outside. He kept his promise that the boy would be the first to know. Immediately, the lad ran to town to share the news with his friends and everyone else he came in contact with.

The wedding ceremony was performed two days later, with Salmon officiating. Nazim and Eliana pledged their love for one another and vowed to spend the rest of their days in perfect union on the banks of the pools of Heshbon, with the majority of the town in attendance. A huge meal was provided at the inn shortly after.

That night, Eliana and Nazim lay together in the bed they now shared. She slept peacefully in the arms of her husband. He stroked her hair as he held her, thinking that he had never seen such beauty. Though he was at perfect peace, sleep refused to claim him. He had only thought he had loved before, but he had never felt a love so pure and genuine as what he felt for Eliana now.

Salmon had approached him after the ceremony, while Eliana was being loved on and congratulated by the people who had watched her grow from a child into the beautiful bride she had become. Nazim replayed the conversation in his mind.

"I have never been happier over a union other than my own," he joked. Nazim scoffed.

"You are just glad you no longer have to worry about me tracking you down," he joked back. Salmon laughed, clasping his shoulder.

"Avi, the men, and I will return to the Israeli camp tomorrow. I would like to leave knowing the people of Heshbon and Bashan are left in the care of someone who can restore peace and trust to these lands. I have sent word to Joshua of all that transpired, and though I realize what an asset you would be on the battlefield, he agrees that we would be honored and rest easy knowing you have charge of the two cities."

Nazim looked at him in surprise. Never had he expected to hold any sort of leadership over any of the Israeli people. He also realized what an honor it was to be considered for such a position by men such as this.

"If it is any consolation, Joshua would never have agreed without prayer and supplication to Jehovah over the matter," Salmon continued. "If you do not feel it is something you would consider, we will appoint someone else, but…"

"I would be honored," Nazim spoke before he could continue. He felt an assurance wash over him immediately and could not stop the surprise in his voice. Salmon nodded his appreciation and clasped Nazim's shoulder once again.

"I realize we are sworn enemies," Salmon smiled, "though I must admit we make a pretty good team," he smiled.

Nazim scoffed again. "Do not push it," he laughed. Then he continued speaking in complete sincerity. "Will you relay to Rahab that I thank her for her prayers," he requested.

Salmon nodded once again. "I will," he acknowledged. "My brother," he finished quickly, embracing the man before him.

Nazim laughed. "I suppose we are, but brothers do not have to be friends," he reminded him. "Eliana told me of a man called Joseph who had some terrible brothers."

Salmon laughed aloud. "Right you are," he acknowledged as the two embraced in another quick hug.

Salmon announced at the dinner that evening that Nazim would now rule over both Heshbon and Bashan, with his primary residence remaining with his wife and Reuben in Heshbon. Nazim would also be appointing an aide to assist him in the near future, whose primary residence would be in Bashan so that both cities would have someone watching over them at all times.

Nazim could not believe where his journey had brought him. He had come to this place seeking an idol, a god that he could destroy. He had found the living God who had kept him from being destroyed. He had searched for a people he had longed to ruin. He had found a people who had been delivered from ruin. He had arrived angry, bitter, and distraught. He lay here now, happy, content, and elated with the woman he held and would forever hold in his arms for as long as Jehovah allowed. The woman he would cherish for the rest of his days. The woman he would protect, honor, and sacrifice his life for if need be. Openly and in perfect union with Jehovah God. He loved this feeling of contentment and peace. He knew that he would never wander again. The wandering soldier had found peace, a living God, and his home.

Epilogue

It was late when Salmon arrived back at the camp with Avi, Garrick, Zebulun, Asher, Azariah, and Hallel. The men retired to their own tents, Salmon sneaking quietly into his own dwelling attempting not to awaken his sleeping toddler. Rahab lay curled in her normal position sleeping peacefully. He knew he should not awaken her, but he could barely wait to share the news with her that he knew would thrill her soul.

He carefully lay down beside her, and immediately she sensed his presence. She turned to him without words, embracing him for several moments. Finally, she pulled away and looked into his face.

"I have missed you," she whispered.

"As I have you," he spoke as he kissed her gently.

"You were gone for so long, but Joshua continually assured me you remained well. Are you well?" she asked, searching his eyes.

"I am very well," he whispered back, "especially now that I am back with you in my arms," he smiled. "But I am glad you are awake; I have some news I could not wait until morning to share with you."

Rahab pulled away, looking into his eyes, a puzzled expression on her beautiful face. She sat up on the cot. "What is it?" she asked.

"I met someone in Heshbon. I had been told of his presence there, but before I told you anything I had heard, I wanted to see for myself if the stories I had been told were true. I am happy to report, that they are," he smiled caressing her face.

Rahab thought for a moment before looking at him again. "Who?" she asked. "Who did you meet that would have anything to do with me?"

"I was told of a wandering soldier who had given his life to Jehovah. He fought alongside me in the battle against Kylus, and he now rules over our people in Heshbon and Bashan," Salmon continued.

"A wandering soldier," Rahab whispered slowly. She could not believe what her heart was telling her. "Salmon, do you mean?" she asked.

"Rahab, Jehovah has heard and answered your prayers. Nazim has given his life to our God. He thanks you for the prayers I assured him that you have daily prayed, and I assured him that you had forgiven him when he shared the burden on his heart over his treatment of you."

She embraced her husband. How good could Jehovah possibly be? She knew that a miracle as big as the crossing of the Red Sea had been performed when Jehovah had reached the heart of Nazim.

Salmon lay down with his wife positioning her head on his chest as he continued to speak. The beating of her beloved's heart calmed her. She thanked Jehovah for bringing her soldier safely home and for the salvation of the wandering soldier she had once known. Tears wet his chest as she clung to him. The love she felt for this man was pale in comparison to the love she knew her God bestowed upon her. She was so blessed, and she acknowledged as much in thankfulness to Jehovah now.

"I also got to perform a wedding while I was there," Salmon continued. He is now married to Eliana, the granddaughter of Eli, and I must admit, I have yet to see a more perfect union other than our own. And though things are rather strained, I feel something is happening between our Avi and Eliana's friend, Uma, in Heshbon. Though I imagine time will tell, Avi will return soon in my place to check on Nazim and his rule there. Just to make sure things are going well. Rahab?" he asked suddenly, as he sensed her steady breathing.

She lay on his chest, sound asleep in perfect peace. Salmon kissed the top of her head amazed at the love he felt and the God he served before falling into his own peaceful slumber.

Edom placed a plate of food in front of the coarse man who had settled at the corner table. It was late, and he was ready to close his doors. He would not have served the man, but compassion stirred within him at his unkept appearance. The tunic he wore was worn through, and the hood that covered his face, dirty and tattered. He seemed to have been traveling for quite some time. "Will there be anything else?" Edom asked.

"What town am I in?" the man questioned as he began to quickly eat the food in front of him.

"Bashan," he answered.

"Do you have a leader?" he asked, pushing another spoonful of stew down his throat.

"A newly appointed one," Edom answered. He had begun to feel a bit apprehensive at his guest's odd questions. "Perhaps you have heard of him. He was formerly known as the 'wandering soldier' from Jericho. Now he is simply called Nazim."

The man dropped the spoon into the bowl suddenly, and stood slowly, pulling the hood from his head revealing his face. One eye shone brightly, but where his other eye should have been, was nothing more than a scar where the skin had been brought together. "Well, is that not something," he smirked. "Nazim made his way to the top. Fetch him, now," he demanded as he looked down at the short, stubby man.

"I...I cannot, for he resides in Heshbon. He checks in with us often and should be returning soon," Edom stuttered in sudden fear.

"Then fetch me a room," he demanded. "I will wait for his soon return," he spoke with malice.

Edom quickly began clearing the table and prepared to show this stranger to a room in the back.

"May I have a name, for the room?" he asked hesitantly. The stranger hesitated before speaking. Finally, he gave his name.

"Malik," he answered simply. "My name is Malik."

www.ingramcontent.com/pod-product-compliance
Lightning Source LLC
Chambersburg PA
CBHW060524260626
47161CB00003B/755